Chasing Shadows

by

Cat Jameson

Cover Art by *Teddi Black*

The Wild Rose Press, Inc.
PO Box 708
Adams Basin, NY 14410-0708
Visit us at www.thewildrosepress.com

Publishing History
First Edition, 2025
Trade Paperback ISBN 978-1-5092-6019-5
Digital ISBN 978-1-5092-6020-1

Published in the United States of America

Dedication

Write what makes you happy.
Write what makes you laugh.
Write what makes you sing.

To those who gave me the advice that got me out of my own head and made this book possible.
You know who you are. Thank you.

Chapter One

Annie O'Toole dashed through the luxurious hotel lobby, silver stilettos flashing as she skirted the ridiculously overdone fountain of Italian marble and swerved round the bellman in her path. She reached the heavy brass doors to the ballroom just as a thunderous round of applause erupted on the other side. Tugging them open, across a sea of people, she spotted a teary-eyed Emily Goldstein making her way off the platform.

Damn it to hell. She'd missed it. After all the angst, all the agonizing, she'd missed the very reason she'd finally convinced herself to come. She slumped against the door and glared at the figure speaking into the microphone, inviting St. Louis's upper crust to enjoy the remainder of the evening's festivities. Kurt Cochrane. Director of Legal Services of Missouri. Genius. Lover. Prick.

Even on her best night, Annie could do without black-tie balls and fancy awards ceremonies. She'd much rather be working on her cross-exam of the cop in Monday's burglary trial or curled up on her couch ranting at the idiot defense lawyers on TV who sat there, useless, while their clients confessed.

But the Justice for All Ball, the St. Louis legal community's annual fundraiser for Legal Services, was a cause Annie believed in. Add in the fact that Andrew Goldstein, her late, beloved mentor, was the evening's honoree and blowing tonight off hadn't really been an option. So, she'd pulled up her big girl panties, steeled herself to face The Prick and come out to support Andrew's widow, Emily.

At least that had been the plan. Instead, she'd lost track of time and missed the entire presentation. Glaring in disgust at the crowd hiding Emily somewhere in its midst, she decided to fortify herself with a drink. Then she'd find Emily, offer her good wishes, and get the hell out of Dodge. With Mr. How-Many-Ways-Can-I-Screw-You-Over running the show, exiting the ball well before midnight was the obvious choice. She headed toward the bar.

"Annie O'Toole! Don't you sneak past without saying hello." A large woman in heavy make-up and a full boutique of costume jewelry blocked her path.

"Myra." Annie forced a smile.

"Ed, look who's here!"

Ed, rotund and watery-eyed, was holding forth about his glory days at Notre Dame to a tall man wearing an expensive-looking tux and a glazed expression. Everyone in the room knew that speech by heart, having been regaled by it every time they had the misfortune of running into Ed and Myra. The couple turned up at every one of these events, collecting encounters with community leaders and politicos as eagerly as others collected baseball cards.

Ed glanced round. "Annie! You're looking lovely tonight, my dear."

"Hello, Ed. So sorry I can't stay to chat," Annie said with feigned regret. "Em's waiting for me." She turned to make her escape but caught a glimpse of Tuxedo Man slowly backing away while the couple's attention was on her. Taking pity on him, she leaned back in. "Oh, but did you hear the latest about Kurt Cochrane? Caught in bed with a married woman."

Myra gasped and Ed's eyes popped.

"It's true. *In flagrante*, as they say. Can you imagine?" The man had made his escape, so she moved to do the same. "But please, not a word to anyone about Kurt's little problem. Not something he wants spread around, I'm sure."

"Oh, of course not, darling, of course not. Wouldn't think of it," Myra bobbled, her gaze already darting around the room in search of someone to impress with her insider's knowledge of the private lives of those seated on the dais.

Annie's twinge of guilt was fleeting. After all, she'd only spoken the truth, the whole truth, and nothing but the truth. She should know. She was the one who'd caught him.

****

Michael Grayson leaned against the bar and checked his watch. It hadn't moved since the last time he'd checked it. Another thirty minutes. By then he would have mingled sufficiently, been seen sufficiently to serve his purpose. The stock scare seemed to have stabilized with his announcement of a hefty donation to Legal Services, but his PR people insisted he cement it with an in-person presentation. Not that the market cared about Legal Services. Nor did he, for that matter. He just needed a venue to show investors he hadn't been slowed by his little encounter with the wrong end of a gun. Assured that Grayson Aeronautics was still firmly under its founder's brilliant control, they could all relax and return to business as usual. Or so his PR team was hoping.

He'd been amused at Peter's choice of recipient for his largesse. Lawyers of all people. And bleeding-heart lawyers at that. Of course, he knew about Peter's streak of social liberalism—the man spent his spare time volunteering at some youth center for gang members, for God's sake. But Michael didn't mind as long as he got what he was paying for—positive publicity.

He scanned the crowd as he waited for his drink, keeping a wary eye out for the gaudily dressed couple who'd pounced on him like some long-lost relative. God, he hated these society events. The only point seemed to be shopping for 'friends' with impressive credentials to add to one's social résumé. He didn't give a damn about his social résumé and wasn't interested in being added to anyone else's.

On second thought, to hell with thirty more minutes. One last circuit of the room ought to be more than enough to ensure that all the gossip columnists got a good look at him out and about, all hale and hardy, glad-handing Joe Schmoe, lawyer for the underprivileged. And if he was showing up at a charity event this unrelated to his business, he had to be fully recovered, right? Right.

The bartender handed him his drink. Michael dropped a tip into the jar and moved to one side, making room for the next person in line. He had just lifted the golden elixir to his lips when something slammed into the middle of his back, sending his drink flying and the dull ache in his side roaring to full-fledged, hurt-like-hell pain.

"Goddamn it!" He gasped as golden droplets of twelve-year-old bourbon dripped down the front of his tux. "What the—?" He turned with a scowl, but the string of curses ready to launch died unspoken.

She had the greenest eyes he'd ever seen, framed by a tousle of chin-length reddish gold curls that caught the dancing light from the chandeliers.

"Oh, my God. I'm so sorry. I'm such a klutz." Apologies tumbled out in a cascade of distress and self-abuse as she grabbed a stack of bar napkins and frantically tried to clean the front of his tuxedo, leaving tiny dots of wet, white paper across his chest.

He took a deep breath—inhale 1-2-3-4—breathing in a spicy, sexy scent that shot straight to his gut—exhale 1-2-3-4. The pain in his side eased.

The top of her curls barely reached his lapel. Short women had never been his type but, even drenched in alcohol and recovering from a gunshot wound to the gut, he had to admit this particular petite member of the species sported a killer body. She wore a short, shimmery, emerald green sheath of a dress that showcased great legs and strappy silver stilettos that showed off the ruby red polish on her toes. He closed his fingers around her hand and stilled it against his chest.

"Really, it's okay."

"It's not," she protested, cheeks pink with embarrassment. She pulled her hand loose and tossed her wad of soggy napkins into the wastebasket by the bar. "I'll pay to have it cleaned. It's the least I can do." Her gaze finally lifted to his and her eyes widened. "Oh! It's you."

"I'm sorry, have we met?" His voice came out husky and he quickly cleared it.

The pink in her cheeks deepened. "Not really. I just

saw you trying to escape the Henkes."

"The Henkes?"

"We just l-o-o-ve meeting new people, darling. It's what we do, isn't it, Ed?" She mimicked to a tee the irritating nasal tone of the woman with the overdone face who'd trapped him for a good twenty minutes before he escaped.

He laughed—carefully. "A fellow victim, I presume?"

"I was making my own escape when I ran you over. At least I distracted them long enough for you to get away." Her embarrassment gave way to a sparkle of mischief. "Been there, done that too many times not to feel sympathy for any creature trapped in the Henke web. But you might have moved a little faster. I had my own getaway to think about."

"If you were moving any faster, one of us might have been injured." His gaze fell on the glass lying on the floor. He debated whether to pick it up. Bending hurt.

Following his line of sight, she spotted the glass where it had rolled next to a large Ficus tree.

"Well, at least the glass didn't break," she muttered and snatched it up. She looked back over her shoulder as she turned toward the bar. "What are you drinking?" She winced. "Or, maybe I should say… wearing?"

He looked down at his ruined tux, then back up at her with a rueful grin. "Bourbon. On both counts."

He leaned against a pillar and watched her talking to the bartender. Her dress dipped tantalizingly low in back and curved seductively over a very nice ass. His desire to escape the premises seemed to have evaporated. Go figure.

She returned to his side with a glass of wine in one hand and his replacement drink in the other. "Try to hold on to this one, okay?"

He lifted an eyebrow. "Keep your distance and I just might be able to handle it."

"Deal." She clinked her glass against his—with a ringless left hand, he noted—then leaned forward and whispered, "But if the Henkes head this way, you're on your own."

"One save per person is your limit, is it?"

"Absolutely. The first time they get you, it's a blindside. You don't know the danger. Now you know, so watch your step."

Because he was enjoying the teasing light in those green eyes, he saw the exact moment they went flat. Surprised, he turned to see what or who had brought about the abrupt change. The Director of Legal Services strode toward them.

"Michael." Kurt Cochrane's smile broadened as he shook the hand that only minutes ago had presented him with a very large check. "What are you doing over here all by yourself?"

"I'm not." He nodded toward his new companion, those glorious eyes now shadowed and unreadable.

Cochrane peered around the potted Ficus. Hostility shot between the two.

"Annie. I didn't think you were coming tonight." Cochrane's smile wavered, but he recovered and pasted it back in place.

Annie made no such effort. She glared back at him. "That seems to be a common mistake with you, doesn't it, Kurt?" Her voice had turned to ice.

The man cleared his throat and turned his attention

back to Michael. "Annie is a longtime supporter of Legal Services, so I'm sure she can answer any questions you might have. Neither of us would want clients in need to lose the support of generous people such as yourself over a misunderstanding or a lack of information." He shot a warning look in her direction.

Her grip tightened on the stem of her wine glass, another drink disaster in the making.

"Appreciate the hospitality," Michael said, clapping Cochrane on the shoulder and turning him back to the party. He took a couple of steps with the man to get him moving, wished his organization the best and, with a handshake, dismissed him.

Cochrane took the cue and faded into the crowd. Michael turned back to the woman who had already aroused his body and now aroused his curiosity. Anger still smoldered in her eyes.

"I think we're even now," he said. "You saved me from the Henkes. I saved you from Cochrane. But if you don't ease up on the stem of that goblet, we're going to have to buy stock in a dry-cleaning company."

A weary humor doused the sparks in her eyes. Her shoulders dropped, a tension spring released. "That obvious, huh?"

"Only to the extraordinarily observant."

She extended her hand. "Well, Mr. Extraordinarily Observant, I'm Annie. Michael, is it? Do you go by Michael or Mike?"

He looked at her closely, but her expression remained open and relaxed. An odd, unfamiliar feeling flitted in his stomach. Women had never been hard to come by, even before money came along to sweeten the draw. His lean, dark good looks had served him in good stead in that department, even when he seldom had more than fifty dollars to his name. But it had been a long time since he'd been able to enjoy the company of a woman who had no idea who he was or what he could do for her.

"Mick actually," he replied, surprising himself. No one had called him Mick since his test pilot days. Then just to double check… "Have you been here the entire evening?"

"No, I just got here." She sighed in exasperation and combed the fingers of one hand through her gloriously disheveled curls. "I wanted to be here for Emily when they presented the award in Andrew's honor, but I can be such an idiot sometimes and, sure enough, I wound up missing the whole presentation."

He let out a breath. She hadn't heard him introduced or seen him present the check to Cochrane. She might really, truly, not know who he was. He smiled a slow smile and took the next logical step.

"So, what do you say we blow this pop stand?"

"What?" She looked up, startled.

"Leave. Go. Depart the premises in favor of somewhere a little more private and a lot more fun."

Her eyes narrowed, suddenly suspicious, a potent reminder that, in her eyes, he was not most eligible bachelor, billionaire CEO, Michael Grayson, but a total stranger. And from the look she was sending him right now, she wasn't a woman to blithely leave a party with a total stranger.

Tipping his head to one side, he put on his best little-boy-begging look. "Come on. Neither of us wants to be here. Why not save what we can of the evening? There's a nice jazz bar just downstairs. No Henkes. No

Cochrane. Just good bourbon, good music, and good company."

She considered him, her expression giving nothing away. She was probably a wicked poker player.

"I do love jazz," she finally conceded, with a shadow of a smile.

He grinned. "Clearly you are a woman of excellent taste."

She laughed. "Well, since you put it that way—I'm in." She set her drink on a nearby tray and accepted his outstretched hand. As he turned them toward the exit, she said, "So, you got a last name, Mick?"

"Not tonight." His answer caught them both by surprise.

Annie stopped in her tracks. "Come again?"

He sighed. "I'd just like to get to know each other a little better before we invite all the family skeletons to the party. Do you mind?"

Sharp, green eyes darted to his left hand, evenly tanned and ringless.

"I'm not married and I'm not a serial killer—both facts you can check with your buddy, Cochrane, if you want." He was banking that her dislike of Cochrane exceeded her suspicion of him.

She snorted. "You think Kurt wouldn't have sucked up to Ted Bundy?"

He winced. "Good point. Look, we're just going downstairs for a drink. What's the possible risk?"

"Yeah, that's what all the victims thought."

He chuckled. Enjoying her wit. Hoping she'd save her better judgment for future occasions and take the longshot tonight.

She eyed him a beat longer, then sighed. "Oh, what

the hell. Game on. Anonymity-R-Us."

Score.

He grinned. "I admire your spirit, Annie."

****

They were halfway across the room when she whirled, bumping headlong into his chest. Thankfully, he'd left his drink behind, but his side registered the hit.

"Oh, damn it, I'm sorry." She took a quick step back. "I have to find Emily. I can't leave without even letting her know I came."

The image of the small, mouse-colored woman in a plain brown suit who'd been honored earlier wavered, then settled in his memory. An unlikely fit with the vibrant redhead in shimmering emerald.

"Is she a close friend?"

"Well, actually, it was her late husband I was close to." Standing on tiptoe, she strained to search the crowd over the wall of people. "There she is." She grabbed his wrist and dragged him through the crowd of gowns and tuxedos. Sprinkling apologies like fairy dust, she cut a swath through the sea of people as effectively as any running back. "Sorry. Excuse me. I beg your pardon."

They emerged victorious at the far corner of the massive ballroom, his side none too happy about the treatment. The mouse-colored woman stood red-eyed amidst a circle of well-wishers. Dropping his hand as suddenly as she'd grabbed it, Annie swept the mouse into a quick, fierce hug, murmuring something in her ear. Then just as quickly, her respects having been properly paid, she flashed him a smile, grabbed his hand, and turned for the dash back through the tuxedoed defensive line.

"How about we take a shortcut?" he said, spotting

an exit sign behind the dais and opting to avoid the pain of battle for return yardage. He motioned her through the side door into a service hallway.

"Do you know where you're going?" she asked in a dubious tone.

"Nope."

"Well, that's encouraging," she muttered.

"Fear not. I have strong homing instincts."

He led them through a series of hallways, at last pushing open a doorway. They were standing in the hotel laundry room.

"And to think I was worried," Annie commented wryly. "Unusual décor for a bar, don't you think? Chez Laundry. I feel a whole new trend coming on."

"Smartass." He did an about face and shoved her playfully back out the door.

A few more right turns, spiced with Annie's caustic commentary on male navigational skills, and they suddenly emerged through a service door to the skittering harmonies of a jazz trio.

"*Voilà*." He threw out his arm with all the pride of personal ownership. In fact, he did own the bar into which they'd just emerged, as well as the hotel in which it stood.

He just had no intention of letting his companion know that.

Chapter Two

The clink of glasses punctuated a symphony of voices and laughter as Annie followed Mick to a secluded back booth. Sliding into the leather seat, she sighed. "Safe at last."

"I'll drink to that." He signalled to the waitress. "What's your pleasure?"

"Bourbon, of course. After all, it's not just for drycleaning anymore."

"You mean some people actually drink it?"

"Absolutely. You should try it sometime."

He chuckled and placed their order while she enjoyed the view. This was so not how she'd envisioned this evening turning out when she'd dragged herself out of her apartment to face her cheating ex. The dread she'd been marinating in all day had completely dissipated, leaving her almost giddy. So much so that she was probably grinning like a maniac at this man who'd done nothing more than be nice and buy her a drink. She tried to tone it down.

"So, Mick whoever-you-are," she said, "what do you do for a living?"

He hesitated for a beat. "Design airplanes."

She grimaced. "Really? I hate airplanes."

He lifted an eyebrow. "What exactly do you hate about them?"

"That they leave the ground. You really ought to

do something about that."

He laughed—a rich, deep, laugh that rolled over her like a massage, releasing the last remnants of tension from her body.

"I'll work on it." A smile lingered on his lips. "How about you, Annie whoever-you-are? What do you do for a living?"

"Oh, I'm a lawyer like everyone else upstairs." She waved a hand dismissively, much more interested in hearing about him. "So how did an airplane designer wind up at a gathering of law-types?"

"Aeronautical engineer. It's what we 'airplane designers' like to be called."

"Ah," she nodded knowingly. "Like a janitor preferring to be called a sanitation engineer."

His retort was interrupted by the waitress delivering their drinks. Once the server was gone, Annie dropped the dig and circled back to her question.

"So, seriously…what brings an aeronautical engineer out to a legal shindig like this?"

"Legal Services is a pet charity of a friend of mine. He's been pestering me about supporting the cause. I figured I'd buy some good will by showing up here."

"Oh? What's his name?"

"Huh-uh." He narrowed his eyes and shook a long finger at her. "Anonymity-R-Us, remember?"

"Sorry. Asking questions is an occupational hazard." She drummed her nails on the polished tabletop. "Any suggestions for safe topics that will keep this one-night stand totally anonymous?"

Her unfortunate choice of words hung in the air between them. *Damn it.* Why had she said that?

The slightest hint of a smile flirted with the corners

of his lips. "Is that what this is? A one-night stand?"

"I…didn't mean it that way," she stammered, feeling stupid. "I don't expect—I mean—that didn't come out right at all."

He laughed. "You know, I can't say I've ever really had a one-night stand. One that stayed just one night, that is. Unless you count paying for it in the Navy, which I don't."

Her embarrassment dissolved under his easy humor. And okay, the bourbon probably helped, too. She found herself smiling back at him.

"I've always liked the idea of disappearing into the sunset before things turn ugly. Leaving some man forever dreaming about me—the one who got away." She took another sip of her drink and changed topics before she tumbled too far down that maudlin rabbit hole. "You were in the Navy? I thought you were into planes, not boats."

"*Ships*. Boats are for fishing." He lifted his glass. "And some of those ships are aircraft carriers. That's where I spent most of my stint. Navy pilot."

"Really? Do you still fly?"

"Just for myself."

"You have your own plane?"

He shrugged. "A little one." Leaning forward, he turned the topic back to the very one she'd been trying to avoid. "So, what about you? Ever succeeded in keeping a one-night stand one night only?"

She sighed, resting her chin in her palm. "Nope. I always wind up staying too long at the ball." God, she sounded pathetic.

"Well, not tonight, you didn't. You made your escape well before midnight." He lifted his glass in a toast to her.

"Ah, but I brought the prince with me." She managed a smile. "That's against the rules, you know. Now he'll see me turn into a pumpkin and I'll have ruined everything."

He lifted an eyebrow. "I don't know about that. I happen to love the taste of pumpkin."

She laughed. And wondered how a simple eyebrow movement could be so damned sexy.

"Okay. I gave you two facts about me," he said. "Now you owe me two facts about you."

She thought for a moment. "I own my own dog, and I used to be a starving actress."

"An actress? Really?" He sounded impressed.

"A starving actress," she corrected. "A few seasons of summer stock. Some community theater work. I loved everything about it except the paycheck. There was none." She shrugged. "So, I took the next most logical step. I became a lawyer instead."

He cocked his head. "A trial lawyer?"

"But of course. Why spend your life in a musty old law library when you can have the courtroom as your stage and an audience summoned to attend your performances under penalty of law?" She stretched her arms out wide and grinned at her handsome companion. Her toes tingled from the golden liquid that had magically disappeared from her glass.

His smile widened. "Indeed. And the dog?"

She let her arms drop into her lap. "A Great Dane named Darrow." She hadn't noticed his signal to the waitress, but another drink suddenly appeared before her.

"Darrow, as in Clarence?"

She nodded, lifting the new drink in a toast. "To Clarence Darrow. My hero."

Their glasses clinked.

"So, who's your hero?" she asked.

"Orville and Wilbur Wright, of course," he replied, lifting his glass to hers.

Dutifully, she toasted the Wright brothers. After which, they toasted in turn Martin Luther King, Jr., Chuck Yeager, Ruth Bader Ginsburg, and the entire space program, one astronaut at a time.

Swallowing the last drops of her third—or perhaps her fourth?—drink, she realized she was in no condition to drive home. Nor did she want to. Taking a deep breath, Annie leaned across the table, looked into those gorgeous eyes, and did something she'd never done in her life. She propositioned a total stranger.

"So, tell me, Mick No-Last-Names. If I were to try to seduce you tonight, what would my odds of succeeding be?"

There wasn't so much as a beat of hesitation.

"Bet your next month's paycheck on it," he answered with a slow smile that ought to have been illegal. "You'll double your money."

She resisted the urge to crawl across the table into his lap. "Well, then…"

Clearing his throat, he stood and tossed a couple of bills on the table to cover the cost of their drinks. Taking her hand, he pulled her to her feet. "I hear they have rooms here," he said.

"Do they really?" She grinned. "How very convenient!"

****

The elevator ride to the ninth floor was a bit of a

blur. Annie had a vague impression of mirrors and glass and lots of brass, but mostly her attention was on wicked, smoke-grey eyes and that bad-boy crooked smile. He unlocked the door, then stood aside to let her enter first, his hand brushing the small of her back, setting off tingles with his touch.

The room was a luxurious one, but the décor couldn't hold its own with the competition. Mick closed and bolted the door, then leaned back against it. He just stood there, watching her, looking for all the world like the cat about to swallow the canary. And she had no doubts about who the canary was in this equation. He moved toward her, and she could have sworn the temperature in the room shot up with every step. In one last pause of exquisite anticipation, he stopped inches from her.

"Last chance to leave the ball," he said, his voice rough with arousal.

She wet her lips. "It's not midnight yet. And I still haven't kissed the prince."

His eyes darkened. Sliding his hands up either side of her face, he bent his lips to hers. The merest touch. The briefest taste. A kiss that floated on air and left her drifting along with it. Gently, he moved his lips across and around hers, slowly, leisurely, teasing her with a promise held just out of reach.

"But this prince will never be satisfied with just a kiss," he murmured. His hand moved to the back of her skull and tightened, pressing her mouth hard against his own. His kiss turned hungry and insistent, as his other hand slid down her back and yanked her close against him.

The lovely slow simmer she'd been enjoying

bubbled over and raced across her skin in all directions at once. She slipped her hands behind his neck and hung on, her toes barely touching the ground as his mouth moved across her neck and shoulder, leaving a trail of fire in his wake.

****

Michael couldn't remember when he'd been so turned on by a woman. One kiss had turned into a full-body sensory experience—raising the hair on his arms and sending a flush of warmth rushing through his veins and into his groin. The urge to throw her on the bed, rip her clothes off and bury himself inside her was overwhelming. Also unacceptable. He grasped for control. With a deep breath and more effort than was reasonable, he released her and took a step back. Keeping his gaze on hers, he removed his jacket and tie, then paused.

"Your turn."

"What?"

She sounded a little shaken too.At least he wasn't the only one knocked off kilter.

"I removed two items of clothing. Now it's your turn."

She took her own deep breath. "Right. Turns again." Her gaze moved slowly down his body, then lifted back to his face. "But you have more clothing than I do."

He grinned. "Life isn't always fair, is it?"

With a put-upon sigh, she leaned down and removed the silver stilettos. "We do what we can with what we have."

"Life's crosses to bear," he agreed, unbuttoning his shirt and cuffs.

"Pretty sure this is one cross I can handle," she murmured, watching his shirt drop to the ground. Stepping forward, she ran her hands across his bare chest and shoulders.

He wouldn't have been surprised to see actual sparks flashing from her fingertips, given the effect of her touch on his skin. He pulled her against him, his hands sliding down over her hips to cup her ass, drinking in the feel and smell of her. But without her heels, she barely reached the middle of his chest—which meant everything he wanted to touch and taste required bending. He grabbed her hand and led her to the bed.

"Climb up," he ordered. "I want you at eye level."

She laughed. "I'm not that short."

He wrapped a fist in her tousled curls and pulled her to him. Bending his mouth to her ear, he sunk his teeth into her earlobe. She jumped.

"Get on the damn bed," he whispered into her ear.

She scrambled onto the bed.

"Much better," he murmured.

He ran his hands up her thighs until his fingers brushed the tiny swath of lace beneath the shimmering fabric of her dress. She inhaled sharply as he slid his fingers between the lace and the silk of her skin. He loved the way her breath hitched at his touch. He slid the lace slowly down her legs.

"I think you just stole my turn," she breathed, her palms on his shoulders as she stepped out of the thong.

"Royal prerogative. The prince makes the rules—and can change them." He let the lace fall to the floor and ran his fingers lightly back up her legs, enjoying the subtle shifting of her body in response to his touch.

"Don't princesses get to make rules too?" she murmured, her eyes closed. "Or am I Cin—"

He pressed his fingers to her lips, cutting her off mid-syllable. "Sin is exactly what you are…temptation incarnate."

Her lips curved. "My, you do credit me with extraordinary powers."

He brushed his lips beneath her earlobe. "How would you feel about turning those extraordinary powers over to me for the night?"

She opened her eyes. It appeared to take a bit of an effort. "Hmm?"

"Are you amenable to being my royal subject for the night?"

She stilled. A beat of silence stretched between them.

"Depends on what you mean. Are we talking 'safe word' kind of subject?" she finally asked.

He smiled. "No safe word required."

Her eyes narrowed. "Is that because you are the serial killer I suspected and I'm going to die no matter what?"

He clicked his tongue. "Damn. Shouldn't have used my credit card to pay for this room. What was I thinking?" His hands moved to her waist, and he kissed the hollow of her neck. "Looks like I'll have to let you survive the night after all." He traced a slow finger down to where her cleavage disappeared in the fabric of her dress. She shivered. His pulse kicked up a beat.

"So?" he asked again.

She shot him a half-apologetic look. "I'm not a very compliant person."

He lifted an eyebrow. "Ah, but that's what makes it

interesting. Stepping out of your comfort zone heightens the experience." His fingertip slowly circled first one nipple, then the other, through her dress.

Her eyes fluttered closed. "You make it really hard to think straight."

He stepped back, lifting his hands up in the air. "Far be it from me to confuse the decision-making process. Take all the time you need."

She shot him an exasperated look, then bit her lower lip, considering him. Finally, a half-smile flitted across those lips. "What the hell—so long as no safe words are required—long live the prince."

His cock saluted her decision. Affecting a calm neither he nor his anatomy felt, he moved away from her and sat in the chair by the window. Crossing one ankle over his knee, he took his sweet time perusing her, his gaze raking her body. She fidgeted.

"Stand still," he ordered.

She froze.

He let the tension build for a long minute, then said. "Take off your dress. Slowly."

****

It was one thing to get naked with a guy who was also getting naked with you. It was entirely different to be posed up here on a stage while he watched from a distance. She swallowed, her mouth suddenly dry.

He did that sexy eyebrow lift. "Did you not hear what I just said?" She sucked in a breath. Okay. Stepping out of her comfort zone was the point, right? Doing something she'd never done? Well, this little striptease for an audience of one—whose last name she didn't even know—certainly was that. Ignoring the flutters in her stomach, she slipped out of first one sleeve, then the other, and let the top of her dress fall to her waist. His jaw tightened. Her heart pounded. With excruciating slowness, she slipped the dress over her hips and let it drop in an emerald pool at her feet. His eyes gleamed like a predator who's just spotted a rabbit.

Damn. Taking her clothes off in front of a guy had never had this kind of effect on her before. She clenched her thighs together and focused on remembering to breathe.

"What does my temptress want tonight?" His voice was soft and low, reverberating in all her private places.

She pulled herself together, cleared her throat, and managed a halfway insolent look. "I thought you were the shot-caller."

His lips twitched. "I am. And I'm asking you a question. Don't keep me waiting for an answer."

She grinned. "Or what?"

He moved way faster than she'd given him credit for, one arm sweeping her legs out from under her, so she tumbled down on the bed. Before she could regroup, he flipped her over on her stomach and yanked her hips toward him. A sharp slap landed on her bared backside.

"Ow!" What the—?

A strong hand on the back of her neck pinned her in place, while his other hand lightly massaged her stinging cheek. She started to speak, but he murmured, "Shhhhh" and replaced his hand with his lips.

Her prince was literally kissing her ass. And it felt kind of amazing.

His tongue and lips meandered over the landscape of her body, the occasional nip of his teeth causing sharp intakes of breath, while his fingers went on their own exploration. Each brush against her skin fuelled the fire between her legs and the growing ache for his touch in other places—places he circled or skimmed, but never entered. She shivered and shifted restlessly beneath his explorations, wanting—needing—more. He was playing her. Playing with her—every erotic touch followed by a withdrawal, every promising caress slipping away as he intentionally withheld what her body screamed for.

"Damn you," she breathed, squirming under the hand that pinned her in place.

"Now that's no way for a subject to speak to her prince, is it?"

Another slap stung her ass. She inhaled sharply at the surprise of it more than any pain. The sting itself was light. And surprisingly erotic.

His fingers went back to teasing her. "I'll ask you again, Counselor. What do you want?"

"Can I say 'fuck'?" she managed to ask, breathless.

He laughed, a low chuckle that was almost as sexy as his touch. "Only if you use it in a full sentence."

"Finger-fuck me." she whispered.

The words were barely out of her mouth before her wish was his command. The speed and force of the sought-after invasion caught her by surprise. She just managed to choke off the scream that rose in her throat as his fingers expertly found and stroked her G-spot.

"See?" he murmured against the back of her neck, his thumb brushing her clit. "All you have to do is ask."

Her legs spasmed and she twisted the comforter in both fists, gasping at the delicious curling energy building inside her. He said something low in her ear, but whatever it was wafted by without registering on her part, an omission that earned her stinging backside another swat. A part of her brain protested that she really shouldn't enjoy that, but her body ignored it.

"I said," he repeated in her ear, "roll onto your back. Now."

She managed to do so, her body revolving around his gyrating fingers like a merry-go-round anchored at her center.

"Now sit up."

The man was a goddamn traffic cop, using his fingers to direct her movements from inside her own body. She pushed herself up until she was sitting on his hand, those long fingers of his now pressed even deeper inside—still moving. Still driving her wild. She moaned.

"Stand back up on the bed." His voice was hoarse.

"I—I can't." Her voice trembled as much as her body.

That apparently wasn't the right answer, because his fingers drove up inside her, propelling her to her feet by sheer force. She gasped and grabbed for him to steady herself.

"Put your foot on the bed and use my shoulders," he ordered.

And the man practically lifted her off the ground. She wasn't quite sure how, but sure enough, she was once again standing on the bed in front of him, clinging to his shoulders, not trusting her trembling legs to hold her up.

His mouth found first one aching breast, then the other, each rough lick of his tongue and scrape of his teeth over those sensitive nerve-endings spiralling her higher. Good Christ, the man had talents. His fingers quickened, in and out, twisting and turning with each re-entry, while his thumb teased her swollen detonation button—until detonate she did.

She cried out as her knees buckled and her entire body shook with the power of her orgasm. He caught her when her legs gave out, steadying her as she went to her knees, where tremor after tremor rolled through her. Her body curled in on itself until her forehead rested on the bed, her fingers digging into the bedcovers.

He clicked his tongue. "Did I say you could sit down?"

"Go to hell," she managed between the aftershocks that rocked her body.

She heard the soft clink of metal, followed by the shirr of leather sliding against fabric. Oh, hell no. Spanking was one thing—a thing she was surprised to find she kind of enjoyed—but no way was she letting him use his belt on her backside.

She gathered her strength and pushed herself up onto her knees. He was sliding the belt back and forth through his palms.

"Give me your hands," he said.

Backside, hands…didn't matter. No belt-whacking. She shook her head. "Huh-uh."

That eyebrow went up again.

"Did you just tell me no?"

"You're not hitting me with that belt," she warned.

His voice softened. "Of course not. Now, give me your hands."

She sat still for a moment, taking in this man who had already moved her way out of her comfort zone and more than rewarded her for the leap of faith. He was pretty gorgeous—with those broad shoulders and the light shirring of dark hair across that muscular chest. Her insides went gooey all over again and, ignoring the judgy voice in the back of her head, she extended her hands.

He wrapped the belt around and between her wrists, her heart rate kicking up a notch with each new loop of leather pulled tight against her skin.

"Do you like being tied up?" he asked, running a finger over her breasts as he tugged her forward with the tail of the belt that bound her wrists.

"This is new territory for me, so…?" She left the question hanging in the air, though the hitch in her breathing probably provided a pretty clear answer.

He smiled that slow, wicked smile of his again. "Well, we'll just have to make sure of it, then, won't we?"

****

The man more than delivered. Several orgasms later—more than Annie had experienced in a week with The Prick—they both lay sprawled and spent, his belt hanging over the bedpost. Never in her life had Annie even imagined a night like this—tied to a bed, spanked, ordered around—and loving every minute of it? She might not be able to get her head around it, but her body had no such dissonance. A deep sigh of satisfaction escaped her lips. His eyes were closed, but he tightened the arm wrapped around her and pulled her against him.

"You okay?" he asked.

"Pretty sure I passed 'okay' several orgasms ago," she answered, snuggling against him and running her fingernails lightly over his perfect abs.

The man must live at the gym.

He nuzzled her hair. "Glad to hear it. I'd hate to think I was the only one enjoying a stellar night."

She propped herself on her elbows and studied him.

He opened his eyes. "What?"

She shook her head. "This is just all such a surprise."

He laughed. "I know. I might have to rethink my antipathy to charity fundraisers."

She poked his ribs. "I'm not talking about that. I'm talking about the whole giving-up-control-thing. I never imagined I'd like that—or even consider it. I really don't like being told what to do. And before tonight, I'd have said any man who tried to spank me would wind up with a knee to his balls."

He gave her a long, considering look, then dropped a kiss on her shoulder. "Then I'm even more honored you chose to surrender control to me—not to mention passing on the knee to the balls. They thank you, too."

She continued to study him. "You just don't strike me as a guy who would go for passive women."

He smiled. "You're a good judge of character, Counselor."

"Then why…?" The question hung in the air.

He shifted until he was facing her. "Do you ride horses?"

"Planes and horses? The intrigue grows," she mused. "I used to ride horses." One of the few good memories of her childhood.

He ran a fingertip down her arm. "A trail horse will give you a nice smooth ride. A pleasant afternoon. But it's nothing like the adrenaline rush of riding a spirited horse, one that doesn't relinquish control until you

28

prove you're capable of handling her, worthy of her."

A little curl of arousal perked up low in her belly. "And I'm the spirited filly in that equation?"

He grinned. "A very spirited, very gorgeous filly."

She couldn't help smiling back. "You're pretty gorgeous yourself, cowboy."

Leaning in, she pressed a kiss on that magnificent chest. Then another. And another. Slow, lingering kisses across his chest and down his muscled torso. He shifted a bit under her touch.

"Now who has trouble holding still?" she murmured against his skin.

"Your fault," he answered, his hand moving into her hair.

She reached the red, raw scar on his side. She'd noticed it earlier, but being otherwise occupied and incapable of coherent conversation at the time, had let it go. Now she re-focused. "So, what happened here?"

He lifted his head and watched her trace the outline of the scar with her fingertips. With a sigh, he let his head fall back onto the pillow. "Just some minor surgery."

She replaced her fingers with her lips.

"A kiss to make it all better?" he said with a smile.

"Absolutely," she murmured against his skin. "A kiss is the oldest and most potent of magic. It's in all the fairy tales."

He chuckled, then tensed as her kisses shifted to even more sensitive areas. She loved the way he reacted to her touch. It made her feel sexy and powerful. But before she could do more, he took her by the shoulders and rolled them, so their positions were reversed.

"Now why did you do that?" she asked with a little

pout. "I was just getting started."

He kissed the soft notch in the center of her collarbone, his tongue lingering and sending shivers racing out in all directions. "Because chivalry requires that ladies always go first," he answered, boxing her in with his elbows.

She laughed. "I have. Numerous times, thank you very much."

"Every time," he responded, nipping at her neck.

"I guess it would be rude to argue with the rules of chivalry."

"Very rude," he agreed.

Then his talented tongue and fingers moved lower... then lower... and lower again... until her whole body was once again engulfed in wildfire—and all conscious thought left the room.

Chapter Three

Michael opened his eyes to sunlight and solitude. The scent of warm spice lingered—on the sheets, the pillows, on his own skin. He listened for the sound of movement or running water in the bathroom. Silence.

He lifted his head. "Annie?"

No response.

He let his head fall back to the pillow, his mind roaming through scenes from the evening before. The night had certainly exceeded his expectations. She had exceeded his expectations. Not only was she sexy as hell, she was also funny, smart, and smart-mouthed. And most of all real. No agenda, no expectations. No act designed to impress or entrap. A rare find indeed. And now she was gone.

He climbed gingerly out of bed. The combination of adrenaline and testosterone had proven a potent analgesic last night, but this morning his side was getting its revenge. He was sure his surgeon would've had a few words to say about his activities of the night before, had he been inclined to tell her about said activities, which he was not.

He moved carefully to the coffee pot, still hot and half-full. As he poured himself a cup, he spotted the note tucked beneath his watch. A single folded sheet of crisp hotel stationery with 'Mick' written in neat block letters across the front. Anticipation bloomed as he reached for it, expecting a phone number or e-mail where she could be reached. After all, a night like the one they'd just had bore repeating. Numerous times, if he had anything to say about it. He flipped open the note.

My Dearest Prince—
It was an incredible night and one I'll never forget.
Farewell,
—A

Well, hell. She'd actually done it. Ridden off into the sunset. Or sunrise, to be exact. She'd finally succeeded in keeping a one-night stand one night. And damn his luck, it had to be with him. He re-read the note. He had to admit it was classy—like the woman herself—but still. Ruefully, he lifted his coffee in a toast to the petite redhead he was pretty sure he'd never forget either.

"Farewell, my lady, he murmured.

He folded the note and stuck it in his wallet, before moving to the window. It looked across a four-lane thoroughfare to the manicured grounds of the Arch. The towering silver sentinel gleamed in the sunlight. A tugboat muscled an empty barge three times its size up the Mississippi River. Another barge, heavy with cargo and riding barely above the water line, floated past on its own, heading south on its way to the Gulf.

Commerce, transport, life was going on around him. The world was at work and so should he be. After all, if he was well enough to give a gorgeous redhead multiple orgasms, he was well enough to run his company. He stretched, feeling good in spite of his side's complaints, and turned toward the shower.

****

Annie circled her block twice before the parking gods smiled upon her. The downside of living in an 1890's-era neighborhood, built before cars were a thing, was that garages and driveways weren't a thing either—making a daily quest for street parking very much a thing. But she loved the character of the area and of her little two-story, shotgun-style duplex with its not-quite-level wood floors and tall, rattley windows that flooded the place with light—so she would continue sucking up to the parking gods and make do.

Darrow welcomed her home with his sonorous bass drum of a bark, guaranteed to wake up her plex mates. Not that Andrew and Stephan wouldn't applaud her early morning return in last night's evening attire, but then there'd be questions like 'so, what's his name?' and 'when are you seeing him again?' none of which she wanted to deal with.

She kicked off her shoes and hurried to unlock the back door into the so-called 'sunroom'—a glorified back porch enclosed to hold a washer/dryer and, in her case, Darrow's doggie bed and a plethora of chew toys. The outside swinging door gave Darrow 24-hour access to the fenced backyard she shared with her plex mates—who considered Darrow as much theirs as hers—so she never had to worry about him when she had to work late…or got the chance for a once-in-a-lifetime one-night-stand.

"Be still, you big idiot." She gave the squirming giant a hug and a good scratch to calm him down, then headed for the coffee pot.

She opened the freezer and surveyed her stash: Hazelnut, Irish Cream, Chocolate Raspberry… She settled on Crème Brulée and, in a matter of minutes, the aroma of delicately flavored coffee wafted through the room. With an anticipatory sniff of percolating caffeine, she collected her shoes and headed upstairs.

She cast a longing eye at the wrought-iron bed. Visions of wrapping herself in that creamy down comforter and sleeping off the combined effects of too much alcohol and too little sleep danced through her head. Unfortunately, that wasn't an option. She still had to prepare for tomorrow's trial. There would be no rest for the decadent this morning.

She grinned. Okay, so she felt like hell this morning, but wow... the night before had so definitely been worth it. Still smiling, she cranked up the tunes and went into a private strip tease that would have driven her handsome prince wild.

Kurt Cochrane, eat your heart out.

****

Two weeks later, Annie's perspective had changed. She may have fantasized about being the 'one-who-got-away' but she was the one who couldn't get this man out of her head. She didn't know his last name, but she knew the arch of his eyebrow, the way his lips felt against her skin, the still-raw pattern of the scar that crossed his left hip from his recent surgery. She knew the smell of him, the silky tickle of his dark hair against her cheek, the delicious strength of his hands on her body. The rich music of his laugh, the way his eyes sparkled with mischief and darkened with desire were oh, so familiar. She just didn't know his name.

And whose fault was that? Slipping out before dawn might have been cute and sassy given their whole 'leaving-the-ball-before-midnight' repartee, but geez, girl—talk about not thinking things through. This was her life, not some children's fairy tale. Who met the man of her dreams and then slipped away without letting him know how to reach her? Cute, sassy, and stupid.

Annie sighed and slammed closed the case file she'd been staring at, unseeing, for the last fifteen minutes. She leaned back in her chair, rubbing her hands across her face.

"You okay?"

She looked up at the lanky blond leaning against her office door. "Hey, Jonathan."

"Hey, back. You didn't answer my question. You okay?"

"Yeah." She sighed again, something she'd been doing a lot lately. "Just tired."

"You look like hell."

"Gee, thanks," she said acidly. "Your concern is touching."

He shrugged. "I'm making a coffee run. Want anything?"

"Yes," she said, putting her palms on the desk and standing up. "A change of scenery. I'll come with you. I could use the break."

"What are you working on?"

She opened, then closed her mouth. She didn't even know the name of the case file she'd literally just had in her hand. God, she was pathetic.

"Um, the Joiner case," she said, pulling a case name out of the air as she plucked her purse from the coat rack in the corner.

"The Grayson CEO shooting?"

"Right. Monday, I'm deposing the great man himself."

Jonathan snorted. "I'm surprised the high and mighty deign to show up for something as mundane as depos. I mean, if there aren't millions of dollars at stake. Then again, I guess even they take getting shot kind of personal. Wonder what he's like?"

"Arrogant, self-absorbed, too busy to be bothered with a petty nuisance like me."

Jonathan shot her a look. "You met him already?"

"No, but I know the type. I grew up with it, remember?"

"Oh, right. I keep forgetting you're the poor little rich girl. You seem so normal."

"Thank you," she said, absurdly pleased. She'd worked hard to be normal.

"So how does your grandmother feel about you defending a guy who shot one of the elite?"

"That would assume she knows I'm defending a guy who allegedly shot one of 'the elite' and me actually speaking to her to find out how she feels about it, neither of which is likely."

"Still no contact with the old lady at all?"

"None."

"Harsh, O'Toole, harsh." He shook his head. "She is your gran, after all."

"We're not talking rocking chairs and chocolate chip cookies here, Jonathan. She's the original ice queen, iron lady, bitch from hell. You don't talk to her without her taking over your life. With her, it's all or nothing and I've had way too much of the all. Nothing is a blessing."

"Suit yourself. Just seems a shame to walk away from all that money over a tiff."

"A tiff? She destroyed my family and... oh, forget

it," she muttered and yanked open the door to the coffee shop.

"I'm just jerking your chain." He gave her hair a tug. "At least now there's some fire in your eyes instead of that vacant stare you've been walking around with the last week." He surveyed the menu board above the counter as if he didn't know it by heart. Without looking at her, he continued, "You sure you're okay?"

"Yes, I'm o-kay," she gritted out between clenched teeth, as irritated by how stupid that sounded as by just how un-okay she felt.

"O-kay, then." He rolled his eyes and turned to place his order.

She sighed. Again.

"The usual, Annie?" the barista asked.

"Yes, please."

Jonathan threw a look of pity her way.

She shrugged. "What can I say? I'm in a rut."

"Hey, when you find something good, no reason to let it go," the barista countered.

Good advice. Unless you hadn't bothered to find out the something's last name. Annie ground her teeth. Again.

They collected their respective caffeine delivery options and claimed a table by the window.

"Good thing your kid is a lousy shot," Jonathan said, jumping as usual into the middle of a conversation and expecting her to follow. "If Grayson had died, they'd have gone for the death penalty for sure." He punched her lightly on the shoulder. "And then you wouldn't get the fun of trying his case. So hey, good luck all the way around."

"Oh, yeah. I feel really lucky."

"C'mon. You can't tell me you're not psyched about this case. I know you've been gunning for a murder case, but a famous victim and all the press to deal with—it's still a big step up for a newbie."

"I'm not a newbie anymore," she protested. "I've been here three years now."

"Three whole years. Wow. Figured you'd be running the place by now."

"Smartass."

"Hey, if you'd taken any one of those big law jobs you got offered, you'd be lucky to carry the partner's briefcase to a deposition after three years. This is cool stuff you're doing. And a major vote of confidence that Jackson is letting you run with it on your own. You know that. So why are you moping around like somebody killed your dog?" He frowned. "I mean Darrow's okay, right?"

"Darrow is fine. I am fine. Everyone is fine," she snapped. Then unable to stop herself, the rest bubbled out, fast and frustrated. "You want to know why I'm moping around? I'll tell you why I'm moping around. I met the man of my dreams and had the most spectacular sex of my life."

Jonathan choked on his iced coffee.

Annie plunged on, staring morosely into her latte. "I don't know his name, where he lives, where he works, or have any way to contact him. He doesn't know my name, where I live, or have any way to contact me. We're two barges passing on that damn river. One headed upstream, one down. Doomed to never meet again."

"Whoa…" Jonathan wheezed, sucking air back into his lungs. "What the hell are you talking about?"

She dumped the whole spectacular, sordid story. To his credit, he listened without interrupting until she slumped back in her chair and drained the last of her latte.

Then he said, "So that's it? That's what you've been moping around about for two weeks?"

She sighed again and nodded.

"Okay."

She waited for the follow-up, but it never came.

"That's it? Just, 'okay?'"

"What do you want me to say?"

"I don't know. Something."

"Look. You're not dying, your dog's not dying, nobody's dying. You hooked up with some guy, had a great time, and are wishing you could do it again. Post-coital depression. I get it." He grinned and wiggled his eyebrows. "But if you are in need of… relief… I am willing to sacrifice myself for the cause."

She threw a sugar packet at him. "It's not just about getting laid, asshole—and even if it was, your train left this station years ago and it's not coming back."

He shrugged. "Not my fault you missed your chance."

She glared. "And not mine that our one kiss had all the spark of a wet firework."

He wagged a finger at her. "I happen to be a great kisser. I can give you a long list of references to back that up."

She held up a hand. "Spare me your resume, Romeo. Been there, done that. And that assessment was mutual, if you recall."

He shrugged. "Truth. But I'm still willing to help

out a friend in a pinch."

She rolled her eyes.

He dropped the teasing. "So, what's got you so wrapped up about this guy?"

She stared out the window, mulling the question. Finally, she said, "Remember the Fourth of July fireworks over the Mississippi—that incredible grand finale set to classical music performed by the symphony?"

One eyebrow lifted. "Yeah…"

"It was that."

"Well, shit."

"Exactly."

Chapter Four

Back in her office, Annie dug out the Joiner file. Jonathan was right about this case. It was a big deal. She'd been on intake the morning the complaint came through, but once she'd learned the press was all over it because the victim was some big shot corporate mogul, she'd expected it to be reassigned to a more experienced attorney. But Jackson had said it was hers to keep if she wanted it. And she wanted it.

Not that she knew anything about the corporate mogul in question. She never followed the news, but Jonathan had given her the lowdown on Michael Grayson. Of course, she knew of Grayson Aeronautics. Sort of. It was a landmark in St. Louis and one of the largest employers in the city. The morning traffic report always included an update on the roads heading into or out of Grayson Aeronautics. But that's where her familiarity ended. She hadn't even known there was actually a Grayson involved with the company and wouldn't know the man if he was standing in front of her. But she was about to meet him very soon. And he was not happy about it.

The prosecutor had made that clear. 'Mr. Grayson is a very important man.' 'Mr. Grayson can't be expected to drop everything and appear on your schedule.' 'The least you could do is arrange the deposition at a time and location convenient to Mr.

Grayson.' His obsequiousness only strengthened her resolve to treat Grayson like every other victim in every other case. If the average Joes of the world had to show up at the public defender's office for a deposition, then so could Michael Grayson. She was sick to death of rich people getting their way while everyone else got run over by their limousines. Screw 'Mr. Grayson.' He was coming to visit the public defender's office Monday morning—under order of a subpoena.

She opened the manila envelope of media coverage the office investigator had pulled together and fished out the thumb drive hiding at the bottom of all the newspaper clippings. She plugged it into her computer and more than a dozen video files popped up. Seriously? Shootings happened every day in St. Louis. Most got barely a line or two of news coverage, if that. But let one of 'the money guys' get scratched by a bullet and the media machine practically wet itself.

Grinding her teeth at yet another example of the ever-present double-standard, she opened the first video file on the list. The low, musical voice of Tina Hoff, Channel 7's busty, blonde news anchor filled the room.

"And this just in—founder and CEO of Grayson Aeronautics, St. Louis philanthropist Michael Grayson, was shot tonight in the city's Central West End. Police say the shooting appears to have been the result of an attempted robbery. Mr. Grayson was rushed into surgery. There is no word yet on any suspects."

Annie froze. There, in the corner of the screen behind Tina's talking head, was a headshot of the man who'd had her tied to his bedpost. The same silky, charcoal hair. The same smoky grey eyes. And beneath the photo the name, "Michael Grayson, Grayson

Aeronautics CEO." A rushing noise in her ears drowned out the voice of the police chief giving his take on the situation.

Mick. Michael. 'I design airplanes.' CEO of an aeronautics company.

She flashed on the fresh scar above Mick's left hip. Michael Grayson had sustained a through and through gunshot wound to his left side just above the pelvic bone.

Hyperventilating, she dumped the envelope of news articles on her desk and scrabbled through the clippings until she found one with a picture. There he was again. Her mystery man, her fabulous one-night-stand man, her 'no-last-names' man. Her ever-so-charming prince.

'Mick' was Michael Grayson.

'Let's not bring all the family skeletons to the party.' It hadn't been some playful game. He really hadn't wanted her to know his name. He was too important, too privileged, too goddamned special to let her know his real identity. After all, what was she? Some low-level public interest lawyer. Just a night's free entertainment. He didn't want any entanglement, any messy follow-up with the likes of her. A quick lay and out, free and clear. That's all she was to Mr. High-and-Mighty so why bother getting to know last names?

Anger bloomed as the rant in her mind picked up steam. Never mind that she'd been the one to suggest their one-night stand. He was the one who'd lured her away from the ball with his slick, sneaky invitation to get away from Kurt Cochrane. He was the one who'd seduced her with that sexy eyebrow and bad-boy gleam in his eyes. Guess he thought he didn't have to worry about running into the likes of little Ms. Nobody again. Well, Mr. Hotshot was in for a bit of a surprise now, wasn't he?

Her anger vanished as the reality of that surprise rushed back. Oh. My. God. She had slept with the victim in the case of her career. She'd had sex with the state's star witness against her own client—*after* she'd been assigned the case. For God's sake, she'd kissed the scar that was her client's handiwork. Allegedly.

And Monday morning, he was showing up in her office for her to take his deposition.

****

"You what?!?"

Annie flinched.

"I didn't know who he was, Jackson. I truly didn't. I would never have… I didn't know, I just… I didn't know." She squeezed her eyes tightly closed, willing the tears not to fall and embarrass her further. As if that were possible.

Jackson Winrod, Chief Public Defender for the Twenty-Second Judicial Circuit, sat behind his desk and stared at her in ominous silence, the calm before the storm. She didn't have to wait long for it to break.

"You didn't *know* who Michael Grayson was? The Michael Grayson whose picture has been on the front page of every newspaper in the country the last month? The Michael Grayson *your* client is charged with shooting? You didn't know who he was? That's what you're telling me?"

"It's the truth, Jackson. I feel like—"

"I don't want to hear how you feel, O'Toole," he bellowed, rising from his seat and looming over her like a towering avenger. "It's your goddamn feelings that got us into this mess!"

She cringed.

"God in heaven, woman—what possessed you to sleep with a guy without even bothering to find out his name?" He was shouting now, his voice probably resonating throughout the office.

She started to stammer something, but he cut her off.

"Don't answer that." He threw up a hand. "I don't wanna know. What I want is for your personal life to stay personal. Like we don't have enough of a credibility problem as it is. Most of our clients already think we're in bed with the prosecutors, but not you, no, you're in bed with the victim. And the famous victim, to boot!" He glared at her, radiating fury.

"Jackson—" She stopped.

"What?" he snapped.

"I'm...I'm sorry." It sounded so lame, so completely unequal to the situation, but it was all she had.

"Jesus, Mary, and Joseph," he muttered, dropping back into his chair.

Annie forced herself to breathe.

Finally, he said, "Depos are Monday?"

She nodded, not trusting herself to speak.

"Okay. First things first. I have to visit your client. He has to be told you have a conflict with his case and just what that conflict is—and not by you. I don't want you discussing your sex life with your client. Not that I want to be discussing your sex life with your client but, thanks to you, somebody has to." He glared at her. "If he agrees, you'll do the depos on Monday as planned. But I want Clark in there with you—a second set of eyes on the case and on you.

"After that, you're off the case and Clark will take it from there. If Joiner's not okay with you even doing the depositions—and I wouldn't blame him—" his glare intensified, "he gets Clark immediately and both the depos and trial date will have to be postponed. Which means you'll have to tell the court why we need a continuance."

Annie opened her mouth in horror at both options. "But—"

"Don't go there, O'Toole." His hand flew up again. "Do not even go there. You're the one who decided to bare your ass. Don't expect me to cover it for you now."

Her face grew even hotter and she closed her mouth.

"Does Clark know about this?"

The whole office knew they were besties.

"Um, sort of."

"Sort of?" he growled.

"He knows about my, um—well, you know—the… event. But he doesn't know it was Grayson. I didn't know—when I told him about…it." Her face burned and she kept her gaze on the wall above Jackson's head.

"Well, bring him up to speed. I'll see Joiner tonight. And until I say otherwise, you're busted back to docket duty. Be thankful you still have a job."

"Yes, sir." She knew better than to argue. She turned toward the door.

"O'Toole?"

"Sir?"

"From now on, you damned well better be asking for an ID and running a computerized conflict check before you climb into bed with anything but that Great

Dane of yours. You got that? I am not having this conversation with you again. *Ever*."

"Yes, sir."

****

Jonathan was Annie's best friend at the PD office—one of her best friends, period—but even he wasn't cutting her any slack on this. He sat in the rocking chair Annie kept in the corner of her office, slowly shaking his head in rhythm with the squeak of the rocking until she snapped.

"Would you stop that?"

"What?"

"Stop shaking your head in that condescending, can-you-believe-she's-such-a-screw-up way."

"Well, if the shoe fits…"

"This is not my fault," she protested. "I didn't know who the guy was, okay?"

"Yeah, got that. And that's the screwed-up part. How could you not know you were jumping Michael Grayson? I mean the man's been featured in every 'Most-Eligible-Bachelors' list for like the last five years. You gotta come out from under your rock and start paying attention to the world, girl. You're a danger to yourself."

"I don't need any more lectures," she snapped. "Jackson covered that department just fine."

"I bet he did." Jonathan gave a long, low whistle and chuckled. "Wouldn't have minded being a fly on the wall to watch that ass-whooping. Or better yet, Jackson's meeting with Joiner about your sexual forays into the dark side. Bet that'll be a fun conversation."

Annie jumped up and paced. "Enough, already. You're supposed to be helping me here."

He tipped back the rocker and propped his feet on the edge of her desk. "Well, the way I see it, you've got two choices. You can do nothing and just enjoy the shock on his face when he walks in and finds you at that deposition table Monday morning—which, frankly, is my vote, since I now get to be there to see it and I think that's gonna be a life moment—"

She threw him an exasperated look.

"—or you can try to reach him and give him fair warning. After all, there's nothing in this for him but public embarrassment. It's as much to his benefit to play it cool as it is yours, right?"

She stopped pacing and stared at her reflection in the glass of her framed diplomas. "You're right. I need to call him. I need to let him know."

Silence.

"Oh, God, I do not want to have this conversation. What exactly do I say? Hey, Mick, it's me, your anonymous one-night stand from the Justice for All Ball. Funny thing. Turns out I'm the defense lawyer for the guy who shot you. See you at the depo. *Christ*."

"Yeah, well. Have fun with that." Jonathan unfolded his lean frame and reached across her desk. "I'll just take the file and start getting up to speed. Later."

"Thanks for all your support," she snapped at his back as the door swung closed behind him.

She plopped into her desk chair and stared at her computer. Finally, she typed in 'Grayson Aeronautics' and hit the search button. There were listings for the Grayson Aeronautics Executive Leadership Center, Defense Division, Commercial Division, and Grayson Aeronautics Enterprises, but no just General

Information listing. She opted for the most likely-sounding candidate and jotted down the number for the Executive Leadership Center.

She stared at the phone. Then at the ceiling. She ran her fingers through her hair, taking deep breaths, and praying for a reprieve. None came.

Okay. Better just to dive in and get it over with. Like jumping into icy cold water. Do it and be done. Rip off the band-aid. It was just a phone call. Just. A. Phone. Call.

She picked up the phone. And set it back down. Several seconds passed. She gnawed on her lip, ran her fingers through her hair again, stared at the ceiling again, and at last picked up the phone again. Taking a deep breath, she punched in the number.

Twenty minutes later, Annie had made her tortuous way through a half dozen different automated answering systems—not surprisingly they had no 'if you slept with the CEO and now need to disclose your identity, please press one' option—and a host of useless receptionists, not one of whom had been able to put her in touch with their boss. Instead, she'd been transferred from what turned out to be a training department to a design department, back to the executive leadership center, and then, when she disclosed that she was from the Public Defender's Office, to the government affairs department, before finally reaching someone who actually knew the number for the executive office suite. Accessibility to the public was obviously not part of the company's mission statement.

"Michael Grayson's offices. This is Myriam. May I help you?"

The smooth, professional tones froze Annie's

blood. This was it. She cleared her throat. "Yes. Um, Michael Grayson, please."

"Who's calling?"

"Annie O'Toole."

"And what is this regarding?"

"I'm a…a friend…of Mick's—er, Michael's. I just need a quick word with him."

"I'm sorry." The voice cooled by several degrees. "Mr. Grayson is very busy today. If you're a… friend… of his, you might try reaching him on his private number. Good day."

The phone line clicked, and she was listening to a dial tone.

Okay, now she was pissed. She punched in the number of the executive office suite again.

"Michael Grayson's offices. This is Myriam. May I help you?"

"This is Annie O'Toole again, the caller you just hung up on. I am the attorney who has Mr. Grayson under subpoena to appear in my office Monday morning for a deposition. I have information he will need before that deposition. And I guarantee he will want to hear what I have to say before he shows up for that deposition. Trust me, you do not want to be the one who keeps him from receiving that information. Now, please put me through to Michael Grayson."

There was silence on the line for a moment.

"Hold, please."

"Thank you." Annie squared her shoulders and took a deep breath.

"Legal Department, Susan speaking. May I help you?"

"Legal? I didn't ask for Legal, I was on hold for

Michael Grayson."

"Is this the attorney calling about the deposition for Monday?"

"Yes, but— "

"Please hold."

The phone went dead for another thirty seconds, then a deep male voice came on the line. But it wasn't the right deep male voice.

"Harrison Stewart."

"I'm sorry. I was holding for Michael Grayson and was apparently transferred to you by mistake. Can you transfer me back?"

"Is this A.J. O'Toole?"

"Y-e-s," she said slowly. She signed all her pleadings A.J. O'Toole. "Who is this?"

"Harrison Stewart. General Counsel for Grayson Aeronautics and Michael Grayson's legal advisor. I have your subpoena right here. Is there a problem with the deposition?"

"Um… No-o." The man must think her a complete idiot.

"Then why are you calling, Counselor?"

"I, uh, I just needed to go over a few things with Mr. Grayson in advance of Monday's deposition. Is he available?"

The silence was deafening.

"I'm sorry, Ms. O'Toole, but I don't think it's appropriate for you to be 'going over things' with Mr. Grayson in advance of your deposition. I am his legal advisor and any communication regarding this matter needs to go through me. I'm sure you can understand that."

Yep, he thought she was an idiot.

She gave it one last, desperate shot. "Why don't you let Mr. Grayson decide that? We, uh, we crossed paths at the Justice for All Ball the other night and I... Look, please, just tell him that Annie called and let him decide if he wants to call me back."

She left her cell number and hung up, knowing full well the message would never be delivered. No lawyer worth his salt would give his client the choice of chatting with opposing counsel. She slumped back in her chair.

Monday morning was going to suck.

Chapter Five

It did. Mother Nature must have known what the day held in store and chose not to waste any sunshine on the occasion. Scattered raindrops streaked the windows, accompanied by soft rumbles of distant thunder, a joint opening act for the sea of ominous grey thunderclouds swelling in the west.

Darrow's ears twitched with each new rumble. He lay on the floor and watched her curled up on the couch, hugging her second cup of coffee like a junkie cuddled up to the needle. It wasn't a pretty picture. Annie wore a ragged, green-striped bathrobe long past its prime and her uncombed hair was even more Medea-like than usual. Her eyes were puffy and rimmed with red from a night of too little sleep and too many tears.

The truth was, before she'd learned who he was, she'd missed Mick terribly. And beneath the anger and embarrassment that followed the bombshell revelation, the fantasies she'd nourished of some future romantic reunion lay curled and cringing, awaiting the final nail in their coffin.

So, the tears had poured forth, staining her cheeks and pillow, and leaving her with a hangover-quality headache this morning. Now, not only would Grayson be shocked to discover she was Joiner's lawyer, he'd take one look at her ravaged face and wonder what in

God's name he'd ever seen there to interest him for even one night.

She sniffed and slurped her coffee, wondering if it was heresy to wish for the whole second-coming apocalypse thing to get a move on. Or maybe just an earthquake. An earthquake would do it. They'd been predicting the New Madrid Fault would go and take St. Louis with it for years now. Why didn't you think of that, Mother Nature? Earthquake, tornado, flood —why could a person never conjure a good natural disaster when she needed one?

The doorbell stopped her musings. Darrow scrambled to his feet as she glanced at the clock. Visitors at 7:00 a.m. could not be good. She set down her mug and shoved past Darrow to peek through the peephole. Jonathan. Of course. With an irritated sigh, she unchained and unbolted the door. After pulling it open, she turned back to retrieve her coffee.

"Ball of fire, isn't she, boy?" Jonathan paid Darrow the duty owed to pass—a good scratch from ears to wagging tail—then stepped into the living room. He held out a white bag. "I brought donuts."

She turned. "Donuts?"

"Still warm."

She snatched the bag and sank back onto the couch, inhaling the fragrant scent. "You are a good soul, Jonathan. Or at least a semi-decent one part of the time. Okay, rarely, but every now and then, you come through and for that, I'm appreciative."

"I'll take that," he said comfortably, settling himself in the armchair.

Annie allowed the warm sugar to dissolve on her tongue before she looked across at her colleague. "So, what are you doing here, really?"

"Really?"

"Really."

"I thought you might need a bit of a boost to get you up and out of here this morning."

"You thought I was going to bail."

"You? Of course not." He sounded a bit too nonchalant.

"You did. You thought I was going to bail." She glared at him. "I can't believe you thought I'd do that. I mean, this sucks. Big time sucks. And if I were the kind of person to ever bail, this would be it, believe me. But I am not that kind of person. And I'm really offended you thought I would be."

"I just thought you might need a boost." He spoke extra slowly as if she were a mentally ill client. "So, I'm here—as your friend—to give you a sugar-loaded, lard-laden boost, and make sure you get your ass to the courthouse today."

"Because you thought I was going to bail."

"Absolutely."

She snorted and reached for another donut, breaking off a bite to appease Darrow who was demanding his share.

Jonathan snagged one for himself. "You didn't even think about bailing? Not a little?"

"Of course, I thought about it. I'm not an idiot." She sighed and took another slurp of caffeine. "But I can't. As Jackson said, I'm the one who... well, never mind what Jackson said. The point is, I will be there."

He looked at her dubiously. "Yeah, you definitely look ready to depose the guy who swept you off your feet in the case of your career."

"I will be ready," she said defensively. "I just needed a…"

"Boost."

"Right."

****

The long, black limousine rolled to a stop, looking out of place next to the Depression-era criminal courts building. Long past its prime, the seat of justice was now pollution-gray, its stone façade adorned with tired gargoyles and chipped columns.

"I've no idea how long this will take, Angelo," Michael said. "I'll call when we're finished."

The husky chauffeur closed the car door and cast a baleful eye at the motley crew of bystanders gawking at the limo. "I'll just wait until you're inside, sir."

Michael sighed. The man had gotten positively grandmotherish since the shooting. "We'll be fine, Angelo."

"Yes, sir," Angelo said, falling into a military at-ease stance, his back to the limousine, and making no move to get in the car.

"Fine," Michael muttered irritably. "Sure you don't want to hold my hand and walk me to the prosecutor's door?"

A touch of a smile flitted across one corner of the ex-Marine's mouth. "I doubt they'd let me through security, sir."

Angelo never went anywhere without packing his own personal armory.

"Well, I guess I can be grateful for small gifts, then."

"Yes, sir."

Sporadic raindrops sprinkled around them as they

climbed the worn marble steps and stepped through the oversized brass doors. The wide hallway was filled with people waiting their turn to get through security. Bored, brown-shirted deputies moved the line through at glacial speed, stopping now and then to chat with passing courthouse personnel while the line came to a grinding halt. Beyond the metal detector, clusters of St. Louis's finest, holstered weapons on their hips, leaned against the marble walls, conversing in low tones while they waited to be called into court. Farther down the corridor, a lawyer in a rumpled suit gesticulated angrily at a client wearing a 'Fuck the Police' t-shirt, while several women in tight, short skirts and heavy make-up sulked against one of the wide windowsills.

Michael was taking in the odd mix of tension and lethargy when, at the far end of the hall he caught a glimpse of reddish-gold curls. He stepped quickly to the side to get a better look. And there she was. Annie.

She looked every bit as stunning in her black, tailored suit as she had in that emerald green, backless cocktail dress. She was carrying a stack of files and talking to a tall, lanky man who leaned by the elevator door. As if pulled by the force of his gaze, she turned her head, and their eyes met. A silly grin spread across his face.

But she didn't smile back at him. Instead, she dipped her head, breaking the connection as the tall man glanced his way. Then the elevator door opened and the two of them stepped inside. Without a backward glance, she disappeared. Again.

She wouldn't even acknowledge him? What the hell?

"We're up." Harrison nudged him forward through

the security line.

Their first stop was the prosecutor's office on the top floor. There the Honorable Francis Nicoletti spent a tiresome fifteen minutes sucking up before introducing the assistant prosecutor handling the case, an Ichabod Crane look-alike by the name of Randall. The latter reviewed their previous statements and what to expect in the deposition, then escorted their group to a back elevator.

When the doors re-opened, they found themselves in very different surroundings. In stark contrast to the towering ceilings and marble floors of the halls of justice above, the ceiling down here was stained and peeling and the institutional linoleum floor yellowed with age. Scarred wooden benches, overflowing with the city's down-and-out, lined the wall outside an equally scarred door marked Public Defender.

The prosecutor led their group to an unmarked door at the far end of the hallway. It took him a couple of tries before the loose doorknob caught. When it did, he stood to one side and waved them through into a sad excuse for a law library. Sagging shelves were crammed with more books than they were designed to hold and an old table that had seen better days sat in the center, ringed by a handful of mismatched chairs.

Standing in a doorway leading into an adjacent room was the same lanky blond man Michael had seen upstairs. His heart leapt as he tried to figure out how to find out more about Annie without crossing a boundary she apparently didn't want crossed. Still. He began forming the question: *By the way, what was the name of the redhead you were just talking to upstairs? Thought I recognized her from somewhere…*

"Are you doing these?" Randall addressed the man in the doorway. "I thought this was O'Toole's case."

"It is. I'm coming on as co-counsel," he said. His response was addressed to the assistant prosecutor, but his gaze was on Michael.

Michael knew when he was being sized up. It happened in every business deal, each taking the measure of the other. But this examination held a touch of amusement he didn't quite understand.

"Are we ready then?" The prosecutor was all business.

"Yep. We'll start with Mr. Grayson."

"Harrison Stewart, personal counsel to both deponents," Harrison said, introducing himself since the prosecutor hadn't seen fit to. "I'll be sitting in as well."

"Fine." The lanky blond spared the lawyer the briefest of glances before returning his focus to Michael.

Again, Michael felt the touch of amusement in the man's gaze.

Slowly, deliberately, he did his own sizing up of the man in the doorway. "You obviously know my name, but I didn't catch yours."

The amusement increased. "Sorry about that. Jonathan Clark." The man had a firm handshake and friendly, un-intimidated gaze. "Mr. Ashton, you can have a seat out here while we depose Mr. Grayson. There's coffee by the window—though I can't say I recommend it—and a restroom down the hall to your left."

Peter surveyed the battered chairs available and gingerly lowered himself into one.

"Ready, Mr. Grayson?" Clark seemed to be

working at keeping a smile from spreading across his face as he motioned Michael through the doorway.

The inner room was a replica of the outer—mismatched bookshelves lining the walls and a scarred table in the center where a court reporter was setting up his stenography equipment. At the far end, her back to a narrow, ground-level window, stood a petite woman in a tailored black suit. Tousled reddish-gold curls provided a familiar frame for wide, emerald-green eyes that watched him, her expression unreadable.

Michael froze mid-step. What the hell?

The prosecutor almost collided into his back, teetering on his toes and quick-stepping to one side as Clark rocked back on his heels, hands in his pockets, watching them all with a grin he no longer attempted to hide.

The woman squeezed her eyes shut, took a deep breath, and stepped forward, extending her hand.

"A.J. O'Toole. I represent Mr. Joiner and will be conducting your deposition today." Her voice was tight, but even and professional, betraying none of the shock flooding his system.

"You?" he finally choked out." You are O'Toole?"

"I am." She let the hand he'd ignored drop back to her side. "And you, it turns out, are Michael Grayson. So, we have a deposition to conduct." Stiffly, she motioned toward the chair closest to the court reporter. "Would you have a seat, please?"

Confusion and anger flooded through Michael's veins at her matter-of-fact demeanor. "No, I will not have a seat, goddamn it. What the hell is going on?"

"Is there a problem?" Randall asked, looking from one to the other.

"Damn straight there's a problem." He kept his gaze locked on Annie, his voice edged with steel. "You are defending the guy who shot me—have been defending him all along?"

Her voice dropped to almost a whisper. "I'm sorry. I didn't know who you were."

"You two know each other?" asked the assistant prosecutor, in obvious confusion.

Clark coughed into his fist and emerged with a grin. "Their paths have crossed."

"What's going on?" Peter Ashton appeared in the open doorway.

"I'm sorry, Mr. Ashton," Jonathan intervened, steering Ashton back out into the anteroom. "You'll have to wait out here."

"Everybody, wait out there," Michael barked. "Outside. All of you." He jerked his head at the court reporter, who promptly got up and scurried into the anteroom.

"But s-sir—" the befuddled prosecutor stammered.

"Did your boss not just say, moments ago, that I was to tell you how I wanted things handled and you would see that it was done?"

"Well, yes, sir, but I'm sure he never envisioned—"

"Out."

"Michael, what is going on?" Harrison Stewart leaned in. "What are you doing?"

"You, too. Out."

"Michael?" The lawyer looked at him in amazement. "This is not—"

"Just for a minute." He placed a hand on his lawyer's arm, his gaze never leaving Annie's. "It's all right. Go."

The man stiffened. "This is against my advice, I hope you know."

"I know. Do it anyway."

The man had worked for him long enough to know that argument was futile. Shaking his head in exasperation, Harrison jerked his head at the prosecutor and headed to the door.

The prosecutor held his ground. "Sir, I don't think—"

Clark leaned over. "I don't think we want to piss this one off," he whispered into Randall's ear. "Let's just give them a minute."

The prosecutor hesitated, then followed the others to the door. "I'll be just outside here, Mr. Grayson. If you want anything, I—"

Clark gave him a gentle push out the door.

"Have fun, you two." He smiled broadly and pulled the door closed behind him.

****

A heavy blanket of silence settled over the room as the two stared at each other. Thunder rumbled outside the window. Annie was the first to look away. Crossing her arms in front of her, she turned to stare out the window.

Finally, she said over her shoulder, "I didn't know who you were. You know that."

"Right." His sarcasm was palpable. "You were just defending the guy who tried to kill me. No reason at all for you of all people to have any idea who I was. So, what was the point? Just a kick to see if you could pull it off? Hey, I fucked the guy my client shot?"

She whirled to face him. "I did not—"

"A bet? Some defense lawyer double-dare with

your buddy Clark out there? He seems to be getting a big kick out of this little reunion. Was he in on the joke?"

His eyes had flashed with heat when he'd first entered the room—and not the good kind—but now they were flat, devoid of any emotion whatsoever. Nausea crawled up the back of her throat and tears filled her eyes as rain pounded against the window. Furiously, she blinked them away. For God's sake, Annie, get a grip.

"Did you think this might actually help your case?" He strolled toward the table, his voice sardonic and contemptuous. "Convince me to drop the charges or agree to some slap-on-the-hand plea bargain to avoid the fun the press will have with our little *tête-à-tête*?" He leaned down and pressed his palms against the table between them, his eyes level with hers. "Well, forget it, love." His voice went as flat as his eyes. "You should have done your research first. I don't give a damn what the press says about me, and I don't make deals with people who fuck with me. Ever."

Anger struggled with pain and Annie grasped onto it with her whole being. She needed anger right now like she needed air. Anger was the only way she would survive having her heart sliced open by the man who had wormed his way inside it in just one night.

"You arrogant bastard. Do you think I wanted this? Planned to destroy my reputation and my career for the pleasure of a night with His Majesty, Michael Grayson?"

A streak of lightning flashed, bright and deadly.

"If you hadn't been so coy about making sure your one-night stand didn't know who you were, neither one of us would be in this mess. You think my heart didn't stop when I sat down to prepare for this deposition and saw your face on the news?"

The storm growled and rattled the window.

"And you got right on the phone to let me know about our little problem, didn't you?" Michael sneered. "Sorry, sweetheart, that one doesn't fly."

She exploded. All the anxiety, all the frustration, all the pain she'd endured since the morning she'd walked out of that hotel room coalesced into an explosion that overwhelmed even the thunder crashing against the walls of the courthouse.

"You asshole!" she spat, gripping the back of the chair in front of her so tightly her knuckles turned white. "You live in a goddamned ivory castle that mere peons aren't privileged enough to access. Did you ever consider that?" She gave the chair a shove and it banged against the table as she paced furiously behind it. "Ask your precious Myriam why I didn't call. Or how about Susan in Legal?" Her voice rose with every word until it was an octave above normal.

Anxious voices rose outside the door, and she stabbed a finger in its direction.

"Ask your precious Harrison Stewart out there if I tried to reach you. Or every one of your other fifteen receptionists in your piss-poor Executive Training Center or goddamn Government Affairs Office —" she swept her arms wide to encompass his entire company — "or in fricking hell... because that's pretty much been my life since you came into it, with, with... with your sexy eyebrows—" she sputtered and waved her hands, the anger fizzling.

One lifted at that.

"—and your bad-boy smile and your, your..." Energy spent, she dropped into the chair at the end of the table and pressed her palms against her eyes. "Oh, why the hell couldn't you just be Mick, the airplane designer?"

Seconds ticked by with the staccato of raindrops against the glass. Neither of them moved.

Finally, he said, "So what do we do now?"

She sniffed and rubbed the back of her hand across her nose. "We have to do this deposition."

"Are you kidding me?" he asked incredulously.

"No, I'm not kidding you. I didn't go through this hell so you could walk out of here without being deposed. We're doing this."

Now it was his turn to take a deep breath. "If you really didn't plan this, why the hell didn't you just get off the case?"

Annie massaged her temples. "I am getting off the case, but it was too late for anyone else to be ready to do the depositions this morning. That's why Jonathan is here. He'll be taking it over after today. James was okay with that as a compromise."

"James?"

"My client."

"The punk who tried to kill me, you mean. Like I give a damn what he thinks."

"He's my client. It's his call," she said wearily.

"Clark." Michael began to pace the small space. "He knows?"

"Yes."

"Who else?"

"Well, my client."

He snorted.

"And my boss, Jackson Winrod."

"Your boss?"

"Yes." She lifted her head and gave him a sardonic look. "I know this comes as a shock to you, Grayson, but you're kind of a big deal and so is the case of the guy who shot you. My boss is watching this one very closely."

"Right." Michael laughed without humor. "Getting to defend the guy who tried to kill me was a big career-boost for you, I suppose."

"*Was* being the operative word. Sleeping with the victim is kind of a career-killer."

Michael watched her. She sighed, straightened her shoulders, wiped her face one last time, and finally met his gaze.

"So, shall we get this over with, Mr. Grayson?"

He gave a short, humorless laugh. "Oh, yes, Ms. O'Toole, let's."

He crossed to the door and yanked it open. The group huddled around the door trying to overhear stumbled back. He jerked his head at the collective.

"Let's do this."

The prosecutor and court reporter filed in, each careful not to look too closely at either of the room's combatants. Harrison gave Michael a quizzical look, but didn't speak, while Jonathan's eyes flitted first to Annie, his earlier humor tempered by concern. She gave him a weary shrug and he squeezed her shoulder before glancing back to Michael with a rueful grin.

"Michael, what is going on?" Peter peered in the door.

"Don't worry about it. It's under control." Michael closed the door on his colleague and seated himself at the head of the table, still acting like the one running the show—even though it was not his to run.

Of course he did. Asshole.

****

"We are here for the deposition of Michael Grayson in the matter of State of Missouri vs. James Joiner, Case Number 24CR-2342."

As Annie ran through the preliminaries that started every deposition, Michael realized that anyone walking in right now would see nothing but a typical deposition of another crime victim. He couldn't help but be impressed at her ability to slide this professional veneer in front of the raging storm he'd just witnessed. She was an excellent actress. The question was, which was the act?

"Please tell us in your own words about the night you were shot. I'll have some follow-up questions when you're finished."

He took a deep breath—and inhaled her scent. That soft, delicate spice. His train of thought derailed.

"I… um," He cleared his throat, irritated at how easily she unsettled him. "I'd had dinner with Peter and a couple of potential investors. Peter and I were walking back to the car when Joiner stepped out of an alleyway and shot me. After that, things get a little blurry."

"Did the shooter say anything before he shot you?"

Annie was watching him, leaving the notetaking to the court reporter. Professional and intent sure beat the hell out of tear-filled and hurt. Maybe. Then again, maybe not. Up was down and down was up and he didn't know what to think.

"No, he didn't say anything."

Her glance flicked to his cuff. "You're wearing a gold watch today with what appear to be diamonds circling the face."

She'd left her good-bye note beneath that watch while he lay asleep in the bed behind her, naked and satiated from their night of lovemaking. He toyed with the idea of throwing in that tidbit of information just to watch those green eyes shoot sparks again, but she was already moving on. If she was troubled by any of the same memories as he was, she hid it well.

He let it go.

"Were you wearing a watch the night you were shot?"

"I was."

"This same one?"

"Yes."

"But he didn't ask for the watch?"

"He seemed more interested in shooting me."

She ignored his sarcasm. "And he didn't take it from you once you fell?"

"Obviously not." What was the big deal about the watch?

"What about your wallet? Did he take that?"

"No."

"How much cash did you have with you that night?

"I'm not sure. A few hundred, I imagine."

"You typically carry a few hundred in cash with you?"

"Yes."

"Credit cards?"

"Yes."

"And all of those were left in your wallet as well?"

"Yes."

"Was anything at all taken from you?"

"No."

"Was anything demanded of you before you were shot?"

"Not that I recall." Come to think of it, that was a little odd, wasn't it?

"What about your companion, Peter Ashton? Did the man who shot you take anything from him that you know of?"

"No. At least not before he fired. I can't say what happened after."

She switched subjects. "Can you describe the man who shot you?"

"Late teens. Black, about six feet tall. Skinny. Wearing a red baseball jacket that was too big for him. Baggy jeans. White tennis shoes."

"Dark or light skinned?"

"Light."

"Any facial hair?"

"No."

"Any other distinctive marks or characteristics you recall?"

"He had a gold incisor, right side."

"Did you give the police a description of the man who shot you that night?"

"I was a little indisposed. Peter gave them the description. When I woke up after the surgery, the police asked me if I agreed with his description, and I did."

"Is that the way it was presented to you? 'Here's what your colleague said, do you agree?'"

"Yes."

She frowned. "Did you remember anything about

your assailant apart from what Mr. Ashton had already provided to the police?"

Michael considered. "No."

"Were you ever asked to view any photos to see if you could pick out the shooter?"

"Yes."

"How many photos did you view?"

"Just the one."

"Not a group of photos?"

"No. Just the one of the guy they arrested."

"What did they say when they showed you that photo?"

"That this was the guy Peter identified and did I agree."

Her lips pressed a bit tighter. "Did you see the gun?"

"Just the flash when it fired."

"Where did the flash come from?"

"His left side. When he stepped out of the alley in front of us, his hands were in his jacket pockets. Then, he yanked out the gun and fired."

"With his left hand?"

"Yes."

"So, he was left-handed?"

"He shot me with his left hand. I didn't get the chance to ask for his autograph, so I don't know which hand he writes with."

She let his sarcasm slide by without response. "About how far from you was the shooter when he fired?"

Michael considered. "Six or seven feet maybe?"

"What do you remember after the shot was fired?"

Michael cast his mind back. "Mostly pain. Peter's

voice. A woman screaming."

"'Peter' being Peter Ashton?"

"Yes."

"What do you remember him saying?"

He shook his head. "I'm not sure. Calling my name, I think. As I said, it's blurry."

"The woman screaming. Do you know who she was?"

"No."

"Was there a woman in your party that night?"

His gaze met hers, wondering if the answer mattered to her. "No. There was no woman in our party."

"Were you aware that a woman called 911?"

"No, I wasn't," he admitted, surprised. "I assumed Peter called."

"So, you have no idea who she was?"

"No."

"Had you ever seen the man who shot you before?" she asked, switching topics again.

"No."

"Have you had any contact or interaction with any gang members that you're aware of?

"You mean other than when one shot me?"

She gave him an exasperated look. At least something finally broke through that professional façade.

"Before this incident, had you had any contact or interaction with anyone who may have been a member of a gang?

"No. That's Peter's area, not mine."

She cocked her head. "How so?"

"He volunteers at some community center that

works with gang members. I don't know which one."

"Have you ever visited this community center with him?"

"No."

"Attended any event supporting that or any other organization that works with gang members?"

"No. Charity events bore me." He gave her a deliberately long look. "Though every now and then one surprises me."

A slight blush crept across her cheeks, but her voice remained even and professional. "You mentioned having a few drinks prior to the shooting. What were you drinking?"

He had to give her credit. She was good.

"Bourbon."

Not just for dry cleaning anymore.

"How many had you had?"

He considered, casting back in his memory. "Three, I think?"

"What size?"

"Singles."

"Over what time period?"

"One with dinner, two after."

"How long were you there after dinner?"

"Around an hour, hour and a half?"

"Was Mr. Ashton drinking as well?"

"He had a glass of wine at dinner. Nothing afterward. He was driving."

She looked down and flipped through her notes. She turned to the prosecutor. "I'm finished with this witness."

He suspected she was finished with him as well.

Chapter Six

Michael walked out into the hallway. It was Peter's turn to be examined, and Michael needed the time to walk off his confusion. The row of defendants on the benches in the hallway had lessened considerably. One boy who looked barely fourteen sat with his elbows on his knees, staring at the floor. On the other end of the same bench, a homeless man in an army jacket and grizzled beard slept with his arm thrown protectively across the plastic bag that no doubt contained all he owned in the world.

Michael crossed to the door marked Public Defender and pushed it open. It appeared that everyone who had been on the benches outside was now crowded into the small lobby—filling the plastic chairs, perched on the windowsills, leaning against the walls. The switchboard rang nonstop. As he waited for the harried receptionist to get free, he watched a roach crawling along the baseboard.

"Can I help you?" she finally said, as she scribbled down a message.

"I'd like to see Jackson Winrod, please."

"Do you have an appointment?"

"No. But I believe he'll want to see me."

She glanced up and her eyes widened. Annie might not have known who Michael Grayson was, but her receptionist obviously did.

"Yes, sir. One moment, sir. I'll be right back." The woman abandoned the ringing switchboard and scurried down the hallway. A moment later, she was back, opening the door into the narrow hallway. "Straight back, last door on the right."

He followed her directions and found the door in question open. This office was larger than the others he'd passed along the hallway, but no more luxurious. Sitting behind a cheap, pressed-wood desk was a large pro-football-player-sized black man with grizzled gray hair and reading glasses perched on the edge of his broad nose. He was coatless, his shirtsleeves rolled up to reveal thick forearms as he sorted through a stack of files.

Michael rapped on the door jamb. "You Winrod?"

The man removed his reading glasses and eyed him a beat too long to be entirely polite.

"I am." He rocked back in his chair and pursed his lips. "You Grayson?"

Looked like Annie wasn't the only one in the office with an attitude.

"I am," he answered.

"Come on in then, and close that door."

Michael shut the door and took a seat across from the man charged with defending St. Louis's poor against the power of the state. The latter leaned back in his chair and laced his fingers over his stomach.

"What can I do for you, Mr. Grayson?"

"Annie O'Toole. She said she's getting off my case."

"That would be correct."

"Is that her choice?"

"I decide case assignments."

"Did she want off the case?"

"I didn't ask."

Michael considered for a moment, then opted for the direct approach. "Did she plan this for some tactical advantage?"

Winrod's lips tightened. "Is that what you think?"

Michael shifted in his seat irritably. "I don't know. Even that night, I was surprised she didn't recognize me. It's just so rare anymore. But now, knowing she was on this case all the time, it seems impossible she wouldn't know."

"But you didn't tell her who you were."

"No." Michael looked away. "It's not often I get the opportunity to be with someone who…" he trailed off.

"Who doesn't know you're rich and famous," Winrod finished for him.

"She seemed genuine. But now, I don't know." He looked back at Winrod and narrowed his eyes. "Which is why I'm asking you. Was I set up? I want to know the truth."

Winrod took a deep breath. "Mr. Grayson, I apologize for what happened. It is against the policy of this office and the ethical code of professional responsibility for any lawyer to have a sexual relationship with a party or a witness on a case. I can assure you that actions have been taken to address this unfortunate misunderstanding, both as to the handling of this case and as to the lawyer involved. Beyond that, this is a confidential personnel matter that I cannot discuss with you."

Michael let his gaze play over Winrod's face. "But you know who I am."

A quizzical look came into the man's dark eyes. "Of course."

"And you know what I can do."

Now it was Winrod's eyes that narrowed. "I have a pretty good idea, yes."

"You're appointed by the Public Defender Commission, aren't you?"

"I am." The man's words were clipped.

"Which is appointed by the governor."

"It is."

"And I just happen to have the governor's personal cell phone right here." Michael touched the phone on his belt.

The gesture was subtle. The threat was not.

Winrod's poker face vanished. The man glared at him. "I don't give a damn whose number you have in your cell phone. I have a job to do." He leaned forward, his powerful forearms flexing as he rested them on the desk. "And if doing it means losing it, so be it. Now if there's nothing further, you apparently have calls to make, and I have work to do."

Michael smiled and rocked back in his chair. "I think I like you, Winrod."

Winrod snorted. "And I think you're a son of a bitch."

Michael laughed. "Now I know I like you. I won't be making any calls. I just don't like being played."

"None of us do." The man behind the desk spoke slowly, deliberately, and with emphasis.

Point taken.

Michael hesitated, then asked, "Will this hurt her career?"

Winrod busied himself with the files on his desk.

"That remains to be seen."

"Other than being taken off this case, are there any other changes in her assignments?"

The older man paused and pursed his lips. "Her case assignments are public record, so I suppose I can answer that. I'm moving her back to docket duty for a while."

"I'm guessing that's a pretty big step down from a high publicity shooting."

"Most would see it that way."

"Because of me."

Winrod didn't respond.

Michael took a deep breath. "Leave her on the case."

"I can't do that. "

"Did Joiner want her off?"

"What Mr. Joiner did or did not say to me is confidential."

"Of course, it is. God knows we have to take care of the poor guy who tried to kill me."

Winrod opened his mouth, but Michael held up a hand before the man could launch into a speech about defendants' rights.

"You told me this was your choice. That means it wasn't Joiner's. He must have wanted to keep her on the case, or she wouldn't have been doing the depositions today, right?"

Winrod said nothing for a moment. "Annie is a talented lawyer. Her clients are generally very pleased with her services."

Michael wasn't surprised by that. He'd seen her skills firsthand. "Leave her on the case," he said. "And don't bust her down to docket whatever."

Winrod gave him a quizzical look. "Why?"

Michael stood with a weary sigh. "Because appearances to the contrary, I prefer not to ruin people's careers before I know for sure they deserve it." He headed for the door.

"Grayson."

Michael stopped and looked back.

"A deer in the headlights," said Jackson.

"What?"

"That's what O'Toole looked like when she came into my office after seeing your mug in those news clips. A goddamn deer in the headlights."

The balloon that had been steadily expanding against Michael's chest wall since he'd walked into that deposition room, eased ever so slightly. "Really?"

"Really." Winrod sighed. "Annie's more than a good lawyer. She's good people. Pays zero attention to the world around her, God knows. And she can be a little too ready for a fight. But she doesn't have a devious bone in her body. When she comes at you, she does it head on and you know exactly who and what you're up against."

Michael gave Winrod a nod. "Thanks," he said, as a tiny bit of hope took up residence in his gut.

The nod was returned, then followed by a gruff, "Now get out of my office. I have work to do."

Michael stopped briefly at the receptionist's desk before heading back to wait for Peter and Harrison, where he poured himself a cup of coffee, took one sip, and threw it in the trash. He answered several e-mails, made a call to finalize a bid proposal that was going out tomorrow, and debated what to say to her when she came out of that room.

At last, the door opened. Harrison, Peter, and the assistant prosecutor all filed out, followed shortly by the court reporter, who—to his chagrin—closed the door behind him.

The prosecutor was the first to speak. "As soon as we receive the transcripts of the depositions, I'll forward copies to both of you. You can review them, note any corrections that need to be made, and then sign off on them."

Harrison slipped a card out of his coat pocket and handed it to the prosecutor. "Just send them to my attention, please. I'll see they're reviewed and get them back to you."

"Fine." Randall shoved his glasses back up his nose and glanced nervously at Michael. "Is everything all right, sir? What happened before—is there anything I can take care of for you?"

He shook his head. "Everything's fine." With one last glance at the closed door, he clapped Harrison on the shoulder. "C'mon. Let's blow this pop stand."

****

As the door closed behind the last of their witnesses, Annie let her head drop back over the edge of the chair. "This has to go down in history as one of the worst days of my life."

Jonathan laughed. "I think Grayson might fight you for that. Did you see his face?"

"Y-e-a-h." She lifted her head and shot him a sardonic look. "Remember me, the one on the receiving end of the rage? So glad my public humiliation could at least offer you entertainment."

"Me, too. That was priceless. But it sounds like you dished out a fine helping of rage right back." He grinned. "Hey, you should've sold tickets. I'd have paid good money for the full feature and I bet the rest would have as well."

She dropped her head back down and closed her eyes. "Go to hell."

"Lighten up. You did good." He dropped his feet to the ground and stood. "Buy you a drink?"

"Definitely."

"McDowell's? That'd put you within staggering distance of home."

"Perfect."

He extended a hand and pulled her to her feet. She rolled out her shoulders and gathered up her file.

"So, what do you think of the case?" he asked, as they crossed the now-empty anteroom.

"I don't know," she said. "The motive is supposed to be robbery, but the kid walked away from a roll of bills, credit cards, a diamond watch—not to mention what Ashton had on him—and never even asked for anything. Just came out of the alley, firing." She looked up at her companion. "Sounds more like a hit to me."

Jonathan nodded. "My thought exactly. If he'd shot another street kid, I'd tag it as payback. But he didn't. And that's what just doesn't fit. Why would some street kid have it in for Grayson?"

"I guess you should ask him. He's your client now."

"Oh. Yeah." He shifted uncomfortably. "I'm sorry about that.

She sighed. "No need. I'm the one who screwed up—no pun intended. So, no guilt. Meet you there?"

"Yep." He peeled off into his office and she headed on back toward hers.

"Hold on, please." The receptionist raised a hand to the woman at the window and signalled Annie.

She backtracked. "What's up?"

"Michael Grayson left this for you."

Annie looked down at the business card Marsha handed her. Scribbled across the bottom of the card, below his name, title, office number and address, was a phone number, and beneath that, 'Private cell #.'

"O'Toole!"

She looked up, startled.

"You sleepwalking?" Jackson leaned out of his office, glaring at her. "When I talk to you, I expect an answer."

"I'm sorry. I didn't hear—"

He waved her into his office.

"You're off docket duty. Despite your—" he appeared to struggle for a word, then skipped it and continued, "—this kid really wants you on his case. I mean really wants you on the case. He looked like an abandoned puppy who'd just been kicked when I told him I had to take you off. So, you and Clark are on it together until or unless the kid changes his mind about you. But you will do nothing—and I mean nothing—on this case without Clark's knowledge and preferably his presence. And if the case goes to trial, you will be background support only. Are we clear?"

"Yes, but why?" she sputtered.

"Because I said so," he growled. "You got a problem with this arrangement?"

"Uh, no. No, sir. None at all."

"Good. Now get out of here."

****

She found a parking place just around the corner

from McDowell's and was digging out change to feed the meter when her phone rang. She glanced at the caller ID and blew out a breath. *Oh, hell, no, not today, Satan.* Her day had been hellish enough.

She ignored the call, but the voicemail chime dinged as she stepped onto the sidewalk. She fed the meter, debating whether to listen or just delete. At least there was alcohol just a few steps away. She hit play.

"Annabel, I need to speak to you as soon as possible. This is no time for juvenile sulking. Call me."

The icy, birdlike voice of Eleanor Barlow, her not-so-beloved grandmama, was still imperious. Still demanding. No matter how old the woman got, some things never changed. For several weeks after their final blow-up, she'd left similar messages, sometimes several a day. Never apologizing, never seeking forgiveness or reconciliation. Just Grandmother being Grandmother, demanding that Annie 'get over herself' and fall in line like a good, little soldier. Turned out, she just wasn't army material.

The idea of begging must have been more horrifying to Eleanor's queenly sensibilities than being ignored. The calls had ceased, and they'd gotten used to pretending the other didn't exist. So why was she reaching out now? Annie was mildly curious, but not enough to warrant returning the call. She'd severed that tie, and it was staying cut. She hit delete and headed inside.

The Irish pub was one of Annie's favorites. Not only was it, as Jonathan so eloquently put it, within 'staggering distance' of home for her, it was low-ceilinged and low-lit, with a cozy, womblike feel. A place to slide into a relatively private, high-backed booth, enjoy Irish whiskey and Irish music, and cocoon oneself away from the cold, cruel world.

"Grayson talked to Jackson?" Jonathan was incredulous. "What did he say?"

"I have no idea." Annie gratefully accepted her Irish coffee from the waitress and, eyes closed, savored a slow, delicious sip. "Mmmm." She shivered, licking whipped cream from her lip and sinking back into the seat with a sigh. "God, that's good."

Jonathan snorted. "Focus, please? Jackson? Grayson? The future of your career?"

"Jackson didn't even tell me about it. Marsha did. She said Grayson sauntered in like he owned the place and said he wanted to see Jackson. She asked if he had an appointment. He said no, but 'Winrod would want to see him.'" She took another sip and muttered, "Arrogant bastard."

"Which he did," Jonathan pointed out.

"Well, duh."

"And you have no idea what he said?"

"None. All I know is that Jackson stopped me on my way out and said I was out of docket purgatory and cleared to work with you on the case for as long as Joiner is okay with it. But you're trial counsel. '*There will be no more public scenes,*' to quote Jackson. Which suits me just fine."

"And me." Jonathan settled back in his seat with a self-satisfied grin. "You can do the scut work, and I get the glory."

She made a face at him, then turned serious, drumming her fingers on the table. "Why would Jackson do that? It had to be something Grayson said."

Jonathan shrugged. "Maybe he's just a decent guy

after all. There are a few rich people who are, you know, despite your personal experience in that arena."

"Trust me, he wasn't feeling warm and fuzzy about me when he walked out of that deposition. I was there for the full feature, remember? You just caught the trailer." The cruelty of his accusations cut almost as deeply in Annie's remembered replay as in their original airing.

"The guy was blindsided," Jonathan pointed out. "He was caught completely off guard and blew. Then he cooled off and realized you weren't the Queen of Devious after all, just illiterate and living in a cave."

"Go to hell." She threw a straw at him, which he ducked.

A moaning guitar rift announced that the house band was warming up for their first set.

"Sounds like we're already there." Jonathan hated Irish music. "I'm outta here," he said, standing up and pulling out his wallet. He tossed a couple of bills on the table to pay for their drinks.

"Bombshell at two o'clock," Annie murmured into her coffee.

Jonathan's head snapped up. A smile spread across his face as he spotted the well-endowed blonde placing an order at the bar.

"Then again, it would be rude not to even give the band a chance, right?"

Now it was Annie's turn to snort. The new pretrial receptionist oozed sexuality. She spoke in a breathy whisper and had a habit of slowly wetting her lips before she spoke. Add those 38D cups to the equation and the pretrial office suddenly had an influx of lawyers stopping by to double-and triple-check the pretrial release conditions for their clients.

"You know your IQ drops fifty points every time you talk to her," Annie said.

Jonathan grinned. "Good thing I have so much to spare, then, huh? Catch you later." He slipped away and in a matter of seconds reappeared at the bar beside the blonde.

Annie sighed. She'd gotten her dreams of happily-ever-after ground into the dirt today, while Jonathan was probably going home with his own personal centerfold. Life was so not fair. She sat, letting the combination of Irish whiskey and the bittersweet lilt of the music work its healing magic on the tension burrowed between her shoulder blades. After a bit, she dug a pen out of her purse and snagged a bar napkin. The first case she'd inherited with an entire case theory scribbled on a handful of bar napkins had flabbergasted her. But at some point, she'd succumbed to the practice as well. Inspiration hit when it hit.

She wrote ROBBERY? in all caps in the center of the napkin. Around, above, and below, in tiny, barely legible script, she jotted down everything that didn't fit:

Fired before even demanding stuff
Didn't take anything??
LOTS of valuables left behind
Wallet = several hundred $$ & credit cards
Diamond watch
Ashton's stuff
Why? No interruption
No provocation for shot

She looked at the list. Nope. Robbery just didn't fly here. Something else was going on. She flipped the napkin over and wrote HIT? in the center, then repeated the exercise.

Only one shot—non-vital area

V clearly alive when shooter ran away—time for clean-up shots but none taken

Why leave? No interruption

No attempt to take out Ashton. Why leave a live witness?

No previous contact / connection between V & D

Hired hit?

V's enemies = $, could get professional hitter

D = young, amateur

A hit made no more sense in this case than the robbery motive. Unless…

She had a flash of her grandmother ruthlessly running roughshod over anyone who had the misfortune to get in her way. What if Grayson was the same? What if he'd bulldozed over some little guy, some street kid's mom or dad or older brother, someone too insignificant to even be on Grayson's radar, but not too insignificant to pick up a gun and stalk the man to a public place. Payback. The thought of her grandmother's soul in that body, behind those eyes, that smile, made her nauseous. Surely, the gods could not be that cruel.

Then again, look at the joke they'd already played on her.

Chapter Seven

The next morning, Michael strode into his office in a foul mood.

"Good morning, Mr. Grayson."

"Morning," he muttered, then stopped and turned back to his assistant. "Have I had any calls from Annie O'Toole?"

"The lawyer for that guy who shot you?" Myriam's dark eyes narrowed. "She's a sneaky one—trying to pose as a friend of yours to get past me. Like I'd fall for that."

So, she had tried to reach him.

"What did she say?"

"She just asked to speak to you as if I'd put any Tom, Dick or Jane who called right through to the CEO. When I asked what it was regarding, she claimed to be a friend of yours."

"But you didn't put her through."

"Of course not. I told her if she was a friend, she should try reaching you on your private line—which, of course, she didn't know." She sniffed. "Really, how stupid do these people think I am?"

Michael stifled a sigh. "When was this?"

"Friday. Both calls were on Friday."

"She called twice?"

"Immediately after the first. The second time she was all uppity and threatening. 'I'm the lawyer who has

87

him under subpoena. I have information he needs to know before the depositions. You do not want to be the one who keeps him from getting this information.'" She rolled her eyes. "So, I forwarded her to Legal."

Michael bit back the curse that rose to mind. Sometimes Myriam could be too efficient. "If she ever calls again, put her through."

"To Legal?"

"No, to me. Immediately, no matter what I'm doing or who I'm with."

"Y-yes, sir," Myriam stammered.

"And if she wants my private number, give it to her. For that matter, even if she doesn't want it, give it to her." After their last meeting, he wouldn't be surprised if the number he'd left wound up in the trash. "And get me Jacobson."

****

Streeter Jacobson was the Director of Security for Grayson Aeronautics. Unbeknownst to most of the employees there, he also handled a different kind of investigative work. Few of those who did business with Grayson Aeronautics had any idea just how much the CEO knew about their lives—from the street they'd grown up on to the professions and proclivities of their college drinking buddies.

It wasn't about holding the information over their heads or threatening exposure of the skeletons in their closets. It was about understanding their developmental DNA—the people, places, and events that had shaped them, the subtext that motivated them, the brass rings for which they still pined. With that information in hand, Michael could compose a strategy that hit all the right chords for each particular audience of one. And

Jacobson was a wizard at providing that 360-degree perspective. They made a good team. The fact that he was also one of Michael's closest friends was just an added bonus.

The man in question rapped on the door jamb. "You ready for me?" His frame had thickened some since his Navy SEAL days. He was pushing sixty now, the crew-cut more salt than pepper, skin creased and leathery from a life of too much exposure to sun, salt, and wind.

"Yeah. Come in." Michael closed the file on new helicopter modifications one of his engineers had recommended.

Jacobson dropped another folder in its place and helped himself to a chair. "The info on the new Northwest marketing exec. Summary's on top."

"Anything interesting?" Michael flipped open the folder for a quick skim of the top page.

"Not really. Has an eye for the ladies."

"Don't we all?"

"And the one on Eleanor Barlow."

A second, much thicker, folder followed the first.

"Ah, yes, the matriarch of Barlow Industries."

"This one is scary. Watch your back if you're looking to do business with her."

Michael raised an eyebrow at the man who, years before, had single-handedly rescued him from an off-the-books North Korean mission gone bad. "Eleanor Barlow scares you?"

"Didn't say that. I said she's scary. Likes to ruin people just to prove she can. And she usually can."

"Okay, then. Good to know." He set both files on top of the design modifications. "I have something a little different for you." Michael shifted in his chair, irritated by his own embarrassment. "It involves a woman."

"Aw, shit, Mike. What have you done now?"

Reminding himself he was the boss, not the kid called into the principal's office, he briefed the older man as briskly and professionally as possible.

"And you want to know if this was a setup."

"Exactly.

"What's your gut say?"

"That it wasn't." He shifted his gaze out the window and shrugged. "Then again, that might just be what I want to believe."

"I asked what your gut says, not your dick."

Michael rolled his eyes. "Just see what you can find out for me, okay?

"Sure." Streeter rose but turned back at the door. "I'm serious as a heart attack about that Barlow woman. Don't trust her. And don't turn your back on her."

"As long as she's not carrying a .38, I think she'll be an improvement over what I've been dealing with, don't you?"

"Not so sure about that. At least with punks like Joiner you know where you stand. Eleanor Barlow is the kind that serves you caviar with one hand and slides a knife in your ribs with the other."

"Warning taken."

Streeter turned sideways to allow Michael's assistant to enter as he made his exit. "Hello, Myriam."

"Mr. Jacobson."

"You ever gonna call me Streeter? We've only known each other like five years."

"Good-bye, Mr. Jacobson."

Streeter rolled his eyes and headed out the door.

Stifling a chuckle, Michael turned his attention to the woman who ran his life. She still seemed a little subdued at having gotten it wrong on Annie's call, a mistake that really could not be laid at her door. He'd gotten it wrong on that front himself.

"Coffee?" he asked, extending an olive branch as he crossed to the coffee bar in the corner of his office.

"Thank you, no."

She sniffed again, but her shoulders seemed to relax a fraction of an inch. Since that was about as relaxed as Myriam ever got, he considered the matter behind them. He filled his own cup and returned to his desk.

"Okay. What's next?"

Myriam launched. "Here is the draft agenda for next week's board meeting." She handed him a thin manila folder. "And the proposed format for the annual report, both of which need your approval." A second, thicker manila folder followed the first. "You have a ten o'clock with Peter to review the marketing campaign on the E-7, then a lunch meeting with Senator Johansson who is in town for his fundraiser this evening. That's at seven, by the way, at The Granville. Black tie." An invitation fluttered down atop the growing stack of manila folders as Myriam consulted her daytimer. "And, last but not least, your hospital board meeting this afternoon has been moved downtown."

He looked up. "Why aren't we meeting at the hospital?"

"Dr. Roethemeyer is receiving some sort of award at a medical conference there. They moved the meeting so she could attend both events. Angelo has your itinerary."

Michael pulled the stack of folders toward him. "I used to have time to actually design airplanes," he grumbled.

"Yes, sir. Success can be such a cross to bear." She pressed her lips together in a thin line, turned on her heel and left, closing the door behind her.

"That's not what I meant," he muttered.

Though, of course, it was.

****

"Annie O'Toole," Annie said into the earpiece propped on her shoulder as she flipped through the stack of messages Marsha had shoved in her hand the moment she returned from court.

There was a beat of silence on the other end.

"Annabel."

Pink message slips fluttered across the top of Annie's desk at the familiar, cultured birdlike voice in her ear.

"I would apologize for bothering you at work, but your unwillingness to take my calls left me no other choice." The tone of voice conveyed no apology. It never had.

With effort, Annie unclenched her jaw enough to reply. "I don't take your calls because I don't wish to speak with you. That doesn't change with my location. So—"

"Do not hang up on me." The voice was old, but still sharp, still used to being obeyed.

"We have nothing to say to one another."

"You may have nothing to say to me, but I have something to say to you."

When hadn't the woman had something to say her?

Annie's nails tapped an impatient rhythm on the scarred desktop. "If I let you speak your piece, will you stop calling?"

Another beat of silence.

"It appears you won't have to worry about my bothering you much longer. The doctors seem pretty sure of that, at least."

Annie stopped tapping. "What's wrong?"

"A long, depressing story for which you have neither time nor interest. But the punchline is—I'm dying. Sooner rather than later, they tell me. And there are things we need to discuss."

Annie swivelled to stare out the window. She may not have seen her grandmother for years, but she could not conceive of a world devoid of the indomitable force that was Eleanor Barlow. The woman had always seemed immortal. She tried to think of something appropriate to say and failed.

Her grandmother spared her the necessity. "I'm sending Carter down for you Saturday morning. Flying would be more efficient, of course, but I know better than to expect that. So, Carter will pick you up. Expect him at eight. We'll lunch at one."

"You still have Carter?"

Her grandmother's driver had been one of the rare bright spots in a childhood with too few of them. Her grandmother ignored the query.

"Do not disappoint, Annabel. Riding off into the sunset may seem like a grand, dramatic gesture, but it is a childish response that, in the end, just leaves you with regrets and questions no one is left to answer. I will see you Saturday."

The phone clicked off and Annie was left listening

to the dial tone.

She flung open Jonathan's office door with such force that it banged against the wall and almost bounced back into her face. "Coffee. Now."

Jonathan jumped at the noise, his elbow catching the cup of cold coffee on his desk. He grabbed for it as it wobbled, righting it just in time to keep it from spilling its contents onto his keyboard. "Geezus, Annie."

"Sorry. I need caffeine. Whipped cream. Chocolate. Now."

"Can't." His gaze was already back on his computer monitor.

"Jonathan, c'mon. This is serious. I just—"

"I said, I can't." He looked up, scowling at the interruption. "Motion for new trial due today." He glanced at his watch. "In a little over two hours to be exact. So run along and play and let the grown-ups get some work done."

"Oh." She bit off her whine.

Motions for new trial were one of the few things that carried a drop-dead filing deadline even a judge couldn't extend. Failing to file one on time was one of the few unforgivable—and unfixable—sins in the practice of criminal defense. It even trumped her call from a supposedly dying grandmother.

She sighed. "Want anything?"

"Huh-uh." His back was to her, fingers typing furiously.

She shut the door, more softly than she'd opened it, and headed down the hallway alone.

****

"Annie! Wait up."

She turned on the steps of the courthouse as one of the sex crimes prosecutors headed her direction. Phil Goodwin had pestered her relentlessly to go out with him for most of her first year at the defender office. Now he just smirked in her direction, choosing to interpret her rebuff as evidence of a deeply embedded character flaw.

"What's the story with you and Michael Grayson?"

"What?" Her collar seemed to grow tighter around her throat.

He smirked even more. "Come on. It's all over the courthouse—that royal row the two of you had at his depo yesterday? Grayson throwing everybody out of the room and you two going at it? Obviously, there's some history there you haven't disclosed. Nicoletti's thinking of filing a bar complaint."

He was obviously hoping she'd rise to the goad and reveal something juicy. He cocked an eyebrow at her, waiting. Why was that particular gesture so sexy on some men and simply smarmy on others?

"Did it suddenly become unethical to raise your voice to a witness?" She managed to keep her voice cool and unruffled. "Guess you're going to have to give up cross-examination altogether."

"I'm serious, O'Toole," he pressed, ignoring the dig. "I don't know what you're hiding, but it's obviously something big and it involves one of this city's most prominent names. Nicoletti's not going to let that slide by unnoticed."

She shrugged. "No great conspiracies to uncover, I'm afraid. Just a little misunderstanding. Sorry to disappoint." She made a show of looking at her watch. "Sorry I can't stay to chat, but I'm late."

"Don't say I didn't warn you," he called to her back as she headed on down the steps.

She waved her hand without turning, neither pausing nor slowing her pace until she'd reached the end of the block. There she paused and took a deep breath. Phil was just trying to get a rise out of her. The city's top prosecutor wouldn't do anything without talking to Grayson first. And Grayson wouldn't want her hauled before the bar for any kind of disciplinary review. Grayson was the one who told Jackson to put her back on the case. Grayson was the one who…

Her thoughts froze as an image of steely grey eyes and a voice tinged with ice slammed into her brain: *You should have done your research first, love. I don't give a damn what the press says about me, and I don't make deals with people who fuck with me. Ever.*

A wave of nausea enveloped her. Could he have set her up? Was he that devious? Had he gone out of his way to arrange for her to stay on the case just so he could pull the rug out from under her? But he'd *told* Jackson to leave her on the case. Jackson could attest to that if it ever came to any kind of hearing.

And who would the world believe—the guy who worked in the courthouse basement defending the 'scum of society' or the billionaire philanthropist who'd been shot and almost killed by the guy they were defending? Who was she kidding? An ordinary joe couldn't fight these people. And any who tried, sure as hell couldn't win. All she'd wind up doing was costing Jackson his career, too. It was her grandmother all over again. The rich did what they wanted to whom they wanted, and the little guy invariably wound up being crushed like an irksome June bug.

A headache started to bloom behind her eyes as she stepped off the curb to cross the street. The screech of tires had her head snapping up just as someone yanked her bodily back onto the curb. A black limousine sped past, barely avoiding flattening her onto the pavement.

"Rich bastards. Drive like maniacs," a rough voice sounded behind her as the steel hold on her released.

She looked around.

The man's clothes marked him as one of the central post office's loading dock guys, but his size looked more like bouncer material—a fact for which she was extremely grateful, having just been bodily lifted out of harm's way by those bulging arms.

"You okay?" he asked.

"Yes. Thanks."

"Rich bastards," he repeated. "Think they own the roads along with everything else."

"No shit," she muttered, mirroring his scowl if not the depth of his growl.

"Looks like the coast is clear," he said, motioning her on across the street and falling in step beside her. "You're a pretty a little thing." He grinned down at her. "Maybe you should buy me a drink out of gratitude."

A voice cut off her reply.

"Annie?"

She looked up and there he was, not twenty feet from her, his hand on the door of the entrance to the hotel that housed her favorite coffee shop—or at least the one closest to the courthouse.

Annie stopped mid-step. She wasn't ready for this. Not now. Not yet.

"Hey, you're not sleepwalking again, are you, love?" Meaty fingers snapped in front of her face, bringing her attention back to the man who was waiting for her response.

"I'm sorry," she said. "The doctor says alcohol interferes with my anti-psychotic meds, so I'd better not. But thanks again for saving my life."

"O-kay." He gave her an odd look and picked up his pace. "Uh, you take care of yourself."

She'd had a lot of practice deflecting pick-up lines.

She hadn't had a lot of practice dealing with a gorgeous, but possibly evil prince who might be plotting to destroy her career.

The prince in question moved toward her. "Hello."

Why did he have to smell so good?

"Hi."

"So, come here often?" A shadow of the crooked grin that kept sliding into her dreams touched his mouth, a hint of irony playing around the edges.

"Almost every day," she admitted.

"Every day?"

There was that sexy eyebrow lift. Goodwin just could not pull that off.

She forced her thoughts back to the conversation. "Coffee. I'm addicted."

"Ah. Another secret you failed to disclose."

She bristled. "I didn't—"

"It was a joke. A bad one, admittedly, but this is new territory for me. Sorry."

"Me, too," she mumbled, looking at the sidewalk.

"Did you get the card I left for you yesterday?"

"I did. Thanks." Oh, what the hell. She just wasn't hard-wired to pussyfoot around. "Why did you do that?"

"Do what?"

"You took my head off in that depo room. You made it crystal clear you think I set you up, not to mention that you would gladly destroy my career without a blink. Then you turn around and tell my boss to put me back on the case and leave me your private cell number like I'm supposed to call you up for a good time? What am I supposed to do with that? What the hell do you want from me??"

Incredibly, he laughed.

She stared at him. "Did I say something funny? Because, believe me, I could use a good laugh now, so by all means—let me in on the joke."

****

Michael was again struck with how vibrant and real this woman was compared to those who filled the hallways of his life. In a nano-second, the slide show of Annie O'Toole flashed through his mind: Stunning, clumsy, and teasing at the ball. The ice queen putting Kurt Cochrane in his place. And finally, his deliciously seductive subject for one amazing night. At their second meeting, she'd gone from cool, professional attorney-at-law to a hellcat ablaze with anger and back again, all in the space of a few minutes. The woman had more sides than the Pentagon and all of them fascinated him. So, what was the harm in getting to know her a little bit better while he waited for what he really hoped would be Streeter's confirmation that Annie O'Toole was agenda-free?

He tilted his head toward the hotel entrance. "How about we see if we can get through a civil conversation and go from there? Buy you a coffee?"

She studied him for a moment. "I don't think so."

His heart sank.

"But you can buy me an extra hot cinnamon and hazelnut latte, with whipped cream and cinnamon sprinkles."

He laughed and opened the door. "After you, Counselor."

She looked just as good in today's pantsuit as she had in yesterday's pencil skirt. Frankly, he couldn't imagine anything she wouldn't look good in.

"I talked to Myriam, my assistant. She confirmed that you did try to reach me before yesterday's deposition."

"And?"

"And I'm sorry she didn't put your call through. It won't happen again."

"You're sorry she didn't put my call through?" Annie glared up at him. "How about being sorry for accusing me of being a lying slut? Could we perhaps start there?"

"I didn't call you—"

"The hell you didn't."

For someone so small, she radiated a lot of energy and right now all of it was angry and focused like a laser on him.

"I admit I said some things that were a little harsh, but—"

"A little harsh?" Her eyebrows shot up. "Are you really that much of an ass the rest of the time that the things you said to me yesterday only qualify as a little harsh on the Grayson scale?"

"Hey!" Now his anger was rising as well. "I had a right to be pissed. I was completely blindsided walking in and finding you representing the guy who shot me. How was I supposed to react? 'My, isn't this a coincidence, imagine meeting you here?'"

"I didn't say you didn't have a right to be pissed given what you thought were the circumstances, moron." She ground her teeth. "I said the decent thing to do now that you know the actual circumstances, would be to apologize for the awful things you said to me."

"Did you just call me a moron?" He stared at her.

"If the shoe fits," she muttered.

Nobody had called Michael Grayson a moron since boot camp. He began to laugh. He hadn't realized how tiresome it was to have the world tiptoe around him until this petite redhead had blown into his life and done anything but—even after she knew who he was.

Now she was the one staring at him. "You know inappropriate affect is a sign of mental illness. Maybe you should see somebody about that."

He laughed again. "I apologize for implying that you were—in your words—'a lying slut.'" He extended a hand. "Truce?"

She watched him, apparently waiting for the punchline. When none came, she shrugged and took the hand he extended.

"Truce."

His fingers brushed the wrist he'd wrapped with his belt before tying her to the headboard. Desire flared at the memory. Shit. He dropped her hand.

"So, what are you doing down here?" she asked, leading the way to the coffee shop tucked in the corner of the lobby.

He forced himself to focus on the conversation at hand. "Hospital board meeting."

"Is this side trip going to make you late?"

"Not by much. They can take care of the preliminaries without me. They'll wait on the major decisions until I get there."

"Of course, they will. You're Michael Grayson. The world waits for you."

"One of the perks of the pocketbook," he said lightly, perusing the drink options on the board.

She suddenly looked up at him. "You didn't happen to arrive in a black limousine, did you? With a driver?"

Surprised, he looked down at her. "Yes. Why?"

"Figures," she muttered.

"What?"

"Hi, Annie. The usual?" The perky barista, who looked all of seventeen, interrupted his follow-up question.

"Yes, please."

"And for you, sir?" The girl turned to him, obviously having no idea who he was.

Annie smirked. "You may be hot stuff everywhere else, Grayson, but here I'm the fair-haired one and you're the nobody."

Michael rolled his eyes and ordered a black coffee. He paid for their drinks and debated whether to wait for Jacobson's report or go with his gut now. He opted for his gut.

"Would you like to go to a fundraiser for Senator Johansson with me tonight?"

"What?" She turned, mid-sip, a fleck of whipped cream on her upper lip.

He very much wanted to lick it off. Instead, he cleared his throat. "Senator Johansson. Do you know who Senator Johansson is?"

"Of course, I know who he is," she snapped. "I'm not a complete illiterate living in a cave."

"Just checking," he said mildly. "Given recent history, I don't want to take anything for granted."

"Smart ass," she mumbled into her latte.

"He's having a fundraiser—a dinner—tonight. Come with me."

"What makes you think I'm a supporter of Johansson?"

He had no doubt she was buying time. He could respect that.

"It makes no difference to me—or to Johansson—whether you're a supporter or not. It won't be your money going to his campaign. It will be mine. It's simply a chance for me to spend an evening with a woman who intrigues me."

Interest and disappointment chased one another across her face. "I can't. I'm back on the case. I can't go anywhere as your date or your guest, or whatever. Nicoletti's already making noises about filing a bar complaint against me and I can't give him any more ammunition."

Damn. He hadn't considered that implication when he'd told Winrod to put her back on the case. Of course, he also hadn't considered the possibility he'd be asking her out in just twenty-four hours' time either.

"A bar complaint about what?" he asked, buying a little a time of his own.

She raised her eyebrows and stared at him. "Well, it was obvious to everyone in that depo room that something had gone on between us before that day. The courthouse is abuzz with our little scene. Nicoletti wants to know what it was and whether there's any way he can use it against me. One of his prosecutors just filled me in on that fun tidbit." She looked away and bit her lip. "You know—I kind of wondered if you were setting me up, having me put back on the case just so you could pull the rug out from under me in a bar complaint yourself."

"Jesus." He sighed. "Things have gotten complicated, haven't they?" He took her by the shoulders. "Listen up, A.J. O'Toole. I am not trying to set you up. Scout's honor. I told your boss to put you back on the case because I was the one who proposed keeping things anonymous and I didn't feel right letting that derail your career." He grimaced. "Though I have to say, the idea of you getting a career boost out of helping the guy who shot me doesn't exactly feel right, either."

She smiled wearily and, tilting her head to the side, brushed her soft curls against the top of his hand. "I really am sorry you were shot."

"Me, too." He moved his thumb across her cheek. "Not only did it hurt like hell, but it's playing havoc with my social life." With an effort, he dropped his hands. "Look, don't worry about Nicoletti. I'll take care of him."

"Another perk of the pocketbook?"

He didn't miss the sarcasm. "You don't think very highly of rich people, do you?"

"Nope." She didn't mince words.

"Can I ask why?"

She laughed, but there was no humor in it. "Let's just say I've been run over by them too many times."

"Money isn't all bad, you know. It can do good things, too."

"So, the rich keep saying. Sorry. Experience teaches me differently."

"Come tonight," he urged. "Give me a chance to change your perspective."

She ran her fingers through her hair, her expression a study in desire and frustration.

"I like you, Mick—Michael. I really do—even though you're rich and even though you called me a lying slut."

He opened his mouth to protest.

"And I would love to go with you tonight," she plowed on, not giving him the chance. "But I can't. Jackson has given me a chance to redeem myself on this case and I'm not going to let him down."

He closed his mouth and rocked back on his heels, considering his options. "There's no prohibition on public defenders supporting political candidates, is there?"

She looked confused. "Of course not, but—"

"And you would have no control over who you might run into at a political fundraiser, would you?"

A rueful smile lifted the corners of her mouth. "I suppose I wouldn't."

"I hear Johansson has done some preliminary work on expanding the public interest student loan forgiveness program. Someone practicing public interest law might want to visit with him about that."

She cocked her head. "They might indeed."

"The fundraiser is at seven at The Granville. The green dress would work very nicely. Your ticket will be waiting for you at the front desk—not delivered by me." He grinned. "Nice running into you, Counselor. Perhaps our paths will cross again sometime."

With a wink, he turned down the hallway toward the meeting rooms.

Chapter Eight

Annie eyed herself in the mirror, gnawing on her lower lip as she twisted around yet again to check the back of her dress. She'd called the hotel to confirm the details for this evening's event and, with that information in hand, had opted for the long black gown in lieu of the short green one. A $5,000-a-plate dinner required elegance, not sassiness. As granddaughter of the matriarch-from-hell, the appropriate attire for every conceivable social event had been pounded into her brain right alongside multiplication tables.

She'd had to dig deep into her closet for this one, not to mention giving it a spritz of perfume to chase away the musty smell. Public interest lawyers didn't get a lot of call for formal evening wear. But when her grandmother had shipped the last of her things in a final, unspoken farewell, the formal wear had been included—and wasn't that handy now? This had been one of her favorites. The ebony silk, shot through with silver thread, caught the light as she moved, and the way it hugged her curves all the way to her ankles made her feel very Audrey Hepburn-ish. She considered adding the long black gloves to complete the effect but decided against it. Too much Audrey, not enough Annie.

She fiddled with her hair. Should she try to sweep it up? She glanced at the clock. Not enough time, and she was never very good at that anyway. Instead, she added a little mousse, scrunched the curls, and tucked one side behind her ear. Then fluffed it out again. And tucked it back again. Definitely back. It showed off the earrings better. She added her mother's diamond necklace, taking a moment to run her finger across the familiar piece she'd never gotten used to seeing at her own throat. Then, with a deep breath and one last spin before the mirror, she pronounced herself done. She picked up the silver clutch she'd dug out along with the dress, dropped in her lipstick and wallet, grabbed her keys, and swept out the door, grinning at her own giddiness.

This wasn't smart. She knew it wasn't smart. But she'd found a way to spend an evening with the man she'd been fantasizing about for weeks now—who miracle of miracles still wanted to see her—without jeopardizing her job or her law license, and she was grabbing it with both hands.

****

He saw her come in. He'd barely taken his gaze from the door since his own arrival so that wasn't unexpected. Her appearance was, though. She hadn't worn the green dress, but he couldn't be disappointed. She looked stunning. For someone who professed to dislike rich people, she certainly knew how to dress and move like one. She radiated elegance, the diamonds at her ears and throat catching the light along with the silver threads in her dress. He started toward her, then stopped. This was supposed to be an accidental meeting. He had to play his part.

Senator Johansson was welcoming all the guests as they entered. Michael couldn't help noticing he was more effusive over Annie than his less attractive contributors, holding her hand in both of his much longer than was necessary. Michael didn't care for the way her eyes sparkled above her smile as if she was genuinely enjoying her conversation with the notorious ladies' man. He moved toward them.

"Looks like an excellent turnout, Tom," he said, clapping a hand on the older man's shoulder.

"Michael." Johansson turned, keeping Annie's hand firmly in one of his. "I want you to meet Annie O'Toole, a lovely young woman who has the good sense to support me for the Senate."

Michael extended his hand, forcing Johansson to release hers. "Counselor. We meet again."

"Mr. Grayson."

She accepted his handshake, her eyes cool. The actress was in full force tonight. At least he hoped that coolness was for the benefit of any onlookers and not actually directed at him.

"Now here I thought I was going to have the honor of introducing you to the most beautiful woman in the room and it turns out you two already know each other."

"Ms. O'Toole is the public defender defending the punk who shot me."

"Oh." Johansson's eyes widened, his gaze darting between the two. "Well. I'm sorry. This is… a bit… awkward."

Michael put a hand on the senator's shoulder. "It's not a problem, Tom. Truly. She's just doing her job. No different than running into the lawyer on the other side of a civil suit and God knows, we've all done that enough, haven't we?" He looked over at Annie. "You wouldn't be uncomfortable joining the senator and I for dinner tonight, would you, Ms. O'Toole? We have a vacant seat at our table, I believe."

"Not at all." She grinned. "I promise to save the cross-examination for the courtroom. And please, call me Annie."

"Splendid," said Johansson, the tightness around his mouth relaxing into a relieved smile. "Do join us. Michael's plus one had to cancel, and it's bad form for my own table not to be full after I've harangued everyone else about filling theirs. Not to mention that you'll be much easier on my eyes than Michael here."

"Hey," Michael protested.

"Sorry, old chap. It's a fact. You're just not my type."

"I'm heartbroken." Michael looked at Annie. "In the meantime, can I get you a drink, Counselor?"

"That would be lovely. Thank-you."

"Follow me. We'll leave the senator to finish his hosting duties. Catch up with you at dinner, Tom."

The senator kissed Annie's hand gallantly and made Michael promise to behave himself, before turning to greet the next round of arrivals.

"Ironic, his warning me to behave around you, when you were the one screaming obscenities at me just yesterday," Michael murmured, leading her through the growing crowd.

"Yeah, I'd say I was sorry about that, if you hadn't started it. I am sorry your plus-one stood you up, though."

He grinned. "I'm not quite so heartbroken about that—since she never existed."

"Hmm," she murmured demurely. "Now who's the

lying slut?"

His response was a combination snort and choked-down guffaw that turned into a coughing fit.

"You okay, sir?" the bartender asked. "What can I get you to help that cough?"

"Bourbon," he wheezed, shooting Annie a look heavy with blame.

She smiled serenely and ordered a glass of white wine.

When he'd recovered, he said what he'd been thinking since she walked through those doors. "You look stunning tonight."

"Thank you. So do you."

He smiled and lifted his drink in a toast. "Don't we just make the perfect couple then?"

"Well, other than that little detail that I'm defending the guy accused of trying to kill you"—she returned the toast with a sardonic smile—"absolutely."

They drank, watching each other over the rims of their glasses. He was glad she hadn't worn her hair all pinned up and sprayed stiff like every other woman in the place. It fell in soft curls around her face, tucked behind one ear where a diamond earring sparkled. He wanted to bite that earlobe, to wrap his fingers through that hair, to feel that body beneath his again. Michael took a deep breath as his groin tightened uncomfortably. *Back away from the cliff there, boy.*

He steered the conversation to a topic he could count on to be anything but arousing. "You always say 'accused of'—like they have the wrong guy behind bars. Joiner confessed, you know."

"You don't think the police could get a confession out of a scared teenager, guilty or not? You've been living in your castle too long."

He gave her a skeptical look. "Are you saying the police beat a confession out of him?"

"I'm not saying anything about Mr. Joiner's case. It would be an ethical violation for me to discuss the specifics of his case with you." She looked at him pointedly. "I'm saying that it is hardly unheard of for the police to elicit false confessions, especially from a defendant who is young and terrified in a case they're under a lot of public pressure to solve." She extended an index finger from around her glass and pointed it at him. "That's not some bleeding-heart defense lawyer making excuses, Grayson. It's a proven fact. Try reading something other than your bank statement sometime and you might learn something about the injustices on the other side of the moat."

"Now just a minute—"

"Well, there's the man of the hour." A hand clapped him on the back, cutting off his irritated retort. "Glad to see you out and about again."

"Frank." With a sinking stomach, Michael acknowledged the silver-haired man.

Now *this* was about to get awkward.

"Listen, I am so sorry about that deposition fiasco. Randall told me that upstart of a public defender turned the whole thing into some kind of circus. That was simply inexcusable, and I promise—"

"Frank," Michael cut him off before the head prosecutor could dig himself into a deeper hole. "Have you met Annie O'Toole?" He inclined his head toward the woman at his side, heretofore ignored by the newcomer. "The upstart public defender in question?"

Francis Nicoletti slowly turned his head and stared.

"Mr. Nicoletti," Annie said smoothly, a gleam in her eye that didn't give Michael comfort they were going to get out of this without a scene. "It's so nice to finally meet you. Hard to believe I've been there three years now and I've never once come across you in a courtroom. But then I guess yours is pretty much just a political post, isn't it?"

Michael winced. She wasn't going to make this easy.

"What the hell are you doing here?" Nicoletti snarled.

"I'm sorry," she said, meeting Nicoletti's angry stare with one of her own. "I didn't realize the democratic process was off-limits to public defenders."

"Listen, Frank, it's okay—"

Annie cut him off, putting up a hand. "No, I want to hear his answer. Obviously, our head prosecutor thinks public defenders should not be allowed to participate in the electoral process. I'd like to hear him explain that to me."

"Who do you think you are, giving Michael Grayson orders?" Nicoletti's voice rose a notch. "You ought to be back in some jail cell with the scum you represent."

"Oh, Christ." Michael downed the rest of his whiskey.

The evening was about to go to hell in a hand basket.

"So, the top law enforcement official in this city doesn't believe in the Constitution? Is that what you're saying, Nicoletti? That we should all just ignore that little amendment guaranteeing the right to assistance of counsel before the state can lock you up and throw away the key? They call that a police state and I'm sure you'd feel right at home there." She stood toe-to-toe with the man, her voice heavy with sarcasm, completely unconcerned that her adversary was one of the most powerful politicians in the city. "Has it ever occurred to your political pea brain that the founding fathers put that clause in there to protect the average joe from people exactly like you?"

"Don't spew your bleeding-heart gibberish at me, young lady. I was practicing law when you were in grade school."

"You're right. It's been a lot of years since you had Con Law. Maybe you need a refresher course."

"What is going on?" Johansson hurried over at the sound of raised voices. "Is there a problem here?"

Nicoletti and Annie both ignored him, continuing to spit at each other like a couple of angry cats.

"What do you say I get you a drink, Senator?" Michael put a hand on his shoulder. "These two are going to gnaw on each other for a while and I think we'd best leave them to it."

"But—"

"Occupational hazard. Let's go."

The senator cast a worried look over his shoulder as Michael steered him away from the snarling pair. "Are you sure we shouldn't try to intervene?"

"Absolutely." Michael said. "You can trust me on that."

He watched from a safe distance, while she and Nicoletti went several more rounds. Her color was high and her eyes alight with righteous indignation. She leaned into the fight, passionately arguing for what she believed with complete disregard for what it could cost her personally. He'd never met a woman like her. She was beautiful, brilliant, and badass. And he wasn't about to let her get away—case or no case.

Nicoletti finally threw up his hands in exasperation and stomped toward the bar, leaving Annie looking after him with a satisfied smirk on her face. Michael shook his head and ordered the prosecutor a drink.

"That goddamn woman," the man growled as he reached the bar, "is completely out of control."

Michael nodded sympathetically and pressed the glass into his hands.

Nicoletti took a gulp. His face was flushed, and beads of sweat ran down his neck into the collar of his tuxedo. "I'm going to see she's disbarred. You can count on it, Michael."

"Sorry, Frank. I can't let you do that."

"Why in God's name not?"

Michael looked over at Annie, the picture of elegance once again, chatting pleasantly with an elderly woman in a silver evening gown.

"Because as soon as this case is over, I intend to ask her out." Michael grinned. "Go figure."

****

"You told him *what*?" Annie stared at Michael in horror.

"That I intend to ask you out as soon as this case is over. There's no problem with us dating at that point, is there?"

They were outside the hotel, Michael having insisted on walking her to her car. She'd considered splurging and going for valet parking, but it would have taken a week's worth of coffee money and, considered in that light, she was more than willing to walk a block in heels.

"No," She groaned, "but I can't believe you told him that. It'll be all over the courthouse by morning. Do you have any concept of what it's like being in that kind of fishbowl?"

"Yes, actually," he said sarcastically. "I think I might have some idea."

"Well, then why would you do that to me?"

"Is the idea of going out with me so distasteful that you wouldn't want anyone to know it might even be a future possibility?"

"That's not what I'm saying. I just don't want the whole world evaluating every move I make on this case to see if I'm handling it any differently because of you."

"I didn't tell him you wanted to go out with me. Or that I'd ever even spoken to you about it, for that matter. I just said that I intended to ask you out once this case is over. It was my way of guaranteeing that Nicoletti leaves you alone." He shrugged, as if that settled the matter.

"Excuse me?"

"Nicoletti was after your ticket—you told me that yourself—and you certainly didn't go out of your way to endear yourself to him tonight. All I did was give him a reason to leave you alone."

"That reason being the guy with the pocketbook wants it so."

"Is that such a bad thing?"

"Yes. Yes, it is—and so is the fact that you don't even recognize it as a bad thing." She'd stopped walking now and stood facing him, her voice heating up all over again. "Do you really think it's okay to just throw your money around and force everyone to fall in line? How would you feel if someone did it to you? Do you have any idea what it's like to be on the receiving end of that kind of bullying, day in and day out, having no say in your life?"

"Whoa, hang on a minute. We're talking Nicoletti here. I thought you hated his guts."

"It doesn't matter whether I hate his guts—which I do. What matters is…I don't want to start hating yours." Her voice cracked at this as her eyes filled with tears. "Goddamn it!" She brushed the tears away with the palm of her hand.

"What the hell are you crying about?" He stared at her in bewilderment.

"Just forget it." She waved a hand as if to erase their conversation. "It's been a long day and I'm obviously a little over-emotional." She sniffed. "This is my car anyway. Thanks for walking me out." She dug out her keys and unlocked the door. "Good night."

"Wait just a minute." He grabbed her arm and turned her back to face him. "You can't just break into tears, then tell me good night and drive off. What's going on? What did I do?"

She sighed and lifted her gaze to his. "You're rich, Michael. That's what it comes down to. You're God-awful, outrageously rich and that's how you choose to live your life." She looked down. "Even if we didn't have this case between us, it wouldn't work. We live in two different worlds."

"So, you're writing off anything that could ever be between us because I have more money than you do." His voice was hard now, angry.

"Mick–"

"I never pegged you for an elitist snob, Annie O'Toole."

"I'm not!"

"Really? What would you call someone who judges people based solely on how much money they have? You don't know anything about me, where I came from, what's important to me. But you don't have to, do you? All you need to know is my bank account. And with that all-encompassing information, you get to label me as some kind of blight upon society."

"That's not—"

"Oh yes, it is. That's exactly what you meant." His eyes flashed. "Well, I've got news for you. Even if I had been born with a silver spoon in my mouth—which I wasn't—you'd have no right to define me by how many millions I happen to have made. If I treated anyone else that way based upon their lack of money, you'd have my head on a post and justifiably so. Well, prejudice is a two-way street, sweetheart, and it's just as ugly both ways."

"It's not that you have the money…" She struggled to explain. "It's that you use it to bully people. To push people around like you just did Nicoletti. Do you see nothing wrong with that?"

"Not a damn thing. I think stopping a politician who wants my support from going after your law license because you had the audacity to stand up to him and be proud of defending poor people—including, I might add, the S.O.B. who almost killed me—is a very justifiable use of whatever influence I might have. And I don't think it's unreasonable to expect someone of your intelligence to understand that." He angrily jammed his hands in his pockets. "So, get this goddamn case over with as soon as possible so we can figure out where the hell this thing between us is going." With that, he strode off into the night, not once looking back.

****

Annie drove home on auto-pilot, her mind reeling with successive waves of hope and nausea. She'd seen up close and personal the kind of strings money could pull, the doors it could open, the boulder-sized obstacles it could toss aside as if they were made of cotton candy. Her father had been one of those 'obstacles.' Ripped out of her life and tossed aside without a second thought by the matriarch who thought him unseemly, unworthy to stand in the spotlight that was the Barlow dynasty. With a flick of her bejeweled finger, her grandmother had dispensed with him.

But she'd lost her only grandchild in the process. That at least, she hadn't been able to control. Annie straightened her shoulders and glared at the road disappearing under her wheels in the night. Annie O'Toole would not be bought—not by her grandmother and not by a gorgeous billionaire with a killer crooked smile.

Most of the stoplights had switched to flashing yellow this time of night and she was tempted to kick up her speed and take advantage of the clear pathway home. Nothing like a good fast drive to clear one's head. But she couldn't afford the hike in insurance another ticket would bring, and her friends had all flatly refused to fix any more tickets for her. Resisting temptation, she glanced over at the neon lights of a twenty-four-hour grocery. Ice cream. Ice cream was what she needed right now.

She swerved sharply across four lanes of nonexistent traffic and swung into the parking lot. Grabbing her silver clutch, she marched inside and headed straight for the frozen foods aisle, a woman on a mission. At this time of night, the place was empty, except for one wide-eyed cashier and a pair of stock boys who gaped at her around the tower of flavored waters they were building.

She perused her options. Cherry chocolate chip or fudge brownie? The man of her dreams or her grandmother all over again in pretty packaging? Snagging the cherry chocolate chip, she slammed the freezer door and headed to the checkout. Wouldn't her grandmother just love the idea of her winding up with the likes of Michael Grayson? She could just see that self-satisfied smirk. *'What a perfect match, Annabel. I knew you'd come around.'* Grinding her teeth, she slammed the ice cream down on the checkout belt.

The cashier flinched and cleared her throat. "Will that be all?"

Get a grip, Annie. It wasn't this poor woman's fault she was falling for the world's sexiest puppet master.

"Yes, thanks."

"Umm, your dress is beautiful. Special occasion?"

Annie forced a grin. "Nope. I always dress like this to come to the store. It's my one big outing, you know?"

The cashier chuckled and relaxed a fraction. They exchanged the usual cashier-customer chit chat as the woman rang her up and Annie dug out the ridiculous purchase price. There went a couple of lattes this week, but she had no regrets. Unlike valet parking, quality ice cream was worth the sacrifice. Gathering up her medicinal remedy, she flashed a smile at the two stock boys who hadn't taken their gaze off her since she'd walked in, and headed back to the car.

It was running. And the door was locked.

"Goddamn it! Not again."

She banged her fist on the door, cursing her own stupidity. Why did she keep doing this? Other people managed to be preoccupied about all sorts of things and still remembered to grab their keys when they got out of the car. She slumped against the door and stared at the empty parking lot.

Jonathan was going to kill her, dragging him out here this time of night. She flipped open her phone case and then, with another curse, snapped it closed. Jonathan wasn't here. He was in Kansas City for a jury selection workshop and wouldn't be back until Friday. Well, double damn it.

Michael's face flitted across her mind. Bet it had been a lot of years since the mighty Michael Grayson had gotten a call to come deal with a locked car in the middle of the night. It would serve him right, though. After all, it was his fault she'd needed to make the ice cream run in the first place. Without letting herself even consider the fact that she was obviously grasping at any excuse to see him again, she pulled up the private cell number she'd entered in her contacts—for purely professional reasons, of course—and punched it.

Her mind raced as it rang. He probably wouldn't even come. He'd roust some minion with power tools to take care of it. That's what the rich did, passed their problems down the line, never hesitating to screw up some little guy's plans in lieu of interrupting their own schedules so much as a fraction.

"Grayson." His voice was deep, rich, tantalizing.

Her mouth suddenly went dry.

"Michael?"

"Yes? Who is th—Annie?"

"Yeah. Um, I have a bit of a problem."

"Are you all right? What's wrong? Where are you?" His voice took on a worried, urgent tone that warmed her heart.

"I'm fine." She fingered her earring, staring at the cracks in the pavement beneath her heels. "Just uh, stupid. I've locked my keys in my car. I was wondering if... I'm sorry, this is really stupid, but I'm kind of stranded, and—"

"No problem." The deep voice was brisk now, energized. A man with a problem to fix. He probably thrived on fixing problems. "Where are you?"

"In the parking lot of the twenty-four-hour grocery on Lindell in the West End. Do you know it?"

There was a beat of silence. "You went grocery shopping? Now?"

"I needed ice cream," she said defensively.

"I see." His amusement fairly oozed through the phone. "Okay, I'm about twenty minutes from you. Wait inside the store for me. I'll give you a call when I get there. This is your cell, right?"

"Right. And, uh, thanks."

"See you soon."

****

Michael blew past the speed limits. In no time, the lights of the 24-hour grocery came into view. Braking, he cruised into the parking lot and coasted to a stop beside the woman in the evening gown perched on the hood of a baby blue bug eating ice cream out of the carton with a plastic spoon. One more picture added to the increasingly memorable photo album of Annie O'Toole.

He climbed out of the car. "Meant to tell you before—I like your ride."

She looked at his sleek and obviously very expensive, black sports car. "You dissin' my baby?"

"Never in a million years. My first car was a bug and they've held a special place in my heart ever since." He grinned, leaning against his own baby.

"Notice you're not still driving one, though."

"Got tempted away by speed. It's one of my addictions."

She nodded. "I can respect that. Mine, too."

"Happy to take you for a spin sometime."

"Perfect. You can take me to my house to pick up an extra key."

He bowed. "Happy to be of assistance to a damsel in distress."

She capped her ice cream, tucked it back in her grocery bag, and slid off the hood of the car, the silver in her gown sparkling in the parking lot light. He stifled a grin, imagining the stir she must have made in the grocery looking like that. He turned to open the passenger door for her.

"Can I drive?"

He looked over his shoulder. "This? My car, you mean?"

She grinned wickedly. "The very idea just makes you cringe, doesn't it?"

"No, of course not, it's just that—"

He never let anyone drive this car. He never let anyone touch this car. He…was an obsessive ass about this car. He knew it. And so, obviously, did she. He looked down at the pixie in evening wear.

"You're doing this to make me crazy, aren't you?"

"Right in one." She stood with one hand on her hip, the other rhythmically swinging her grocery bag back and forth, her diamond necklace sparkling as brightly as her eyes. "This is a test, Mr. Billionaire Boy. You all about the money and the fancy cars or about sharing with us little people?"

He cleared his throat and crossed his fingers. "Can you drive a stick?"

She snorted. "Of course."

He tried not to grind his teeth. He could do this. It was a car. Just a car. He could buy a dozen more just like it if he wanted. It took unbelievable effort, but he managed to walk around the car, and open the driver's door… for her.

"Great! This'll be fun." She shot him a megawatt smile and slid inside.

He just stood there, stroking the key fob in his pocket like some lucky talisman as she began adjusting his seat. Her seat. The driver's seat.

She peered up at him. "Are you getting in or do you want to wait here while I run home?"

He rounded to the passenger side and climbed in.

"Afraid I might not come back?" She pressed the Start button and the motor roared.

"Wouldn't that be witness tampering?" He concentrated on the banter, hoping to take his mind off the fact that someone else was behind the wheel of his baby. "Luring a state's witness out to some isolated parking lot in the middle of the night and then stealing his car, leaving him abandoned with no way home?"

"Mmm."

She navigated to the parking lot exit. But instead of pulling out, she rolled to a stop and turned to him, her face serious for the first time since he'd arrived.

"I shouldn't have called you. I mean, I know this was not a good idea. Totally apart from the fact that it's a tremendous inconvenience, it's really bad manners to ask favors of people you've just pissed off." She took a deep breath and touched his hand where it rested on his thigh. "But I'm glad you came."

The issue of who was driving dropped off his radar. All he saw were wide, uncertain green eyes pulling him to a place he was more than ready to go. He leaned across and gently brushed his lips against hers.

"No inconvenience at all. Princes are supposed to take care of their subjects." He smiled. "Now whaddya say we blow this pop stand?"

She grinned and punched the accelerator. She knew how to drive; he had to give her that. She handled his baby well, shifting smoothly, giving her enough speed to make it interesting, not so much as to make him crazy. And she looked damn good doing it, too. He almost regretted it when she pulled to a stop in front of a two-story brick duplex with tall, arched windows and a tiny front yard enclosed in a spiked, black, wrought iron fence.

Old St. Louis was almost all brick, the result of a mandate passed by the city fathers over a century ago after the Great Fire took out most of downtown. Of course, when the New Madrid fault finally gave, all those fire-resistant buildings would tumble to the ground like so many toy blocks, but the builders had done their best to fight the devil they knew at the time.

Still, Michael loved the old city neighborhoods and was absurdly pleased she'd chosen to live in one of them instead of some cookie-cutter suburban high-rise.

"Home sweet home." She killed the engine and set the parking brake. "I'll be right back."

"You have keys to get in? They're not on your car key ring?"

"I keep an extra key under the mat."

She climbed out of the car. He followed.

"You know that's not safe, don't you? That's the first place a burglar would look."

"I'm kidding. I'm the one who defends those burglars, remember? I do keep a key where I can get to it, but it's not exactly under the mat. It's around back. You don't have to come."

He ignored her and moved to open the wrought iron gate for her, inhaling her spicy scent as she brushed past him. He didn't know what that scent was, but he was thinking about buying the company. An uneven brick sidewalk snaked through the breezeway between buildings, so deep in shadows that he could make out very little beyond the shape of the woman in front of him. A second gate squeaked open.

"Brace yourself," she said.

"For what?"

Her answer was a piercing whistle, followed by a deep bark, the rattle of a door, and a blur of a large animal racing across the yard toward them.

"What the—?"

"Whoa, Darrow. Sit. S-I-T."

She reached out and grabbed the dog as it raced toward him. She managed to hold on to his collar—no small feat, since he was the size of a small pony. The animal wriggled and danced beneath her grip, alternating between cheerful barks and licks at his owner and suspicious sniffs and low growls at the newcomer.

She clasped the huge head in both her hands and kissed the flaring nose as two glittering eyes glared over her head at him. "Hold your hand out, so he can smell you."

"Are you sure? I'd rather not lose one," he muttered.

"Stop being such a chicken. He's a pussycat."

"Right. With a mouth the size of my head."

She grabbed his hand and pulled him forward. The dog sniffed his hand, arm, chest and crotch, before deciding to ignore the new guy and go back to begging for more of Annie's attention. Michael let out the breath he hadn't realized he'd been holding.

"When you said you had a Great Dane, I must admit I failed to quite grasp the full effect."

She laughed as she scratched the dog's ears with one hand and worked at his collar with the other. "Aw, he's a sweetheart. Not bad-tempered, just doesn't like rules. I think that's why we get along so well." She grinned and held up a key she'd removed from its clip on the beast's collar. "Ta-da! The key to my castle."

Chapter Nine

"You just left him standing outside? Seriously?" Jonathan shot Annie an incredulous look as they walked across the parking lot to the St. Louis Medium Security Institution—still known to locals as the Workhouse, even though forced labor hadn't been a part of its operations for many years. "You left a billionaire in a tux standing out in your backyard in the middle of the night with that giant animal of yours?"

"Well, what was I supposed to do?" Annie shifted her files and reached for the door handle. "Jackson would have been packing up my office if I'd invited him into my house. I'd already crossed the line by calling him to come rescue me when I locked my keys in the car. Which I would not have had to do if you'd been in town." Now it was her turn to shoot him a look—this one heavy with blame.

"Right. *Mea culpa.* For a day or two there, I forgot I only live to serve you." He followed her into the depressingly institutional waiting room. "As apparently does the billionaire CEO of Grayson Aeronautics, riding to your rescue on his 530-horsepower steed. You know, for somebody who professes to hate rich people, you're keeping some strange company these days."

Her retort was cut short by the guard working the front desk, a heavy-set woman squeezed into a uniform never designed to fit a woman's curves.

"Who you here to see?" Warmth and welcome were not part of the service here.

"James Joiner, please." Annie signed her name in the heavy visitor's log, then scooted it over to Jonathan to do the same while she dug out her driver's license and bar card for the guard's perusal.

"Joiner, huh? Popular boy today."

"Oh?"

Annie's senses jumped to alert, but she knew better than to show too much interest. The last thing most guards wanted to do was pass on information a defense lawyer might find useful.

"Some hotshot private lawyer taking him off my hands?"

The woman snorted. "That one don't have any money. Just another preacher tryin' to save his soul. Don't know why they bother."

Jonathan sighed wearily. "Please tell me it was at least a real preacher and not some lay do-gooder without any preacher-parishioner privilege. Confession may be good for the soul, but it sucks for the case."

A twitch that might have been a grin touched the guard's lips but faded before it could be fully identified. "Brother Adams. Runs that Northside Community Center. Always goin' on about keepin' the peace between the gangs. Lost cause if you ask me." She slid the aged logbook back under the counter. "But whether he's a full-fledged legal preacher, I couldn't say. Guess you might want to check that out." She started to turn away, but Annie stopped her.

"Could I check the log while you're calling Joiner down? I have an intern who was supposed to do some visits for me. Just want to make sure he's keeping up."

"Suit yourself." The guard dropped the logbook back on the counter, then picked up the greasy wall phone and growled at her counterpart on the other end to send Joiner back down to the interview room.

Annie flipped the book back to the day of Joiner's arrest. Page by page, she ran her finger down the entries, jotting down dates and names on her legal pad. When she was done, she slid the logbook back across the counter and rejoined Jonathan in the waiting area. She passed him her notes. He scanned the semi-legible scribbles, then stood and turned toward the guard.

"Hey, have I got time for a smoke before Joiner gets here?"

She snorted. "You got time for three. Shift change. Gonna be a while."

"Of course, it is. My timing is always impeccable that way," Jonathan replied. "C'mon, O'Toole. You can brief me on this guy's case while I feed my addiction."

"Right. 'Cause I only live to serve you." She shoved her legal pad back into her file and followed Jonathan outside.

"You don't smoke," Annie said to her co-counsel.

They'd moved to the side of the entrance, out of sight and hearing of the guard.

"Really? All this time I've been laboring under the delusion that I couldn't quit. So, talk to me."

"Adams has visited James every week since his arrest. And his Northside Community Center is the very same place where Peter Ashton volunteers," Annie said excitedly. "That can't be a coincidence. James is the only inmate to receive a weekly visit from the reverend, so this isn't just a regular check-in on parishioners."

"That assumes the reverend has other parishioners

here. We don't know that for sure."

Annie rolled her eyes. "Gimme a break. The man works with gang members in one of the highest crime areas in the city. How many gang members in your caseload, Mr. Clark? 'Cause I got a ton in mine. Nobody who works with that population has only one parishioner in the Workhouse."

Jonathan shrugged a concession.

"But wouldn't you think he'd be avoiding Joiner like the plague out of deference to his rich supporter," Annie mused, "instead of showing up here every week like clockwork to tend to his spiritual needs?"

Jonathan's gaze met hers. "Unless his visits aren't about Joiner's spiritual needs at all."

****

Attorney visits took place in the inmate side of the long room designed for family visits, its two halves divided by a row of windows. The thick glass was always covered with palm prints. Annie usually tried not to look at them.

The guard ushered them inside. "Joiner'll be down in a minute." She grunted and locked them in behind her.

Jonathan pulled three molded plastic chairs from the row of windows into a small circle while Annie snagged the only potential writing surface in the place—a grimy TV tray the guards used to hold their coffee when on family visit duty—and added it to their makeshift office.

"God, I hate the smell of bleach," she said.

Jails and prisons reeked of it.

"All part of the ambiance," said Jonathan, stretching his long legs out in front of him. "At least it's private. More than you could say for the old jail. I always found it so easy to get clients to open up to me sitting in the center of the cell block with the guard ten feet away. Something about those whispered conversations that just built trust, you know?"

"At least they had chairs. Out in Montgomery County, all I got was an upside-down bucket inside my client's jail cell."

"That bucket was your own fault." Jonathan wagged a finger at her. "You had choices. You could have sat on the bed with your client, like the guard told you."

Annie shook her head. "That guard was beside himself because I refused to sit on the bed. Or on that metal toilet. Can you imagine? Conducting an interview sitting on a toilet?"

"Not sure the bucket was all that much of a step up, but still, you get props for sticking to your principles. Such a glamorous gig we have. Can't imagine why we have trouble recruiting people, can you?"

The door on the cell pod side of the room opened and a gangly teenager in an orange jumpsuit and flip-flops two sizes too large, shuffled in. He hesitated when he saw Jonathan there.

"Hi, James," Annie said. A slow blush crept up her neck as she realized they hadn't seen each other since Jackson had been out to discuss her sex life with the teen. "Um, come on over. This is Jonathan Clark. He's the attorney who'll be working on your case with me. If you want me to stay on the case, that is. I mean, um, I believe, Mr. Winrod told you about him, right?"

She was blushing to her rosy, red roots. Thank God Jonathan had stood to shake hands with Joiner, so neither of them was looking at her.

James and Jonathan both sat. If James had any reaction to Jackson's news that his lawyer had had an anonymous one-night-stand with the man he was accused of shooting, it was long gone, which was bizarre in and of itself. Annie was used to clients coming on to her, something she'd learned early on to quash. But she didn't have another client in her caseload who wouldn't have made some sort of remark on this situation. Not so with James, though. He met her gaze with his usual quiet politeness. Not a trace of a leer or knowing twinkle in those wide eyes. Not so much as a whiff of anger or suspicion. It was a little unnerving.

"We, um, we did the depositions of, um, of—that I—and um, Mr. Winrod—told you about." *For God's sake, O'Toole, pull it together.*

Jonathan interrupted her stammer. "Before we get into that, since I'm new to your case, would you mind just giving me a rundown of the day of you got arrested?"

Annie blessed Jonathan's usually sarcastic, obnoxious heart.

"Like, all day?" James asked.

"Yeah. Just start with when you got up and go through when you got arrested. You were living with your mom, right?"

"Yeah."

"Just the two of you there? Nobody else in the home with you?"

"No, just us."

"Okay. Go ahead."

James looked over at Annie who gave him an

encouraging nod. "It's okay, James. Everything you tell Jonathan is just like what you tell me. It's confidential, just between us. We just need to know everything we can about what happened so we can prepare the best defense for you we can."

The boy shifted in his seat and looked at the floor.

"What time did you wake up that day?" Jonathan prompted. "Do you remember?"

"Around ten, I think."

"Was that when you usually woke up?"

"Yeah."

"And I'm sorry I don't already know this—still catching up on your file. Were you in school or working anywhere? Any place you had to go every day?"

"I worked at the taco place over on Kingshighway. But I was off that day."

"Know it well," Jonathan said with a grin. "Great tacos. Okay. So, after you woke up at ten, what did you do?"

"Ate breakfast. Watched some of my mama's shows on the TV with her."

This time Jonathan just waited, without further prodding.

"Little Wayne come over that afternoon."

"Who is he?"

"Just a guy I know. Lives in the neighborhood."

"Do you know his last name?"

"Nah."

Nobody knew last names. Last names could get a person killed.

"What did he want?"

"He was headed over to pick up some money a guy

owed him. Wanted me to go with him."

"Did you know the guy who owed him money?"

"Yeah. Guy named Xander."

Another no-last-namer. One for whom Little Wayne apparently wanted back-up.

Methodically, Jonathan led the taciturn teen through the same story he'd given Annie. The two boys had gone to hit Xander up for the money owed, but he wasn't home. They hung out with a couple of other guys they knew on one of the street corners, then went over to a girl's house. Played some cards, listened to some music, smoked a little weed. Around nine o'clock, James had been ready to go, but Little Wayne was still holding out hopes of getting lucky, so James left on his own. He was headed to the bus stop when a slew of police cars went screaming by. He detoured over to the West End to see what was going on. It was there one of the cops had nabbed him as a possible suspect.

All depressingly ordinary and mundane and life-shattering.

"Why'd you say you did it, if you didn't?" Jonathan asked softly.

James stared at the floor. "They kept sayin' they had a witness who identified me, and it was only gonna be worse for me if I didn't come clean while I still could. They said if the guy died, I'd be looking at the death penalty unless I took responsibility and said I did it. They kept sayin' things would go a lot easier if I just admitted it. So, I did."

Jonathan sighed. "You and a whole lot of others, my friend."

Books had literally been written about how easy it

was to elicit a false confession using a lethal combination of threats and promises of leniency, especially if you were dealing with a kid. And eighteen or no, James Joiner was in all respects still very much a kid.

Annie had gotten her grounding again as Jonathan and James talked. Now she picked up the reins, switching subjects. "James, I noticed in the visitor's log that Reverend Adams has been coming to see you a lot since you got arrested. Did you know him from before?"

Now James fidgeted. "We met once or twice."

"Where?"

"Just around."

"Did you ask him to come visit you every week or did he just do that on his own?"

"He just started coming."

"What do you the two of you talk about when he comes?"

"I dunno. Just stuff."

"Has he asked you anything about your case?"

"Not really."

"Can I ask you something, James?" Annie leaned forward. It was an odd question since that's all they'd been doing since they got there, but she wanted to get his attention.

He looked up. "Sure."

"Do you trust Reverend Adams?" she asked, intently watching the boy's face.

Something flashed behind the brown eyes. Then it was gone.

"Not sure I trust anybody these days. Except my mama. And maybe you."

Knife through the heart there. Thanks, buddy.

"There's a chance that Reverend Adams sometimes works with a friend of the guy who was shot," Jonathan said. "A man named Peter Ashton who volunteers at the Center. He was with Grayson the night he got shot. Have you ever met Peter Ashton?"

James shook his head. "Don't think so."

"Were there any white guys who volunteered up there?" Jonathan asked.

Annie and James both looked at him.

"Hey, just thought I'd narrow the field a little," he said a little defensively.

Most neighborhoods on the north side of the city were black, while most on the south side were white. Segregation might no longer be legal, but its vestiges still dominated the St. Louis landscape, and every resident knew it.

"Ashton's a white guy. Any white guys who volunteered?"

"I wasn't up there a lot, but I did see one white guy. Don't know his name though."

"What did he look like?" Annie asked.

"Older guy. Kinda short and chubby. Had a beard and little round glasses."

Annie smiled. "Sounds like Santa Claus." It did not, sadly, sound like Peter Ashton.

A touch of a smile lifted the corners of the boy's mouth. "Nah. This guy's beard was kinda reddish brown."

"What did he do at the Center?" Jonathan asked.

The boy shrugged. "I dunno. Not sure if he was a regular or just there that one time."

"Do you know when that was?"

137

James looked out the barred windows. "The day before I got arrested."

Annie and Jonathan exchanged a look.

"You were at the Center the day before your arrest?"

"Yeah. I went with Little Wayne."

"Did you talk to Reverend Adams at all then?"

"Nah. He was in the office with that guy with the beard. Little Wayne went in and talked to him though."

"What did you do while they talked?"

"Played foosball."

"How long were they in there?"

"Fifteen, twenty minutes maybe. Not too long."

"Did Little Wayne tell you what they talked about?"

"Didn't ask."

Jonathan leaned forward in his chair. "James, we think Reverend Adams might be coming to see you to get information about the case. Information Peter Ashton, who was with the victim the night he was shot, might want. Has he asked you anything about the case?"

James's gaze slid away to the window again. The kid would make a lousy poker player.

"James?" Annie said. "If he's taking advantage of his position as a pastor, we can put a stop to his visits."

"He's fine," James said, his gaze now dropping to the floor. "So, um, I gotta get back to the pod. Yard time this afternoon."

****

Annie and Jonathan made their way back through security and out to the parking lot.

"Well, that was productive," Jonathan said, the

sarcasm palpable.

"There's obviously something going on with Adams that James doesn't want us to know about," mused Annie, "even though he clearly doesn't like the man. Did you see his reaction when I asked if he trusted him?"

"Oh, yeah."

"If Adams is out here every week bugging him for some kind of confession, wouldn't he want us to pull him off?"

"You'd think. Not to mention that the police already have his confession so that would be a pointless endeavor on Adams's part. Unless he's trying to get some other information about the shooting. Something the police don't yet have."

Annie looked at him. "Like who put him up to it?"

Jonathan shrugged. "It's one possibility. We both know the facts don't fit a robbery, no matter what the police fed the media."

Annie stared out the window. "I don't know. I just don't see James as a hitman, even an amateur one. He's just too…" she searched for the word. "Sweet."

Jonathan snorted. "News flash. My murder clients are some of my favorite people. Doesn't mean they didn't kill somebody."

"You think he did it?"

"No idea. But no way the state's version of the story adds up."

She huffed out a breath. "I need ice cream. How do you feel about a stop before we head back?"

Jonathan pretended to consider. "I feel very good about it."

Business was booming at the popular frozen

custard stand when they arrived. It nearly always was. Jonathan squeezed his car into what might charitably be called a parking spot in the gravel lot and they joined the long line of people in need of therapeutic custard.

"So, are you going to Chicago?" Jonathan asked.

She'd filled him in on her grandmother's call.

Annie sighed. "Leave it alone, Jonathan. We're supposed to be talking about Joiner."

"And so we shall, as soon as you obtain your sugar fix and we retire to someplace private and appropriate for confidential discussions," he said, looking pointedly at the crowd of people around them. "In the meantime, we will make small talk like normal humans do. Like, for example, the fact that your grandmother is dying and has asked you to come visit her on her deathbed."

"Jonathan—"

"I'm serious, Annie. This is a big deal and you're playing it off like your hair appointment got cancelled—some minor inconvenience interrupting your schedule."

"She's probably not even really dying. Knowing her, it's just another manipulation to get me back under her thumb. She's too mean to die. Heaven wouldn't have her and if the Devil let her into hell, she'd probably stage a *coup* and be running the place in a week." She turned to eye the menu. "Strawberry Massacre or Cookie Dough Concrete?"

"Jeez, O'Toole. And you say I'm cynical."

"Strawberry Massacre it is. Seems more appropriate to the occasion, don't you think?"

"Could you move about ten feet away from me? I don't want to get singed when you get struck by that lightning bolt the Almighty is aiming at your head right now."

Annie rolled her eyes and nudged him forward as the line moved. They placed and collected their orders and retired to one of the picnic tables scattered around the grounds.

"You should go," Jonathan said for the umpteenth time in as many different ways.

She glared at him. "Why?"

"You know why." He gave her an exasperated look. "She's your grandmother. You're her only living relative and she's dying. She's asked to see you. You go. That's what good people do and you are good people. Death is forever, Annie. No second chances, no do-overs. This is it."

She stared into her cup, nudging a piece of fudge brownie around with a spoon. "You don't know my grandmother."

"Doesn't matter. This isn't about who she is, it's about who you are. And the O'Toole I know and love would not let her only living relative die alone because she's still pissed about ancient history."

Annie ground her teeth. "It is *not* ancient history. And you have no idea what that woman is like."

"No, I don't." He looked at her. "The question is, are you like her? Because it sounds to me like ignoring a dying old lady is exactly the kind of thing your grandmother would do. Is that the person you want to be?"

Annie stared at him, anger fading into horror. "Oh, now that is so below the belt."

Jonathan shrugged. "I have been told that's where I do my best work."

She swivelled on the bench, placed her boot against

his hip, and shoved. He slid right off the end of the bench and landed in the gravel, just managing to hang onto his custard.

****

Across the road, a man in a grey sedan chuckled. He jotted a note on his pad, then waited and watched as the man on the ground got up, dusted himself off, and followed the redhead back to the car. They pulled out of the parking lot, making a right onto Chippewa.

After a beat, he swung his own car from the curb and followed.

Chapter Ten

Jonathan never took the same route to anywhere, insisting that exploring alternate routes gave him a better grasp of the city—which was probably true. It also meant that going anywhere with Jonathan took two or three times as long as the direct route. But sometimes his odd detours led to surprising synchronicities.

"Wait!" Annie pointed. "Turn there!"

"What? Why?" Jonathan's query cost them the turn.

"That's the street they live on—James and his mother. Maybe we can catch her at home and see if she has any info on Reverend Adams."

"Worth a shot." Jonathan made a U-turn at the next opportunity. "Should we call first?"

Annie flipped through the file. "No phone listed. Street address is 5817."

Jonathan pulled up in front of one of the four-family flats that dotted the landscape of many of St. Louis's older neighborhoods. The building had seen better days, as had most of the vehicles sitting out front. The Joiners had the end unit. A window was open, and the sound of a TV wafted past the satellite dish attached to the side of the building. A good sign—though they knew from experience it didn't mean their knock would be answered. This time, it was.

A short, wide woman opened the door. She was

dressed in a flowered housedress and faded slippers. Her gray hair was cropped short, revealing a pair of startlingly beautiful diamond studs completely out of sync with the rest of her attire. Annie had long ago been taught to tell at a glance the difference between rhinestones and the real thing and these were definitely the real thing.

"Mrs. Joiner?"

Jonathan handled the introductions while Annie processed the rest of the woman's jewelry collection. A luxury watch. Large ruby ring. And those expensive diamond earrings. WTF?

Mrs. Joiner was as polite as her son. She invited them inside and seated them on a lovely cream-colored leather couch that dominated the small living room. Across from them, affixed to a wall with peeling paint, perched an outrageously large flat-screen television.

Mrs. Joiner picked up a remote and muted the blaring buzzers of a game show. "You want some iced tea?"

Annie and Jonathan had learned early on in their careers that it was never a good idea to partake of food and drink in the homes they visited. One never knew the extent of the rodent infestation at play in the next room. Then again, most of the homes they visited didn't have creamy leather couches and flat-screen TVs the size of Annie's car.

"That would be great," said Annie, grasping at the chance to peruse the rest of the room without appearing rude.

"Uh, none for me, thanks," said Jonathan, shooting a glance at Annie.

"Be right back."

Annie quickly began jotting down an inventory of the room. It was an odd mix of thrift store finds and top-of-the-line chic. A worn rug and raggedy recliner shared the living room with the leather couch. Over here a tarnished floor lamp of indeterminate metal, topped with a faded shade that may once have had a color, and there a gleaming table lamp with an intricate stained-glass shade that would have looked at home in her grandmother's house.

Mrs. Joiner returned with Annie's iced tea and one for herself.

"Sure you don't want nothin'?" she asked Jonathan. "Ice water? I could make a quick pot of coffee if you'd like?"

The caffeine addict in Annie wondered which end of the line Mrs. Joiner's coffee pot hailed from.

"I'm fine," Jonathan assured her. "Appreciate you seeing us without any notice. We would have called first, but didn't have a good number for you."

"Oh, I have a new number I ought to give you folks." She pulled a sleek smart phone from the pocket of her housedress. "Just got it last week. Still haven't figured out how to work this thing. Didn't need all those new-fangled features, but…"

She read them the number scribbled on a piece of masking tape stuck to the back of the phone. Annie jotted it down.

"You have some lovely pieces here, Mrs. Joiner," Annie ventured, unsure how to ask about the bizarre mix of outrageously expensive and depressingly poor furnishings.

Mrs. Joiner smiled shyly. "I do, don't I? It's the darndest thing. That nice Brother Adams from up at the

145

Northside Community Center? Ever since James got locked up, he's been comin' by to check on me. And bringin' me these lovely things." Her eyes widened with the impossibility of it all.

"Really?" Annie asked, swallowing her astonishment and scooping up the gift the universe had just handed her. "Like this lovely couch? And that gorgeous lamp over there?"

Mrs. Joiner nodded. "Ain't they just as pretty as can be? And these nice earrings and this watch," she added, fingering her earlobes with one hand while extending her other arm for them to see. "Seems like every week, he's showin' up with somethin' new just for me." She leaned forward in her chair and lowered her voice as if sharing a secret. "Said he's got some nice donor at the Center who heard 'bout my James gettin' locked up for that shootin'—which he didn't have nothin' to do with—" she looked at them both sternly, then her face relaxed back into a smile—"an' he just wanted to do somethin' for me."

"Wow." Jonathan looked round. "That's very generous. Did he give you that TV, too? It's a beauty."

"Yes, sir, he did. With my cataracts, I couldn't hardly see my shows on that little one we used to have. James always said he wanted to get me a real big TV so I could watch my shows." Her voice softened with a tinge of sadness. "And now here it is and he's not here to enjoy it with me."

"Did James spend a lot of time up at the Northside Community Center before his arrest?" Annie asked.

"That's the funny thing. He only went up there a coupla times I know of. Told me he didn't care for Brother Adams, though I don't see why not." She gestured round the room. "I mean, surely he has to be a good man to do all this for somebody like me he don't even know!"

"He must indeed," Annie agreed, an idea starting to gel in the back of her mind. "I wonder how he knew what you'd like. Like that you needed a bigger TV because of your cataracts."

"Me, too! Every single thing he's brought is somethin' I've always wanted. I used to tell James, I'd say, before I die, I want a genuine leather couch. I used to clean houses before my hip started givin' me trouble, and one of the ladies I worked for had the most beautiful creamy leather couch. Soft as butter. I always wanted one just like it. And now, here I got me one, sittin' in my very own livin' room. Unbelievable."

"Did you know that Brother Adams has been visiting James at the Workhouse? Pretty regularly. Do you think James might be giving him ideas of things you'd like?" Annie watched her closely, looking for a reaction.

She showed no surprise at the news. "Could be. James always acts surprised when I tell him what new thing Brother Adams brought by, but that boy always did keep his secrets to hisself and I'd never be the wiser. Every year, he'd surprise me with somethin' for my birthday he'd been workin' on all year, and I never knew a thing about it even though he was makin' it right here in my own house. James is good with his hands. Likes to carve things out of wood. He made that there." She pointed to a delicate carving of a dancer Annie had placed on the expensive side of her inventory.

"Really? He made that??" Annie's awe was

genuine. "That's amazing! It's beautiful."

"Wow. Your son is a wonderful artist," Jonathan concurred.

Her smile was wide, her pride in her boy's talent evident. "He's been tinkerin' with wood since he was old enough to hold a carvin' knife. Draws good, too. But mostly he plays with the wood pieces we find thrown out round the neighborhood."

Annie thought of the sculptures that dotted her grandmother's house and grounds. She doubted there was a piece there purchased for less than $5,000 and James's dancer was every bit as good. But instead of collecting large checks from rich patrons vying to own his masterpieces, he was stuck carving his gems from thrown away bits of wood scavenged from the vacant lots that dotted the ghetto in which he lived.

"Is James right or left-handed?" Annie heard Jonathan ask. She pulled her gaze from the dancer and her mind back to the case.

"Right-handed."

Unlike their shooter.

"Was he ever in a gang?"

Mrs. Joiner sighed and gazed out the window. "I don't know that he was ever in a gang. But he wanted to be. We used to argue 'bout that all the time. I kept tellin' him those boys are trouble and just gonna land you in jail, you keep runnin' with them. He wouldn't listen. James always wanted to be a part of something, y'know? I sent him to high school out in the county— part of that diversity program, you know?" The question was rhetorical, because she didn't pause for a response. "I thought he'd get a better education, keep out of trouble, make some friends who didn't have juvie records already." She plucked at a loose thread on her housedress. "But I think it kinda backfired. He never really fit in at that school. He couldn't hang with the other students after school or go to much of the outside stuff 'cause the bus couldn't bring him home that late and we didn't have a car. And the neighborhood kids here gave the deseg kids kind of a hard time." She shook her head "He was in a hard place. But he graduated. I insisted on it. Said he'd break my heart if he dropped out, so he didn't, even though I know he wanted to. Proudest day of my life when I watched my boy walk across that stage to get his diploma. I only went to the eighth grade myself." She looked up at them with a sad smile. "I thought he was gonna make it outta here. Then this." A single tear escaped down her cheek. "I'd gladly give back all these nice things to have my boy home."

Annie reached over to lay her hand across the old woman's. "I'm sure you would, Mrs. Joiner. That's what we want, too. That's why we're here. We need your help."

The older woman wiped her cheek and straightened her shoulders. "Tell me what you need."

****

"Somebody's buying his silence," Annie said, as soon as they were back in Jonathan's car. "What else could it be? If it were really a 'concerned donor' who believed James was being railroaded, wouldn't he be hiring James some hot shot private lawyer to try to save his skin instead of buying pretty baubles for his mother?"

"I think he passed 'baubles' my fantasy TV ago," said Jonathan. "There's money behind this." He looked over at Annie. "Grayson Aeronautics' kind of money."

Annie stared at him. "You think Michael is buying the silence of the guy he thinks shot him?"

"No, you moron. Sheesh. Grayson isn't the only big money involved with Grayson Aeronautics. I mean, have you seen the salaries of guys like Ashton and his other top execs?"

"No. Have you?"

"Well, no," he admitted, "but you know they have to be big enough that a leather couch is chump change. Everything here is pointing to Ashton. He was with Grayson the night he was shot. And he's the connection between Grayson and Adams. He's got to be the one funnelling money through Adams to buy off James by giving his mother everything James could never afford to get her."

"So, you think Ashton hired James to shoot Michael?"

"Hired someone. I'm not sure it was James, but since he's the one who got picked up and confessed, it's certainly in Ashton's best interest to keep him quiet and let him take the rap." Jonathan nodded to himself as the light turned green. "It all fits."

"Except for a motive," Annie pointed out. "Ashton's been one of Michael's right-hand guys for years. Why would he want Michael dead? And let's face it, if he did want Michael dead, wouldn't he hire a professional, instead of some amateur street kid like James?"

Jonathan blew out a breath. "No clue on either front."

Both were silent for a bit.

"Review time. What do we know about Ashton?"

Jonathan asked.

"Impressive CV, as I recall. Ivy league all the way, Wharton MBA—all the right checks in all the right boxes to be where he is now."

"Assuming it's all genuine. We can't afford to take anything for granted. Remember our motto." He placed his hand over his heart and intoned in melodramatic fashion, 'In God we trust, all others we cross-examine.'"

"'And sometimes even God doesn't get a pass,' I know. We should get t-shirts. Oh, wait! We already did." Annie smiled. "But you're right. Maybe the guy's been running a ten-year con. That's something we can have Charlie start on, make sure his bona fides really are bona fide." She made another note on her legal pad. "Charlie can also dig into the Northside Community Center and Mama Joiner's beloved Brother Adams."

"All well within Charlie's wheelhouse, which brings us to the elephant in the case." Jonathan shot Annie a glance. "Most of this isn't in any of our wheelhouses. I mean the shooting itself, sure. But if the motive is high-dollar white-collar, uncovering that is a paper game. One for which we don't even speak the language, much less have the resources to investigate."

Their office had one of the best street crime investigators in the state, but the operative word was street crime. Give him junkies to flush out or angry family members to sweet talk, street rumors to track down or forensic evidence to review, and Charlie could always deliver. But the man knew even less about the corporate world than Annie did.

They needed someone knowledgeable in the world of international business, someone at home in the culture, fluent in the language, who knew both the rules and the many circuitous routes by which the rules got broken. Someone who could spot the inconsistencies, the little details that didn't quite fit, those tiny oddities that could generally be counted on to go unnoticed, but that any good dowser would recognize as a place worth digging deeper.

A tingle of dread formed in the deep recesses of Annie's mind as the thought spiralled on to its conclusion. Someone who knew how to dig out the dirty secrets and hidden motivations of some of America's wealthiest corporate moguls. Someone at home in the Machiavellian maneuvering of multi-national corporations and mahogany boardrooms.

Damn it to hell. She needed her grandmother.

She tried to say it out loud, but the words stuck in her throat. She gave herself a mental shake. This wasn't some academic exercise. Someone was trying to kill Michael. Someone other than an awkward adolescent locked safely away in a cell out at the Workhouse. It was someone Michael knew, very possibly someone wining and dining with him daily. Someone just waiting for another opportunity.

She cleared her throat, took a deep breath and tried again. "It's my grandmother's wheelhouse. Corporate espionage is smack in the center of her wheelhouse."

Jonathan threw her a dismissive glance. "Annie, we're not talking about sharing trade secrets out of school here. We're talking about murder for hire. You want to drag your dying granny into this?"

Annie fought down the urge to vomit all over Jonathan's front seat. "When will you get your head around this? My 'granny'—who would have you stripped and flayed for calling her that, by the way—is not some mildly eccentric family matriarch. She's the evil genius in the Bond movies, a high-class mob boss. Hell, she probably has her own hit men on the payroll. And I guarantee they won't be teenaged wannabes, but true professionals in every sense of the word." She pressed her fingers against her eyes.

Jonathan coasted to a stop at a red light and stared at her. "You don't mean that."

"I absolutely mean that. How can I make you understand this? Her one and only moral code is to be the richest and most powerful of them all. Period. And she will run over anyone—anyone—who stands in her way, without so much as a backward glance."

"I thought it was 'the fairest of them all.'" Jonathan grinned, a weak attempt to lighten the mood.

"Definitely important, but secondary to money and power. Lessons made very clear to me growing up, believe me. But here's the thing: she's brilliant. Devious and dangerous and brilliant. If anybody could dig up dirt on Ashton or anyone else at Grayson, it would be her."

The light changed and they moved again.

"Believe me, I'm open to other ideas if you have any, but Eleanor Barlow happens to be the only corporate Machiavellian I have on speed dial."

Jonathan cleared his throat. "I'm still trying to wrap my head around the idea of your Gran as an evil genius-slash-murderer."

"Well, it's true. At least the evil genius part. I'm guessing on the murderer part, but I certainly wouldn't put it past her."

"Do you think she has a file on me? You know,

best friend and confidante of her wayward granddaughter?"

"Probably," Annie muttered. "She has files on everyone."

"Lovely. I'm feeling all warm and fuzzy about your family, O'Toole."

"Can't say I didn't warn you."

"*Touché.*" He inhaled deeply. "But she's also sick now. If she's dying, whatever her talents may once have been, she may no longer be able to pull the strings she once did."

Annie snorted. "I'll believe the dying thing when she's underground—and even then, I wouldn't count her out. She probably has a whole cryogenics setup just waiting."

"You really think she's lying to you about being sick?"

"I'd bet my paycheck on it." She winced, recalling the gleam in Michael's eye, delivering that same line in a very different context.

"Well. Okay, then. When can you talk to her?"

Annie stared out the side window, numb, as the reality of what she was about to do sunk in. "Tomorrow, I guess. She's sending a car." She pressed her fingers against her temples. "I'd planned to send Carter packing without me, but now… looks like I'm the one that needs to be packing."

"She's sending a car from Chicago? What, did you lose your license and not tell me?"

The shadow of a smile flitted across Annie's face. "No one drives themselves in Grandmother's world."

"No private jet, then?"

"She knows I won't fly."

"But she has a private jet."

"Of course, she does."

"Of course. What was I thinking?" He swung into the lot behind the courthouse. "What do we tell Jackson?"

"I'll let him know my grandmother is sick and I'm headed to Chicago. May or may not be back on Monday depending on what I find there."

"You don't think we should fill him in on this?"

Annie ran her fingers through her curls. "What can we say? He's already gotten so much heat over the office defending the 'punk who shot Michael Grayson.' You've heard what the pundits are saying about the use of taxpayer funds for this. Do you think he's going to be super-enthusiastic about us going all corporate espionage on Grayson Aeronautics?"

Jonathan blew out a breath. "Yeah, hardly."

"Let's leave it for now. It is the truth. I did get a call that my grandmother is sick and I am going up to see her. And, if all goes as planned, it will be Eleanor Barlow, not the Office of the Public Defender, digging into the dirty laundry of Grayson Aeronautics. James will simply be the beneficiary of what she uncovers."

"Not to mention Michael Grayson."

Annie hesitated, then voiced the question that had been coiled in the back of her mind since they'd left Mama Joiner's house. "Should I tell him? Warn him? I mean, what if we don't find who's behind this before…" She left the unthinkable unsaid.

"What would you say? We don't have a name or a motive or a speck of evidence, just a gut feeling that things don't fit. Hell, for all we know Adams just has the hots for Mama and is using her son to wiggle his way in."

"And happens to have a secret donor willing to bankroll his love life?"

"Wouldn't be the first time a so-called minister has diverted donations to live high on the hog and buy presents for his lady friend. Look, you know the rules as well as I do. If we had definite information that Grayson was in danger, we could reveal it. But anything short of that has to be kept confidential. And we're far short of that. We're chasing shadows here. They might turn out to be something. They might just as easily turn out to be nothing more than our overactive imaginations." Jonathan blew out a breath. "Let's see what Charlie can dig up. You go work your grandmother and I'll take another try at James over the weekend. See if I can get him to open up a little more. We'll take it day by day." He glanced over at his passenger. "It's all we can do, Annie."

She stared out the window, silent for a time. Finally, she said, "Do you think there's any conflict in what I'm doing here? I mean, yes, I'm trying to save Michael, but finding out who's behind this will help James, too, won't it? With that info, we could get him a deal to turn state's evidence. He might wind up looking at five to ten, instead of life." She searched Jonathan's gaze. "I need some objectivity here, because, frankly, I'm anything but at this point."

"Yeah, I got that." He shot her a sidelong look. "But truly, everything we're doing at this point is what we need to be doing for James. If that changes down the road, I will personally kick you off the case. Okay?"

Annie took a deep breath and nodded. "Okay, yeah. Thanks."

"Now get out of my car. I have a date."

"Of course you do." She climbed out and then leaned down to the window. "And let the record reflect that, once again, you're getting laid and I'm getting the shaft. This is a trend that has to stop."

"Hey, it was your getting laid that got us both into this mess. This is all just payback."

She flipped him off over her shoulder and headed to her car.

Chapter Eleven

"Hey, Joe. Need you to run me a plate." Streeter Jacobson took a sip of his coffee while the usual stream of invective came and went, then continued, unperturbed. "Illinois. EJB-005. I'll hold."

While he waited, he jotted down a description of the man standing at Annie O'Toole's door. Black male. Mid-sixties. Approximately 6'1." Fit. Close-cropped gray hair. Clean-shaven. A black suit that looked damned uncomfortable for a Saturday morning but went with the black limousine parked out front.

Joe came back on the line. "Registered to one Barlow Industries."

Streeter choked on his coffee. "Did you say Barlow?"

"Yes, asshole. I said Barlow. Barlow Industries. Now go away and leave me alone. You ask too many damn favors."

"Yeah, you get way more than you give and you know it," Streeter retorted. "Pair of hockey tickets headed your way. You can thank me later." He disconnected the call as the door to the duplex opened and the driver disappeared inside. He jotted down the time of entry and drummed his fingers on the steering wheel, mulling this new twist.

He didn't have long to mull. In less than five minutes, the front door opened and Ms. O'Toole herself emerged, looking lovely in an elegantly simple, Royal blue dress and heels. The sun caught the gold in her reddish curls. Mike did have good taste in women, Streeter had to give him that. The driver followed her out, carrying a suitcase. She locked the door behind them while he loaded the luggage in the trunk.

He couldn't hear their conversation, but they laughed and chatted easily. These two looked like they'd known each other a long time. If so, O'Toole's association with Barlow was not a new development. Damn. Mike was not going to like this news.

The limousine rumbled to life as Streeter reached for his phone. Punching in his assistant's number, he pulled from the curb, careful to keep far enough back not to be noticed. Anybody who worked for Barlow was probably well-trained in spotting a tail.

"Yeah."

"Such a professional way to answer the phone."

"Your name came up on the screen. It's not like I didn't know who I was talking to."

"I bet nobody working for Barlow Industries answers the phone that way when they see Eleanor Barlow's name on the screen."

"I bet anybody working for Barlow Industries would be crapping their pants if they saw Eleanor Barlow's name on the screen. Did you call for a reason or just want to dole out some shit this fine morning?"

Streeter grinned. Hiring Remi Jackson had been one of the best things he'd ever done. Smart, scrappy, and nosy. Kindred souls, the two of them. He thought of her as the daughter he'd have wanted, if he'd ever wanted children. Not that he'd ever admit any of that to Jax, as she preferred to be called.

"You started on the O'Toole background yet?"

"Not yet. Is it a rush?"

"It is now."

"Oh? Things get interesting out there this morning?"

"They did indeed. Ms. O'Toole was just picked up by a limousine registered to Barlow Industries. Looked like she and the driver are old friends."

Jax whistled. "That is a twist. I'll start on her right now."

"Give me a call when you know something. I doubt somebody sent a car all the way from Chicago just to drive her to the airport, so I may be in for a road trip. I wanna see where this is going."

"Need anything from me trip-wise?"

"May need another tail if I get made. I'm guessing they're headed back toward Chicago, so you might roust a crew up that way and have them on standby."

"Will do. Anything else?"

"Go earn your pay." He hung up before she could retort.

Sure enough, the limousine swung north onto I-55. Headed to Chicago.

Nope, Mike was really not going to like this.

****

Time turned on its heels as the limousine passed Lincoln Park. They swung onto Burling Street and suddenly there it was—Annie's personal hell, wrapped in a multi-million-dollar bow. Four stories high, with a wrought iron widow's walk atop its broad expanse, the mansion looked as if it had stood for generations. It hadn't. Eleanor built the place herself, recreating the glory days of the Vanderbilts in her own little corner of the world. She'd been disappointed at having to settle for just eight city lots on which to build her showplace, but she didn't want to locate any farther out of the city. Life required such unfair compromises. Still, its measly 25,000 square feet managed to provide plenty of places for an unhappy little girl to hide. Annie knew them all.

The automated iron gates slid closed behind them as Carter eased to a stop under the portico. Annie stared up at the stone facade. It had been years since her dramatic exit down those steps, but sitting here now, it felt like she'd never left. The life she'd built for herself in that interim felt like someone else's. Distant. Inconsequential. Irrelevant.

Carter opened the car door and handed her out into the afternoon sun. "You're in your old room. I'll bring your things up."

Annie took a deep breath, fighting the urge to dive back in the car and scream, 'Run for it!' Instead, like the grown-up she pretended to be, she walked up the steps, pushed open the ornate double doors and, on her own two legs, stepped back into the jaws of hell.

It was as lovely as she remembered. Sunlight streamed through the fourteen-foot windows and the scent of the many extravagant fresh flower arrangements tickled her nose. A tall man, thin and slightly hunched, appeared in the stairwell, a little out of breath.

"My apologies, ma'am. I heard the bell of the car coming through the gate but was in the wine cellar. Miss Barlow, I presume?"

She extended her hand. "The name is O'Toole, actually. Annie O'Toole. And you are…?"

"Jenkins, madam." He took her proffered hand

awkwardly, dropping it as quickly as possible.

She'd forgotten one didn't shake hands with servants. She'd forgotten a lot about living like Eleanor Barlow lived. She'd worked hard at forgetting it.

"Nice to meet you," she said, moving on from her *faux pas*. "I understand I'm in my old room. Since I know the way, just tell me where lunch will be served, and you can get back to your wine cellar." She'd known better than to expect her grandmother to be waiting for her. She would see her granddaughter at the appointed time and not one minute before.

"Lunch will be served on the South Loggia, ma'am."

She nodded. "The South Loggia it is."

She headed up the marble staircase that was the central showpiece of Barlow House. Its intricate ebony and gold banister spiralled upward, four stories tall, in an open and stunning geometric display. As she ascended, it occurred to her that Michael Grayson would probably be right at home in this gilded birdcage of a house. Well, hell.

****

Her grandmother didn't look like she was dying. The woman sat at the table, sipping her iced tea and perusing her paper, looking exactly as she had the day Annie walked out.

Called that one, Jonathan. Two points for me.

Annie crossed the wide balcony spanning the back of the mansion to the far end where her grandmother sat.

"Hello, Grandmother." She gave the papery cheek the expected kiss, a matter of protocol, not affection.

"Annabel," the older woman murmured, studying

her granddaughter. Finally, she asked, "Would you like some iced tea?"

Annie sat. "Coffee, please."

"It's too warm for coffee. Angela, bring my granddaughter some iced tea and then you may serve our lunch."

"Yes, ma'am." The girl, who looked to be barely eighteen and a nervous wreck, headed for the French doors in the center of the long balcony.

"Excuse me. Angela, is it?" Annie said, catching the girl before she could make her escape. "I don't want iced tea. I'll have a coffee. With cream, please."

The girl's eyes darted between the two women locked in a power struggle over beverage choices, with her job very possibly hanging in the balance. Annie felt for her but knew better than to give an inch.

"Coffee," Annie repeated, softly.

A wry smile lifted one corner of Eleanor's mouth. "Coffee it is, then."

Angela fled.

"I must admit, I'm surprised you came," Eleanor said, moving past Annie's errant choice of beverage.

"Likewise."

"Hoping to get back in my good graces now that I'm at death's door so I don't cut you out of my will?"

"We both know I have never been in your good graces, and I assume you cut me out of your will long ago, if I was ever in it. But you did say you were dying, so, yes, I came. Though you appear to be the picture of health. Did you just tell me you were dying to see if I'd come back?"

Eleanor laughed. It wasn't a pleasant sound. "Oh, I have missed our little *tête-à-têtes*. If I'd known a little thing like dying would bring you home, I'd have done it years ago."

"So, you really are sick? What's wrong?"

Eleanor looked out over the lush gardens and gestured with her glass. "Did you see the pavilion? I had it installed the summer after you left. It's an antique. Hand-forged, they tell me."

Annie followed her gaze to a wrought iron pavilion at the back of the expanse, beyond the long reflecting pool lined with statuary. It would have dwarfed her living room.

"It's lovely," Annie said. And waited.

"Pancreatic cancer."

Two words that took the breath away. One of those silent diseases that showed few symptoms until it had spread too far to stop.

Annie cast about for something to say. "When did you find out?"

Eleanor turned back to her. Now that she knew what to look for, Annie could detect a faint tinge of yellow to the aged ivory skin and the slightest of shadows beneath the ice blue eyes.

"A month ago. They said I have about four months, and that's 'being generous' according to the doctors. Of course, that was then, so I suppose I'm down to three now." She sipped her tea with no display of emotion whatsoever. Still, she seemed…tighter. As if the iron control that was her trademark had been upped a notch or two.

"I'm sorry."

Eleanor lifted one perfect eyebrow. "I very much doubt that."

Annie blew out a breath. "I wanted you out of my

life because when you were in it, you seemed to think it was yours to run. But I have never wished you dead. I hope you know that."

Eleanor sniffed. "I simply wanted what was best for you. You were the one who insisted on fighting me at every turn."

Annie sighed. "Do you really want to rehash our lifetime of disagreements? I'm happy to oblige—after all, I do argue for a living now—but I doubt that's why you called me back."

Eleanor pointed a manicured finger across the table. "You are more like me than you want to admit, Annabel. Stubborn. Iron-willed. Once you set your mind to something, there is no stopping you. You get that from me, not your flibberty-gibbet of a father."

Annie's eyes narrowed. "I think it best we leave my father out of this discussion."

Eleanor waved a hand dismissively. "I thought it best we leave your father out of everything, so on that at least we can agree."

Annie clenched her teeth shut, reminding herself the woman was dying. Let it go, Annie.

Angela returned with her coffee and more iced tea for Eleanor, as well as a salmon salad for each of them. When she had completed the serving of their lunch, she faded back out of view, if not earshot, and her grandmother continued.

"There are matters to be settled," her grandmother went on. "I didn't build this empire to have it sold off in a corporate garage sale." She pinned Annie with piercing blue eyes that had not weakened with age or disease. "Whether you want it or not, this empire will be coming to you."

Annie choked on her salmon. "You don't mean that."

"I may not want to mean it, but my choices are limited now, aren't they?"

Annie felt, but did not react to, her grandmother's barb. She always felt them.

"I've never wanted your money. You know that. I've seen firsthand the pain it can inflict, and I much prefer the life I have now. Besides we both know I haven't the first clue about running your businesses."

"This is your life, Annabel. You were born into it, and you will inherit it, most likely before the year is out." The older woman leaned back and took a breath. "But I do agree that you are not capable of running the businesses. You have neither the interest nor the experience. In that respect, you have definitely been a disappointment."

Another casual sting. Would she ever get old enough or calloused enough that the barbs just bounced off, without drawing blood?

Eleanor continued, more indifferent than oblivious to the impact of her words. "So, I am putting things in order. As much as it pains me," her grandmother grimaced, "I'm arranging a merger that will ensure my companies remain viable and well-managed. You will have fifty percent ownership, serve on the Board of Directors and be the public face of Barlow Industries— charity events, endowment presentations, speaking engagements, and such. I assume those, at least, you can handle." She sniffed again, in case her disappointment over the limited span of Annie's abilities had not been made clear.

"You will also hold veto power over any board

decision to dissolve any part of Barlow Industries. If you ever choose to exercise that veto, it will trigger a dissolution of the merger, and you'll have to run the companies yourself or find someone else competent to do so. But it shouldn't come to that. The potential cost and fallout would be too much. The purpose of the clause is to stave off any thoughts of dissolving or breaking things up. My version of a nuclear deterrent. And you will live in Barlow House at least six months out of the year. If you want to spend the rest of your time in St. Louis, or Europe, or in Antarctica for that matter, you are free to do so."

Annie blew her curls out of her eyes, primarily because her grandmother considered the habit crude. The woman had absolutely no morals, but oh-so-many rules.

"I don't want this house," she said, "and I don't want to be on any board or oversee your companies or be 'the face' of Barlow Industries. I thought I'd made that crystal clear. My life isn't in Chicago. It's in St. Louis, where I have a job twelve months out of the year. Give it to someone who wants it. Give it to Carter."

Eleanor glared at her. "Give this"—she waved a thin arm across the property—"to my chauffeur? Don't be ridiculous."

"Ridiculous would be giving it to someone who doesn't want it, will not live here, and will sell it as soon as possible." She was sounding petulant now but couldn't help it.

"This house is entailed." Her grandmother practically spit the words. "You will not sell it. Not now. Not ever. And you will take your seat on the board."

"I will not. If you couldn't control me in life, what makes you think you can control me once you're dead?" It came out sounding harsher than Annie had intended but was a true statement of her feelings, nonetheless.

"Because for reasons beyond my comprehension, you appear to care a great deal about legal defense for poor people."

Annie froze. An all-too-familiar knot began to form in the pit of her stomach. "And that has what to do with our conversation?"

"The arrangements include a $50 million trust funding a capital indigent defense center in St. Louis."

Annie sucked in a breath. Jackson had been lobbying for a capital defense unit since before she'd started law school. Though desperately needed, it was a politically unpopular cause and never one that made the priority list of the state legislature. Private funding from a perpetual trust would be an incredible gift to indigent defense.

But Annie knew her grandmother. "And the catch?"

"As I said, you will take your seat on the board of this new company created from the merger I'm negotiating. You will maintain Barlow House as the showplace it is, and you will also host at least one corporate or charity event here every June and every December."

Annie opened her mouth.

Her grandmother held up a finger. "And it must cost at least $1,000 a plate. No lemonade stands on the lawn. June is a perfect time to show off the gardens and the house is lovely decorated for Christmas."

Right. Because party planning for posterity is what she'd be worried about if she got the news she was dying in a few months' time.

"And if I don't?"

"The $50 million goes into a fund for the St. Louis Prosecuting Attorney's Office. Mr. Nicoletti has explained to me the need to significantly expand the war on drugs and gangs in the St. Louis area."

Annie dropped her fork. "You're shitting me."

"Don't be vulgar."

"You met with Nicoletti?"

"Really, Annabel. Do you think I know nothing about your life simply because you choose not to return my phone calls?"

Motherfucker.

The French doors slammed as she blew through them, just like old times.

****

The old new butler eventually found her in the old new Pavilion, which she decided was one of her new favorite places to hide. She wasn't sure if he'd been looking that long or was just naturally asthmatic, but once again he was out of breath and agitated.

"Ah, Miss Barlow, er, O'Toole. My apologies, madam, for interrupting your reverie."

A nicer name than a rant, which is what she'd been doing the last hour and a half. Some of it aloud, some not. She wasn't sure which had preceded Jenkins's approach and didn't care. It wasn't like he didn't know his employer was a bitch-from-hell. No one could work in this house fifteen minutes without figuring that out.

"Mrs. Barlow asked me to tell you that she'll be

tied up for the remainder of the day but will be expecting you at seven in the drawing room. She said to tell you there will be guests for dinner. She will have clothes laid out for you in your room."

Of course, she would.

"Thank you, Jenkins."

"Can I get you anything? It's a bit warm out here. Perhaps a nice glass of iced tea?" he inquired solicitously.

Annie found she had a new aversion to iced tea. "No, thank you. Is there a car I might borrow for a few hours?" She needed to get out of this place for a bit. She needed to breathe.

"I'm sure Carter would be happy to drive you wherever you'd like to go, ma'am."

"I meant a car I could drive myself."

The man's eyes widened, even as the rest of him seemed to shrink into itself. He opened his mouth to speak, then closed it again.

"I do know how to drive," she assured him. "I even have a license."

He swallowed rapidly. "Oh, of course. I didn't mean to, just, um, I would need to check that with Mrs. Barlow…"

Annie sighed. "Never mind. I'll just go for a walk."

"Yes, ma'am." He bowed away with a soft sigh of relief at an encounter with his employer avoided.

Annie stomped toward the house to change.

Chapter Twelve

Streeter jotted down the time the woman exited the mansion. She'd changed into slacks, flats, and a loose, brightly patterned blouse that would be easy to spot along Chicago's sidewalks.

"Thank you for that, my dear," he muttered as he stuffed his notebook in his shirt pocket.

He shot a quick text to the man he had watching the back, snagged his day pack, and climbed out of the car. She was half a block ahead of him now, setting a brisk pace. He crossed to the opposite side of the street as his phone vibrated against his belt. He checked the caller ID. Jax. He switched on his earpiece.

"Yeah?"

"You still lounging around Chicago while we peons work?"

"Not as much lounging as I'd like. Our lady has apparently decided we're going for a walk."

"Lucky you. How hot is it up there today?"

"Hot enough. What'd you find?"

"You sitting down?"

"No. As I just pointed out, I'm walking."

"Sucks for you. Get this, Annie O'Toole is Eleanor Barlow's granddaughter."

Streeter stopped dead in the middle of the sidewalk. Un-fucking-believable. Man, had they missed an important piece of information in compiling

Barlow's file for Grayson.

"I thought the granddaughter was estranged and living back east somewhere."

"She was. Did her undergrad at Brown. A few seasons of summer stock theater. Worked as some kind of coordinator for a women's shelter in New York. Then she up and changed her name to O'Toole and came here to go to law school at Washington University. Graduated in the top ten percent of her class, so it sounds like she got her grandmother's brains at least.

"Married an O'Toole?"

"Nope. She was named Barlow at birth and there's no father listed on her birth certificate. But here's where it gets interesting. There was a Lee O'Toole who was a rising star in the Chicago theater scene around the right time to have been her dad. He had a sister who died as a little girl. Her name was Annabel."

"Bit of a stretch, don't you think?"

"Nope." The gloating came through his earpiece loud and clear. "I found an old picture of said Lee O'Toole at a charity event for the Twilight Theater covered by the *Chicago Examiner*. And who should just happen to be on his arm in that photo? Lenora Barlow. Daughter of Eleanor, mother of Annabel, who was born nine months later."

He had to give the girl props. She was good. "Nice work," he conceded. "Shoot me the picture. Maybe we'll get lucky and there's a resemblance. And see what else you can track down on him, is he still alive, his whereabouts when she changed her name. Maybe they reconnected and she decided she liked Daddy more than Grandma."

His earpiece chirped. He glanced at the incoming text. It was from his man watching the Barlow gates.

—Grayson just arrived—

WTF? Mike said he had an upcoming meeting with Eleanor Barlow, but he hadn't said it was this weekend. Of course, Mike didn't usually keep him informed of his schedule, but this was about to get really sticky.

"I gotta go. E-mail me the rest," he told Jax. "And call Myriam and tell her to text me Grayson's itinerary for today and tomorrow. ASAP."

"It's Saturday. You know that right?"

"Her cell's in my card index. Use it."

He hung up and, with one eye on O'Toole striding ahead as if she was in some power-walking competition, hit the speed dial for Michael's cell. The call went straight to voicemail. *Shit.* This day was turning into royal clusterfuck.

"You're gonna want to step out of that meeting to someplace private and give me a call. Got some new Barlow intel you need to know ASAP. Call me. Now."

He hung up and sent the same info in a text, but had little hope he'd be hearing from his boss soon. Grayson was one of those people who considered it rude to check his phone while talking with someone else, a plus for the one meeting with him, a pain in the ass for the one outside trying to get in touch.

The woman ahead broke stride and swerved into the coffee shop on the corner. Streeter followed. He stood two back from her in the line, ostensibly perusing the pastry selections, but his senses were entirely tuned to his quarry. His men always claimed he had more than the usual five, and truth be told, some kind of sixth sense had saved his and their asses on more than one mission. He wasn't superstitious, but he did trust his gut and his gut told him all was not well with the lovely Ms. O'Toole today. The easy laughter and teasing demeanor he'd observed between her and the driver this morning were gone. Now she was wound about as tight as it was possible to be. He could almost see the rays of anger or frustration or—something—pulsing from her. Looked like the meeting with Grandma hadn't gone so well.

She reached the front of the line and put in one of those ridiculously complicated orders that got on his nerves. Waiting at the pickup counter, she took out her phone and texted, fingers flying over the keys. The lady had speed when she was pissed.

One more advantage of black coffee, the guy who took his order handed it right back to him. No waiting for all the fancy blending, pouring, stirring and shaking. As a result, their orders came up at the same time. She headed for a table on the sidewalk. Streeter followed a bit more leisurely. He took a seat closer to the building, out of her sight line, but close enough to hear her ranting to someone about getting her life fucked over.

Yep. He'd called that one right.

****

Eleanor Barlow was a petite woman with a ramrod straight back and silver hair.

"Mr. Grayson. It is nice to finally meet you."

"Likewise." He accepted the beringed hand, noticing the impressive ruby and diamond bracelet around the frail-looking wrist. He knew from her file that this was a woman who liked to impress. He could accommodate that.

"Your home is stunning, Mrs. Barlow. I understand

you designed it yourself?"

He wasn't lying. Full of natural light, unique architecture, and one-of-a-kind pieces, 'stunning' was an apt description.

"Thank-you. It was a process I enjoyed. We'll talk in the library."

She led him across the marble floor of the foyer, with a circle of gold flames at its center. They passed an impressive spiral staircase and entered a large room with floor-to-ceiling, glass-enclosed bookcases—probably filled with the signed first editions Streeter said she collected. An Italian marble fireplace taller than his hostess spanned the far wall.

A butler appeared with a tray of iced tea and coffee.

"I also have several single barrel bourbons you might enjoy, if you'd prefer," his hostess said as she accepted an iced tea from the butler.

His drink of choice. Apparently, he wasn't the only one with an ace investigator on the payroll. "Coffee is fine."

"Well, then, you can explore the bourbons with dinner this evening." She took a seat behind the elaborately carved desk, its light feminine lines a counterbalance to the weight of the books that surrounded them.

Michael settled into the proffered chair in front of her. "I'll look forward to it. In the meantime, what can I do for you, Mrs. Barlow?"

"Not one for small talk, are you?"

Michael grinned apologetically. "Not especially."

"Neither am I. I've been doing a little research on you, Michael Grayson."

No shit. "Find anything interesting?"

"Quite a bit. You are a brilliant businessman. Not afraid to take risks, but seldom foolish ones. You're good with people when you want to be, but not overly concerned about what they think of you, a delicate— and important—balance. You're innovative. Not one to sit on your laurels. You surround yourself with smart people. You've built an impressive résumé for yourself."

"Why do I feel like I'm being evaluated for a job I haven't applied for?"

Eleanor smiled. It was not a comforting gesture. "Perhaps because you are."

He lifted an eyebrow. "And perhaps you'd better explain."

An hour later, Michael had to admit he was intrigued. Barlow Industries was a major player in a number of arenas, including several that meshed nicely with his own companies. The merger of the two would diversify his holdings and give him a much wider range of control over his suppliers—both pluses. The downside was that it would mean partnering with the devil, Eleanor Barlow herself. And that, he knew from Streeter's intel, was a leap too far.

Still, he couldn't help asking, "So what do you see as your role in this new company?"

"I will not have a role. I'm retiring. That's what this proposal is all about."

"Pardon my candor, but you don't seem to be the retiring type."

"Circumstances sometimes change our plans." Her words were clipped, making it clear that further inquiry was unwelcome.

He knew from Jacobson that Barlow Industries was thriving, so it must be Eleanor Barlow herself who wasn't. Some diagnosis that foretold an inability to continue at the helm in the not-too-distant future?

"However, my granddaughter will retain a fifty percent share in the combined companies and will have a seat on the Board of Directors."

And here it was. The catch. No way, no how, was he giving anyone fifty percent of any company he ran. He couldn't run it if he didn't own it. But now wasn't the time for arguing the details. He was still getting the lay of the land.

"I don't believe I know your granddaughter. What is her role in your business?"

"She's an attorney."

Of course, she was. Lawyers seemed to be first and foremost in his life lately.

"Does she serve as your General Counsel then?"

"No. She is not involved in the business, at present." Eleanor sniffed. The topic had hit a nerve. "And she will not take one in the new company created by this merger, other than to sit on the board."

One director among a dozen. He could live with that, he supposed, if she backed off the 50-50 ownership split. Assuming the granddaughter wasn't as difficult as her grandmother. He'd have to get Streeter doing some digging on that.

"Anything else?"

"She will have veto power over any decision to dissolve any of the companies that come to you as part of Barlow Industries."

Michael choked on his coffee. "Excuse me?"

Eleanor sipped her iced tea as her bombshell

settled. "Mr. Grayson, I am presenting you with the deal of a lifetime and you and I both know it. While I will not be participating in the running of my companies going forward, it is not unreasonable that I wish to protect my legacy. This is how I do that."

"And you know as well as I do that nothing in business is static. We can't lock into stone that your businesses will remain unchanged for eternity going forward. That would be utterly foolish, not to mention potentially bankrupting."

"I did not say the businesses had to remain unchanged. I said, if you decide to dissolve any one of them, my granddaughter will have the right to veto that decision."

"But—"

"And"—she held up a finger to stop his interruption—"should she exercise that veto, her decision will trigger a dissolution of our merger agreement and those companies that came to you as Barlow Industries will return to her, free of any claim or control by Grayson."

Michael stared at her. "That would be a nightmare, and you know it."

"Indeed, it would."

Understanding dawned. "Which is exactly why you want it in there. So we never go there."

"A small price to pay for the deal of a lifetime, don't you think?"

Michael assessed her through narrowed eyes. "You are a cunning old bird, Mrs. Barlow."

"I'll take that as a compliment."

He hadn't meant it as such. Still… "It is intriguing," he said, truthfully, "but your price is too rich for my pocketbook."

She picked up a thick binder from the corner of her desk and crossed to him with it. "I'm sure you'll want to do your own investigation of Barlow Industries, if you haven't already, but this should give you a rather substantial head start in that endeavor. As you'll see, given the value of Barlow Industries, my price is most reasonable. I'm giving you first chance at this because I want my companies to continue to thrive and I believe you and Grayson Aeronautics are the best fit. But, if you don't want the deal, so be it. I'll take it to Pan-Air instead. John Williams has been trying to get his hands on my companies for years. I'm sure he'd be happy to have them handed to him on this particular silver platter."

And there was the knife Jacobson had warned him about. Pan-Air was the biggest aeronautical company in the country. Grayson was growing, but they were still the new kid on the block and had a way to go to be a threat to Pan-Air. Not so the reverse. Especially if Pan-Air joined forces with Barlow Industries. That was a powerhouse that would wipe him off the map.

"You don't fuck around, do you?"

"I do not. And since time is something of the essence in this matter, I will need your answer by Friday."

"You can't be serious." This kind of merger typically took months, if not years, to sort and he was supposed to decide if he was all in within a week?

"Deadly serious," she replied, flatly. "As I said, time is of the essence, and I need the future of my companies decided. I don't expect all the details to be sorted by then, of course," she said, waving one hand dismissively as though those details weren't the difference in the life and death of a company like his. "I'll accept a binding letter of commitment as sufficient to get things underway." She stood. "I look forward to seeing you at dinner, Mr. Grayson. You'll get a chance to meet my granddaughter then."

He'd been dismissed. He tucked the binder under one arm and walked over to set his coffee cup back on the sideboard, his mind racing. One week meant identifying priorities among the endless list of things he'd normally want reviewed and calculated for a deal this size. He was mentally flipping through his roster of people, deciding who to bring in on this, when a picture caught his eye. He bent for a closer look. The woman in the picture looked to be in her early twenties. She was laughing and shading her eyes against the sun. And she looked eerily familiar.

"My daughter," Eleanor said. "Lenora."

His gut slowly tightened. "She is lovely. Tell me, does your granddaughter look anything like her?"

"The spitting image, as they say, though I have no idea where that expression came from. Except for her hair. Annabel did not get Lenora's dark hair, I'm afraid."

"Annabel," Michael repeated, the tightness creeping upward toward his chest. "Would your granddaughter's hair be red by any chance?"

Eleanor shot him a look. "You know her? She does live in St. Louis, but I doubted your paths had crossed."

"Did you now?"

He stared at the picture, his mind reeling. The refreshingly 'real' A.J. O'Toole was a fucking fraud. Miss I-Didn't-Know-Who-You-Were, with her bleeding heart for the cause of poor people bullied by the rich, was the scion of Barlow Industries. Checking him out at her grandmother's behest, no doubt. She had pulled the wool over his eyes like he was a complete neophyte. He wanted to put his fist through the mahogany paneling, but the last thing he needed was for Eleanor Barlow to see that he'd been taken in by her charade.

"Our paths have crossed," he said, swallowing the bile that rose in his throat. "So, Annie is here this weekend?"

"Annabel," she corrected, emphasizing the proper name. "And yes, she arrived this afternoon."

"Come to see you often, does she?"

"She is my granddaughter," Eleanor demurred.

"The same granddaughter you want to put on my Board of Directors."

"I only have one granddaughter. I believe I've given you a very reasonable proposal, Mr. Grayson, but if you don't want it…"

"I know." He grimaced. "My competition is waiting in the wings to snatch it up."

She smiled. "I look forward to seeing you at dinner, Mr. Grayson."

"Where I'm sure a good time will be had by all." He made his exit before she had a chance to respond.

Chapter Thirteen

Michael had his phone out before he reached the car, a text and voice mail from Streeter both highlighted on his screen. He stabbed the call back button as he climbed in the car.

"Hey, boss." Streeter answered on the first ring.

"Don't 'boss' me, you goddamn banana!"

It was a stupid insult, but one that stung a Navy Seal—the name used for wannabes who hadn't yet made the cut.

Streeter sighed. "Sounds like you already found out my news."

"That Annie O'Toole is Eleanor Barlow's granddaughter? Yeah. A tidbit of information that might have proved fucking useful before I walked into that blindside. Isn't that what I pay you for?"

Streeter took a breath. "If I'd known you were meeting with Barlow today, I might have been able to give you a bit more of a heads up, but truth is we only found it about an hour ago. I've been tailing O'Toole since eight this morning when a limo registered to Barlow Industries picked her up in St. Louis and drove her here. I put Jax to work tracking down the connection. She called me with the news just as O'Toole was walking out the back of the mansion and you were going in the front. She just now went back in the same way."

"Like bloody synchronized swimmers, aren't they?"

"Looks that way."

"Where are you now?"

"Watching the taillights of your limo."

"Meet me back at the hotel. I'm at The Shubik. We need to figure this out."

Michael hung up, dropped his phone back in his coat pocket, and stared out the window. How could they have missed this? For Christ's sake, he'd had a stack of briefing papers an inch thick on Barlow. More to the point, what was the game? Clearly, he'd been hoodwinked, but to what end? How did Annie's subterfuge help Barlow's push for the merger of their companies? Especially since she planned to reveal the con at tonight's dinner. Was it all just to throw him off his game in the negotiations? Pretty elaborate scheme for a very small advantage. Or was Annie checking him out on her own, knowing what her grandmother had in mind, without giving Barlow a heads up either? More likely. Seduction as a power move was the oldest game in the book. He flexed his fingers, resisting the urge to curl them into a fist and punch something.

His phone rang again.

"What?" he growled.

"Whoa. You sound ready to bite someone's head off," said a voice that wasn't Streeter's.

Michael glanced at the caller ID. "Harrison? Sorry. I thought you were someone else."

A chuckle. "Well, glad I'm not whoever the someone is. Listen, Myriam told me you're in Chicago?"

"I am."

"Well, so am I. And there's someone I need you to meet. How's tonight?"

"I have a dinner at seven." He rubbed his forehead. "Who is it?"

"A bit complicated to explain. But important. Let's meet for drinks after your dinner. Just text me when you're done."

"Do we have to do this tonight?" He closed his eyes and rested his head on the back of the seat. "It's been a bit of a day."

"Sorry, but I think you'll agree this can't wait. I'll explain tonight. Just text me when you're finishing up."

"Fine," he sighed, and clicked off. Because why not pile more onto his plate today?

When the knock he'd been expecting came, Michael swung the door of his suite open without a word and turned back to the mini bar. Streeter followed, dropping his bag on the floor beside the table. He shrugged out of his jacket and moved to the wall of windows framing a magnificent view of Lake Michigan.

"Hard to believe that's a lake," he said. "Looks just like a lot of oceans I've seen."

"Yeah, well. Looks can be deceiving, can't they?" Michael set a beer for his security chief on the table, a little harder than necessary, and took a long pull off one of his own. "Want to tell me what happened? How the hell did this get missed?"

Streeter turned. "Can I point out that you just gave me the assignment on the girl?"

"You can. And can I point out that you'd already completed the investigation on Eleanor Barlow, and the fact that her granddaughter was the lawyer defending the guy who tried to kill me somehow got missed?"

"You can."

"Well, thank you, Mr. Jacobson. Now what the hell happened?"

Streeter took a pull from the beer. "We missed it. Got no excuses. We knew she had one granddaughter, Annabel Barlow, estranged, who'd settled back east and seemed not to have any contact with her grandmother, so we didn't follow up on her. She'd changed her name by the time she started defending the kid who shot you, so we didn't make the connection. Our mistake."

"No shit. I'm guessing you weren't the one who did that particular piece of the investigation. So, who botched it?"

Streeter ignored the query, which didn't come as a surprise to Michael. Streeter had always protected his crew—from higher ups as well as outside threats—and that hadn't changed with his switch to a civilian occupation.

"Here's what we know," he said instead. "It looks like Eleanor's daughter, Lenora, got knocked up by an actor, name of Lee O'Toole. They met at a charity function to raise money for the old Twilight Theater. Needless to say, the grand dame did not approve of the liaison."

"And?"

"Near as we can tell O'Toole got blacklisted from the entire Chicago theatre scene. His last production ended about six months after that charity function and there's no record he ever worked in any Chicago productions after that, which is odd since he was something of a rising star when he met Lenora."

"Mama Barlow's doing?"

"Expect so. As a big contributor, she'd have the clout to get it done." Streeter consulted his notes. "He next shows up in New York. Did a few minor gigs there, but none seemed to last long, and he never broke out of the pack. That's where the trail goes cold. I've got people trying to track down what happened to him from there."

"That's it?"

"Again, we only learned of his existence an hour ago, and I've spent that hour tailing his daughter and talking to you."

"Right," Michael muttered and sat at the table, motioning for Streeter to do likewise. "Okay, my turn." And he proceeded to brief Streeter on his meeting with Eleanor Barlow.

"She's either dying or lying to you. Or both," said Streeter. "Both is definitely not out of the question with her. But there is no way Eleanor Barlow is just walking away from Barlow Industries. Not willingly. And they're not in financial trouble. We researched every angle on that one. Did it myself." He looked meaningfully at Michael. "They're solid and growing."

"That's what I thought. She has to be sick—"

"Not just sick. Dying," Streeter broke in. "She'd rule that company from a hospital bed and probably do it well. The only way she lets go is if she's looking at an ironclad, irrevocable death sentence and is out to protect her legacy."

"Which would also explain why her 'estranged' granddaughter has returned to the nest. Circling the money. She appears to be the only heir. So much for despising rich people." Michael's tone was bitter.

"We all despise rich people, Mike. I just hadn't the

heart to break it to you."

"I'll remember that come bonus time."

"I've got Jax digging into the girl's background. We'll figure it out."

"Her name is Annie," Michael snapped. "Not 'the girl.'"

Streeter gave him an odd look. "Right. Annie."

Michael stood up. "Get yourself a room here and keep me posted." He glanced at his watch. "I need to think before this goddamned dinner tonight."

Streeter collected his bag and started toward the door, then turned. "I don't know yet what's going on with Annie. But just from my observations today, she's a lot closer to her grandmother's chauffeur than she is to her grandmother, which may say something about who she is as a person."

Michael frowned. "Why do you say that?"

"When the two of them left St. Louis this morning, she was laughing and teasing the old man—very much at ease. When she came back out of Barlow House just before you got there, she was seriously pissed. No idea about what, but she was hot. Sat outside the coffee shop and ranted on the phone to someone about getting her life fucked over. Her words."

"Yeah, well. I know the feeling."

"Just saying. Eleanor Barlow is the last person in the world I'd want as my grandmother. Don't write her off just yet. Let me figure this out."

Michael raked his fingers through his hair. "Call me when you know something."

"Will do."

****

Streeter punched speed dial as he walked to the

lobby.

"Hey, boss."

Jax always picked up. Another reason he liked her.

"Caught up with Grayson."

"How'd he take it?" He could hear the wince in her voice.

"Pretty much like you'd expect." He blew out a huff. "We've got to get this mess sorted—like yesterday. Anything new on your end yet?"

"Got the court documents on her name change. The reason listed for the change was that she was 'a victim of abuse by a family or household member.'"

"Seriously?"

"Seriously. The section of the statute cited includes emotional abuse, as well as physical. But the only family she was known to have around that time was her missing father and dear old grandmama. And since the name she chose was her dad's, I'm guessing he wasn't the bad guy in this."

"Could have been a live-in boyfriend."

"Could have, but we haven't found one yet. I've got the list of every place she's ever lived. Putting Tony on finding anybody who might have known her there."

Streeter nodded. "Good call. He's good at sweet-talking little old lady neighbors. When can he get out there?"

"Already on his way. Ought to be able to hit the streets first thing in the morning."

"Excellent. And daddy dearest? Any update on him?"

"Dead. Finally located a death certificate. And why the hell don't we have a national repository of death certificates in this country? I mean, if I knew where the guy died, I wouldn't need the damn thing in the first place!"

He ignored the rant. It was a familiar one. "And?"

"He died in New York City some six months before Annie changed her name to his."

"Cause of death?"

"Suicide."

Streeter whistled. Part of the picture was starting to come together at least. "So, she took his name to honor the old man's memory."

"Looks like."

"Any evidence of contact between them?"

"Not yet. That's on Tony's list of info to ferret out."

"Ok. I want phone records for both Annie O'Toole and Eleanor Barlow over the last two to three years at least. We need to figure out their relationship, starting with how much contact they have. Call Carlo. He owes me."

There was a beat of silence on the other end. "You're going to hack into Eleanor Barlow's phone records?"

"No. Carlo is." Streeter collected his room key, hitched his backpack over his shoulder, and headed toward the elevators. God, he was ready for a shower.

"Sometimes you make me nervous, Boss."

"Yeah, well. All the good stuff in life is nerve-wracking. Call me when you have something. I'm out."

Chapter Fourteen

Annie's walk back to Barlow House was far from a relaxing stroll. Most people, surprised with the news they were about to inherit a fortune would be ecstatic, but Annie knew better. There was no take-the-money-and-run scenario with Eleanor Barlow. Just the thought of the intricate plans crafted to drag her back into the life she'd worked so hard to escape made her want to turn tail and run—back to her little place in Soulard, to Darrow and Jonathan, to her cramped, crappy office, her clients, and the gruff big-heartedness of her linebacker boss. To freedom.

But she couldn't. Because someone was trying to kill Michael and she needed her grandmother's help to find out who. And the only way her grandmother was going to lift a finger was if Annie got in line and did exactly what Eleanor wanted. This was an old dance between them, and both knew the steps well.

Her thoughts raced and she struggled to rein them in. *Get a grip, for God's sake. You're not a lonely little girl anymore or some torn-up teenager. Adult here. Lawyer here. Someone others pay to solve their problems.*

Well, okay, they didn't actually pay, because they couldn't, but she was paid to solve problems. She had to stop reacting out of old patterns and look at the situation like the grownup, lawyer, problem-solver she was.

She took a deep breath and considered. What would Eleanor Barlow do if she found herself in this situation? Whatever it took. That's what her grandmother had always done. Say anything, promise anything, buy the time she needed to get the players in place and then pull the lever on the trap door. And she always won. Always.

But this time Eleanor didn't hold all the cards. The clock was ticking, and Eleanor needed to get her affairs settled. Annie chewed on her lower lip. Nothing she did or didn't do this weekend would lock her into accepting this inheritance or the strings attached, but the fact that her grandmother needed her to accept it was leverage. The only leverage she had.

Honesty mattered to Annie. A lot. Largely because she'd experienced so little of it growing up. She'd made a promise to herself she would never play the kind of games in which her grandmother excelled—and she hadn't. But maybe this time the only way to uncover the truth was to lie. Tell her grandmother what she wanted to hear, get the information they needed, and then pull the rug out, in true Barlow style.

She blew out a breath. You want me to be more like you, Grandmother? Be careful what you ask for.

"Jenkins," she said, re-entering the house. 'Tell my grandmother I'd like to speak with her before dinner. She can find me in the music room after six-thirty."

"Of course, ma'am," he wheezed, with a slight bow.

****

The evening gown laid out on the four-poster bed and its accompanying sapphire and diamond choker were more formal than Annie had anticipated. Barlow House hosted dinner guests almost every weekend and one always 'dressed' for dinner here, but the upgrade in elegance had her reconsidering her assumption that tonight's dinner guests were routine. All the more reason to lay her own groundwork before Eleanor's next move.

She stepped into the shower. Now this she missed. Eleanor scrimped on nothing and that included the private baths adjoining each bedroom in the house. Multiple jets of steaming water massaged away her tension. She could have stayed in that spot for days, but she had intrigue to spin. She dressed and did a quick check in the full-length mirror, going over the upcoming scene in her mind for the twenty-seventh time. It sounded convincing in her head.

Time to see if it was convincing enough.

****

"You should wear more of that blue instead of so much green. Green is such a common color for redheads to fall back on."

"Well, we've both long agreed that common is more my style." Annie turned from the music room window and lifted her glass in acknowledgement of her grandmother's entrance. "You look lovely. Can I get you a drink? Alcohol is such a wonderful buffer." And wasn't it handy that Barlow House had a stocked bar in every space where guests might be entertained—a feature Annie had been too young to fully appreciate until now.

"Do we require a buffer?" Her grandmother settled herself in one of the delicate armchairs near the grand piano.

"When haven't we?" Annie knew better than to play too nice with her grandmother. They had too much history for Eleanor to buy that. She had to hit just the right blend of her usual defiance, but with a hint of a potential willingness to play along.

Eleanor sniffed. "Really, you act like inheriting a fortune is a terrible burden. I'd think you'd be pleased at my willingness to overlook your behavior."

Annie fixed her grandmother's usual vodka tonic. "It's not the fortune that's terrible, it's all the strings you attach."

"All you have to do is take your place as a Barlow—"

"The name is O'Toole."

Eleanor's eyes hardened. "Call yourself what you will; you are a Barlow and you will behave as one."

"Or?"

"Annabel, stop acting like a child. Neither of us have time for your tiresome tantrums."

"Well, one of us doesn't," Annie muttered with calculated cruelty, just loudly enough to be heard. She crossed back to the hand-carved bar and added a bit of ice to her drink. She wanted to slug the thing down but resisted. Instead, she turned and leaned against the bar, swirling the ice in her glass. "So, what's in this for me?"

"The Barlow fortune is 'what's in it' for you," Eleanor snapped.

"No, that's what's in it for you. You want me to keep your legacy intact. I don't want your fortune. Money matters to you, not to me. What I want to know is, if I agree, what's in it for me?"

"Fifty million for that capital indigent defense

resource center you appear to want, for reasons I can't begin to understand."

Annie shrugged. "That is a nice touch. But that's for a cause I happen to care about. It doesn't affect me personally, though all the rest of this certainly does."

Eleanor eyed her thoughtfully. "What do you want?"

Annie gazed out the window on the gardens backlit by the setting sun. "Intriguing question. I'll have to give it some thought."

"Please do. As you so eloquently pointed out—one of us doesn't have a great deal of time."

Annie turned back to her grandmother. "I'm sorry. That was cruel. You have a way of bringing out the worst in me."

Eleanor pursed her lips. "I could say the same."

Annie laughed ruefully. "True enough. We're quite a pair, aren't we? I'll give it some thought. I promise." Then she oh-so-casually shifted gears. "In the meantime, I'd be interested in your thoughts on a case I have—one that involves some corporate intrigue, as it turns out. Since that is more your area of expertise than mine…"

She left the sentence hanging, doing her best to appear nonchalant. Annie knew better than to let her grandmother know this was her true ask, the one that mattered. Anything that mattered became a weapon for Eleanor to wield against her.

"I thought you only defended rapists and drug dealers," Eleanor's disapproval broadcast loud and clear in her tone. "When did you foray into the corporate world?"

"When I got assigned to represent the kid charged

with shooting Michael Grayson."

Her grandmother's eyes widened. "You? You are defending the criminal who shot Michael Grayson?"

"I am. And it's allegedly, if you please. Innocent until proven guilty and all that."

"Well, this is awkward." Her grandmother actually seemed nonplussed.

"Why? It's not like he's a personal friend or anything... is he?" Annie hadn't considered the possibility that Michael knew her grandmother. Damn. Why hadn't she considered that?

"Actually, I just met him this afternoon," Eleanor replied. "He's coming to dinner tonight."

Annie's mouth fell open. "He's coming here? *Tonight?*"

Eleanor glanced at the large grandfather clock in the corner. "In about fifteen minutes, to be exact."

"In God's name, why?" Panic squeezed Annie's chest, making it hard to breathe. This couldn't be happening. It couldn't be. Not *again.*

"Because the merger I am planning is with Grayson Aeronautics.

Annie stared at her grandmother. "You have got to be shitting me."

"Annabel! I will not have that language in this house—"

"I can't sit down and have dinner with Michael Grayson," she moaned, her mind reeling. Never mind that she'd done exactly that, just two nights ago. "Not here, not like this!"

"When he said your paths had crossed, I had no idea this was what he was talking about."

Annie's heart plummeted to the bottom of her

stomach. "He knows I'm your granddaughter?"

"He saw the picture of Lenora and of course you look just like her, except for that hair." She pursed her lips. The fact that Annie had her father's hair had been a trial for her grandmother the entirety of Annie's life. "I'd mentioned my granddaughter lived in St. Louis and when he saw the picture, he made the connection, that's all."

Annie's laugh was unnaturally high-pitched. "Oh, that's all. Right."

Eleanor's manicured nails drummed the satin arm of her chair. "Surely you can give the case to someone else. Isn't it a conflict for you to be on the case if we're on the verge of going into business together?"

Annie downed the rest of her drink in one gulp and reached for the bottle to pour another. "Well, here's the thing," she said. "It looks like someone in Grayson's company put a hit on him, which he doesn't know about. Which no one knows about but me and my co-counsel and whoever's behind it. And whoever that is, is very likely still out there and probably planning another go at it since the first one didn't succeed." She turned back to her grandmother. "That's what I needed you to help me figure out. Whatever motive is behind this is probably buried in some corporate something somewhere that I wouldn't recognize if it was staring me in the face, but which you," she gestured with her glass, "corporate badass that you are, could probably pick out in an afternoon." She downed the second drink.

"A hit? You're sure?" Eleanor's eyes were bright and sharp. "How do you know this?"

"I can't tell you. And no, I'm not completely sure,

but all signs are pointing that way."

"Well. We can't have a merger with Grayson Aeronautics without Michael Grayson at the helm. He's the brains of that company."

Annie stared at her. "Really? That's your response. We should rethink the merger, rather than—oh, I don't know—maybe try to save the man's life?"

"Don't be crass, Annabel. The two are one and the same. I need Michael Grayson alive, which means we need to figure this out." She stood. "I have calls to make. Pull yourself together and for God's sake don't drink anymore. I'll see you in the drawing room in fifteen minutes."

Annie had spent a lifetime ignoring her grandmother's directions and right now didn't feel like the time to dispense with tradition. She poured herself drink number three.

How many surprise encounters was Michael going to accept from her? It wasn't like he'd learned about her family from her, with some context and clarity about how and why she'd walked away from this life. No, he would walk in and find her enjoying a Barlow family dinner, dripping in diamonds and sapphires, and discussing the merger of her future company with his own. Could the floor not just open and swallow her now?

****

The butler opened the front door as Michael stepped out of his car. He hadn't planned on a black tie event when he came to Chicago, but Myriam had done her magic, and a tux with all the accoutrements had appeared at his hotel suite within the hour. He used to wonder how she pulled off such miracles. He didn't even question it any longer. He shot his cuffs, squared his shoulders, and strode up the broad marble steps.

"Welcome back, sir. Mrs. Barlow is receiving guests in the drawing room."

The old gentleman led him down a wide hallway of glass mosaic arches, each one unique. In other circumstances, he might have paused to appreciate the intricate craftsmanship, but he wasn't in an appreciative state of mind tonight.

At the doorway, the butler intoned, "Mr. Michael Grayson" and stepped aside for him to enter.

Eleanor Barlow turned from her conversation with a handsome older man whose face had graced many a newspaper. She wore a floor-length, champagne silk gown. A diamond and golden topaz necklace glittered at her throat. The coloring of a rattlesnake. Fitting.

"Michael, have you met our mayor?"

"I've not had the pleasure," Michael said, extending his hand.

And so, the evening's dance began, with each new arrival announced and duly introduced around, before relinquishing the spotlight to the next entrant in Eleanor Barlow's parade—the mayor of Chicago, a U.S. senator and his wife, and a dozen or so more whose names and titles Michael didn't bother retaining.

The one he was waiting for slipped in unannounced, though he was instantly aware of her arrival. Every nerve in his body stood at attention. He turned. She was wearing a sapphire blue gown with one side slit up to her thigh. Even as he longed to wring her neck, his traitorous anatomy responded to her appearance. He flinched at the physical reminder of the rush he'd felt when she'd agreed to surrender to his control. As if. She'd been the one playing him like a puppet all along. He ground his teeth. He'd never laid a belt across a woman's backside, but tonight it was a fantasy he could get behind.

"Annabel, finally!" Eleanor crossed to her granddaughter and took her by the arm. "I was about to send out a search party for you."

Michael tossed off the last of his drink and watched as Eleanor swept her through the round-robin of introductions. Annie avoided his gaze until he was the only one remaining.

"And I understand you two already know one another," Eleanor said as she turned Annie to face him.

"We've met. But I would hardly say we know one another. Annabel." He gave her a curt nod. He thought he caught a flicker in her eyes at his use of her formal name, but he might have imagined it.

"Mick." She answered with a stiff nod of her own, before moving off toward the bar, leaving his old nickname hanging in the air behind her, a pointed reminder that he too had hidden his true identity when they'd first met.

But that wasn't the same thing at all, damn it!

The announcement of a new arrival drew Eleanor away, leaving Michael free to follow Annie to the bar—a moth to the flame. He stepped close behind her and murmured, "I'd say 'what a surprise running into you here,' but that's getting to be a bit overused between us, don't you think?"

She turned and took a quick step back from him. He took one forward. He wanted her uncomfortable. She deserved uncomfortable. He lifted his empty glass in a mock toast.

"Eleanor Barlow's granddaughter. Did not see that one coming. Kudos." He reached round her and set his glass on the bar, signalling the bartender for a refill. He was close enough to inhale her scent, which pissed him off even more. "You know, you really should have stuck with acting. You clearly have a talent for it. Your 'I-hate-rich-people' spiel was most convincing."

"You've met my grandmother," she murmured, collecting her own drink. "Why wouldn't I hate rich people?"

He might have conceded the point if he weren't so goddamned furious. He wanted to hurt her, to humiliate her—and to bend her over that bar and fuck her harder than she'd ever been fucked. He wanted to make her lose her devious little mind, to make her scream his name and crave him as much as he craved her. He took a step back out of self-preservation and glared at her.

"Must have given you quite the laugh, haranguing me about the size of my bank account when your grandmother is literally one of the richest women in the world."

Green eyes snapped to his. "And my bank account was all of $253 this morning. This" —she gestured at the glittering room—"is her world, not mine."

His gaze raked her from head to toe. "And yet, here you are." He flicked the jewels around her neck. She flinched at his touch. "Wearing jewels that could feed a homeless shelter for what, a year?"

She looked away. "Yeah, well… Sometimes life throws you a curveball."

"Tell me about it," he said with a bitter laugh, picking up the drink the bartender had just replenished.

Annie blew out a breath, her gaze moving to her

grandmother on the other side of the room. "She's dying. That's why I'm here."

He turned to watch Eleanor, who had gone back to holding court before a coterie of sycophants. "She looks the picture of health."

"Pancreatic cancer. Apparently, it's a matter of months."

Well, Streeter had called that one. A beat of silence as hope and cynicism waged war within. Cynicism won out.

"And you rushed to her bedside in satin and sapphires to comfort her on her deathbed? Oh, wait, no. It was to attend the dinner party she's throwing to pressure me into the merger of our two companies." He shook his head. "You really expect me to believe you just happened to choose today of all days for your grand reconciliation? I'm not stupid, Annabel. Especially when my man saw you going out the back entrance the very same time I was coming in the front."

She drained the last of her drink and set the glass on the bar a little more loudly than was warranted. Catching the bartender's eye, she signalled for a refill then turned back to him.

"I don't expect you to believe me. Any more than I believed her when she called to tell me she was dying. I wasn't even going to come. Figured it was just another ruse to get me back under her thumb. But she is. Dying." She took a deep breath and looked back at him. "And I didn't know anything about your involvement in any of this. That fun fact I found out all of what, twenty minutes ago?" She picked up the newly filled glass the bartender slid toward her and downed half at one go.

He watched her in silence for a bit. She wouldn't

last long if she kept downing drinks at this rate.

"So why did you come?" he finally asked.

"Hmm?"

"You said you didn't believe she was dying, so you weren't going to come. And yet here you are. Why?"

Before she could answer, the butler announced the newest arrival.

"The Honorable Francis Nicoletti!"

Michael felt Annie's reaction before he saw it. She froze, every muscle in her body stiffening. Slowly, she turned to the door, fury flashing on her face. Well, well.

"Mr. John Williams!"

Now it was his turn to stiffen. Dying or not, Eleanor Barlow was still a master chess player. Williams was obviously brought here to threaten him with the specter of a Barlow Industries-Pan-Air merger. Nicoletti was just as obviously here to threaten Annie, though how exactly, Michael couldn't figure. It was also clear Annie hadn't anticipated Nicoletti's presence here anymore than he'd anticipated the Pan-Air executive's. Maybe she wasn't fully on the inside of Barlow's game?

Then again, maybe that was just wishful thinking.

Chapter Fifteen

Eleanor watched her granddaughter finish off yet another drink in direct disregard of her warning not to drink more. Their time apart had not changed the girl's rebellious streak. The two had started butting heads when Annabel was two, but it wasn't until Eleanor had let slip that she'd destroyed those ridiculous letters from her granddaughter's sperm donor—the only way she ever thought of Annabel's father—that the girl had cut all ties and refused all contact.

It had never occurred to Eleanor that Annabel might have some romanticized notion of lost love between her mother and that idiot actor. She'd bungled that one badly and was running out of time to fix things. She'd been so sure that Capital Resource Center—and the threat of Nicoletti as back-up—would be enough to get Annabel to fall in line, but the girl was nothing if not unpredictable. At least she'd hinted she might be willing to negotiate. Negotiations, Eleanor understood.

Dinner went pretty much as expected. Those who were not pawns in this particular chess game savored their perfectly prepared almond-crusted duck breasts and chatted over their wine. Their counterparts ate the same fare and drank the same rarefied selections, but with considerably less enjoyment.

When the last bites of dessert had been enjoyed, Eleanor led the entourage out to her gardens, past the reflecting pool, softly aglow with underlighting, down the path to the pavilion. The sun had gone down, but dozens of lanterns had been lit, bathing everything in soft candlelight.

****

Michael glanced back at Annie who was slowly bringing up the end of the line. She carried her heels in one hand and a glass of wine in the other. Frankly, he was surprised she was still standing, given the way she'd been drinking. Of course, a drunk woman was often a much more honest one. He slowed his pace, allowing the others to pass him.

"Annabel."

"Don't call me that."

Her slur was pronounced and she mis-stepped on one of the flagstones. He caught her arm to steady her. The touch of her skin sent sparks shooting through his own. He quickly withdrew his hand.

Falling into step beside her, he asked, "So, are you going to be joining my Board of Directors? Inquiring minds want to know."

"I told you. I want nothing to do with any of this."

"And yet, you haven't told dear Grandmama to shove it and headed back home."

"It's not that simple," she muttered.

"I'm sure it's not. Money does 'complicate' things. A little tougher to be quite so pure of heart when you're looking at actually inheriting the fortune in a matter of months as opposed to Grandmama just holding it over your head."

Her head snapped up at that, but he cut off her retort with an upheld hand. "Just tell me what you want."

Tell me what you want, Counselor. Shit. That was a moment he didn't need to be reliving right now. He cleared his throat and changed his word choice. "What's your game? It's not like I'm not used to games. This is the world I live in, after all." The truth was bitter on his tongue.

"My game? You really think this has all been some elaborate plan, do you?" Her words might be slurred, but her fury broke through with cutting clarity. "That I wanted to risk my career and law license for the fun of surprising you at that deposition? Definitely my idea of a good time. How about you? Was that fun for you? But hey, that was nothing compared to my second act, right? Just as we seem to be having a bit of a *détente*— perhaps a chance at something between us—how about I pop out of a cake as Eleanor Barlow's granddaughter with a merger agreement for you to sign. 'Ta-da! Gotcha, sucker!' You think that was the plan? Jesus Christ, Grayson. How stupid are you?" She spun around, almost falling, but righted herself and drunkenly stomped in the direction of the house.

From the sudden silence of the party ahead, it appeared he was not the only one who'd gotten that last earful.

Eleanor Barlow broke the silence. "I must apologize for my granddaughter's behavior." The old woman's voice was tight with displeasure. "She can be a bit on the high-tempered side and sometimes lets her emotions get the better of her. Let's not let it ruin our evening. Come, I have a bit of a surprise arranged." With a flourish she indicated a string quartet in one corner of the pavilion.

Their first chords were soon joined by laughter,

conversation, and the clink of glasses. No one heard the soft splash at the far end of the wide lawn. No one but Michael, who still stood where Annie had left him. He ran.

She floated face down in the reflecting pool, her gown spread on the water like dark wings sparkling in the lamplight. Eerie. Beautiful. Motionless. He never broke stride. The pool was barely chest-deep, thank God. He lifted her out and eased her onto the grass, where she gasped and coughed and vomited all over his rented tux. This woman was hard on tuxes. Still, she was breathing and the depth of his gratitude for that fact—for the very existence of this vomit-covered, soaking wet redhead shivering on the grass beside him—rocked his core.

"Talk to me, Annie. You're okay now. Talk to me." He turned her face toward his.

"Wha-wha... I'm all wet. Wha..." And she faded out of consciousness again.

He fished out his phone, glad for the waterproof features Streeter insisted on, and texted his driver to get him some assistance from inside the house. Within minutes, an older well-built black man with close-cropped grey hair sprinted round the corner.

"Miss Annabel! Is she okay?" The man dropped to one knee beside her.

She lifted her head, mumbled something unintelligible, and rolled over into a fetal position.

"Too much to drink and an unplanned dip in the pool, but okay, I think," Michael answered, checking her pulse and respirations. "I'm Michael Grayson."

"Carter Daniels. I work for Mrs. Barlow. Let's get her inside."

"You lead, I'll carry," Michael said. "I'm already wet and vomit covered. No reason for us both to be."

Carter grinned. "Can't argue with that. This way."

The man led him through a side door and up a back stairway. Practical and plain, it was obviously a servant's passageway. Michael wondered how many times Annie had used that route as a girl to avoid her grandmother, just as they were tonight. Annie's language alone had pissed off her grandmother. Finding her granddaughter passed out, soaking wet, and covered in vomit would not end well for any of them.

They emerged into a wide hallway one story up. His side was almost fully recovered but still, Michael was grateful it wasn't more. Carter ushered him through the first door on the left and closed the door behind them.

He started to deposit his messy cargo on the four-poster bed but had second thoughts about the likely damage to the rose silk spread. He didn't give a fig about such things but had a feeling Eleanor Barlow might feel differently. Carter was one step ahead, grabbing a couple of towels from the bathroom and spreading them across the bed.

"There you go. Lay her there."

Michael did, then stood, stretching out his back and side. He looked down at his own wet and vomit-covered attire. "Think you could find some clothes for me to change into? I'll be happy to have them laundered and returned tomorrow."

Carter sized him up. "I probably have something that would fit you."

"That would be much appreciated. Would you mind bringing them here? I'm afraid I'd create a bit of stir if I run into anyone looking like this." He looked ruefully at the rented tux.

Carter hesitated. "I mean no disrespect, Mr. Grayson, but I don't know you. And I wouldn't want anyone taking advantage of Miss Annabel while she's not herself. I just want to make sure we understand each other on that point?"

Michael looked up at him in surprise. Anger surged at the implication, quickly tempered with appreciation for the man's protectiveness.

Raking his fingers through his hair, he said, "Annie and I do know one another. Intimately, actually." He sighed. "We're... Well, hell, I don't know what we are. It's complicated. But I assure you I would never harm her." Except for maybe taking a well-deserved belt to her backside.

Carter nodded. "I'll be right back. If the door is locked, be aware that I have a key."

"Noted."

He closed the door softly behind him.

Michael dug through the suitcase in the walk-in closet and found a nightshirt with a sleepy-eyed coffee cup across the front. After grabbing another towel and warm washcloth from the bathroom, he went to work.

By the time Carter returned, Annie was clean and curled up under the covers in her nightshirt, snoring softly. Carter pursed his lips, but said nothing, handing Michael a pair of black pants and a white dress shirt.

"Not quite up to what you ruined, I'm afraid. But they should fit. And I hadn't gotten around to opening these, so consider them my gift to you," he said, passing over an unopened package of boxer shorts and a pair of black socks.

Michael laughed. "You are full-service."

A hint of a smile touched Carter's eyes, if not his mouth. "I try. This is to put the tux in." He handed Michael a plastic bag.

"Both will do nicely, thank you. Might I ask, are you by any chance the chauffeur who drove Annie up here from St. Louis yesterday?"

"I am. Why?"

"I just… I was told she was close to her grandmother's chauffeur. That would be you."

A full smile spread across the older man's face. "We go way back. She's a special girl. Why don't you go ahead and take a shower, get cleaned up? I'll watch over Miss Annabel."

"Thank you." He hesitated. "I'm pretty sure Annie would prefer her grandmother not know about the two of us—or any of this, really."

Carter drew himself up to his full height. "I serve Mrs. Barlow." Then grinned and added, "But I've never been one to carry tales she doesn't need to be bothered with."

Michael laughed. "I can see why Annie likes you."

****

He entered the bathroom and had just started stripping off the ruined tux when his phone buzzed on the vanity. He checked the caller ID and grimaced. Harrison. Damn it. He'd forgotten about their meeting tonight.

"Hey, Harrison." He hit the speaker button and continued undressing.

"Michael. Thought I'd have heard from you by now."

"Sorry." He turned the vomit-covered tux inside

out, rolled it into a tight ball, and stuffed it in the bag Carter had provided. "Not sure tonight's doable. When are you back in St. Louis?"

"I'd really rather we meet tonight. We can make it later. What time do you think you'll be free?"

"What's so important it can't wait?"

"I'd rather not go into it on the phone."

Michael glanced at the time and sighed. "Okay, meet me at my hotel in about thirty minutes. I'm staying—"

Harrison interrupted before Michael could finish. "No, I'm sorry. There's someone I need you to meet, and he has obligations here at his club—a place called The Nightingale. I'll text you the address. Just have your driver drop you off. We can talk with him and then I'll drive you to your hotel when we're done."

Michael frowned. "Sounds pretty cloak and dagger. What's all this about?"

"As I said, not a conversation to go into on the phone. I'll fill you in when you get here."

He sighed and rubbed the back of his neck. "Okay. I'll text you when I'm headed your way."

"Sounds good. Thanks." Harrison ended the call.

Michael started the shower, irritated he hadn't just told Harrison to bugger off. He'd had enough of a day as it was. But Harrison generally didn't bother him unless something really did require his attention and if he felt this was that important—well, Michael probably needed to hear it. Didn't mean he had to be happy about it.

He stepped into the multiple streams of hot water and thoughts of Harrison melted away. The shower smelled like Annie. He breathed it in and then flashed to the terrifying image of her floating face down in the pool. He leaned his forehead against the glass tile, his heart racing all over again. What the hell was he into here?

****

Ten minutes later, he returned to Annie's room, the bag of soiled clothing tucked under his arm. "Thank you again for the clothes. I'll have them back to you tomorrow. Minus the boxers, that is."

Carter chuckled. "That will be fine."

Michael turned to look at Annie. She was breathing easily, curled on her side, hands tucked beneath her cheek, her damp reddish-gold curls catching the lamp light.

The older man followed his gaze. "She seems to be resting well now."

"She does." He resisted the urge to drop a good night kiss on her forehead. And when had he ever had that urge with any of the women he'd dated, much less one with red flag after red flag waving in his face? *Fuck.* He wiped a hand across his face and turned back to Carter. "Anyway, thank you again for your help. I'm going to head on out. Would you tell Mrs. Barlow that I got called away unexpectedly?"

"Of course. Would you like me to show you a less conspicuous way out to your car that might avoid any untoward meetings?"

"That would be much appreciated," Michael replied, feeling a bit like his teen-aged self, trying to slip out of Jeanie Goodman's house in the early hours of the morning without running into her parents. Hopefully, his luck tonight would be better than it had back then.

****

The car slowed outside The Nightingale Gentlemen's Club. Music blared from the open doorway and a group of heavily tattooed and inebriated smokers traded loud insults on the front sidewalk. A couple of more mellow patrons leaned against the painted naked lady that adorned the front window, passing a joint between them. Down the alleyway, a man was pissing against the wall of the building.

"Sir?" His driver looked back at Michael. "Are you sure this is where you want to go? I mean, if you're looking for a club, I can suggest several that are of a higher caliber than this place. Nothing wrong with a relaxing night at a club, no sir, but this, well, this... Sir, I just don't think this is a safe place to leave you. That's all I'm saying."

Michael double-checked the address on his phone. This couldn't be right. Tired and exasperated, he stabbed at the call back number and listened as Harrison's phone rang several times before going to voicemail. He took one more look at the alleged meeting place for this mystery business.

"Screw it," he said. "Take me back to—"

The quick pop-pop-pop of gunfire and the shattering of the side window cut off the rest of his sentence.

"Go-go-GO!" he yelled.

The driver floored it, throwing Michael back against the seat just as another *thunk* hit the side of the car.

"Are you okay? Are you hit?" the driver yelled over his shoulder as he maneuvered them out of the area at a speed that was definitely unsafe.

"Yeah. I mean no, not hit. I'm okay. What about you?"

"Fine, fine. Goddamn it to hell! I mean—I'm sorry, sir, sorry for my language, sir—"

"Goddamn it to hell is right." Michael pressed a hand against the scar from his last encounter with gunfire on a city street. "Did you see anything? Who was shooting?"

"No, sir. I was looking back at you and then, bam!"

Michael finally focused on the road ahead of them, which flew by at an insane speed. He glanced over the seat at the speedometer. It was deep in the red zone, pushing 100 mph. He sucked in a breath.

"Looks like you've done some high-speed driving before," he observed, as calmly as someone who'd just been shot at and was now in a car speeding 100 mph down busy city streets could be expected to be. He swallowed the bile rising in his throat and closed his eyes.

The car began to slow its pace.

"Did my share of street-racing back in the day."

"Thank God," Michael muttered. "Your criminal youth may have just saved us both."

The driver chuckled nervously. They reached the parkway and eased into traffic at a more sedate pace.

"Should we call the police, sir?"

Michael considered. The last thing he needed was more publicity along this line. "I'm sure someone at the club already has. Not much we could add to what they'll get from everybody standing out front." Except for possibly a bullet or two of forensic value. He pushed that aside and pulled out his phone.

Streeter was waiting for them at the hotel entrance.

He directed them into the parking garage, where he examined the car while Michael tipped the driver an extra couple of hundred.

"Send the bill for the car repairs to this address," he said, also handing the man a card. "I'll take care of it."

"Appreciate that, sir. Especially since it wasn't even your fault."

Michael hoped he was right, that this was just some random city feud that had nothing to do with him, but his gut was telling him otherwise. He turned back to Streeter. "You done?"

"I am." Streeter nodded to the driver as the man climbed back into the car and pulled slowly onto the ramp out of the garage.

"Find anything?"

Streeter slipped two bullet casings out of his pocket and extended them in the palm of his hand. "Dug one out of the back passenger door. And one out of the back seat." He looked down at the shells in his hand, then back up at Michael. "I'm starting to think you've pissed somebody off, my friend."

Michael stared at the shells as well. "I'm starting to think you're right."

Chapter Sixteen

Annie woke to a harsh, bright light piercing her eyes and the voice of Eleanor Barlow raking across her consciousness like fingernails on a chalkboard.

"Get up, Annabel. We have things to discuss. I've ordered breakfast to be served in twenty minutes. *Twenty* minutes," the disapproving voice emphasized. "In the breakfast room."

Flinging a protective arm over her eyes, Annie tried to muster a response, but the sound of the door made the effort pointless. It was just as well. Her tongue was stuck to the roof of her mouth and her throat burned. Even her eyelids ached. She lay there, willing her abused body to move, but it seemed as pissed at her as her grandmother and refused to do her bidding. What the hell had she done last night?

She didn't make her grandmother's twenty-minute mark, but she did make it in twenty-five, which she considered pretty damn miraculous under the circumstances. She'd spent most of that with her head under the shower, then threw on the first clothes she grabbed out of the suitcase. She hadn't the energy to forage for shoes.

The breakfast room was one of the smaller, less pretentious rooms in the house. Annie had always liked it. She found her grandmother perusing papers at the table in front of the large diamond-shaped window of leaded glass overlooking the patio. The older woman glanced up when she entered, then at the large clock in the corner, and finally back at the disheveled mess that was her only heir. With a heavy sigh, she pointed her pen at the chair opposite her.

"Coffee for my...granddaughter," she said to an invisible servant, the pause making clear just how much it pained her to have to claim Annie as kin. "And bring out her breakfast. Though it's probably cold by now."

A shadow detached itself from the coffee service in the corner and slipped through the door into the kitchen.

Annie sank into the tall chair and gingerly leaned her head back against its gilded edge. Her fingers pressed against her temples, trying to hold her parts together until the coffee arrived. Contrition was called for, but un-caffeinated contrition with this hangover was beyond her acting skills. The best she could do was be silent in the face of the coming onslaught. She steeled herself...but nothing came. She waited. Still nothing. Carefully, she opened one eye and, squinting in the sunlight, peered across the table.

Her grandmother wasn't even looking at her. She was completely focused on the papers in front of her, underlining things and making notes in the margins with one of the special-order pens she had flown in from somewhere far away because Americans didn't know how to make a decent writing instrument.

"Here you go, miss."

"Bless you," Annie muttered, lifting the coffee to her lips. She took a long slow sip, willing the sacred beverage to bring her damaged soul back to life.

"And your breakfast, ma'am." Angela set an omelet bulging with healthy veggies and a selection of fresh fruit in a crystal dish on the table.

No grease-laden, sugar-covered donuts to be had at Barlow House.

Annie inhaled the first cup of coffee and poured herself another before picking up a fork to poke at the overstuffed omelet. Her grandmother's continued silence was making her more nervous than the tirade she'd braced for. Clearing her throat, she shot a glance at the older woman.

"So, about last night—"

"Not now."

Annie had never known her grandmother to skip a good scolding when circumstances warranted it, and often even when they didn't.

"Um, what are you working on?"

"I've received some information pertinent to this hit of yours on Michael Grayson and I'm trying to make sense of it, so please be quiet."

"Oh." Annie picked up her coffee cup with feigned nonchalance. The Herculean effort was interrupted by the old butler who appeared in the doorway.

"I'm so sorry, Mrs. Barlow—"

Michael Grayson shoved past the older man's feeble attempts to stop him. "What the hell do you think you're up to?"

Annie was instantly and surprisingly wide awake. "Michael! What are you doing here?"

Eleanor lifted her gaze from her papers and perused the intruders with that imperturbable calm she should have trademarked. She watched Michael's companion gently remove the old butler from the room, then close the door and stand in front of it in a military 'at-ease' stance.

"Well, this is convenient. It saves me having to contact you."

"I would have thought you'd be expecting news of my untimely death instead," Michael growled.

Annie's heart began to race. "What are you talking about?"

Eleanor Barlow sighed and laid her pen down across her papers. "I suspect he's talking about the attempt on his life last night. Angela, please tell Carter to join us, then bring these gentlemen some coffee. I don't believe I've met your companion?"

"Wait, what?" Annie jumped to her feet. "Attempt on your life? Another one? Are you okay? What—"

"Annabel, sit down and stop being stupid."

"B-but—" Annie stammered.

"*Sit down.*"

Annie sat.

"So, you admit you know about it," Michael said, watching Eleanor Barlow with narrowed eyes and a quasi-military stance of his own.

"Of course, I do."

"But how—?" This time Annie stopped herself in response to Eleanor's glare.

"How?" Michael picked up the inquiry. "Because she's the one behind it. Police picked up a car with a Barlow license arriving at the scene minutes before the shooting went down."

Eleanor laughed, then leaned back in her chair and eyed her guest with lingering amusement. "Mr. Grayson, if I'd wanted you dead... you'd *be* dead. Carter must have been in a hurry indeed to be spotted so easily."

"Carter?" Annie and Michael said at the same time,

but only Annie went on, "What does Carter—?"

"Annabel, for the last time, unless and until you have something productive to add to this discussion, which I doubt very much will be anytime soon, *be quiet*."

There was a quick rap on the door.

Eleanor lifted an eyebrow. "I suspect that's the man in question, if you'd like to ask him about it yourself."

Michael nodded at the man Annie assumed must be some kind of bodyguard. He pulled the door open, one hand inside his jacket. Annie realized he must be armed. Of course, he was armed if he was Michael's bodyguard. And he thought Carter—*Carter*—was a threat? She felt dizzy, though she wasn't sure if it was the hangover or the surrealness of the scene. She picked up the goblet of orange juice and downed it as Carter stepped into the room.

The chauffeur nodded politely at Michael and his companion before turning to his employer. "You called, Mrs. Barlow?"

"It appears someone spotted you last night and Mr. Grayson has now concluded you were part of a plot on my part to have him eliminated. Would you care to disabuse him of that notion?"

A flush crept across Carter's face. He winced. "I'm sorry, ma'am. This is… unfortunate."

Michael exploded. "What the hell is going on here?"

Eleanor Barlow nodded at Carter. "Please fill Mr. Grayson in on your activities last night before he becomes apoplectic." She picked up her pen and turned her attention back to her papers.

"Of course." He turned to Michael. "I overheard your phone conversation last night about meeting someone after the dinner party in a situation that seemed to make you a little uncomfortable. I believe you asked, 'why all the cloak and dagger' or something along those lines."

Michael shot a surreptitious glance at Eleanor Barlow, but she seemed uninterested in the conversation.

"Go on," Michael said.

"Mrs. Barlow had informed me earlier of concerns about your safety."

Annie cringed as Michael shot a surprised look at his bodyguard.

"So, I decided it best to take precautions. I substituted one of my guys for your hotel driver. Someone who's good in a crisis. Just in case."

Michael lifted an eyebrow. "So, he wasn't just 'an old street racer.'"

Carter grinned. "Oh, yes, he was. Juice was one of the best. He's kind of a legend."

"Please get on with it, Carter." Eleanor sighed without lifting her gaze from her papers. "We don't have all day."

"Yes, ma'am. Sorry. I had Juice drive you the long way around, to give me time to get there first and check things out. Unfortunately, I didn't have enough time to be as thorough as I would have liked. My apologies."

Eleanor capped her pen. "What Carter is skirting around is the fact that he found and disarmed one shooter before you arrived, but didn't have time to discover there was a second. Unfortunately, both managed to escape."

Michael and Annie both stared at Carter. Michael was the one who spoke.

"You're a pretty full-service chauffeur."

"Carter is my chauffeur, bodyguard, and assistant in a number of areas." Eleanor said. "So, you took the matter to the police? I have to say I'm surprised, given the stock price fall the last time you were shot. A reprise won't exactly be good for business."

Annie resisted the urge to throw a cup of coffee in her grandmother's face. Everything was a business calculation to that woman, including—no, *especially*—life and death.

"We didn't go to the police. For precisely that reason," Michael replied.

Annie ground her teeth at the pair of them and reached for more coffee.

"Then how did you learn of Carter's involvement?"

Michael gestured toward the man at the door. "Streeter Jacobson. My... Carter. Minus the chauffeuring. He has a lot of contacts in a lot of police departments. Apparently, The Nightingale has enough criminal activity to warrant routine photo sweeps of license plates in its vicinity. Streeter called in a few favors and got the roster. When a Barlow Industries vehicle showed up just before the shooting, on the very night Barlow Industries tried to strong-arm me into a merger of our companies... Well, let's just say that was a bit too coincidental to ignore."

Eleanor's gaze moved to the stocky man standing beside Michael. "I see. Please take a seat, gentlemen. It hurts my neck to keep staring up at you and we have things to discuss." She motioned to Carter, who pulled additional chairs over to their breakfast table, then returned to his position by the door.

"Will there be anything else, Mrs. Barlow?" Carter asked.

"No thank you, Carter. But stay close."

"Yes, ma'am."

"Angela?" Eleanor called irritably. "I said coffee for our new arrivals, please."

Angela scurried over to pour two more cups of coffee, then refilled Annie's cup, before Eleanor waved her away.

"Enough. Leave us. We have business to attend to."

"Yes, ma'am" came the quiet murmur and the girl once again faded into the shadows.

****

For the first time since his arrival, Michael did more than glance at Annie. She stared vaguely in the direction the servant had taken. He suspected she was suffering from a hangover of epic proportions. The glittering jewels and elegant attire of the night before had been replaced with cream-colored leggings and a baggy, navy blue sweater. Her curls were damp and her feet bare. She sat with one leg tucked under the other, clutching her coffee like an anchor in stormy seas. It was the first time he'd seen her without makeup. She had a light sprinkle of freckles across her nose. He liked them. A lot.

"So." Eleanor began after the servant made her exit. "Just how much do you know about these attempts on your life?"

Michael turned his attention back to the woman who, until a few moments ago, he'd been fairly sure was behind said attempts. She watched him with the sharp stare of a predatory bird.

"That's what I came here to ask you." He wasn't laying any cards on the table until she had shown hers.

A begrudging smile lifted one corner of the old woman's tight mouth. "When Annabel told me about the hit—"

"Grandmother!" Annie shot her own green-eyed daggers of warning across the table.

Streeter turned to Annie in surprise. "You knew the first shooting was a hit?"

"And when were you going to tell me?" Michael said, his anger rising, freckles or no freckles.

Annie looked from one man to the other, then shot another glare at her grandmother. "I can't tell you anything. Case confidentiality."

"Oh, give me a break! Someone is trying to kill me, but keeping that punk's secrets is more important than warning me?"

Streeter was a bit less emotional in his response. "But you told your grandmother. Why?"

"Because she needed my help." Eleanor said. "My granddaughter's expertise does not extend to corporate espionage and its like." She sighed, her disappointment in this truth evident. "If she was going to solve the case, she needed someone more knowledgeable in that arena than herself. And what better someone than her own grandmother?"

Streeter turned to Annie. "So that's why you came up this weekend?"

"Yes, that's why I came," Annie snapped. "I am trying to save your life, Michael, whatever you might think, and I'm also trying not to betray my client. If I had proof your life was in danger, I could have told someone, but I don't have proof. Just a hunch. And hunches don't waive client confidentiality. I'm sorry, but that's the law." She slumped back in her chair and ran her fingers through her damp hair. "Of course, after Grandmother sprang her surprise merger plans this weekend, I'm off this case anyway, so… whatever."

Michael stopped pacing and shot a look at Eleanor. "She didn't know about the merger?"

Eleanor avoided his gaze. "I invited my granddaughter up this weekend to discuss the future of our company."

"*Your* company," Annie muttered.

Eleanor ignored Annie's clarification, forging on as if she hadn't spoken. "During our discussions, Annabel revealed that someone was trying to have you killed, which would, of course, ruin the entire point of the merger, so clearly we had to get to the bottom of this."

"Clearly," Michael said dryly.

"And?" Streeter was always one to cut to the chase.

"Well, this is where things get interesting," Eleanor said, picking up her pen and pulling her papers toward her. "Mr. Grayson, please stop pacing around like an angry badger and sit down at the table like a civilized person."

Michael growled something that did indeed sound a little badgerish, but he and Streeter both sat.

"You are familiar with Sirapul?"

Michael frowned. "The Russian bank?"

"Yes." Eleanor said. "Does Grayson Aeronautics have a relationship with Sirapul?"

"Of course not," Michael said.

"I realize none is publicly reported. But there are public relationships in business and there are private ones."

"The answer is still no," Michael snapped. Her assumption that he operated one set of books for the public and one in the shadows pissed him off. Of course, that was probably how Barlow Industries did things, so there was that to consider in this merger business, once they'd sorted out who was trying to kill him. His head pounded and he found himself empathizing with Annie having to deal with all this mid-hangover.

He resisted the urge to look at her and addressed her grandmother. "As I'm sure you know, a significant portion of our business is designing aircraft for the U.S. military. I couldn't qualify for those contracts if I was also doing business with their biggest security threat. So, no. Not public, not private, not off the books or under the table or in the shadows. No. Period."

"Well, then you may be surprised to learn that at least one server owned by Grayson Aeronautics is communicating on almost a daily basis with a server owned by Sirapul—and has been for the last thirteen months."

Streeter and Michael exchanged shocked glances.

"Viktor Kostrokovaz, the primary owner of Sirapul, is, as you may also know, thought to be closely associated with FSB."

"What's FSB?" Annie asked, looking completely lost.

"Successor to the KGB," Streeter replied.

"Of course," Annie said faintly.

"How do you know this?" Michael demanded.

Eleanor removed her reading glasses and sat back in her chair. "There is a group of cybersecurity experts who monitor odd occurrences around the world. They're not associated with any government or organization. They come from many different countries and walks of life. But, on the side, so to speak, they have joined forces and keep an eye on things. And when they find odd things, they sometimes alert persons to whom that information might be relevant. I have a contact among that group, so I reached out to him last night. I received his response early this morning."

"Where is this server? The one supposedly owned by Grayson?" Streeter asked.

"There's no supposed about it, Mr. Jacobson. This group is very thorough and they don't speculate. If they say it's a Grayson server, it is a Grayson server." She consulted her notes, "It's housed somewhere near a place called Defiance, Missouri. Rather an appropriate name for an off-the-books operation, isn't it?"

"Defiance?" Streeter looked at Michael. "Isn't that where the old Daniel Boone farm is? Little town about 40 miles west of St. Louis. There's nothing there but some wineries and the Daniel Boone site as far as I know. It's a tourist site surrounded by farmland. No business to speak of."

"And definitely no Grayson business," Michael added. His head spun.

"No Grayson business you were aware of, you mean."

"You're saying this server is connected to Grayson's network?" Streeter asked.

"No. It is a stand-alone server. It's only contact or connection appears to be with Sirapul."

"Then how can they say it's a Grayson server?"

"It was purchased by and is registered to Grayson Aeronautics."

"By whom?"

"That, I'm afraid, is for you to find out."

Streeter pulled a small pad from his shirt pocket and jotted down notes.

"What exactly is being communicated between these two servers?" Michael asked, dread pooling in the pit of his stomach.

"No idea. All they can tell is that encrypted communication is happening. But the fact that someone associated with Grayson is secretly and actively communicating with or through a Russian bank whose owner is considered the financier of much of the work of the FSB tells you a bit about what you may be dealing with here."

Michael stared out the diamond-shaped window, his fingers drumming the table in a short, staccato beat. "Thirteen months." He looked over at Streeter.

Streeter nodded. "That occurred to me as well."

"Why? What happened thirteen months ago?" Annie asked.

"A top-secret military contract." Michael answered curtly.

"Ah," Eleanor nodded. "Someone is selling secrets about your new military contract to the Russians."

"But Harrison doesn't have access to any of that information," Streeter said to Michael.

"Harrison?" Annie's eyes widened. "Harrison Stewart, your GC? You think he's involved in this? Why?"

"He's the one who arranged Michael's presence at the club where the shooting happened last night."

"Said he had someone I needed to meet there," Michael added, "but he could have been duped as well. We don't know that he was in on it."

"Have you heard from him since?" Eleanor asked.

"No." He glanced at Streeter. "I tried calling him last night, but it went to voice mail."

"Amateur," said Eleanor with a look of disgust.

"At least they're consistent," Annie muttered.

Michael shot her a sharp look. "What do you mean?"

Annie took a deep breath. "The first shooting looked a lot more like a hit than a robbery, but it was amateurish. No kill shot, a witness left behind, and not even a decent attempt to make it look like a robbery. Nothing taken, despite lots of value for the picking. Not even a demand for anything."

Eleanor picked up the narrative. "Likewise with this Harrison fellow. A professional would have called you the instant shots were fired, warning you away. Then, if you had been killed, there's proof he tried to save you. A nice touch for inquisitive authorities. If, on the other hand, the attempt failed, his warning places him clearly on your side, someone you can trust, someone who may even have faced danger right along with you. How terrible for the both of you. This Harrison did none of those things. *Ergo*, amateur."

Michael was disconcerted at how easily Eleanor slipped into the mindset of a professional killer. Streeter had said she was scary. The more time he spent with her, the more he understood the accuracy of that assessment.

"Wouldn't be the first time the Russians reeled in an amateur," mused Streeter. "And of course, they'd be interested in intel on new military designs. But what does killing Michael get them?"

"Oh, I doubt very much the Russians are behind these attempts," Eleanor replied. "They don't use inexperienced street thugs. They use professionals who get the job done quickly, neatly, and with a viable cover story to avoid suspicion. This looks like someone gone rogue for reasons of their own."

"Such as?" asked Michael.

Eleanor shrugged. "Who knows?"

The group fell silent as three of their number contemplated the craziness of it all. The fourth calmly sipped her coffee.

Streeter was the first to break the silence. "Even if Harrison is involved, he can't be working alone. As you pointed out, he doesn't have the access."

"What about Ashton?" Annie said. "Does he have access?"

"Ashton?" Eleanor asked.

"Peter Ashton," Michael answered. "He's my marketing director. He was with me when I was shot...the first time." And how surreal was it that he now had to clarify among multiple attempts on his life? He mulled Annie's question. "Peter has more access than Harrison because he's involved in the pitches we make to the defense department. Internal marketing stuff. So, he knows big picture capabilities, but none of the design details I suspect the Russians would be after. Why?"

"Just his connection to Northside and all those expensive gifts to James's mom." Annie spoke absent-mindedly, her thoughts already moving on as she refilled her coffee.

All turned to Annie and silence settled as they waited for her to expand on this new tidbit of information. She glanced up.

"Oh, shit. I mean—I shouldn't have—I wasn't thinking, I—"

"Annabel," said Eleanor in that voice that brooked no disagreement. "What are you talking about?"

Annie shook her head, pressing her fingers to her eyelids. "I spoke out of turn. I can't say anything else. Attorney-client—"

"—goddamn privilege." Michael completed her sentence. "Yeah, got it. Streeter, look into Peter's connection to some place called Northside—probably that youth community center he's involved with—and whatever 'gifts' you can trace going in or out of there to that Joiner kid's mom."

Streeter jotted another note on the pad. Annie squeezed her eyes closed and rubbed her temples, hunching even lower in her chair until she was practically in a fetal position. Michael might have felt a smidgeon of compassion for her if his own life hadn't been the prize hanging between her divided loyalties. Under the circumstances, he really didn't give a shit about her confidentiality scruples.

"We need to bring the FBI in," Streeter said.

Michael noted the tightening of Eleanor's lips. "You disagree?"

"That's your decision. Just be aware that if news of this gets out and Grayson's share values dive, I will be rethinking my merger offer."

"For God's sakes, woman, you'd rather he just get killed than risk a drop in share value?" Even Streeter's legendary patience was wearing thin.

Eleanor leaned back in her chair. "I think the Russians themselves will be eliminating that particular risk shortly. They're not stupid. They'll be watching their recruits in this operation very closely, so I expect they know exactly who is behind these amateurish attempts. And they will not like it. These are the kinds of 'coincidences' that make people curious and suddenly what was operating nicely under the radar is instead under a microscope, putting their whole operation at risk. I suspect it's just a matter of time before the Russians themselves will be cleaning up this problem, at which point the attempts on Mr. Grayson's life will be at an end."

"You think the Russians will kill the guys trying to kill me," said Michael.

"I do."

"But wouldn't that also blow their larger objective? If they kill their contact, they lose their access."

"Would they? You yourself said that neither of these persons—Harrison or this Ashton person—have the access needed, so they have to be either recruiting or already working with a third person who does. You think the Russians can't find that person?" She raised a silver eyebrow. "No, I suspect your Harrison friend will be found dead of a heart attack in the very near future. Or perhaps a car accident. Either way, I think we can rely on the Russians to remove him from the equation in short order. Though it would be prudent to watch your back for a week or two until they finish the job."

Michael and Streeter looked at each other. Michael was starting to believe Eleanor Barlow's statement that if she had been the one behind these attempts, he would indeed be dead right now.

Streeter was the first to speak. "Even if you're right, the underlying espionage will continue."

"One would assume."

"Well, don't you think we should be doing something to stop that?" Michael asked. The more time he spent with this woman, the more he could understand why Annie might have a less than stellar opinion of the values and motives of the uber-wealthy.

"That is not my concern." Eleanor sipped her coffee delicately. "What does concern me is the value of Grayson Aeronautics. Headlines about military contracts compromised by internal company espionage would most certainly impact both current share value and the company's ability to land future military contracts. Do you disagree?"

Michael sat back. She was right on that front. That kind of news would kill the military business that made up a good portion—the growing portion—of Grayson Aeronautics business. It could kill the future of the company. But he couldn't just ignore the espionage. Systems might be compromised, possibly even sabotaged. He had to do something, but what? Maybe he should cut Annie a little slack. Being caught in the middle sucked.

"So, what do you suggest?" he asked.

"Oh, I have no suggestions. I'm strictly an observer here, passing on the information I was able to obtain. Use it as you choose. Do keep me posted though. As you know, I also have some decisions to make. And now, I have another appointment so I shall have to bid you both good day. You are welcome to stay here and sort your next steps. I suspect your hotel is under surveillance and probably not the safest place to return to." She rose from the table and turned toward the servant's door in the corner of the room. "Angela!"

The young woman materialized in an instant.

"These two gentlemen will be staying a bit longer. Please see they have whatever they need." She turned back to the two men. "Good luck." And the grande dame made her exit.

No one moved or spoke for a bit.

Finally, Annie broke the silence. "Well, I think I've done about as much damage as I can do here, so I'll just go turn in my law license." She pushed away from the table and stood.

"Annie, wait—" Michael started.

She paused and looked back at him.

But what could he say? That he wanted her desperately, but wasn't sure he could trust her?

She gave him a half-smile. "Stay safe, Michael." And she too was gone.

Michael muttered a curse and rubbed his hands over his face. How the hell was he supposed to figure out his love life in the middle of this mess?

Streeter rose. "Let's move this conversation to the garden."

"You think a stroll in Mother Nature will make this all better, do you?"

"Can't hurt." The man jerked his head toward the door where the serving girl hovered.

Michael caught the cue. Too many ears in too many corners inside this place, and probably all of them reporting to Eleanor Barlow.

Chapter Seventeen

Annie pushed open the door to her room. It took some searching, but eventually she found her phone. There were three missed calls from Jonathan and a text in all caps: CALL ME!

She punched the speed dial, then crossed the room to the window, staring out at the elaborate gardens that, if Grandmother had her way, would soon be her responsibility. Ironic, since she killed every plant she touched.

"Where have you been? I've been trying to reach you since last night."

The familiar voice, redolent of the life she had worked so hard to build, had tears welling up in her eyes. She dashed them away.

"Sorry. Long story."

"Well, I caught up with the not-so-Reverend Adams at the Workhouse yesterday and we had us a bit of a chat…"

"Jonathan, stop. You can't tell me anything else about the case. I have to get off. Now."

There was a beat of silence on the other end of the phone. "You just got back on."

"Yeah, well. That was before my grandmother decided to merge her companies with Grayson Aeronautics and put me on the board."

"You're shitting me."

"I am not. That's what I was trying to tell you yesterday. Though I didn't know then it was Grayson she was planning the merger with. Weren't you even listening?"

"Looks like I missed the lead. Sorry, you were a bit... whatever. So, you're going to inherit after all? I thought she'd disowned you."

"Blood trumps all in the Barlow world, it seems. That's why she wanted me up here this weekend. She really is dying. Pancreatic cancer. Two, maybe three months at most, the doctors say. So, she's 'protecting her legacy,' as she puts it. And since I'm her only heir, I'm being dragged right into the middle of it all."

"Wow. I mean, just wow. That's like winning the lottery, only a bunch of times in a row."

"Trust me, there'll be a whole lot more strings attached."

"Hey, can you pay off my student loans?? Is it crass to ask that?"

She couldn't help laughing, hungover and heartsick though she was.

"Seriously, are you okay? You don't exactly seem elated at the prospect of being crazy rich. I mean, I know your gran is dying and that's a sucky way to get rich, but it's not like the two of you were close. I thought you hated her guts."

"Oh, I do. Believe me. There's just... a lot to sort out."

"I bet."

"I'm not sure when I'll be back now. Or frankly, if I'll be back." She sighed. "I need you to tell Jackson I have to get off the case. And tell James for me. Tell him I'm sorry. About all of it. All of this mess."

"What do you mean 'if you'll be back?' Now that you're rich, you're bailing?"

"I have no idea what I'm doing." She squeezed her eyes shut at the painful truth of that. "But I'm pretty sure Jackson won't want me back."

"What? Why the hell not?"

"There've been some...developments."

Resting her aching head against the cool glass of the windowpane, she watched Michael and his bodyguard stroll out to the Pavilion as she filled Jonathan in on the second shooting and what appeared to be a Russian connection.

"Wait, so he's there? Right now??"

"He is." Her heart ached as she watched him below, much more than a glass window between them now.

"Shit. What did you tell him?"

Annie turned away from the window. "Too much. Grandmother spilled the beans about the first shooting being a hit before I could stop her, and things just rolled from there."

"Annie!"

"I know," she muttered, despair permeating the simple syllables.

Jonathan was silent for a beat. "You know, all we really have to say is that your family is now in business with Grayson. That alone is enough to conflict the case. Definitely from you, but possibly from the whole office. Especially if the case is turning into some international spy intrigue—which I just have to say is a bit surreal. Even Jackson will agree that's way beyond our expertise or funds to investigate. He'll jump on the chance to farm it out to some well-funded corporate types looking to burnish their *pro bono* credentials. We don't have to say anything else."

God, she loved Jonathan.

"I don't want to drag you into my screw-ups. Truly, I appreciate it, but—"

"Have you told Grayson anything James told you?"

"Of course not." Not that James had ever told them anything of actual value to the case. That was part of the problem.

"So, all you've told him is our theory about it being a hit."

"Well, I did mention the gifts to James's mother."

She cringed just repeating it. The duty of confidentiality extended to all information obtained in the course of representation, including information obtained from witnesses.

"Sheesh, Annie. I mean, he already knew about Peter's connection to Northside, but the stuff Mrs. Joiner told us?

"I know. I know!" She squeezed her eyes shut. "I was just thinking out loud. They were talking about Harrison Stewart being involved and—"

"Wait, what? Grayson's lawyer at the depo? How is he involved?"

"He's the one who set up the meeting last night where the shots were fired at Michael's car."

Jonathan whistled. "This just gets weirder and weirder."

"Doesn't it, though?" Annie sighed.

"Hey, remember James talking about seeing some lawyer out at Northside when he went out there with Little Wayne the day before the shooting? Chubby guy with a reddish-brown beard, he said."

"Oh my God. It was Harrison!"

"So, Harrison is behind the hit on Grayson. But why?"

"None of this makes any sense. Michael said Harrison didn't have access to the plans for the military, contract they think this Russian connection is probably about, so if it was him, he has to be working with someone else. That's how I stepped in it. I asked if Peter did."

"Fair question, though. What did they say?"

"Big picture stuff, general capabilities. He put together the marketing presentation for the Defense Department, but no detailed plans. And then he asked why I asked about Peter."

"And you answered."

"It wasn't even conscious. I was just running the scenario in my head. Only out loud." She banged her forehead not-so-gently against the window glass. "Talk about amateur."

"Okay. Look—"

She could almost hear his mind racing.

"—I'll talk to Jackson tomorrow, just about the merger situation, and we'll get the case conflicted out of the office. Nothing's going to happen on it for a while after that because whoever gets it will need to get up to speed. In the meantime, I assume your billionaire boy has a few investigative resources of his own he'll be putting on this. No doubt they'll be able to uncover anything he might have learned from you soon enough."

"Of course they will. Because I told them to where to look!"

"Would you shut up? My point is we don't have to

do anything right at this moment other than get off the case. Let's let the dust settle before we go blowing up your legal career. When you get back, we'll crack open a bottle of the most expensive whiskey I can find— which you're buying—and sort the rest out. Okay?"

She took a deep breath. "Okay. You're a good egg, Jonathan."

"So I keep telling you. In the meantime, take care of you. After all, I'm counting on those student loans being paid off and you're the only soon-to-be-rich person I know, so don't screw this up, okay?"

Annie smiled. "I'll try. And Jonathan? Thanks."

"Yeah, well. Payback's coming, sweetie. Later."

Annie dropped the phone on the bed, catching sight of herself in the mirror. Her shadowed eyes and makeup-free face stared back at her. Wow, really dressed to impress there, Annie.

She picked up the gown from last night that lay crumpled on the floor, an offense Grandmother would consider much more egregious than breaking client confidentiality. It was wet. Oh, God, had she spilled wine all over herself? Horrified at the images that possibility called to mind, she frantically ran her hand over the dress. The entire dress was soaked. The. Entire. Dress.

What the hell had happened last night?

Chapter Eighteen

Stepping into the gardens inevitably brought to mind the scenes played out on that same stage the night before. The one of Annie floating face down in that damned reflecting pool would haunt Michael for a while.

His cell phone rang and he glanced at the caller ID. Myriam. A Sunday morning call from his assistant was never good news.

"Myriam. What's up?"

"Good morning, sir. I wanted to make sure you'd heard about Harrison."

The back of his neck prickled. "What about Harrison?"

Streeter looked up sharply.

Myriam took a deep breath before she responded. "He was killed in a car accident driving back from Chicago early this morning."

"Harrison is dead?" Streeter and Michael locked gazes. "What happened?"

"They think he must have fallen asleep at the wheel. It was a one-car accident, and he was alone. Nobody saw it happen, so it's speculation, of course. Could just as easily have been a heart attack, I suppose. You know he didn't take care of himself."

He heard a muffled sniffle and the rustling of tissues.

When she continued, she was back in professional mode, though her voice was strained. "His daughter called. I had the office phone forwarded to my cell in case you needed something while you were out of town."

"Wow. I'm so...sorry. Please send flowers to the family."

Another sniff. "Already done, sir."

"Of course, it is. Thank you." He shifted gears. "I also need you to clear my schedule for this next week. Cancel my appointments." He glanced at Streeter, who nodded his approval.

"All of them?"

"Yes. Eleanor Barlow has made a proposal I need time to sort through."

"Of course. I'll see you tomorrow then?"

"I probably won't be coming into the office. Too many distractions. Just let anyone looking for me know I'll get back to them next week."

"Under the circumstances," she hesitated, then said in a quieter tone, "do you think it's a good time for you to be out of the office?" Myriam often disapproved of Michael's behavior, but she was seldom this direct about it. She was clearly shaken.

"I know the timing is not ideal, but Eleanor Barlow has me under a strict deadline and the only way I can sort through everything is to knuckle down and do it. Without interruptions. I'll be in as soon as I can. In the meantime, I trust you to take care of whatever needs to be taken care of. I don't suppose they know yet when any services may be held?"

"No, sir. His son lives in London, so it may take a bit to get everyone home."

"Okay. Keep me posted."

He ended the call and turned to Streeter. "One-car accident driving back from Chicago early this morning. No witnesses."

Streeter shook his head. "Man, did Barlow ever call it. She couldn't have been more spot on if she'd planned it."

"Think she might have?"

"No." Streeter shook his head. "I've no doubt she's capable of it. But if she was behind it, she wouldn't have laid that scenario out for us. She'd have just done it."

"Agree." Michael pursed his lips. "It's going to look very odd if I'm not at the funeral."

"Let's cross that bridge when we come to it. If Harrison was acting on his own, then—as Barlow predicted—you may be safe at this point, Russian spying aside. But just in case he wasn't, I still want you to lay low for a while until I see what I can find out."

Michael ran his hands through his hair. "I still don't see what killing me gets them. The rest of it makes some sort of surreal sense, I suppose. But what would killing me have gotten Harrison?"

"Time is my guess." Streeter said.

Michael frowned. "Sorry. Not following. What do you mean 'time'?"

"The E-7 design isn't finished yet, right? Aren't your hands still all over it?"

"Yes. So?" Michael's insistence on being hands-on in the design process pissed a lot of people off. It was inefficient. It was micro-managing. It was x, it was y, it was z. A long list of complaints he'd heard over the years and knew by heart. None of them mattered. It was his company, and design was both his passion and his genius. He got to do way less of it than he'd have liked these days, but a few projects he kept hands on. The E-7 was one of them.

"So, killing you shuts it down—which is why the Russians wouldn't be behind it. They need you finishing those designs. But what if Harrison or Peter—or whoever—doesn't have their access person fully on board yet and the Russians are putting pressure on them to deliver something they can't? We both know Peter promises the moon. And God knows, lawyers make bluffing a way of life. But if you're out of the picture, everything stops cold. Nothing anybody can do. The Russians are just going to have to tread water until things get sorted out, if they ever do."

Michael looked at Streeter. "Eleanor Barlow is good. You're better."

Streeter snorted. "Not sure I want to even be evaluated on the same scale as that woman, but thanks."

"So, where do we go from here?"

Streeter stared at the intricate ironwork of the pavilion in silence for a moment. Finally, he said, "While the Russians may not want you dead, I suspect they're watching you very closely right now to see if Harrison's bungling blew their cover. And if they figure out the game is up, they'll shut it all down."

"What's wrong with them shutting it all down?" Michael grumbled. "Isn't that the goal?"

"Not with the mole undiscovered and still in place, it isn't. That's just pushing the problem down the road."

Much as he'd like to, Michael couldn't argue. "So, what do you suggest?"

"Make everything look like business as usual. No

big changes, nothing to tip our hand that we know anything is up. Let it be known that you're working from home to knock out this Barlow proposal, but also get on the phone and bitch to some people about being caught near another street shooting—not that you were a target—just in the wrong place at the wrong time and how you have to start picking better places to hang out, blah, blah, blah. Don't keep it a secret."

"I don't exactly want to broadcast it. I just got the stock stabilized from the last scare."

"I'm not saying take it to the papers. I'm just saying mention it to a few people, who might in turn mention it to a few other people, and it might eventually reach someone that matters. Make sure you include Peter in that number, just in case he is involved."

Michael's jaw tightened. "Right."

"The compound should be safe, given the security measures already in place."

Those security measures—fences, sensors, cameras, guards—had been quite the point of contention between Michael and Streeter, as was Streeter's insistence on calling Michael's home 'the compound.' Michael thought the measures intrusive and over-the-top. Streeter insisted they were standard operating procedure for protecting someone rich and famous and Michael was both, whether he thought of himself that way or not.

Streeter continued ticking off next steps. "Call Mrs. C and give her the week off so you can work uninterrupted on this Barlow thing. Nobody in or out but me and Jax."

Michael raised an eyebrow. "You really think my

housekeeper is in league with the Russians?" His housekeeper was a sixty-year-old grandmother who spent her spare time making baby quilts for orphans in Africa.

"I'm not saying everyone around you is a suspect. I'm saying everyone around you is a potential source of information to those who are. Information that seems harmless to the person passing it on can be useful to those who may have more nefarious motives. The fewer people in contact with you, the fewer potential sources of information."

"I get it. But what intel could Mrs. C possibly pass on? That I don't pick up my socks? Besides, I told her she could bring her grandsons fishing at the lake this week."

Streeter shot him a look of exasperation. "Someone's trying to kill you and you're worried about cancelling a playdate?"

Michael ignored him, his eye caught by a movement in the upstairs window he now knew was Annie's. "And then there's the question of Annabel Barlow O'Toole," he muttered.

Streeter followed his gaze to the woman in the window. "Still some unpacking to do there, but I have to say, nothing this morning set off any conspiracy alarms for me. If she's acting, she's damned good at it."

"That's the problem," Michael said. "She is damned good at it."

"Why don't you offer her a ride back to St. Louis? It'd give me a chance to talk with her a bit more, since you'd be busy playing pilot."

Michael sighed. "She won't. She hates flying."

Streeter laughed. "Ah, the ironies do keep on

coming." He clapped Michael on the shoulder. "Nothing like falling for a woman who hates the very thing your life is all about. Good job there, bud."

Michael rolled his eyes. "Glad you can find some enjoyment in my predicament. Besides, you drove up. What about your car?"

"It's yours, not mine, so what do I care?" He chuckled at Michael's expression, then turned serious again. "I'll have Jax arrange a driver to get it home. I want to get a look at Harrison's office as soon as possible. We also need to go over that plane of yours with a fine-tooth comb before take-off, just in case any of these amateurs know someone who knows aircraft."

"You do know how to cheer a guy up," Michael said.

"I do my best." Streeter glanced at his watch. "If you want any fond farewells with the lovely Ms. O'Toole, now would be the time." Streeter settled into a glider. "Not like I don't have a few things to occupy my mind here, so take as long as you need. Within fifteen minutes or less."

Michael flipped him off and headed for the house.

****

Keeping Grayson safe was top of Streeter's to do list, but flushing out the mole and determining the extent of the breach was a close second. He mentally ticked through his available resources. In addition to Jax and his corporate security staff, he had a roster of other professionals he maintained for their fields of influence or expertise: off-the-record regulars who would trade information for favors—police contacts, hackers, low-level employees at regulatory commissions, and even some not-so-low-level political staffers who would occasionally spill some inside scoop of interest to Grayson's projects. There were also a few ex-military colleagues who could be counted on not to ask a lot of questions. But there were a few who didn't show up on any list, people with skillsets not often called upon in civilian life.

David Aylesbury was in the latter category. He was never a field guy. He was the brains in the background—Naval Academy grad, Georgetown Law, followed by a long line of Foreign Service and CIA posts overseeing US operations in most of the world's hotspots. He was widely expected to be named CIA Director one day, but he took an unexpected off-ramp and went to work for an old Georgetown classmate instead. Everyone thought he'd lost his mind until that old classmate happened to find his way into the presidency of the United States.

One major newspaper had referred to David as 'the most powerful man you've never heard of." But that had been years ago. Aylesbury was now pushing eighty and officially retired, though rumor had it he still did a little 'consulting' on the side. Streeter hoped the rumor was true. He pulled out his phone.

"Aylesbury." The deep baritone had not weakened with age.

"Hello, David. Streeter Jacobson here. Was hoping you hadn't gone and changed your number on me."

"Streeter Jacobson? My God. What rock did you crawl out from under? I haven't heard from you in years."

"Yeah, well, we don't exactly run in the same circles anymore, sir."

"Don't 'sir' me. We've been through too much shit

together for that."

Streeter chuckled. "We did have our share. And now here I am back with more."

"Oh? Something interesting I hope."

"Could be. Don't suppose you'd be up for a quick flight to St. Louis, would you? Always easier to talk business in person and you could spend a few days catching up with old friends, enjoy some toasted ravioli, maybe visit the top of the Arch—"

"Well, I haven't been over that way for a while, it's true. Might be I could find some time for a visit." The old man knew better than to press if Jacobson wasn't offering details over the phone. "When were you thinking?"

"How's this afternoon look? I can send a plane."

David laughed. "You never did believe in letting moss grow. And working for that fancy aeronautics company, I suppose you have all the planes you need just waiting at your beck and call."

"Mike lets me play with a few of his chess pieces now and then."

"Good man, Grayson. He was lucky to have you as a mentor."

"Just as I was lucky to have you."

"How do I say no after that kind of suck-up?" David chortled delightedly. "Ah, what the hell. Order up your plane, Jacobson. I'll fly out of Midway."

"Midway? You're in Chicago? I thought you were kicking back on your acreage in Tennessee these days."

"Got bored. You can only look at so many cows. And it's easier to meet up with people in a city with a decent airport close by."

Retired, my ass. "Sounds like you could just as

well have stayed in DC."

"Well, a wise aunt once warned me it's never a good idea to live too close to your children."

Streeter laughed. The old man had no children of the regular definition, but the beltway was thick with his progeny.

"Some of us hunt you down anyway."

"Always happy to hear from those who don't abuse the privilege. It's the ones who have me on speed dial I like a little distance from." The old man chuckled. "So... logistics?"

"Well, as it turns out Mike and I happen to be in Chicago with a plane waiting for us at Midway as we speak. Think you can be ready to go in an hour? If not, we can arrange a different ride back for you."

"I'm not doing anything but twiddling my thumbs and listening to Sara ordering more shit we don't need off some cable shopping network. I'll be glad to get out of the house and she'll be glad to be rid of me for a while. An hour it is. Any idea how long this visit might last?"

"Well, there's at least a week's worth of sights to enjoy. After all this time, you wouldn't want to cut things too short."

"Let's plan on a week then and adjust as needed. And I'm going to hold you to those toasted ravs."

"Never doubted it, sir. Text me your address and I'll send a car for you."

Streeter hung up the phone and breathed a silent sigh of relief. If anybody could help sort through the maze in which they found themselves, it would be Aylesbury.

He had the knowledge, the contacts, and the

discretion—all of which Streeter desperately needed right now.

At least something had gone right today.

Chapter Nineteen

Annie answered Michael's knock on her bedroom door with a decided lack of enthusiasm, probably expecting a summons from her grandmother. Her eyes widened when she saw him standing there instead.

"Hi," he said, shoving his hands in his pockets just to have someplace to put them. What the hell was it about this woman that had him feeling like an awkward adolescent? He cleared his throat. "May I come in?"

"Um…sure," she said, stepping back to let him pass. She peered behind him into the empty hallway. "How did you know where my room was?" she asked.

"Ah, right. You probably don't remember."

"Remember what?" Her green eyes narrowed.

He hesitated, not wanting to open that particular can of worms, but unable to think up a viable detour. "I brought you back here last night. After the dinner party."

"You brought me back here? Why?"

He opted for the short version. "You passed out. Carter showed me where to bring you."

She looked thunderstruck. "Great," she managed to get out, after a bit. "Well, that's just great."

He started to change the subject, but she interrupted.

"Do you happen to know how my gown got wet last night?"

Well, damn. "You, um, sort of decided to go for a swim in the reflecting pool."

She gasped. "I did not!"

"Well, no—not exactly," he conceded with a grin. "There wasn't really any deciding involved. You fell into the reflecting pool."

She gaped.

"If it makes you feel any better, I have a matching drowned tux."

"Wait, you fell in too? We fell in together?"

"No, mine was very much a deciding. I jumped in. After you. A lady shouldn't swim alone. Especially when she's unconscious."

Her mortified face convinced him to tone down the teasing and stick to just the facts. He relayed the story as quickly and dispassionately as he could, omitting that he was the one who'd undressed her and cleaned her up, and blurring the details about the argument that had triggered her dramatic exit back to the house in the first place. No need for a reprise of that right now.

Annie looked a little green. She pressed her lips together and swallowed hard, before mumbling something that vaguely sounded like, "Thanks."

He let it pass and changed the subject. "Harrison is dead."

Annie gasped. "What?"

"Myriam just called. A one-car accident between here and St. Louis sometime in the early hours of the morning. Exactly as your grandmother predicted."

She sank onto the bed. "Wow."

"Indeed." He gave her a minute to absorb the U-turn, before continuing. "Streeter doesn't want to tip our hand that we know this is anything more than a run-of-the-mill car accident, so the Russians don't pull their operation before we have a chance to identify the mole and the extent of the compromise. That means we all need to keep up appearances as if everything is normal."

She gave him a skeptical look. "Normal? What about any of this could possibly look normal?"

"Car accidents happen. 'Isn't it horrible Harrison was killed in that tragic accident?'"

"What about the shooting? Hard to pretend that was normal."

"Shootings happen in Chicago all the time. I just happened to be in the neighborhood when some gang shooting went down. Close enough to hear the shots, but never in danger, that sort of thing. So… if anyone asks about your weekend—?"

She inhaled and shoved a curl out of her eye. "Just a normal hellish weekend with my grandmother who has once again decided to ruin my life. Nothing new about that."

He badly wanted to believe that was exactly what it had been. All it had been.

"Right. Thanks. So, uh, Streeter and I are getting ready to head out. He's decided to fly back with me and have his assistant arrange a driver for his car, so…"

"He didn't fly up with you?"

Damn. Why had he said that? He deflected. "He drove up earlier, on other business."

"Isn't a bodyguard supposed to stay with you?"

"He's not my bodyguard. He's my chief of security."

"And your chief of security just happened to be in Chicago on other business when you just happened to get shot at— again—while visiting Chicago?"

Why did this woman have to be so damned smart? He blew out an exasperated breath.

"Streeter oversees a lot of different investigations for Grayson Aeronautics. He doesn't report his every move to me. Had I known he was going to be in Chicago, I would have invited him to fly with me. But I didn't, so he drove up instead and now will be flying back with me." Hoping she'd leave it at that, he added, "You're welcome to fly back with us. You'd be home in an hour instead of five."

She shuddered. "God, no. I hate planes."

"So you said." His gaze locked on hers, a touch of a smile lifting the corners of his lips. "Because they leave the ground."

"Right," she said, with a tentative smile of her own as she followed him into their conversation from the night they met. "You really ought to do something about that."

"I'll work on it." His voice was husky as he reached out and wrapped a silky curl around his finger. It was still damp and cool to his touch.

What was it about this woman that kept him coming back for more, no matter how many disturbing surprises he kept uncovering? She was like one of those Russian dolls—each new discovery revealing yet another identity. And yet, instead of walking the hell away, he found himself desperately wanting to know who was at the bottom of them all. Releasing the curl, he moved his fingers to her chin and tilted her face up to his. Her breath caught. He savored the reaction.

"I may not know fully who you are, Counselor, but I will figure it out. It's what we princes do." He bent and brushed her lips with his own. "Until then, stay safe—because you and I are not done."

It took everything he had to walk away.

****

Annie sat where he left her. She might be twisting in her grandmother's web and her career headed for wreck and ruin, but that brief kiss had reinvigorated a tiny bit of hope in her tired soul. What if—*what if*—Michael still wanted her...even if she was both Eleanor Barlow's granddaughter and defending the kid charged with shooting him?

She ran her fingers through her hair. The odds were long. She knew that. They'd had one amazing, magical night, but had been blocked at every turn since. She wasn't naïve enough to believe all those obstacles would just magically fade away. A lot still stood between them. But hope was a scrappy little bugger and could go a long way on a tiny bit of air. Especially when a handsome prince had just given it CPR.

She pushed herself off the bed and crossed to the alcove her mother had always referred to as her 'reading nook.' Other kids had fuzzy bean bag chairs in their reading corners. She'd had a rose silk Queen Anne. She let herself drop into the throne-like chair and rested her aching head against its high back, idly running a finger along the books on the shelf next to her. Pulling one out at random, her gaze fell on the little box she'd hidden there so long ago.

Memories flooded back as she slipped it out and opened the lid. The little stack of letters, penned in the handwriting of a child and secreted away so many years before were still there. Letters written to a father she would never meet—a father she grew up believing didn't want her or her mother. Letters trying to convince him to come back, to give them a second chance so maybe her mother wouldn't be so sad all the time. Letters that would never be mailed because she'd had no idea where to send them. All because of Eleanor Barlow.

Slowly she closed the box and looked around the room. Every detail had been selected by her grandmother. The colors, the furniture, the pictures on the wall, even the expensive tchotchkes carefully positioned atop the various surfaces. There was nothing of her in this place. Not then, not now. Nothing but a few books and a secret stash of never-mailed letters from a desperately lonely little girl.

But she wasn't that little girl any longer. Determination flared deep in the pit of her stomach. There was no way in hell she was coming back to this gilded cage. Not now, not ever. She was a grown woman and a hell of a lawyer, and—according to her grandmother—had the same steel running up her backbone that the old woman had used to push through every obstacle in her way. Well, now it was her turn.

****

Two hours later, Annie went searching for her grandmother. She found Jenkins in the butler's office off the pantry, sorting through paperwork. She rapped on the door jamb.

"Sorry to bother you—"

The old man glanced up and instantly jumped to his feet.

"Ms. Barlow! Did you ring? I didn't hear the bell. I'm so sorry—"

"No, you're fine. I didn't call." She was definitely

out of practice when it came to living with a house full of servants. "And again, it's O'Toole, if you please. I'm looking for my grandmother."

"Ms. O'Toole, yes, of course. Apologies, ma'am. Your grandmother is resting and unavailable at the moment. But I will be happy to notify her of your desire to see her as soon as she rises."

Unavailable, my ass. This conversation was happening, and it was happening now. "That won't be necessary. Would you let Carter know I'll be ready to leave for St. Louis in thirty minutes?"

"Of course, ma'am."

****

Annie could count on one hand the number of times she'd been in her grandmother's bedroom. As a child, she wasn't allowed and, as an adolescent, it was the last place she'd wanted to be. Now, as a grown woman, she still experienced a touch of trepidation approaching the inner sanctum. She took a deep breath and rapped sharply on the door jamb.

"What?" the familiar voice inside snapped. "I'm trying to rest."

Eleanor Barlow hadn't rested in the middle of the day since she was a toddler, if then. The cancer was taking its toll, whether she wanted to admit it or not.

Annie pushed opened the door and stepped inside. Heavy brocade curtains were pulled across the wall of floor to ceiling windows, but a lamp on the ornate chest of drawers provided a soft illumination. Her grandmother looked small propped against her pillows on the oversized poster bed.

"Carter and I are leaving shortly," Annie said. "I've come to say good-bye."

The woman could still shoot daggers with a look and did. "We agreed you would be staying until we get things sorted."

"No, we didn't 'agree' to that. What you want and what I agree to are not one and the same thing. It's really past time you came to terms with that."

"We have matters to settle, Annabel. You are not a child anymore, for God's sake. You can't just keep running away."

"I'm not running," she retorted, realizing the truth of that statement even as she said it. It felt good. "That's why I'm here—to settle matters before I leave."

The old woman smoothed the cashmere throw over her legs. "You've come to your senses, then?"

"I've come to decisions that are sensible for me," Annie replied. "Whether you consider them sensible is really irrelevant I'm afraid." She leaned against the doorway, arms crossed, affecting a casual demeanor she did not feel. "I have a counteroffer for you."

Her grandmother narrowed her eyes. "What?"

"I'm not moving back to Barlow House. I'm not changing my name. And I'm not giving up my career."

Anger flashed across her grandmother's face.

Annie held up a hand. "Let me finish. If you still want me to be your heir and safeguard your legacy within those parameters, I will take my place on Grayson's board and I will serve as your 'nuclear deterrent.' And while I will not live here, I will ensure that Barlow House is the site of several very expensive, charity events each year—though the charities will be my choice, not yours. Those are my terms."

"And your capital defense center?" her grandmother asked, her voice tight with disapproval.

"Oh, it would be great," Annie admitted. "That was a nice touch and if you want to throw it in, feel free. But as I said before, that's a cause I care about. It won't affect my life personally." As much as she wanted that center, she knew better than to bite on any carrot her grandmother dangled. There was always a hook in the center. "And one more thing."

"What?" her grandmother snapped.

"Regardless of what you decide to do—whether you decide to make me your heir or not—if you leave so much as a cent to Nicoletti or any prosecutorial organization of any kind, I will go on every talk show that will have me to tell the true story of the abuse my family and I endured at the hands of my manipulative, greedy, bitch of a grandmother, Eleanor Barlow."

Her grandmother's sharp intake of breath was audible.

"The media does love a good villain," Annie pressed on, "and I'm sure they won't be able to get enough of all the stories I can tell. I wouldn't be surprised if 'The Real Eleanor Barlow Story' gets picked up and made into a movie. Probably not quite the legacy you had in mind, but hey, you'll be remembered."

For a moment she thought the old woman might levitate off her bed. She had seen her grandmother angry many, many times, but she'd clearly unlocked a whole new level of rage. She had to steel herself not to take a step backward in the face of it.

"How dare—how dare you threaten me?" The old woman practically vibrated. "You wouldn't—you couldn't even if you tried—"

Annie forced a laugh. "You think not? I've spent

my life watching you destroy people. Do you really think I didn't learn how? Or maybe you just never imagined I'd use that particular skillset against you. Ironic, since you certainly never hesitated to use it against me or my parents. I guess that old saying is right: karma can be a real bitch."

Eleanor looked to be on the verge of hyperventilation. Annie didn't wait for her to collect herself.

"So, that's my counteroffer." She ticked the items off once more for good measure. "One: I'll be your nuclear deterrent and charity party planner, but that's it. The rest of my life, and how I choose to live it, is off limits. Two: Leave Nicoletti and his ilk out of our family feud and your carefully crafted reputation can stay intact, whether you decide to make me your heir or not. Use him to screw with me and I will destroy every memory of you. Your call."

She turned on her heel and walked out, leaving Eleanor Barlow gaping like a hungry baby bird.

****

Neither Annie nor Carter spoke much for the first leg of their journey back to St. Louis. Carter was good at fading into the background when his input wasn't required and Annie's thoughts bounced crazily between replays of the scene with her grandmother and Michael's good-bye kiss. Adrenaline raced through her system on both counts.

"Springfield's just ahead. Would you like to make a coffee stop?" Carter's gentle voice broke through the competing narratives.

She laughed. "Need you ask?"

He chuckled and moved into the exit lane.

"Carter, you know my grandmother is sick, right? Dying, actually."

His voice sobered. "Yes, I know."

"Do the other servants?"

"No. She didn't want anyone else told."

"Well, she can't keep it secret much longer."

"I know," he said. "But she wanted things settled before the news got out. To stop the vultures circling, as she put it."

As if she weren't the biggest vulture of them all.

"What about you, Carter? Are things settled for you? I mean, once she's gone. Will you be okay?"

This man had been the one kind soul in her life after her mother died. The possibility that her grandmother might leave him with nothing to support himself in his old age was horrifying. Why hadn't she thought to include something for Carter in her negotiations?"

"Oh, I'll be fine," the older man said with a smile. "I have a comfortable retirement fund, and your grandmother bought me a nice little place years ago."

Her grandmother had actually done something nice for Carter? Maybe hell was freezing over after all.

"Well, good. I'm glad to hear that."

There was a beat of silence as he navigated down the off-ramp. Unusually, he was the one to break it.

"Do you think you'll be back before—?" He left the sentence hanging.

"No," she said. "I won't be back. We said everything we had to say to each other this time."

"I see," he said, a touch of sadness creeping into his tone.

"Carter," she said suddenly, "could we stay in

touch? I mean, I know you were doing a job for all those years, so of course, you're under no obligation. It's just that, I've always thought of you as—"

"I would be honored," he said with a smile, his gaze meeting hers in the rear-view mirror. "After all, you're the closest thing to a daughter I've had."

"And you are the closest thing to a father I've had," she said, tears welling up. She reached over the seat and squeezed the older man's shoulder. "Thank you for being there all those years."

He laid a hand over hers and squeezed. "My pleasure, Miss Annabel."

"It's Annie. Please. Just Annie."

"Annie, it is."

Chapter Twenty

It was late afternoon by the time Carter dropped Annie off at home and she decided to head out to the Workhouse to see James. Jonathan had offered to make this last visit for her, but now that she'd come home, she felt like she needed to do it herself. She owed James that.

He was his usual polite, subdued self…until she told him she had to get off his case. Then he became agitated.

"No, it's okay. I don't care if he's in business with your grandmother or you or whatever. I want you to stay on my case. Please!"

Her heart broke a little as it so often did in this job. These were kids in way over their heads, with few lifelines available to them. He saw her as one of his and panicked at the idea of it being pulled away.

"You'll be okay, James. There's a lot going on in your case that requires an expertise neither Jonathan nor I have."

"Like what?"

Annie took a breath. He was the client. He had a right to know.

"Well, for one thing it appears that the bearded man you saw out at Northside talking to Reverend Adams was Harrison Stewart, Michael Grayson's lawyer out at his company. And it looks like he's the one who put a hit out on Grayson."

"His own lawyer? Man, that's cold."

"Indeed. And then Harrison himself was killed in a car wreck last night."

James whistled.

Annie leaned forward. "James, you know all those gifts Reverend Adams was giving to your mother?"

His eyes flickered ever so slightly and up went the walls.

"Those were to buy your silence so the guy really behind it all could get away with it, weren't they?"

James sat, silent.

"That guy was Harrison Stewart. But he's dead now. There will be no more gifts, no more reason to keep silent." She let that soak in a minute. "Did you ever have any contact with Harrison?"

James shook his head.

"You just saw him that once up at the Center?"

James nodded. His gaze strayed to the barred windows.

Annie let the silence be for a bit, then said, "You know, I smell a rat when it comes to the good reverend. I don't think he's what he pretends to be. Am I wrong?"

James smiled and shook his head.

"I'm not wrong?"

"Nope."

"What's his story, James? What's he playing at?"

James took a breath and looked at the floor. "He's a dealer. Heroin, cocaine, meth. Recruits the guys he comes to visit here to work for him. Promises a lot of money when they get out."

Anger rose from the tips of Annie's toes all the way up her body and exploded out of the top of her head. "The fucking bastard," she swore under her breath.

James laughed, the first time she'd heard that sound.

"Yeah, that pretty much sums him up."

"Did you ever work for him?"

"Nah. I didn't trust the guy. Little Wayne did though. And a lot of others I know. They kept tryin' to recruit me, but I dunno. Just wasn't interested."

"Any idea how Harrison got connected with him?"

James shrugged. "I only saw the guy that one time. Little Wayne said a lot of those guys playin' at volunteerin' at the center was really just buyin' drugs. I guess it covered 'em bein' in the hood."

Annie sat back, absorbing the information. God, this thing just spiralled deeper and deeper.

"What did Adams tell you when he first came to visit you?" Annie thought it was past time to drop the 'Reverend' when referring to this scum.

James looked back at the window.

"Harrison is dead," she reminded him. "He's not going to be taking care of your mama now, if he ever was." She leaned forward and looked intently at James. "You need to tell me the truth so you can get out of here and take care of her yourself."

James was quiet for a minute, considering. When he spoke it was softly, his gaze on the floor. "He said it would be best for me to just be quiet and take this rap for Little Wayne. That he had this rich guy who would take care of my mama if I did. He said I was a first offender so I'd probably get off easy. A few years at most. And Mama would be sittin' pretty with everything she ever wanted." He shrugged. "Seemed worth it to me, I guess. She's been havin' a hard time, you know. Too old to clean houses anymore with her arthritis."

"So, you didn't leave Little Wayne over at that girl's house the day of the shooting after all?"

James shook his head. "We walked over to the West End together. He said he had a job to take care of for the Rev. I assumed he meant a delivery, so I went along. We went into this alley. He kept checkin' his watch. Said he was waitin' for his guy. I didn't have any place to be, so I was cool with that. I was watchin' this girl walk down the road, and all of a sudden I heard a shot. Little Wayne gave me a shove and yelled, 'Run!' so I took off. I don't know where he went, but after a bit, I circled back round to see what had happened. I could hear the sirens and all. Didn't know if anybody had been hit or even really who did the shooting, if it was Little Wayne shootin' at somebody or somebody shootin' at him."

"And it was when you circled back to see what happened that you got picked up."

"Yeah. Pretty stupid I guess."

"How did you know what to tell the police in your confession about the shooting itself?"

"Didn't have to tell them anything. They told me what happened and just kept pushin' me to say I was the one who done it."

Annie stifled a sigh. All the interrogation studies advised withholding details of the crime specifically to see if a suspect's version matched—a safeguard to check on its veracity.

But for cops under pressure to get a confession quickly and close a case—especially a high profile one—shortcuts were tempting. They also led to a lot more false confessions.

Annie considered. "Does Little Wayne have a gold tooth?"

James nodded. "Same as mine. We got 'em done together."

"Is he left-handed?"

"Yeah." He looked a little surprised by the question.

"Do you know if he's ever gone to jail before? Been convicted of anything?"

If he had a conviction, he had a mug shot.

"He got picked up on a stealing last year. Got probation."

"Has he been out to see you since you got locked up?"

James shook his head. "I heard he got a new case out in the county, but I don't know for sure."

Annie noted both on her legal pad, then leaned forward, resting her forearms on her knees.

"James, I have something to ask you, and it's very much out of the ordinary. It turns out that I've become... well, pretty good friends with the guy who was shot, Michael Grayson."

James grinned a little. "So, I heard."

Annie blushed. "Yeah, well. Anyway, I think he might believe me if I told him what you've just told me. And if he does...well, he has a lot of influence. He might be able to get the prosecutor to drop the case against you. I can't promise anything, but I think it's worth a try before I get off your case. But I can't tell him anything you've said without your permission."

"You do what you think is best. I trust you."

"Okay," she said, fingers crossed he was right to do so. "I'll keep you posted."

Chapter Twenty-One

It wasn't the first Sunday Jax had been called in to work for Streeter and she was sure it wouldn't be the last. But it was certainly a first in its own way.

"You bugged the CEO's office." She repeated the statement back to her boss, as if he himself might not have understood it when he said to it her. "And I'm supposed to be monitoring what is said in the CEO's office. For you."

The two were in Streeter's private offices far from the sprawling campus and many eyes of Grayson Aeronautics. He'd purchased the 150-year-old Benton Park three-story before the old St. Louis neighborhood had become trendy. To her chagrin, he'd also opted to keep it true to its rundown roots.

He offered no response to her repetition of this information. His attention was focused on the papers he and Jax had spent the day sorting, both those from the boxes he'd hauled back from Harrison's office that morning and the dozens more pouring in from his roster of contacts to whom he'd been doling out assignments even before Grayson's plane had landed back in St. Louis this morning.

"I just gotta ask—because I both like and actually need my job—does Grayson know you bugged his office?"

"Not yet. But he won't mind. Don't worry about

it."

"Of course. I mean, what could possibly go wrong from bugging your own boss's office without his knowledge or consent?"

She got no response.

"Okay, then. Think I'll just go update that old résumé."

Streeter finally lifted his head. "Hey, did you hear back from Carlo on those phone records on O'Toole and Barlow?"

She sighed. The man was hopeless.

"I did. He said to tell you he's charging you double for this one."

"He got the info?"

"Looks like. But he didn't seem too happy with you.'"

"I'm heartbroken. Pay the man." He checked his watch. "Okay. I'm going to go pick up Aylesbury from his hotel and then head out to Grayson's. Give me those phone records."

She retrieved the file from her desk, and he wedged it into his backpack, already bulging with the files and timelines the two of them had spent the afternoon creating.

"Appreciate the help with all this," he did concede as he headed for the door.

"I live to serve."

"And now and then you actually do. See you tomorrow."

"I can't wait," she said to the receding back of the man she simultaneously adored and so often wanted to strangle.

****

Michael's home was a two-hundred-acre property atop the Mississippi bluffs, formerly a combination park and nature preserve. Michael had made few changes to the grounds, retaining the mix of native Missouri forest, natural meadow, and mown—but not manicured—spaces. There were no fountains, pavilions, or reflecting pools, just a large house of stone and timber with wide windows overlooking the river. That and a state-of-the-art security system around the full perimeter of the property, thanks to Streeter's insistence and Michael's annoyance.

It was early evening when the three men—Michael, Streeter, and David Aylesbury—gathered on the broad stone terrace overlooking the river, a vantage point from which they could at least enjoy a nice view while wading through the muck in which they were mired.

"Start with Harrison's office. What did you find?" Michael asked Streeter.

"Well, the good news is that the man spent a lot of his work hours taking care of personal business. Bad for you, maybe, but good for us because he never threw anything away. Found three banker's boxes in his closet filled with personal bank statements, credit card statements, investment accounts, bills, personal correspondence, you name it. The man also never deleted an e-mail, left his password book lying on top of his desk, and didn't know the meaning of encryption."

"Dream target," David murmured. "Nightmare source."

"Exactly," Streeter said. He pulled a file from the bulging backpack at his feet and spread it open on the table. "So, here's what we've put together so far. About six months ago, Harrison started keeping company with a woman named Anya Sokolov, the daughter of one Anton Sokolov."

David whistled.

Michael looked between the two men. "And he is?"

"Old." David chuckled. "Like me. But before he got old, he was a bigwig in the Russian foreign service. We always knew he was a spy, but he was a good one. We never could pin anything on him."

"So that's it. That's our connection," Michael said. "Might have known it would involve a woman. Harrison was never that political."

"The honey trap," David said. "Oldest tradecraft in the books. Hell, it probably predates books. Seduction is the universal kryptonite."

Michael shifted uncomfortably. He hadn't heard the term before, but instantly got the reference… and it rang a little close to home.

"Looks like they met at an international business law conference in Aspen back in February," Streeter continued. "She appears to have been the pursuer, reaching out to him after the conference and keeping the conversation going. Then in April, she moves to St. Louis and takes a suite at the Chase—at which point Harrison's credit card bills start including jewelry, lingerie, symphony tickets, and frequent dinners at much nicer restaurants than he usually visited."

"The mating rituals of old men," David said with a rueful smile. "We can't offer virility, but we can offer our credit cards."

"From the looks of it, he had it pretty bad. The two were sending lovey-dovey e-mails and texts back and forth several times a day, even after she moved here."

"How did you get his texts?" Michael asked. "We don't have his phone."

"He didn't use an encrypted platform and backed all his texts up to the cloud. Probably a default setting, given his utter lack of security concerns in any other arena. And I have very good hackers on your payroll."

David chuckled appreciatively.

Michael blew out a breath. "You do realize there are some things it's probably best I *not* know?"

"Well, then you shouldn't ask," Streeter answered. "Anyway, mixed in amongst the lust and wining and dining, there are several exchanges where she asks about 'the package for her dad.' Like this one."

Streeter picked up a sheet of paper and read: "*Just got off the phone with Papa. He said we really need that package ASAP. He's under a lot of pressure and things could go very badly if we can't deliver soon. I told him you could do anything you set your mind to and you'd come thru. I know you will. Are you free tonight? Don't leave me hanging.*"

"And his response?" David asked.

"Never anything specific. Lots of 'I'm-working-on-it,' 'should-have-it-any-day' kind of stuff, then he changes the subject back to wining / dining / sexy time."

"Any idea where Ms. Sokolov is now?" David asked.

"She went back to Russia about two weeks before Michael was shot. The first time," he clarified, with a glance in Michael's direction. He flipped through his file. "This was the last text from her: *I can't believe you let me down. You broke my heart. My family is in such trouble over this. I have to go home. I should hate you for this. I'm trying. Anya."*

Michael looked back and forth at the two men. "So, nothing was actually delivered? Maybe we aren't compromised after all?"

"I doubt it's that neat of a bow, unfortunately," David said. He turned to Streeter. "Anything hinting at who he may have been working with to gain access to the designs?"

Streeter shook his head. "I've got Jax going through his phone records now, comparing them with the list Michael gave us of people who had access."

"Of course, those are only the ones with authorized access," David mused. "His contact might be someone who simply has the proximity and means to steal the intel. And then there's still that server."

Michael sat back in his seat. "And that went online thirteen months ago. Well before Harrison ever met his Russian girlfriend." He ran his hands over his face. "This isn't making any sense."

David wandered over to the stone wall that lined the terrace and stared down at the river two hundred feet below. After a bit he said, "What if Harrison is just a side show? Something to distract us from the main event. It's just so damned amateurish. Using unencrypted messages and e-mails to communicate about this package for her father? Her father would have a heart attack at the thought. Unless they were intentionally trying to leave a trail we couldn't miss."

"Setting Harrison up to be the fall guy?" Streeter asked.

"It's one possibility. A built-in detour if we happened to uncover any glimmer of the real thing. But it also increases the likelihood of discovery in the first place, so…" He shook his head. "Another possibility is that Anton's daughter isn't an agent at all but an opportunist who just happened to cross paths with someone who led her to believe he might have valuable information and decided to follow the lead where it took her."

"There was a bug on Harrison's office phone," Streeter said. "Wasn't anything super-sophisticated but gaining access to his office to install something like that would be a bit of a challenge. Especially for someone without any training."

"What did you do with it?" David asked sharply.

"Called Maintenance from his phone and told them the CEO wanted the new department head to have a fresh start without any heebie-jeebies about moving into a dead guy's office—a complete redo—so they had to come get rid of everything in there: furniture, carpet, drapes, and office equipment."

"Oh, well done," David crowed delightedly. "Well done."

Streeter looked at Michael. "Figured you wouldn't mind paying for a little redecoration."

Michael rolled his eyes. "But how could this woman have gotten into Harrison's office to plant a bug? It's a secure area with a twenty-four-hour guard on duty."

"Maybe Harrison took her," David offered. "Sex in the office after hours? You'd be surprised how many people risk their careers for a little bit of extra spice." David's eyes twinkled as he looked from Michael to Streeter. "Then again, maybe you wouldn't," he said with a wink.

Michael's traitorous libido flashed up a full-color fantasy of A.J. O'Toole bent over his office conference table. His lower anatomy happily waved its approval. Fuck. *Focus*.

"But I don't think that's it," David was saying.

"Why not?" Michael asked, clearing his throat.

"It doesn't add up. If she's simply an opportunist, she's unlikely to have that kind of equipment on hand. After all, the bug is only part of the equation. You need the equipment to monitor it and a team with the time to listen to all the incoming and outgoing calls. No small task that."

"Tell me about it," Streeter muttered.

"On the other hand, if she was a professional, intentionally setting Harrison up to send us down a rabbit hole if the real operation were discovered, the bug makes no sense. It makes him look more like a victim of espionage than a player, which runs counter to the purpose of the whole operation."

Michael was starting to see why Streeter had decided to call Aylesbury in. "So, who do you think put the bug there?" he asked.

David took a long breath and exhaled. "My money would be on whoever's behind the real espionage. And I don't think that was Harrison. Or Anya. They're both too amateurish and this target too valuable. But the professionals would want to keep tabs on Harrison, especially once he went rogue with that first shooting."

"So, we're back to someone inside the company who would have access to Harrison's office?" Michael said.

"Odds are," David agreed. "Of course, almost any building can be gotten to eventually—cleaning staff, maintenance workers, service people. There are plenty of ways to infiltrate a work force if you're willing to wait long enough for the right opportunity. But I just don't see Harrison as an important enough target for them to have gone to those kinds of lengths. He wasn't the guy with access, just a go-between." He turned to Streeter. "You didn't find anything in Harrison's cache of documents concerning the server, did you?"

"Nothing."

"I thought not. Okay. Well, thanks to your excellent work, Streeter, I think we can safely eliminate a need to spend any more time investigating Harrison and turn our attention elsewhere. You said the timing of that server going online matched up with when you got this latest military contract?"

"According to Eleanor Barlow's contacts," Michael said.

David chuckled. "Well, I've long suspected Eleanor Barlow's contacts rival the CIA's, so we're probably safe in relying on that timeline."

"You know Eleanor Barlow?" Michael asked, surprised.

"Oh, indeed," David replied. "Would you believe I introduced her to her husband? Not sure she's ever forgiven me for that." He grinned. "Let's just say it did not turn out to be a very equal match."

Michael opened his mouth, but Streeter cut him off.

"I'm sure you two will have plenty to talk about later," Streeter said, giving Michael a sterner look than Michael thought warranted. "But right now we need to stay focused on this." He glanced back at his notes. "The server didn't go through any of Grayson's regular purchasing procedures, so there's no internal record of it. And so far, no luck piercing the identity behind its registration. Everything simply says Grayson Aeronautics. I've got a couple of hackers I can put on trying to break into the thing itself, but I'm not optimistic about their chances. My guys are good, but not quite Russian spycraft good."

"Couldn't we just go out there and get the thing?" Michael asked. "I assume if they found the signal, we could at least track that, couldn't we? Defiance isn't that big."

"You could. But that would also tip your hand that you're onto them," David pointed out. "And your mole will simply burrow deep underground to wait for another day."

Michael stood and began to pace. "So, we're nowhere."

Streeter's phone rang. He stepped into the house to take the call. He returned shortly with what Michael could only describe as a smirk on his face.

"What's got you looking smug?"

"Set a few traps earlier today and it sounds like someone might have stepped in one. At least I hope so. That was Jax. Says she has something we need to hear. She's on her way out."

David looked at Michael. "Maybe we're not quite 'nowhere' after all?"

****

Jax had never met the CEO of Grayson Aeronautics, much less been out to his estate, and really would have preferred to keep it that way. Unfortunately, Streeter had responded to her news with a terse 'get your ass out here' and hung up on her. And so, here she was, knocking on the door of a billionaire's mansion, dressed in leggings, a 'First-Class Smart-Ass' t-shirt, flip-flops, and a faded baseball cap holding her ponytail in place. Nobody could say she didn't know how to make a first impression.

Grayson himself opened the door. Of course, he did.

"Jax. It's nice to finally meet you." He extended a hand.

"Hello, sir. L-likewise," she stammered.

"We're out on the terrace," he said, gesturing toward the far end of a magnificent great room with a soaring timbered ceiling and a fireplace as big as her kitchen. A set of paned-glass doors were open to the evening breeze. "Can I get you anything? Coffee? Water? Or you're welcome to join the rest of us in something stronger."

"I wouldn't mind a something stronger, if you're offering," she managed. "Sir."

A moment later, fortification in hand, she followed Grayson out to the terrace where Streeter perched on a stone wall talking with an elderly, impeccably-dressed gentleman.

"David, my assistant, Jax. Jax, David Aylesbury."

"Hello, my dear." The man stood in true southern gentleman style to greet her. "I understand from Streeter that you have quite a talent for investigation."

Jax glanced in surprise toward her boss, a man not known for compliments. "Well, I'm glad to hear he thinks so," she said.

"Don't go swelling her head," Streeter muttered.

"Have a seat." Grayson indicated a chair for her and sat down himself. "So, what have you got for us?"

"Well." She looked at Streeter, who nodded his go-ahead. "We, er, Streeter—put some bugs in place earlier today just to see what we might pick up. Including in, uh…" She glanced again at Streeter, unsure how much to disclose.

"Your office, Mike," he said.

"You bugged my office?" An executive eyebrow arched.

Jax cringed.

"I did," Streeter replied, nonchalantly.

"You might have told me, don't you think?"

"Just did. Go on, Jax."

And that, appeared to be that.

Jax swallowed and went on. "So, I was checking the tapes before I headed out and heard this." She hit play on the digital recorder.

The three men leaned in to listen. The sound of a door opening and closing, followed by footsteps crossing the room. A slight jangle of what sounded like keys followed by the quiet click of a lock and the sound of a drawer sliding open.

"What the—?" Michael said.

Streeter held up a finger to shush him.

A rustle of files, then a softly whispered 'Shit!' The sound of a drawer sliding closed. Then another drawer opening, a repeat of rustling files, and closing. The sequence was repeated four times—four file drawers worth—followed again by the brief jangle of keys and the click of a lock turning. Footsteps. A door opening and closing. Then silence.

David Aylesbury turned to Michael. "I assume you have a locked file cabinet in your office?"

Grayson's face was grim. "I do."

"And the designs to the new military plane—?"

"On a secure laptop usually kept locked in that cabinet, at least until I retrieved it this morning as soon as we got back."

"What time was this?" Streeter asked Jax.

She checked her notepad. "Two-thirty-three p.m."

"Thank God, we got there first," Michael said.

David checked his watch. "Three hours ago. Whoever it was is long gone by now."

"I can pull up who was in the building at that time," Streeter said. "Employees have to input their PIN to enter the building after hours—evenings and weekends. It's a starting point."

"It is indeed," David said. "And, while I am sure your hackers are very talented, Streeter, I do know some I expect are a little more familiar with Russian cyber-spying techniques. Why don't I call in a few favors and see what we can find out about that server?"

"Delighted to clear that particular playground for you and your friends," Streeter said.

David Aylesbury turned back to Grayson. "Michael, if you don't mind, I think I'll take a rain check on dinner and see if I can get this project underway."

'Of course. We appreciate your help more than you know."

Streeter rose with him and Jax followed suit.

"I need a minute with Mike," Streeter said. "Can the two of you wait for me outside? Won't be long."

"Sure," Jax answered. "Mr. Grayson, thank you for your hospitality.

He gave her a wry smile. "Half a drink isn't much in response to all the work you're doing for me. Maybe when this is all over, I can at least spring for a celebratory dinner."

"We shall hold you to that." David took her arm and looped it through his own as if he were escorting the Queen Mother into a state dinner. He winked at her. "In the meantime, we shall entertain ourselves just fine," he said to Streeter. "Take your time."

****

Streeter waited until the two had gone, then turned to Michael. "Carlo managed to get those phone records on Annie and her grandmother, though we're paying him a pretty penny for the job."

Michael's gut clenched. "And?"

Streeter handed him the file. "I only had a chance to skim them, so feel free to review more carefully. But they go back three years and, according to Carlo, up until last week, there weren't any calls between Annie and her grandmother at all."

"None?"

"None."

"What happened last week?"

"Several calls started coming into Annie from her grandmother, none lasting more than thirty seconds. If I had to guess, given the consistent length, I'd say they went to voice mail. Then last week, there was one call from Eleanor's cell to the Office of the Public Defender. Can't say for sure she got connected on through to Annie, but the call lasted a couple of minutes, so...likely. And that's it."

"That's all? That's all the contact?"

"That's it. She may be Eleanor Barlow's granddaughter, but it looks like she really did cut ties with all things Barlow years ago. All evidence points away from her plotting with her evil grandmother to overthrow the kingdom of Grayson." He clapped the younger man on the shoulder. "Congratulations. May the two of you live happily ever."

Michael laughed, relief flooding him, bringing with it a lightness of heart he hadn't felt since he'd walked into that deposition room. "I'll take it," he said as his phone rang.

"Good. I'll let myself out," Streeter said, with a nod toward the ringing phone.

"Grayson," Michael said into his phone as he closed the door behind his chief of security.

"Um, hi. It's me, Annie." Pleasure shot through at her call, for the first time unaccompanied by any tempering concerns or wariness.

"Hello, you," he said. "Did you make it home yet?"

"I did, thanks. So, um, I'd like to talk to you about some things."

"Things?"

"I went to see James today. And then Jonathan came over and we talked. And...well, we have a proposal about the case for you to consider."

"A proposal about the case. You and Jonathan." And here he'd thought she was calling because she wanted to see him. He ran his fingers through his hair. "Sure." Because why wouldn't he want to hear more about the punk who shot him? "Can the two of you come out here? Streeter still has me in lockdown."

"Oh."

He sensed her hesitation. "I don't bite, Ms. O'Toole." The words brought a very different image to mind, and his tone softened. "At least not unless you want me to."

He heard her breath catch and smiled.

"Um, it'll just be me, if that's okay. Jonathan has to follow up on some other—"

"Things?"

"Right."

Michael smiled. The evening was looking up. "That works. I'll text you the address. Oh, and bring your ID. The guards will need to confirm you are who you say you are before they'll let you past the gate."

"Of course they will," she said, a touch of her anti-rich-people-snark seeping through.

He laughed and hung up.

Chapter Twenty-Two

"Ms. O'Toole?"

"Yes," Annie answered, passing the guard her driver's license.

The uniformed man inspected it, compared it to her face, and then handed it back. "Mr. Grayson is expecting you. Straight down the lane."

"Thank you."

The exchange was brief and the guard polite, but it was a rude reality check just the same. This is the way rich people lived, behind locked gates with security guards to keep out the riffraff. No friends dropping by unannounced with a bag of donuts here. Visitors had to be pre-approved, added to the list of acceptable admittees, and produce ID for inspection and verification. Even if things could work out with Michael, did she really want to go back to that life? She sighed. Damn it! Why couldn't her prince just be a regular guy? Somebody normal, who didn't live in a fricking gated castle.

With a little less enthusiasm, she navigated the lane the guard had said would take her to the house. Her first impression of the Grayson magnate's choice of abode—a stone and timber house that seemed to grow out of the land on which it sat—was surprisingly positive. But before she had a chance for more than a glance, the front door opened, and Michael walked out, dressed in jeans and a Henley pullover. She realized she'd never seen him in anything but a suit or a tux. He looked good in jeans. Really good.

He opened her car door. "Hi," he said. "Long time, no see."

She swallowed. "Yeah, well. I'd make some crack about our one-night-stand not quite working out that way, but that would just be awkward, so—"

"And I'd say how much I hate that, but I do so hate to lie," he said, with a smile. He extended a hand and helped her out of the car. Then he just stood there, holding her hand in his, looking at her.

"What?" she finally said, unable to stand the heat that gaze ignited.

"Just looking," he said. "I like looking at you. Sorry. Please, come in." He led her up the steps to the house and opened the door for her. "After you."

"Said the spider to the fly?"

"Is that what it feels like?" his voice was soft as she moved past him through the door.

She cleared her throat. "A little."

"And yet, I'm never quite sure who is the spider and who is the fly in this relationship."

This relationship. Why the hell did those simple words have to be so complicated when it came to the two of them?

"Can I get you anything to drink?" He gestured toward his own glass on an end table. "I've already started, I'm afraid."

"I'll pass, thanks. Still recovering from the last one."

"Ah, yes. Sorry. Seems like so much longer ago than just this morning."

"Not to my head, it doesn't."

"Water it is. Sparkling or still?"

"Sparkling, if you have it," she said.

"Make yourself comfortable. I'll be right back."

At least there was no 'ringing for a servant' she noted. She set her purse down on the desk anchoring one corner of the wide room and sank into one of the soft leather chairs. His home was gorgeous, but not in the cold don't-touch-anything style with which she'd grown up. This place invited touch. Cashmere throws in the colors of sunset were draped casually over buttery soft leather seating. One wall was lined with bookcases open to the world without a locked glass door in sight. A few books were even stacked on their sides or tucked in on top of their brethren. A home, rather than a gallery. Without thinking, she slipped out of her shoes and curled her feet beneath her.

"Here you go," Michael said, returning. He handed her a glass of sparkling water over ice, then glanced down at her shoes on the floor and her legs curled beneath her. He cleared his throat.

"Oh, sorry," she said embarrassed, immediately putting her feet back on the floor and reaching for her shoes. "I didn't—"

He stopped her with a touch of his hand. "You're fine. Truly. This is not Barlow House. Be comfortable."

A frisson of warmth ran through her, both at his touch and his insight. "Thanks. It's lovely," she said, meaning it.

He accepted the compliment with a nod, then settled into a chair across from her. "So." He lifted an eyebrow. "Things."

She swallowed. It was an eyebrow, for God's sake.

"Yes. *Things*. I went to see James today to tell him I had to get off his case. You know, because of the... merger issue."

Michael cocked his head. "This business venture is looking better all the time."

Now she was the one clearing her throat. "Anyway, when I told him Harrison was dead, he started talking for the first time since I've known him."

"So, he was working with Harrison," Michael said flatly.

"No. No!" Annie quickly backtracked. She filled Michael in on the entire story relayed to her by James. When she finished, he sat in silence for a moment, staring out the door toward the terrace.

"So, Peter is in this, too," he finally said.

"Well, I don't know that. At least not as far as the shooting. He might have just been buying drugs there. But he does seem to be Harrison's link to Adams, who in turn, was the link to the guy who did shoot you."

"And you believe him—your guy?"

She nodded. "I do. It all fits. Jonathan is tracking down Wayne's mugshot for you to look at. He has the same gold tooth James does. They got them done together. And he's left-handed, which James is not. But most of all, it's all those gifts for Mrs. Joiner to buy his silence. It's not like James had any way of fingering Harrison. But as long as he kept quiet, they'd never get to Little Wayne who could."

Michael swirled the golden liquid in his glass. "It is logical," he said at last.

"I don't expect you to take my word for the gifts. We thought you might want to send your Mr. Jacobson out with one of us to meet with James's mom and see them firsthand."

"I'm actually not worried about you lying to me, Annie—" he gave her a rueful grin—"hard as that may be for you to believe, given our recent history. But I do suspect Nicoletti will need an independent confirmation."

"Of course," she said, trying to ignore the warmth his words ignited. "And, if you do get that confirmation and if the picture of Little Wayne persuades you that you could have been mistaken in your ID of James—?"

"Then I'll call Nicoletti and tell him to drop the charges. I have no desire to put an innocent kid away for something he didn't do." He sighed. "Frankly, at this point, I don't even care that much about getting the punk who did do it. It's the ones behind it I want to string up by their…thumbs."

She wanted to punch her fist in the air and scream 'YES!' at Michael's willingness to let the case against James go, but managed to hang on to a semblance of lawyerly composure.

"The challenge is going to be getting Adams without pinning a target on James. There are too many guys on Adams payroll who might decide payback is in order. I don't want to put him back in jeopardy just when he might finally be getting out from under this."

"Oh, I think Peter can take that particular fall," Michael said, his words edged with a tinge of bitterness.

"You think he'll talk?"

"Peter is many things: smart, creative, a good PR guy. But he is also a coward. At the first glimpse of trouble, he'll fold like a card table with a bad leg. Trust me on that." He stood up. "I need to make a call.

Please, check out the view. It's lovely at sunset," he said, indicating the terrace doors. "I won't be long."

He disappeared somewhere within the house, so she took his advice and wandered out onto the terrace overlooking the Mississippi River below. He hadn't been exaggerating about the view. Taking a deep breath, she felt her shoulders release a notch for the first time since she flipped on that newscast and saw Michael's picture over Tina Hoff's shoulder. Since that moment, a lifetime's worth of crazy-making events had come racing down the pike, one after the other. And it felt like she'd been holding her breath for all of it.

She didn't hear his step behind her, but suddenly he was there, his hands on her shoulders.

She shivered at his touch, despite the warm August air.

He let his hands slide down her arms, then slipped them round her waist and gently pulled her back against him. "I've loved that river since I was a kid. You know, I started out wanting to be a riverboat captain."

"A Tom Sawyer fan?"

"More Huck Finn. Spent a couple of summers working as a deckhand on a tug crew thanks to Mr. Clemens. Fell in love with boats and joined the Navy as soon as I turned eighteen." He chuckled. "My mom was not happy."

"Is she still alive?" Annie asked, trying to picture a teenaged Michael Grayson.

"She is. My dad, too. I think he's more to blame for my love of the river than old man Clemens, though. He had this old fishing boat and whenever the weather was decent, we'd go out exploring."

"You grew up around here?" For some reason, that

surprised her.

"About 60 miles downriver, in Ste. Genevieve. My folks still live there, in the same house I grew up in. I offered to buy them a new place, but they weren't interested. They're dug in."

"You really didn't grow up with money?"

He gave her a squeeze. "I told you. No silver spoon for me. Unlike you, I might add." He dropped a kiss behind her ear, sending shivers down her back. "So maybe I'm the one who should be holding your wealthy upbringing against you?"

"Oh, I think you can check that off your to-do list," she said with a wince. "You did an excellent rendition of that playlist at my grandmother's dinner party."

"You made it a hell of a lot harder looking the way you did in that dress slit up to your thigh."

Annie grimaced. "Can we never mention that dress again, please? Not one of my finer moments."

Michael chuckled and slipped her glass out of her hand. Setting it on the rock wall, he turned her in his arms. "It's been a bit complicated getting here, hasn't it?"

Annie wanted more than anything to just savor the moment, but she couldn't stop herself. "And where is 'here' exactly?"

"Never one to settle for vagaries, are you, Counselor?"

"Sorry. Occupational hazard."

He sighed in mock weariness. "Hazards of falling for a lawyer, I suppose." He wrapped a finger in her curls. "'Here' is just you and me. No secrets. No hidden agendas. No criminal case or conflicts of interest between us. Neither my money or yours—" he gave her a pointed look— "between us. Just us. Enjoying one another. Tonight... and for the foreseeable future."

God, she so wanted to believe that was possible.

He bent and pressed his lips to hers. This kiss was slow and lingering, rich and luxurious, like sinking into a warm bath. The last remnants of tension drained from her limbs and the knots in her stomach dissolved. A sigh escaped her mouth into his and she felt him smile against her lips.

He ran his palms up the sides of her torso, stopping achingly just below her breasts. She shifted, willing him to go higher. She felt the smile deepen.

"Do you want something, Counselor?" he murmured, his lips still on hers. His thumbs moved to circle her nipples. "Maybe this?"

She shivered again. "Mm-mmm..." she answered, revelling in the spiralling sensations his touch ignited.

He lifted his head, a gleam in those grey eyes. "As I recall, you found this a bit... distracting...before."

Her eyelids fluttered closed. "I don't have any decisions to make tonight." Then she opened one eye and squinted. "Do I?"

He grinned. "Depends. How do you feel about exhibitionism?"

Both eyes flew open. "What?"

"Not a large audience, by any means." He turned her toward the river where a tugboat was rounding the bend, pushing a barge upriver. "And they probably won't even look up this way. But still... might be fun to give a show to any who might be."

****

And that's how Annabel O'Toole, Counselor-at-Law, wound up wearing only her jewelry on Michael

Grayson's terrace, giving a full-frontal eyeful to anyone on the mighty Mississippi who might happen to glance up. She couldn't believe she'd let him talk her into this, though actually there had been a lot more touching than talking involved.

The summer evening air kissed her skin, and she had to admit it was erotic, this being *au naturel* in the great outdoors. Michael stood behind her, nuzzling her neck as his hands danced deliciously across her bare skin. It felt like both a caress and a claiming, given their potential audience. An audience that was purely theoretical and highly unlikely, which was the only reason she'd let him get her into this position.

"Any guy looking this way has a hard-on for you right now," he murmured in her ear. "You know that, right?"

"That's an image that should totally creep me out," she said, leaning back into him, savoring all the little fires his touch set off as his hands moved over her skin.

"But it doesn't, does it?" he murmured. "It turns you on. And that turns me on."

He kicked her legs farther apart, like a cop getting ready to bend a suspect over the front of a car. Okay, maybe he was a little bit right. The risk of being seen did add a little extra adrenaline to the potent brew already running through her system.

One hand slipped between her legs as the other encircled her throat. "You know, even when I felt like strangling you, I wanted you."

Her pulse kicked up another notch. His touch was light, and she had no fear he would tighten that grip around her throat—either in play or anger—but there was something about how easily his fingers spanned that vital, vulnerable part of her that weirdly turned her on. What the hell was that about? Some vestigial go-for-the-biggest-baddest-alpha-male-in-the-pack' biological thing?

Suddenly, he pulled his hand from between her legs and wrapped his arm tightly around her waist. The hand on her throat moved to her chin and slowly turned her head.

"Say hello to your audience, Counselor."

Annie opened her eyes. The tugboat was just below them, and a line of figures stood on the deck, looking up directly at them.

"Fuck, fuck, fuck!" She recoiled in on herself—or would have if he hadn't anticipated her response and already locked her in place.

"Oh, no, Counselor," he said, amusement lacing his words as he tightened his hold. "You already signed on to this show, remember? No running out once the performance has begun. That would be rude."

"Easy for you to say," she hissed. "You're hidden behind me."

He chuckled. "Honey, it's not me they want to see. I'm just the one they all want to be."

Then he grasped her wrists and pulled her arms out wide to either side, until she was standing spread-eagle in front of him, like DaVinci's Vitruvian Man—her naked glory fully exposed to the strangers on the boat below.

Oh, my God. A hot blush flamed her face and every other part of her anatomy.

"What are you doing?" she whispered furiously, trying to pull her arms free to cover herself.

It was a futile endeavor.

"You're the star of the show," he answered, clearly enjoying the moment. "You should take a bow."

And he bent her forward from the waist in an elaborate stage bow like she was his personal sex puppet. The muffled sound of cheers wafted up from the water.

He laughed at the elicited response and another flush of hot embarrassment rose from her toes to her curls.

"Sounds like you're a hit, darling," he said, pulling her back upright. He crooked her arms up behind his neck, a position that thrust her breasts even more front and center, in case any of the men below hadn't gotten a good enough look the first time. "Lock your hands and keep them there," he said, his breath tickling her ear as one hand traced a lazy line from her throat to her pubic region. "And stop worrying. They're too far away to see who you are. Relax and enjoy."

He slipped his fingers inside her, slowly, one at a time, until she was filled with the delicious pressure of his intimate intrusion. Then he began to move them, curling into and caressing her G-spot with an expertise that sent her divinely constructed nervous system spiralling. She gasped.

"Open your eyes," he ordered. "Watch them watching you."

She did. Her breath hitched at the row of silent figures below, heads all tilted upward. At her. Oh, God. What was she doing? A deeply rooted flight response warred with the growing arousal coursing through her, but she was going nowhere with Michael's hands on and in her. His fingers began moving faster and harder, harder and faster, feeding the fire on the edge of enveloping her. She tightened her clasped hands behind his neck and hung on, riding the sensations racing from her center to every nerve ending in her skin. The muscles in her legs began to twitch. The hand not driving her to madness locked back on her throat and controlled the direction of her gaze, holding her head in place facing the men on the boat.

"Those men are going to watch you come, Counselor." he whispered, his breath hot against her ear, his fingers drilling even deeper into her. "Aren't they?"

She was beyond speech, gasping for breath, as her body began to tremble uncontrollably.

"Aren't they?" he repeated, as his fingers practically lifted her off the ground.

She nodded, frantic for the release that hovered just out of reach.

"Let them hear you scream," he said hoarsely.

She was still trembling from the orgasm that had just blown through her when he pressed her down over the patio table, flattening her breasts against the warm mosaic tile. She grabbed hold of the edges of the table as he kicked her legs apart and started rubbing himself across her weeping opening, eliciting another series of gasps and jerks and *oh, God's* as the spiral began building all over again.

Suddenly he froze. "Shit! I don't have a condom out here."

The words registered through her haze. She opened her eyes and lifted her head from the table. The men below were still there, still watching. Several gripped the railing.

"I'm on birth control," she panted. "And STD-free.

You?"

His laughter was strained as he fought to maintain control. "Same. So, we're good?"

"We're good."

She gasped, and he rammed them both home.

In case any of the men on the boat hadn't heard her scream the first time, they got a second chance.

Chapter Twenty-Three

Michael once again opened his eyes to sunlight and the scent of warm spice, but this time, the woman he would forever associate with that scent hadn't disappeared with the dawn. Instead, she lay curled next to him, her soft skin warm against his own. He brushed a golden red curl from her eyes and dropped a kiss on the tiny mole beside her mouth that had been flirting with him since he'd first laid eyes on this remarkable woman. Annie warm and naked and asleep in his bed was a snapshot he was more than delighted to add to his ever-expanding mental photo album of Annie O'Toole.

He kissed her eyelids. She sighed and shifted in her sleep. He blew, ever so gently, into her ear. She burrowed into her pillow. He slowly traced a fingertip southward toward the soft swell of her breast. She shivered and opened her eyes.

"Hi, sleepyhead," he said with a smile.

"Mmmm," she murmured in response, her eyes fluttering closed again. He slipped his hand under the sheet and spread his fingers across her belly. She stretched like a cat, arching her back and extending both arms overhead. He enjoyed the show. Immensely.

She curled back into him and whispered, "Coffee."

He grinned and ran his fingertips down her arm. "And here I was thinking we might start the day with something a little…stronger?"

With some effort, she propped herself up on her elbows, shaking the curls back out of her face. Her eyes blinked slowly, and she made a half-hearted attempt to cover a yawn with the back of one hand before sinking back down onto her pillow and muttering something he couldn't make out.

"What was that?" he asked, leaning in closer to hear her.

"Ain't nobody gettin' nothin' until I get coffee," she muttered. "Your call, sailor."

His feet hit the floor.

****

Streeter swung into the circle drive and parked next to the little blue bug. Looked like Mike hadn't wasted any time following up with Annie after getting his report of the night before. He climbed out and was headed to the door when a squeal of laughter came from the direction of the lake, just over the rise. He hesitated, then glanced at his watch.

"Sorry, Mike," he muttered. "Playtime is over."

It was a lovely summer morning, and the happy couple was taking advantage of it. Clothes were strewn about the deck and even from this distance, he could see that what may have begun as a morning swim was quickly turning into something more intimate. He whistled loudly. A scream was followed by a splash.

"What the hell are you doing here?" Mike bellowed.

"Thanks for the love, bro," he yelled back. "We need to talk."

"Well, your timing sucks."

"Yep. Sorry. Some of us have to work for a living."

"Well, hell." More splashing. "Go get some coffee.

We'll be there in a minute."

It was closer to ten before the front door opened. One set of footsteps ran up the stairs. The heavier ones headed for the kitchen and then out to join him in the great room.

"Morning, boss." He lifted his mug in acknowledgement. "Looks like lockdown agrees with you."

"It was about to agree with me quite a bit more before you showed up," Michael grumbled, plopping into a chair and taking a sip from his own mug. "What's up?"

"Got a list."

"Get on with it then."

"First, I'm going to send Jax with Annie to see the Joiner kid's mom this afternoon. My plate's a little full and she does the sympathy bit better than I do anyway."

"I'm shocked," Michael said with a grin. "And sure that will be fine. I'm more concerned with what to do about Peter."

"Number Two on my list, as it happens."

"You think he's the other link with the Russians?"

"If he is, he's another amateur skating round the edges like Harrison. He just doesn't have the access to get what they'd want. I talked to David about it. Neither of us see the Russians expanding the pool of fringe players, unless Harrison brought him in without their knowledge, which is possible. I had Carlo go ahead and pull his bank records. If we find a lot of unexplained deposits, that could point toward Russian cooperation. But I suspect it's more likely he was just buying drugs from the good reverend and thought that's what he was hooking Harrison up for as well."

Michael lowered his cup of coffee. "I don't know. He was the one there when Joiner—or whoever—" Michael caught himself—"shot me. He chose the place we went. Kinda feels like he and Harrison might have arranged that encounter in tandem."

"I'm not ruling it out. But it's also possible he just told Harrison where the two of you would be. Harrison may have sucked at being a spy, but he was a pretty decent lawyer by all accounts. I imagine he could have found a way to work your plans into the conversation without arousing suspicion. Anyway, my thought is to approach Ashton without ever mentioning the Russians," he said. "Just confront him about his involvement with Adams's drug-dealing operations first and see what shakes loose. He's hardly the most stalwart of souls, so I think once the fruit starts falling, we just might get his laundry list of sins back to grade school."

"Looks like we have similar assessments of his backbone."

Streeter snorted. "Just sit through a meeting with the man and it's pretty obvious he has none. Still, I think I'll have better luck shaking him loose on my own. He thinks of you as the civilized executive. He harbors no such illusions about me."

Michael eyed him. "But you are a civilian now. Remember that."

"I know that. Not so sure our friend Peter knows I know that—and that just might be enough. You good with me setting up a meeting with him?"

"You're going to do this in his office?"

"I was thinking I'd call him down to your hangar. Lots of tools and shit out there to add... nuance... to our discussion."

Michael lifted an eyebrow but didn't argue. "Just don't kill him. We have enough shit going on without having to hide a body."

He laughed. "Think Annie would defend me?"

"Defend you from what?"

The lawyer in question was coming down the stairs. She wore a loose, colorful skirt and sleeveless shell that clung in all the right places. Her tousled red hair was damp and her feet were bare and he could absolutely see why his boss was smitten.

"Good morning, Ms. O'Toole," he said.

"Annie, please."

Her cheeks were a little rosy, but he couldn't tell if that was embarrassment or just the aftermath of her little romp with the boss in the lake. Either way, she wore it well.

"I was just reminding him not to kill anyone," Michael said. "He tends to get pissed off easily."

Annie plopped onto the arm of Michael's chair and took the coffee he was drinking out of his hand. "I feel your pain," she said, taking a sip. "I've been told I have the same problem."

"Great. I'm surrounded by assholes." Michael ruffled her hair and got up to go get himself a new cup of coffee. "Refill, Streeter?"

"No thanks, I'm good," he replied, suppressing a smile.

"Are you always on the job this early, Mr. Jacobson?"

"Streeter, please. And yes, I'm sorry to say I am. I just don't usually come knocking at Mike's door quite this early. My apologies for the interruption."

"Apology accepted," she murmured, green eyes twinkling over Mike's coffee.

Michael returned with another cup of coffee and retook his seat, looping one arm casually over Annie's leg. Streeter didn't think he'd ever seen the man this relaxed with a woman. Any woman. Ever. It made his crusty old heart glad.

"Next?" Michael said.

"I got the list of folks signed into the building yesterday when our secret someone made their little visit to your office."

"Wait," Annie said, "what happened?"

"We didn't get to that part last night." Michael kissed her. "I think you were distracting me."

Streeter cleared his throat. "Still here."

Michael grinned. "Sorry. I'll fill you in later," he said to Annie and turned back to him. "So, what did you find? Who was in the building?"

"Only five employees logged in. But here's the punchline. One of them was Harrison Stewart."

"What? He's not dead?" Annie said, her face filled with confusion.

"Oh, he's dead all right," Streeter affirmed. "But somebody used his PIN to get into the executive offices yesterday."

Michael sat back in his chair. "The Russians?"

"We can't rule that out. But whoever this was chose to go in on a weekend afternoon when others were in the building. If the entry had been in the middle of the night, I would have said absolutely it was the Russians. But this? Doubtful. David agrees. He thinks it's more likely our inside employee who just didn't want a record they'd been there."

"Like using a dead man's name doesn't send up red flags?"

"Only if somebody's checking those logs, which generally isn't done unless there's a problem. And even if it is discovered, it's a flag that can't be traced back to them."

"Well, pull his bloody access codes," Michael growled, his frustration palpable. "Christ. Even dead, this man is screwing with me."

"Already done. So, my plan is to contact each of the other four who were there yesterday and tell them you found a security key card on the floor outside the executive office suite when you popped by to pick up some papers last night. You've asked me to make sure it gets back to whoever lost it."

Michael frowned. "I'm not following."

"I ask each of them if the lost card is theirs—"

"Which it won't be because there is no lost security key card," Annie said, catching on.

"Exactly. At which point, I ask for their help figuring out whose it might be. 'The computer froze up before the log-in report finished and I only have these four names, even though it shows a total of five check-ins. Did they see who else was around so I can be sure to check with them too?'"

Michael grinned. "You're a sneaky bastard, Jacobson."

"Well, we'll see if it works. Moving on. David's super-hackers were successful in gaining access to the server overnight."

"Shit, Streeter—talk about burying the lead! That's wonderful. What did they find?"

"Nothing yet, which is why it's number four.

They're in the process of trying to retrieve what's already been conveyed. It'll be a bit still before we know if they're successful. David's question is what you want them to do then—leave it active and continue to monitor communications or disable it? He says they can make it look like an accidental malfunction if you want it taken out."

Michael didn't hesitate. "I want it taken out. Fried to a fucking crisp, if possible. I don't want to risk those plans getting through."

"Okay then. That's it." Streeter stood. "Oh, Annie, is it okay if I send my assistant with you to Mrs. Joiner's this afternoon? I've got a pretty full day."

"Of course."

"Her name is Jax. I'll have her call you and coordinate."

"That'll work. Thanks."

"Later," he said and let himself out.

****

Michael tugged on Annie, pulling her off the arm of the chair into his lap. "You almost got a chance for another round of exhibitionism, Counselor." He slid his hand beneath her skirt, his pace luxurious and excruciating. "And while I thoroughly enjoyed our show last night, I'm not so into sharing with anyone I actually know, or who knows you."

"I still can't believe you did that," she said.

He grinned at her with that wicked, bad-boy grin of his. "We did that. And you thoroughly enjoyed it."

She blushed. "Okay, maybe a little."

He lifted an eyebrow. "The screams were just for show, were they?"

She punched him on the shoulder. "Not that,

moron. That, obviously, I enjoyed a lot."

He laughed and nuzzled her hair. "As did I—and our audience—so all is well with the world."

"Just don't expect it to happen again," she said. "Despite last night—and okay, this morning—I'm not actually an outdoor sex type of girl. Or an outdoor-anything type, actually."

He nipped at her neck. "No camping trips growing up?"

"You've met my grandmother. What do you think?" Annie murmured, leaning her head back to give him better access. Suddenly, she started up. "Oh, wait, I forgot to give Streeter my number for Jax."

Michael pulled her back down. "He has it."

"He does?"

"He does. I gave it to him." He caught her ear lobe between his teeth, and she melted back against his chest. His fingertips drew lazy circles on her skin, each brush a micro-movement higher on her leg.

"Was your dad an outdoors kind of guy?" He brushed a kiss across her lips.

"I don't know," she finally said, when she could gather her thoughts sufficiently. "I never knew my father."

"Oh," Michael replied softly, looking up at her. "Sorry. I forgot."

His fingers continued to caress her skin, and the comment floated by, marinated in the smoky haze of sexual arousal, but something about it flickered and eventually caught her attention. She backtracked, lifting her head to look at Michael.

"What do you mean you 'forgot'?"

"Hmm?" came the response, his mouth otherwise

occupied on her neck.

Annie stilled his hand, and his mouth followed. "We never talked about my dad."

"We didn't?"

"No, we didn't." She sat up. "I never talk about my dad with anyone. Well, anyone but Jonathan. So how did you know I never knew him?"

Michael shifted uncomfortably. "Well, to tell the truth, I did a little investigating. Or Streeter did. At my request."

The sexual haze evaporated.

"You had me investigated?"

"Like your grandmother hasn't been investigating me?" His defensiveness was palpable.

"My grandmother is not me. Investigate her all you like, but you had *me* investigated?" She swung her legs around and pushed herself off his lap. "What, do you have a file on me in your office somewhere?"

He was silent.

"Oh, my God, you do. You have a file on me? So, what'd you do?" she prodded. "Have me followed? Interview my neighbors? Talk to my co-workers? Dig into my transcripts?"

Silence again.

"Holy shit. You did!"

"I didn't know who you were or what you were up to. Whether this whole anonymous one-night-stand thing"—he made a vaguely circular motion— "was real or some kind of set-up." His tone was wary, defensive.

She narrowed her eyes. "When?"

"When what?"

"When did you have me investigated?"

"Well, an investigation spans time. It's a little here

and a little there as things are uncovered."

Now he had the audacity to mansplain to her?

"Defense lawyer here, remember? I investigate cases all the time. My question is when did you start investigating me?" She bit off the 'asshole' that ended that sentence in her brain.

He ran one hand through his hair. "When I found out you were representing the kid who shot me."

She supposed that was fair, though it still rankled. And why the hell hadn't he told her about it? "When did you end it?"

"End?"

"Yes, end as in stop, quit, finish investigating me?" Silence again.

"You haven't ended it?" She stared at him, incredulous. "He's still investigating me?"

"In my defense—"

"There is no defense," she snapped. "You invited me to Johannson's fundraiser, flirted with me, kissed me, all while you were having me investigated? Was someone in the bushes taking pictures of us so you'd have your own little stash of blackmail with which to destroy my career just in case?"

"If you will recall"—his words were now clipped, formal, and frustrated—"I found out all of yesterday that you were Eleanor Barlow's granddaughter. A not-insignificant fact, by the way, and not a discovery likely to motivate me or anyone with half a brain to pull the plug on an investigation of your involvement in her merger scheme. Within hours of that lovely discovery, I learned that my company is the target of Russian espionage, and someone is very likely trying to kill me, so forgive me if I haven't stopped to send Jacobson a memo on the appropriate time to wind down this particular assignment."

She kind of had to give him that. But she sure as hell wasn't ready to let him off the hook. Not by a long shot. "When was his last report?"

"What do you mean?"

"You know exactly what I mean. I work with investigators all the time, remember? They do investigations and then prepare reports about the results of those investigations. When was the last time you got a report from Streeter about me?"

Michael took a slow breath, closed those beautiful grey eyes, and said, "Last night."

For a nanosecond, there was silence.

Then Annie breathed, "You son of a bitch." Her mind raced and she began pacing the room. "That's why Streeter drove to Chicago instead of flying up with you, isn't it? He wasn't up there on some 'organization-wide investigation' you weren't up to speed on. He followed Carter and me up there, didn't he?"

Michael sat silent.

"Didn't he?" She practically screamed the words.

"Yes." He cleared his throat. "When he ran the plates on Carter's car, it came back registered to Barlow Industries. I had just been invited to come discuss a business deal with Barlow Industries, so yes, finding out you had an unexpected connection there was worthy of follow-up in Streeter's mind."

"So, he was sitting outside my house just watching me? He had to have been, to be there when Carter arrived."

Michael didn't say a word.

"For how long? How long has that man been

following me around and spying on my every movement?"

Michael didn't reply quickly enough.

"Answer me!"

He ran his hands over his face. "I don't know. I leave the details of Streeter's investigations to him. I just asked him to find out what he could so I could figure out if you were who and what you said you were or if there was some kind of subterfuge at play."

She flashed to Michael lifting her chin to meet his kiss in her bedroom at Barlow House.

'I may not know fully who you are, Counselor, but I will figure it out. It's what we princes do.'

Oh, God. She'd thought it so romantic, so sweet, the beacon of hope that they might have a future after all. But he was just waiting on his goddamn investigation results! Fury enveloped her. She grabbed a glass bowl off the coffee table and launched it at his head. He ducked. It sailed over the couch and crashed on the floor behind him, the sound of splintering glass filling the room. Before she could reach for anything else, Michael was up and wrapping her in a vise-tight bear hug.

"Annie, stop. Annie! Listen to me."

She fought him. "Get away from me, you bastard. Let me go!"

"Not until you listen to me."

"I've seen this play before, Mr. Grayson," she spat out. "This has been my entire life, and I will *not*, I will not go down that path again. Not with her, not with you, not with anyone. My life is *my* life." A sob caught in her throat and Michael's grip eased.

"Annie." His voice was soft now, placating.

"Don't." She pulled loose from him, and he let her. "Just don't."

"I'm crazy about you, don't you get that?" he said. "My gut has always told me you were exactly who you said you were, but I just needed to be sure I wasn't being played. You of all people have to understand that."

"I don't have to do anything but get the hell out of here." She snatched her purse off the desk, knocking a file of loose papers to the floor. She grabbed for them, catching a few mid-air as the rest floated to the floor. She was debating picking them up or letting His Royal Asshole deal with it, when she saw her phone number on the paper in her hand. Rows and rows of her phone number. She scooped up the rest of papers from the floor and began flipping through pages. Her phone records. Months—no years—of her phone records.

And she'd been worried about making sure Streeter had her phone number. '*He has it.*'

No shit.

She stood and threw the file at Michael's face. He didn't even flinch, just closed his eyes as the papers floated to the floor around him.

"Go to hell," she said and slammed the door behind her.

****

An hour later, Michael hadn't moved from the chair he'd dropped into as the door slammed closed on Annie and his future. In the far recesses of his mind, he vaguely registered the front door opening, followed by his housekeeper's shocked voice.

"Oh, my goodness. What happened?"

He lifted his head and looked at the carnage from

Annie's explosion. The fragments of shattered glass caught the sunlight streaming in through the terrace doors. Strewn papers carpeted the hardwood floor. Shrapnel digging into his heart. He closed his eyes and let his head fall back on the chair again.

"Annie," he said. "Annie happened."

"Annie?" repeated his housekeeper, sounding bewildered. "Who is Annie?"

He blew out an audible breath. "Just the love of my life, who I will probably never see again because I'm a suspicious, self-absorbed twit."

Silence settled over the room once again, eventually broken by the woman's matter of fact, "Well, I'll just get this glass cleaned up so nobody cuts themselves and then I'll sort those papers." She started for the utility room, then paused. "Can I… can I get you anything, sir?"

"A do-over would be nice. Can you arrange one of those for me, Mrs. C?'

She gave a soft sigh.

"Wouldn't life be lovely if we could, sir," she said, and went to collect the broom.

Chapter Twenty-Four

"Hey, you."

Myriam looked up from her keyboard at the familiar voice. Streeter Jacobson was a handsome man, no doubt about it. A woman would have to be blind not to notice and she certainly wasn't blind. Not that she would ever let Streeter know she noticed. Instead, she sniffed at the man's inappropriate informality as she always did, gave him a quick nod, and returned eyes and fingers to her computer.

"Mr. Grayson isn't here."

"Where's he off to this time?"

"If he'd wanted you to know, I imagine he'd have told you, now, wouldn't he?"

Streeter plopped, uninvited, into the chair in front of her desk. "I'm sorry about Harrison."

Her fingers slowed on the keyboard.

"I can't say I knew him all that well," Streeter said, "but he seemed like a good enough egg. Tough, checking out that way."

She blinked rapidly a couple of times. "He was a good man."

"Any word on services, yet?" Streeter asked, his gravelly voice gentler than usual.

She gave up any pretense of continuing to work and let her hands fall into her lap. "No. His children are scattered across the world—literally—so it will take a bit for them to coordinate something."

"Is there a wife?"

"Divorced. A couple of years ago."

Streeter nodded. "I know you worked with him more closely than I did. My condolences."

"Thank you. Was there…anything else I can do for you?"

"I just need to pick up a file I left on the boss's desk over the weekend. Got some new info to add. Kind of a lucky break he's not in. He gets a better report, and I don't have to confess I missed something first time round." He grinned. "Silver linings."

She looked away from the twinkle in his blue eyes. "Well, get on with it, then."

"Yes, ma'am." Streeter ducked into the CEO's office and soon reappeared with a thick file tucked under one arm. But instead of making his exit, he leaned against the door jamb and contemplated her.

"What?" she finally snapped.

"How old are you, Myriam?"

The man could be infuriating. She turned back to her laptop. "That is none of your concern, Mr. Jacobson."

"Oh, but it is."

She looked up, startled. "Why?"

"Because I'm kind of particular about the age span in the women I date."

Her back snapped straight of its own accord, indignation radiating from her core. How dare he openly insult her as too old to be worthy of his consideration? She opened her mouth to cut his oversized ego down to size, but he cut her off first.

"Too much of an age difference and we just don't

speak the same language, share the same history, have the same references, you know? I'm afraid you may be too young for me and that would be a disappointment indeed. So, I have to ask."

She stared at him open-mouthed a beat too long, then caught herself and snapped her mouth closed. Swinging her chair back round to her computer with an angry flourish, she replied, "We are not and will not be dating, Mr. Jacobson, so the query is an irrelevant one."

"Ah, but we might be. Haven't you thought about it? At least once?"

That was a question she was definitely not answering. "That would be inappropriate. Dating co-workers is never a good idea."

"No 'dipping the pen in company ink'?"

She blushed and hated herself for it. "A bit crass for my taste, but yes, that is the gist of it."

Unperturbed by her rejection, he reached down and scooped up her cell phone off her desk.

"What are you doing?" she demanded.

"Just adding my number to your contacts in case you change your mind."

He swiped and tapped, as she stuttered, "I-I already have your number."

"You have my work number."

He set the phone gently back in front of her, bending close enough she could smell his cologne.

"This one is my private number. Just in case you change your mind."

She snatched back the phone and dropped it in her desk drawer. "Good-bye, Mr. Jacobson."

He grinned wickedly. "For now, Myriam. For. Now." And strode out her door whistling, file in hand.

Damn that man. Discombobulated in spite of herself, she grabbed the coffee pot and headed to the kitchen. The half pot she'd made this morning was already gone and, with Grayson out all week, a long, boring afternoon stretched before her.

"Hey, Myriam." Julia, from HR, hoisted her own coffee pot with a grin. "Caffeine makes the world go round, right?"

"Mine, at least."

"Mine, too. Hey, did you get your key card back?"

"My key card?"

"Was it not yours?" At Myriam's blank look, she went on. "Jacobson, the chief of security guy? He called this morning and said somebody dropped a security key card outside Mr. Grayson's office yesterday. Apparently, he stopped by last night for something and found it. Anyway, Jacobson was checking with the folks who came in yesterday to see if it belonged to anyone."

Myriam's blood turned cold.

"He was having trouble with the log-in report freezing up on him again. We've really got to upgrade some of these old systems, you know?" She finished filling her pot. "All yours," she said, gesturing toward the sink. "Anyway, yours must have been one of the names that got cut off because it wasn't on the list, so I told him you were here too. He said he'd check with you. I guess he found whoever it belonged to first."

"I guess so," Myriam said.

"Catch ya later," Julia said and headed back down the hall.

Back in her office, Myriam's mind was in overdrive. If Streeter had run that report, he would have seen Harrison's log-in rather than her own. And he now knew from Julia that she'd been there, but not under her own name. Unless she'd gotten really lucky and Harrison's name was one of the ones left off. Streeter certainly hadn't seemed at all suspicious when he stopped in to pick up that file this morning, flirting with her in that obnoxious way of his just like he always did. But he hadn't asked her about the key card even after Julia had given him her name. Was that because it was all a ruse to identify her as the one logging in under Harrison's ID? Or simply because, as Julia said, he'd already identified the owner so there was no need to?

What to do, what to do? She drummed her fingers on the desk, her mind racing. If it was nothing and she bailed, she'd be abandoning a mission she'd worked on for years with nothing to show for it. On the other hand, if she was compromised, she needed to be bailing and bailing fast. She needed input. Which meant she needed to be somewhere other than here.

Her call was answered on the second ring, but not by Grayson.

"Why hello, Miss Myriam! It's Mrs. C. Saw your name come up on the boss's phone and thought I better pick up for him in case it was important."

She and Mrs. C, whose full name was something long and unpronounceable for Americans who couldn't be bothered to learn such things, had never met in person, but they often spoke on the phone when arranging things to be dropped off or picked up at Grayson's house. The woman was one of those chatty sorts who wore on Myriam's nerves.

"He's not around then?" she inquired.

"Went for a walk and forgot his phone. He's in a

right state this morning, that's for sure."

Myriam tensed. "What's wrong?"

"The old story. Love gone bad. He and his lady had a big falling out. I didn't even know he had a girl, did you?"

"Um, no." This was an unexpected twist. "I didn't."

"He's a private one, that. But when I got here this morning, they'd had a big row and he was moaning about losing the love of his life. He's got it bad for her, I'll tell you. I felt so bad for him. Annie, he called her."

"Annie. Annie O'Toole?"

"Dunno. He just called her Annie. Was beating up on himself for being a 'self-absorbed fool' and messing it all up."

"Well. I'm sorry to hear that."

"Me, too. He's a good man, Mr. Grayson. He deserves to be happy."

"He does. So, um, when he gets back, could you just let him know I need to head home early today? I have a workman coming by to fix a plumbing issue at the house."

"Oh, sure. Plumbers take forever to get, so you gotta go when one's available!"

"Indeed. Thanks for letting him know."

"No worries. I'll tell him as soon as he gets back."

Myriam hung up. It had to be Annie O'Toole. Myriam knew everyone in Grayson's personal address book and the only Annie was Annie O'Toole. It was Annie O'Toole whose calls he'd instructed her to always put through, no matter what he was doing. And Annie O'Toole for whom he'd had her arrange the extra ticket to the senator's fundraiser. She almost laughed aloud at the irony. Grayson had fallen for the lawyer defending the kid Harrison had been bribing to take the rap for shooting him. And now she'd dumped him to boot.

Her phone buzzed again, this time through her encrypted messaging app. She grabbed it and ducked into Grayson's empty office.

"Why are you contacting me in the middle of the day when anyone could walk in?"

The answer was short, sweet, and in Russian. "Our server is screwed."

"What? What do you mean?"

"I mean destroyed. Ruined. Worthless."

"What the hell happened?"

"Unclear. They tell me there was a malfunction that caused damage beyond repair."

A chill ran down her spine. "Malfunction or sabotage?"

"Hard to say."

She had always trusted her gut and her gut was screaming this wasn't another random coincidence. There were too many of them, one right after the other: The security key card. The server. And Grayson's high security laptop moved from where he always kept it. She'd watched him put it away dozens of times and now suddenly it was gone. She'd assumed he'd taken it to work on at home since he was out all week, though he'd never allowed it to leave company premises before, but now—

"I—"

She suddenly remembered Streeter taking her phone 'to give her his private number.' Like hell. He'd done something to her phone. He was probably listening to her call right this very moment.

"I have to go," she said and hung up.

She had to get out and she had to get out now.

The question was how.

Chapter Twenty-Five

"Call for you on three, Annie. Sorry I didn't get a name. It's crazy up here today." It was crazy up there every day.

"That's fine," Annie said and punched the number three line. "O'Toole."

"Annie O'Toole?"

She didn't recognize the voice on the other end of the line. "Yes. Who is this?"

"This is Michael Grayson's assistant, Myriam."

Well, hell. Because her day hadn't gotten bad enough already.

"Mr. Grayson has some papers regarding your client's case—the one charged in the shooting he was involved in? He said it was urgent, but doubted you'd want to meet with him to get them." She gave an awkward laugh. "I'm not sure what's that about, exactly, but, um, I have the papers here at his office for you. He's not in today. Can you come get them? Unfortunately, I have to leave early, so it's a rather short window, but he did really want you to have them today."

It pissed Annie off that he'd expect her to just drop everything and run because he called—or had his bitch of an assistant call—but at least he was clear that she sure as hell wouldn't want to see him. And anyway, this wasn't about her. This was about James. She glanced at her watch.

"I can be there in about thirty minutes. Will that work?"

"It will. I'll meet you in the lobby. Our building can be a bit confusing to navigate."

Much like your phone system.

She grabbed her jacket, checked out at the front desk, and headed to her car, texting Jonathan as she walked. She'd asked him to take Jax to meet Mama Joiner. She figured Streeter's assistant was as involved in Michael's investigation of her as her boss and Annie wanted nothing to do with either of them. But the meeting must have gone well if Michael had already heard from them and was moving forward on James's case.

****

The lobby of Grayson's executive offices was pretty much what she'd expected. All grey and white, glass and steel. Modern. Expensive. Impersonal. Appropriate to a deceitful asshole CEO. She headed toward the reception desk, but a tall, slender, middle-aged woman intercepted her.

"Ms. O'Toole?"

"Yes."

"Hi. I'm Myriam."

The woman was all friendliness and smiles now, the exact opposite of her demeanor on the phone when Annie had been desperately trying to reach Michael before their deposition. Hypocrisy must be endemic at Grayson Aeronautics. Fuckers. She didn't bother to smile, but did accept the hand extended to her. "So. The papers?"

"This way." Myriam ushered her through a door

and down a long, rather austere hallway.

Why hadn't she just brought the papers to the lobby and saved them both some time? What, did she want to show off Grayson's fancy office suite? Like that was going to impress her? Or worse, was this some kind of bait-and-switch to get her in a room with Grayson himself? She ground her teeth. If he had the nerve to try that, the next thing she threw might be the man himself, right through his executive plate glass window.

"Look—" she started to say.

"This is it."

Myriam punched a code into a keypad. A buzzer sounded and Annie heard the click of the lock opening. Myriam stepped back and gestured for her to go ahead. Annie pushed open the door and found herself staring at an airplane. In a hangar.

"What the—?" Annie turned back to Myriam.

The woman held a gun.

Annie stumbled backward and Myriam pulled the door closed behind them. With her free hand, she yanked Annie's purse from her shoulder and tossed it against the wall.

"Into the plane." She gestured at the stairs with the gun.

"I—I don't do planes," Annie said, her throat tightening at even the thought. "Look, I don't know what you want from me, but I'm happy to give it to you. Anything. Just take it, my bag, whatever you want, just—"

Myriam grabbed her arm and twirled her around, shoving the muzzle of the gun hard into the middle of Annie's back.

"Move," she snarled.

Her legs shook, but Annie managed to make it up the stairs and into the plane. It was luxurious. Creamy leather seats. Wide-screen TV. It had to be Michael's. First, he'd broken her heart and now he was going to get her killed. On a fucking plane.

Myriam shoved her into one of the chairs and tossed her a roll of duct tape.

"Tape your ankles together."

"I don't—"

"And shut your mouth or I'll tape it, too."

Annie did as she was told. Turned out, a gun to her head upped her compliance factor exponentially. When she'd hobbled herself to the other woman's satisfaction, Myriam ordered her to toss the roll of tape onto another seat and fasten her seatbelt. Annie didn't think it was a safety concern.

"Hands above your head."

Moving behind her, Myriam grabbed Annie's wrists and duct-taped them together. Annie flashed to the only other instance in her life her wrists had been bound. That time had been erotic. This time, it was terrifying. Context really was everything.

Myriam shoved Annie's hands back down into her lap and then started winding duct tape around her arms and torso, securing her to the seat—until the only thing Annie could move was her head. Finally, she stepped back and eyed her handiwork with a satisfied smile.

"Lovely. You, Ms. O'Toole, are going to be my ticket out of here." And she pulled out her phone and snapped a picture.

****

Streeter took his time heading to the hangar.

Waiting built tension and he wanted Ashton tense. He took the opportunity to check in with Michael.

"Yeah." The voice he knew so well sounded bleak.

"You ok?" he asked.

"Nope. Not even close."

Streeter tensed. "What happened?"

"Annie found out we were investigating her. Following her. The phone records, all of it."

Ouch. "I'm guessing that didn't sit so well?"

"She threw the file at my head and told me to go to hell. After she threw a few other things, that is. Accused me of being her grandmother made over."

"Shit."

"Yeah. I don't think we're coming back from this one. She was… It was…bad." Despair permeated his every word.

"Man, that sucks. I'm so sorry."

Michael inhaled. It sounded like an effort. "Yeah, well. Not your fault. You were just doing what I told you to do."

Streeter considered whether to layer on the news that his trusted assistant was the one accessing the building under Harrison's PIN and decided it could wait. Hopefully in another hour, he'd have sorted Peter Ashton's role in this mess and could swing by for a full briefing and a night of commiseration over a bottle of scotch. Mike sounded like he could use both.

"Listen, I've got Peter waiting for me in your hangar, so I've gotta go. I'll come by after, ok?"

"Sure."

"See you then."

He had just hung up when Jax rang. He answered as he walked. "How was Mrs. Joiner?"

"Enjoying a whole lot of expensive gifts from that douchebag Adams. They're probably right about her son being bribed to take the fall. But Clark chewed me a new one over our investigation of O'Toole. Said it was 'a stab wound to her heart.' Not sure how she found out—and I didn't confirm anything—but thought you should know she knows."

Streeter sighed. "Already do. Apparently, she broke a bunch of shit at Michael's and then threw the file of her phone records at his head."

"Ouch."

He might have smiled at their mirror reactions if the situation had warranted any smiles. It did not.

"Yeah. Not quite the happily-ever-after he was going for," he said.

"Well... moving from lover's quarrels to international spy ring, we got another hit on the bug in Grayson's office. Listen to this." She didn't wait for an answer.

Myriam's voice came through loud and clear, barking at whoever was on the other end of the line for calling her at work where anyone might walk in, followed by a few short sentences in Russian.

Jax came back on the line. "So, definitely an inside Russian mole and someone with access to Grayson's office in the middle of the workday. Any ideas who it might be?"

"Oh, I know who it is." He recognized that irritated voice, even if he hadn't already zeroed in on Myriam with his lost security key card ruse. He filled Jax in. "Call David and bring him up to date. Tell him I'll be in touch later, but I want him to start ruminating on next steps."

"What about Grayson?"

"Going out there when I'm done with Ashton. I'll tell him then. He's got enough to deal with at the moment."

"Roger that. Good luck with Ashton."

He slipped his phone in his pocket and headed downstairs. He was about halfway down the hallway leading to the hangar when a shot rang out, followed by a scream.

He ran.

Chapter Twenty-Six

Michael had finished off his second bourbon and was considering a third when his phone dinged with a text message. He leaned across the couch and picked it up. It was from Myriam. He thumbed it open. It was a picture. A picture of Annie, green eyes wide and terrified, duct-taped to a chair. A chair on his plane.

His breath left him as time froze. The ring of his phone splintered the moment into jagged shards. Myriam's name popped up on his caller ID, as it had almost daily for years.

"Did you get my picture?" his assistant asked in her usual pleasant voice.

"What are you doing, Myriam?" He forced his voice to stay quasi-calm. Even as he asked the question, he was on his feet and moving to his gun case.

"The name is Mischa," she hissed.

He grabbed his keys and was out the door.

"Okay, Mischa. You've got my attention. What do you want?"

He blew through the gatehouse and was pushing ninety by the time he reached the highway.

"Money. And a pilot to fly me to Ecuador."

"Ecuador?"

"Russia would be nicer, but your plane won't go that far without refuelling, will it?"

It would, but he saw no reason to tell her that. He

swerved onto the shoulder to avoid a car passing a trash truck just in front of him, then back onto the road just in time to avoid a header into a bridge abutment.

"How much money?"

"Five million should do. A mere drop in the Grayson bucket."

"You have an account you want the money wired to?"

"I would have, if I'd had a bit more time to plan this getaway," she said bitterly, "but unfortunately that wasn't possible, so it will have to be cash. In suitcases. Rolling ones."

He grimaced. "Getting five mil in cash is going to take some time."

"You've got ninety minutes. For the money and the pilot."

"Let Annie go, and I'll fly you wherever you want."

She laughed. "Not happening. She's my passport out of here. And I want Jerry. Or Andrew."

No way he was letting that plane take off with Annie on it and him on the ground. "I'm not asking anybody else to fly with a gun to their head. You get me or you stay grounded."

There was a beat of silence, during which he held his breath.

"Whatever. You've got ninety minutes." The phone went dead.

His tires left a trail of rubber as he swerved into the executive parking lot and spotted Annie's car. How the hell had she gotten Annie to come out here? He jumped out and sprinted through the door. Streeter practically tackled him.

"It's Myriam. She's got Annie," Michael said, his words tumbling over one another.

"I know. I heard your whole conversation. I activated the remote listening feature on her phone after I saw Ashton lying at the bottom of the steps to your plane with a gunshot to the middle of his forehead."

"Fuck!"

"My reaction, exactly. So, here's what I'm thinking," Streeter was back in mission command mode. "First thing is to evacuate the building so nobody else gets caught in the crossfire. A suspected gas leak. Closing early for the day while we investigate it. I'll take care of that while you make your money arrangements. Jax can be your runner if you need somebody to go pick it up. I need you here."

"That works for me, because I'm not leaving."

Five minutes later, employees streamed out of the building to their cars, happy for an early release while the gas leak was tracked down.

Michael hung up his call to his banker and crossed back to Streeter. "They're getting the money together. They said they'd send an armored car out with it, but I'm not sure how quickly they'll get here. How fast does Jax drive?"

"Like a bat out of hell."

"Jax it is. Also get in touch with Jerry and Andrew. Tell them we're sorting a situation and if Myriam calls and asks them to take a flight this afternoon, they're unavailable."

Streeter looked at Michael. "You're going to be the one flying her, then?"

"If that plane leaves the ground with Annie on it, I'll be the one flying it."

Streeter nodded and reached for his phone. "Well, let's see what we can do to keep it from leaving the ground."

The wide semi-circular reception desk became their command post. While Streeter made the arrangements with Jax and ensured the other pilots would be conveniently out of commission, Michael pulled up the aircraft's design plans on the computer screen so they could delineate sightlines—where they risked being spotted and where they could move unseen.

Streeter moved over beside him. "We need to figure out a way to get me on there, in case you do have to take it up. You can't take out Myriam, protect Annie, and fly the plane simultaneously. Autopilot will only take you so far."

"The baggage compartment," Michael said. "It's accessible from both outside the plane and inside the cabin. Here." He pointed to a spot behind the lavatory.

Streeter leaned forward to peer at the floorplan. "No sightline to that doorway from the main cabin?"

"No. And I don't think she'll be wandering back there. As long as they're on the ground, she's going to be watching those stairs. Ashton being Exhibit A."

"Ashton was more of a surprise than a threat," Streeter said, "but they're one and the same to her."

"The issue is going to be the noise opening that hatch makes," Michael went on. "No way she isn't going to hear that."

Streeter frowned. "Has she flown on this plane much?"

"Not on this one. She made a few trips with me on the old plane, but none since I got this model."

Streeter nodded. "That helps. She won't know what's normal. If we time it with the fuelling and ramp up the noise level, I may be able to slide in under her radar. Is there a latch to open the cabin baggage compartment door from the inside or will I have to dismantle the thing?"

"There's an inside safety latch. Not sure how quiet it is though. I've never used it."

"Okay. I'll be sure to try it before the fuelling noise is over. And pack a few tools just in case it doesn't work."

"And a knife to cut that damned duct tape off Annie. Check the tool shed in the hangar."

Streeter glanced at his watch. "Okay. My gun's in my office upstairs, so—"

"Save yourself the trip," he said, handing him one of the 9mm's he'd pulled from his gun safe, along with a box of ammunition. "I've got another."

"Think you can get it on with you?"

"Well, she doesn't have a metal detector and if she gets close enough to try a pat-down, I may have a good chance at taking her down right then."

Streeter nodded. "Just remember she's a Russian agent, not your middle-aged secretary. I'm guessing she has decent hand-to-hand combat training, in addition to being armed. Be prepared for that."

The front door opened. They both looked up to see David Aylesbury, Angelo in his wake.

"Gentlemen. I hear we have ourselves a situation. Jax called and filled me in," David added by way of explanation, seeing the surprise on their faces. "I hope you don't mind my commandeering your driver to bring me out here, Michael."

"Well done, Jax," Michael murmured. "We can use all the help we can get."

Angelo was always a walking armory, a welcome addition to their little cadre.

"Carry on then," David said. He moved behind the reception counter to look over Michael's shoulder at the blueprints for the plane. "Where are we?"

"I'm going in through the baggage compartment and Mike's going to be flying the plane, if it gets that far," Streeter explained, handing David his phone. "I've got remote listening activated on Myriam's phone, so you can monitor what goes on in the cabin from here."

"Any comms equipment so I can communicate back with either of you?"

Streeter grimaced. "Unfortunately, not. That's all in my downtown office." He pulled a radio off his belt and passed it to David. "But once Michael has his headphones on, you can talk to him through this, at least until he's out of range." He turned back to Michael. "I think we have Angelo cover the stairs—just in case things get wonky and Myriam decides an exit is in order."

"Agree."

"And if she tries to bring her hostage out with her?" David asked.

"Well, the stairs would put the odds in our favor," Michael said, considering. "They're narrow enough, they'd have to come down single file. And Myriam's a good six inches taller than Annie, so even if she's got Annie just one step ahead of her, Angelo should still have a clean head shot."

"Any chance Annie might try to make a break for it herself?" David asked.

"In a heartbeat," Michael said. Passive was not in her playbook.

"Okay, then." David turned to Angelo. "Be alert for that."

"And the fuel tank is here." Michael pointed to the diagram. "Please do not shoot it."

The ex-sharpshooter grinned. "I think I can manage that."

"Can we get pictures of these two women so we're all clear on who's who?" David asked.

Michael answered. "Annie's the short, curvy redhead. She's the one we save. *At all costs.* Everybody got that?" He stared fiercely at each man in turn, burning his point home. "She is the mission and the only mission."

David cleared his throat. "And, just for a clear comparison, Myriam would be—?"

"The tall skinny one. Straight dark hair. She's the one you can send straight to hell."

****

Annie had read somewhere that waiting was a skill, like everything else. Unfortunately, it was not a skill she possessed, even when she wasn't duct-taped to a chair on a plane with an armed crazy woman. But somewhere, in her muddled recall of the crime novel collective, lurked the lore that the victim should try to keep their kidnapper talking. As long as they're talking, they aren't killing you. And getting people to talk was a skill Annie did possess, so use what you have, right? Her professional criminal clients were always contemptuous of the abilities of amateurs. She didn't know if spies felt the same, but figured it was worth a try. She took a deep breath.

"I guess Harrison Stewart got you into this?"

"What?" Myriam said, glancing irritably over at her.

"Harrison Stewart," she repeated. "Michael told me he was behind all this: the spying, the server, the whole thing. He and that Russian spy girlfriend of his. So, I guess they pulled you in, too?"

"Oh, please." Myriam rolled her eyes. "Harrison knew nothing and did nothing."

Bingo. Spies and street criminals weren't so different after all. "Are you sure?" She tried to sound skeptical. "Michael said he talked to some hotshot ex-CIA guy who said that agent, Anya, targeted Harrison specifically. She must have had her reasons."

"Anya is no agent." Sure enough, Myriam's contempt was palpable. "She is a spoiled brat trying to win Daddy's approval. And stupid enough to think anyone on a first-name basis with the guy designing military aircraft must have access to the designs. She is an idiot." Myriam angrily ripped off a piece of duct tape and crunched it into a ball. "Telling her father she could get the plans for Grayson's new E-7 AWAC design. Without a single deliverable in hand. *Idiot*." She practically spat the word this time.

"Um, AW—?"

"Airborne early warning and control aircraft," Myriam muttered. "Force multipliers, for short." She suddenly smashed her ball of duct tape against the window beside her seat, grinding her palm against it as if it were Anya's face. It stuck there when she removed her hand. She seemed weirdly pleased.

Okay, then. Better duct tape smashed onto the window than bullets smashing into my face. Annie tried not to think about Peter Ashton and the sickening thud-thud-thud of his body dropping and rolling down the steps, followed by an equally sickening silence. Or the way Myriam had just gone on about her business placing her ransom call to Michael, as if killing a man was the equivalent of stepping on a cockroach. If Annie had held any hope of appealing to Myriam's sympathies, that went out the window with Peter Ashton's last breath.

Focus, Annie. If Myriam was talking, she wasn't shooting. "So, I guess those are a big deal, these force multipliers?"

"They're airborne command centers that can track anything and everything for hundreds of miles ahead of a fleet. So, yeah. Kind of a 'big deal.'" She shot Annie an Anya-worthy look of contempt. "The Navy's used them for years. But Grayson developed a whole new design he said was a real game-changer. The Department of Defense agreed. They've ordered twenty-five of them and the final designs aren't even completed yet."

"Sounds impressive," Annie said, filling the pause that followed. "I, uh... I don't know much about military planes."

Myriam scoffed. "Neither did Harrison or Anya." She moved to peer out the window on the other side of the plane, then returned to the couch.

Annie noted that she was careful to keep the stairs in sight and, simultaneously, never position herself directly in front of them.

"I doubt she even knew the terminology to describe what she claimed to have until her father told her. But I knew. I knew even before Grayson's precious

Department of Defense did. I had the perfect access point, and the Service had it all before the DOD contract was even signed. They were ecstatic. This had the potential to be as big as anything Robert Hansson delivered, and everybody knew it. My name would be made—a legend. They even decided to set up a separate server just for this project, routed through Sirapol. It was brilliant. And Harrison—" she hissed the name— "had nothing to do with any of it."

"Sounds like they were pretty happy with you. What happened?"

"Anya happened." The words dripped with contempt. "Grayson was taking longer to complete the designs than anticipated and the Service was getting antsy. But there was nothing I or anybody else could do. Partial designs, designs that might be changed completely, were not what they wanted. They wanted the final design, the finished plans, and those just weren't done.

"But everything was in place. You have no idea how long it took to get a mold of the key to the cabinet where Grayson kept the laptop with those plans." She rolled her eyes. "I didn't think he'd ever leave those keys where I could get my hands on them, but I kept watching and waiting and I got it done.

"And then Anya comes blundering into the middle of it all, making promises she couldn't keep and mucking everything up. Her father runs straight to his old colleagues in the Service. His darling Anya has the inside track on Grayson's new designs." Myriam ripped off a larger piece of duct tape, more forcefully than the last, and crushed it between her fingers, kneading it like a stress ball on steroids. "And then I start getting calls.

Why haven't I been able to get these plans? Me, the trained one, the one who has spent my life preparing for this position and assignment. How have I been scooped by this novice who bats her eyelashes and swishes her hair?"

She practically vibrated with anger now. "My work has never been questioned. I have the highest of reputations in the service. And this, this *amateur*, sallies in and claims to have done the job I couldn't?" She smashed the wad of duct tape onto the window beside its brother. "I told them she was a fraud. I knew there was no way she could deliver. Harrison had no intel to share. He was nothing but a liar who wanted to get laid, filling her ears with whatever she wanted to hear. *Idiot*." In her mouth, the word was an expletive, each successive iteration infused with greater contempt.

"But making promises to the Service that cannot be kept?" She shook her head. "That has consequences. Not for Anya, of course. She's under her father's protection. 'It wasn't poor Anya's fault. She was double-crossed. The cowardly lawyer got cold feet.' Such bullshit." She blew out a breath. "So, Anya gets pulled home, and Harrison is hung out to dry. I told them he knew nothing, that he never had, but they didn't believe me. I was just jealous, they said. Jealous! Me, jealous of that empty-headed playgirl." She seethed. "I have never been so insulted in my life."

For a moment, Annie thought maybe Myriam had tried to save the lawyer, but she quickly cleared that up.

"Had they eliminated Harrison immediately, the damage could have been controlled, the entire operation saved."

Ah, there was the Myriam Annie knew and didn't

love.

She rolled a third ball of tape between her palms. "But did they listen to me? Of course not. 'A little more pressure,' they said. 'He'll deliver.' *Pft*. They could have set him on fire and the man would still have had nothing to deliver. *Idiots*." Her expletive of choice expanded to encompass the bureaucrats who mucked up her mission.

Annie waited a beat or two to make sure the diatribe had truly run down before tossing out another serve. "So why shoot Michael?"

Myriam blew out an exasperated breath. "That was Harrison trying to buy himself some time and screwing everything up in the process. With Grayson out of commission, the place was in chaos. Everything to do with the new military program went into lockdown. I suppose even an idiot like Harrison could anticipate that. So yes, they backed off for a bit. But once Grayson had recovered and returned to work, recess was over." She shrugged. "What did he think would happen? They would just forget about him? He might not know anything of value, but thanks to Anya, he knew too much to be cut loose. He had to deliver or be eliminated. There is no in-between."

Annie suppressed a shiver. If Harrison had known too much to be left alive, her odds at this point certainly weren't looking too good. Well, hell. Maybe this whole 'get her talking' approach hadn't been such a great idea after all.

But once started, Myriam was on a roll. "So, what does our brilliant counselor do? He tries to play the same hand twice." She rolled her eyes. "They didn't even argue with me about eliminating him at that point.

But it was too late. The damage was already done. Grayson isn't stupid. Sure enough, by morning the plans were gone. And the server compromised. And Streeter with his 'lost security card' ruse asking about me being in the building the day before. It was over. The whole operation, compromised beyond repair." Myriam made a strangled sound of pure frustration. "I tried to tell them this is exactly what would happen. This was a delicate operation. It needed to be handled with the careful touch of a surgeon, a single point of contact. Any overplay at all and Grayson would be onto us. But what did I know? And so here we are. Years of work down the drain with nothing to show for it. My cover blown so I'm of no further use as an agent. My career is over."

Myriam stopped talking and just stared out the cabin window, the bright-hot anger that had fuelled her diatribe banked into a sort of blank resignation that Annie found even more frightening. Despair in one's captor did not bode well for either of them getting out of this alive. Flashes of 'Murder-Suicide' headlines flitted across the screen of her mind. She shoved them down and cast about for something that Myriam might feel the tiniest bit hopeful about.

"So, you are actually Russian? Do you still have family there? In Russia?"

Myriam looked back, a little startled, as if she'd forgotten Annie was even there. She didn't answer. Instead, she checked her watch again, then picked up her phone and punched in a number. "Where are we?" Myriam snapped to whoever was on the other end of the line. She punched the speaker button and dropped the phone into her lap, while she proceeded to knead her duct tape stress ball.

"Bringing the fuel truck over to the hangar now." The deep familiar voice that came through the phone warmed Annie to her toes. "You okay with us coming on in?"

"Do we need fuel to fly?" Myriam asked, her voice heavy with sarcasm.

"Um…yes," Michael answered.

"Then what do you think?" Myriam snapped.

Annie figured after years of 'yes, sir' and 'no, sir' and 'whatever-you-want, sir,' Myriam must be finding more than a little pleasure in jerking Michael Grayson around now. She could understand that sentiment. But if Myriam irritated him, Michael's voice didn't show it.

"Just want to make sure there aren't any surprises," he said mildly. "One dead guy on the floor is enough, so I'm giving you a heads-up there will be some people moving around and it's about to get a little noisy. Don't be startled."

"Stop patronizing me and get on with it," Myriam snapped, and hung up.

Michael did have a tendency to patronize. And mansplain. And sometimes even defend the wholly indefensible, like investigating the woman he professed to be crazy about. But still he had come riding to her rescue, arrogant asshole or not. Not that she thought there was likely to be much rescuing going on, but it comforted her to know he was out there.

That he was trying.

Chapter Twenty-Seven

Jax arrived with the ransom money packed into two large rolling suitcases. "These have been taking up space in the back of my closet for years. Happy to donate them to the cause."

"If this works, I'll buy you a whole new set of luggage and a month-long vacation to the exotic location of your choice."

Streeter rolled his eyes. "Can we negotiate bonuses later?"

Michael showed Jax and David where to stand so they wouldn't be visible from the plane. Then he turned to the rest of the group.

"All right, gentlemen. Let's do this."

As Michael maneuvered the fuel truck into position, Angelo rolled a generator from the far corner of the hangar close to the side of the plane, careful to stay out of the identified sightlines. On Michael's signal, he switched on the generator just as Michael started the fuelling. The diesel engine roared to life, its ear-splitting noise amplified by the echo chamber of the hangar.

The fuelling process underway, Michael joined Streeter at the outside hatch of the baggage compartment. Angelo picked up the large wrench Streeter had found in the toolbox and, on Michael's signal, banged it hard against the metal side of the generator several times in quick succession as Michael eased open the hatch. The dual metallic clangs blended nicely.

With a boost from Michael, Streeter swung himself up and inside. He disappeared into the interior and a few seconds later, Michael signalled once again to Angelo. Another round of banging covered the noise of the slamming hatch. They all held a collective breath, but there was no call from Myriam or movement from within. It appeared the first step in the plan had stayed beneath her radar.

****

Annie watched Myriam scrolling and tapping on her phone and wondered what she was doing. Coordinating this getaway with her Russian handlers? Or ditching the motherland and the 'idiot' handlers she'd worked for altogether and scrolling through real estate listings for a nice little villa in Ecuador, compliments of her Michael Grayson retirement plan? Either way, she seemed done with talking.

Annie looked out the window at the hangar wall and cast about for something to focus on other than what was coming next. Things like how many duplicate and triplicate forms the IRS required before letting someone walk out with millions in cash. Was there a 'Ransom Money' reporting form banks kept on hand for occasions like this?

Her gaze traveled back to her captor. Was she shooting her mom or sister a message that she had to do a little traveling for work but should have some time off after and was hoping to make it back to Russia for a bit? Did she have social media accounts, and if so, as her spy persona or was there one out there with old friends from high school she never saw in person and an ex-boyfriend she still secretly cyber-stalked?

The thought of ex-boyfriends brought Michael rushing back to mind. Was he as terrified as she was? Nausea crawled up her throat. The deafening fuelling process meant they would be taking off soon. The universe had a sick sense of humor. It wasn't enough that she was about to die at the hands of this bitch who had been her nemesis from the very first time she'd tried to reach Michael. No, she also had to be tortured with her worst phobia as well.

A scene in a jazz bar swam into her adrenaline-overloaded brain. The clink of glasses. The background buzz of laughter and conversations. A handsome man sitting across the table, watching her with sexy grey eyes.

"So, Mick whoever-you-are, what do you do for a living?"

"I design airplanes."

"Really? I hate airplanes. Sorry."

"What exactly do you hate about them?"

"That they leave the ground. You really ought to do something about that."

That laugh settling into the cells of her body like it belonged there, filling spaces she hadn't known were empty.

Tears welled up in her eyes. God damn it, Michael! She didn't want to die in his luxuriant hellscape of a plane. She didn't want her last words to him—his last memory of her—to be that awful scene this morning. Yes, he could be an arrogant son of a bitch, but he was more than that. So much more. And for a brief and lovely moment, she'd had the best of him. Of them.

That's what she wanted him to remember. And maybe, with time, and half a chance, they might have been able to work things out. Now, thanks to Myriam, they had neither. She twisted at her bindings angrily...and futilely.

Myriam spared her a bored glance and went back to her phone. Annie let her head fall back against the seat and stared at the ceiling of her metal death tube. The sudden silence was as jarring as the noise before it had been. Myriam's phone rang.

"Fuelling is finished," announced Michael's voice through the speaker.

"I gathered." Myriam stood and peered out the window. "Where's my money?"

"Just arrived. Do you want me to leave it on the steps for you or bring it on with me?"

Annie's adrenaline spiked another notch. Michael was coming on the plane? Was he flying this thing? The possibility both warmed her heart and terrified her even more. As much as she didn't want to die alone, she didn't want to watch Michael die too, and if he set foot on this plane that became a very real probability.

Myriam appeared to consider her options, then said, "Bring it on with you. But don't even think about trying to be the hero. No weapons, no tricks, or your favorite lawyer is dead. Do we understand each other?"

"We do."

"Good. Then let's get this show on the road."

"I need to file our flight plan. As soon as that goes through, we can be on our way."

"Screw the niceties. Let's get out of here. Now."

"Myriam—"

"Mischa," she growled.

"Mischa. We're fifteen miles from Lambert International Airport. We can't just launch ourselves into the middle of all that air traffic and hope everybody manages to stay out of our way. Do you want this entire endeavor ending with you getting T-boned mid-air?"

Annie started to hyperventilate.

****

Streeter eased out of the baggage compartment into the alcove behind the lavatory. Just around the wall was the kitchen/dining compartment and beyond that, the seating area where Annie's picture had been taken. A sliding door separated the two compartments, though it could be propped open with the flip of a handle.

Carefully, he eased out just far enough for a look. The door was closed. He breathed a silent sigh of relief. This mission just got a whole lot easier. He quickly and silently moved through the near compartment, keeping low to ensure he wasn't spotted through the porthole-shaped window in the door's center.

He reached the door separating him from the two women without incident. Positioning himself to the right of the porthole, he scanned as much of the forward cabin as could be seen without showing himself. Annie was to his left, still duct-taped to the chair. Ducking below the window, he shifted to the other side and surveilled the opposite side of the cabin. Myriam sat on the far arm of the couch, her back to him, facing the door into the flight deck, fiddling with her phone.

The shot was perfect and Streeter didn't hesitate.

****

Michael heard the double-tap and Annie's scream. He took the stairs three at a time and crouched in the doorway, his own gun at the ready. It wasn't needed.

Myriam slumped against the outer wall of the cockpit. A bright spray of blood and brain tissue decorated the wall and a bloom of red spread across her back. One shot to the head, a second to the heart. Two perfect kill shots. Streeter had not lost his touch.

Michael straightened, pocketed his gun, and moved straight to Annie. Her skin was ashen, her eyes wide and frozen on the bloody tableau before her. He knelt in front of her, shifting so his body blocked her view of Myriam.

"Look at me, Annie," he said. "Look at me." He reached out and took her face into his hands. "It's over. You're okay." His fingers tightened in her hair, and he rested his forehead on hers, allowing himself to breathe again as well. "You're okay."

Streeter touched him on the shoulder.

Michael looked up. "Thank you," he said.

Streeter just nodded and handed him the knife. "Get her out of here."

As Michael cut through the duct tape, Annie closed her eyes. Her rapid, shallow breathing began to slow and normalize, but she still hadn't spoken. Finally, he could stand it no longer.

"Talk to me, Annie," he said, as he finished cutting the last of the tape binding her to the chair and reached for her wrists. "Say something. Please."

She took a deep, shaky breath and opened her eyes. "Your personnel decisions suck."

****

It was close to midnight before the clandestine authorities David had called in finished their questioning and gave Michael the go-ahead to take Annie home. He found her sitting on the couch in his office, head back, eyes closed. The adrenaline had drained away, leaving exhaustion in its wake. She looked like death warmed over.

He gently touched her shoulder. "Annie, we can go."

She opened her eyes. "Go?"

"Yes, they've cleared us to leave. Come on, I'll take you home."

She blinked. "My car is here."

"I know. But you're in no condition to be driving. Let me drive you home. Please."

Uncharacteristically, she didn't argue. "Okay. I can get a ride back in the morning, I guess."

"No need. I'll have your car delivered back to you." He hesitated. "But I don't think you should be alone tonight. Come home with me. I have several guest rooms you can choose from—if you, uh…you know—want some space." He had no idea whether their standing had changed or if she still hated his guts. He just knew he needed to be near her, to make sure she was okay.

She seemed to be considering his offer for a moment, but then shook her head. "I just want to go home."

"Okay." He regrouped. "Then I'll stay at your place, on the couch."

"No." She stood and collected her purse and jacket. "I mean, thanks, but I'll be fine."

"Annie—"

"Michael, please." She laid a hand on his arm. "Just take me home. I can't talk about anything else tonight. I can't think about anything else tonight. I just can't. Tomorrow, okay?"

He nodded and swallowed all the things he desperately needed to say. "Of course. Sure. Let's get you home. We can talk tomorrow."

****

Tomorrow took forever to arrive. Michael didn't sleep at all, the hours trudging by in a repeating slide show of Annie O'Toole since she'd entered his life. Images he cherished. Images that stopped his heart. He watched the sun rise from his terrace, forcing himself to wait for a quasi-civilized hour to show up on her doorstep. Eight a.m. was the longest he could manage.

He pulled in behind her car, parked at the curb in front of her house the night before as promised, and rang the doorbell. But when the door opened, it wasn't Annie standing in front of him. It was Jonathan Clark.

"Hey," the man said, kneeing the eager Great Dane out of the way.

"I, uh, brought Annie's keys back."

"Right. Come on in." He pulled the door open wider, revealing the makings of a bed on the couch. So, Annie hadn't wanted to be alone after all. She just hadn't wanted him there. That hit.

Red curls poked around a doorway and froze when she saw him standing in her living room.

"Hi."

"Hi."

Jonathan looked from one to the other as they stared at each other and cleared his throat. "O-kay, then. I'm off to work, so I guess I'll just leave you two to chat." He shot Annie a questioning look. "You good?"

Annie nodded and stepped into the living room. She wore boxers and a green tank top the color of her eyes. Her feet were bare.

"Tell Jackson I'll be in tomorrow."

Jonathan snorted. "I'll tell him you might be in tomorrow. We'll see." He crossed to where she stood and dropped a kiss on top of her head. "I'll be back after work. Call if you need anything. And text me if you want take-out."

"Okay," she answered. "Thanks."

Jonathan gave Michael a stiff nod and let himself out. Looked like Annie wasn't the only one pissed at him.

After a beat of awkward silence, Michael said, "I brought back your keys." He produced them from his pocket. "Car's just out front."

"Thanks," she said.

He set them on the coffee table and cast about for something else to say. "Is that coffee I smell?"

A shadow of a smile crossed her face. "Would you like some?"

He let out the breath he'd been holding. At least she wasn't throwing him out immediately. He had the span of time it took to drink a cup of coffee to convince this woman they belonged together.

"Love some," he said.

She disappeared back behind the doorway. He prowled the small living room, breathing in her essence, exploring her habitat. The décor was bright and cheery, the art on the walls a mix of edgy and whimsical. Eleanor Barlow would have hated everything about it.

Annie returned carrying two mugs of steaming coffee. She handed him one, then sank onto the couch, tucking her bare feet beneath her and brushing an unruly curl out of her eyes, both gestures achingly familiar to him.

"Thanks for bringing my car back."

"You're welcome." Michael noted the shadows beneath her eyes. Looked like the night had not been kind to her either. "Did you get any sleep?"

She smiled ruefully. "Not a lot. When I did, the dreams were… well, let's just say staying awake seemed the better option. But I'm sure that will pass. It's all just really fresh."

"Yeah." He tried without success to pull his spinning thoughts into something eloquent. Giving up, he just let the words pour out as jumbled as they were in his brain. "I'm so sorry, Annie. About all of it. About before—the investigation—and then Myriam…"

She looked down into her coffee. "I know," she said softly.

"I love you. I probably have since that first night I met you. I sure as hell couldn't get you out of my mind. And even when everything got so screwed up, with first the case and then your grandmother, I couldn't walk away from you. I couldn't bring myself to let you go. Even when everything looked like you were playing me for a fool. That's why I had Streeter investigate you. You mattered too much to just give up on. I—"

"Michael, I get it. I do. I mean, of course you had reason to doubt me—reasons multiple, actually—given the circumstances. You did what anybody with your resources would have done." She sighed. "It's just that, it felt like my grandmother all over again, you know? Big trigger for me, that."

"I know. I'm sorry," he said again. Then, taking a deep breath, his heart pounding, he plunged. "So, can we try again? Start over? Give this thing between us a shot?"

****

God, she so wanted to say yes. To run to the arms that had carried her out of that plane when her legs had buckled beneath her, lifting her over Ashton's blood-soaked body at the bottom of the steps. To curl up next to him when she woke in a panic from the nightmares and feel his warmth and strength beside her. He made her feel safe.

But he wasn't. He was the opposite of safe.

"Do you want children?" Annie asked suddenly, looking up at him.

He looked a little surprised at the question, but didn't hesitate. "I do." A beat later, with a little more hesitation, he asked, "Do you?"

She nodded.

"Well, see?" He gave her a tentative smile. "That's one thing we're on the same page about."

"Oh, Michael," she said with a sigh. "Have you given any thought to what life will be like for a child growing up in your world?"

He looked bewildered. "You're asking about my parenting plans?"

She gave him an exasperated look. "No, I'm talking about what life is like for a kid growing up as one of the 'rich and famous.'" She added the air quotes. "Because I've lived it, and let me tell you, it sucks."

"Annie, you were raised by Eleanor Barlow." Michael ran his fingers through his hair. "Of course, your childhood sucked." He looked up quickly. "I'm sorry, I don't mean to be flip about it, I just—"

"The framework is the same," Annie said, brushing aside his apology. How could she make him understand? "When your family is one of the 'uber-wealthy,' you have a spotlight on you. All the time. You get trotted out for pictures at society functions—"

"I would never do that to my kid. I hate those things myself; why would I put my kid through it?"

"Because when you don't, there are articles and blogs and talk shows discussing all the rumors about why your kid is never seen in public. Is she autistic? A drug addict? Estranged? And the more you try to shield her from the publicity hounds, the more they pursue because the gossip rags pay more for photos that are hard to come by. So now your kid is being tracked and followed and harassed everywhere she goes by people who will do anything to get a picture, the more embarrassing, the better." All the memories, the repeated humiliation she'd endured as the adolescent granddaughter of Eleanor Barlow welled up, making her chest tight.

"And God forbid she screws up. What are just typical teenage shenanigans for most kids become an internet sensation for your kid. Too much to drink at a party? There's always someone there happy to snap all the incriminating pictures and blast them over the internet to see how many 'likes' they can rack up. And if they're really lucky, their scoop might even get picked up by the papers and the gossip blogs until your mortified teen becomes a talk show joke that everyone she knows sees and repeats and shares." She jumped up and started pacing, anger rolling over her as hot and fresh as the day it had happened to her—the one and only party of her entire high school career.

"Your kid can forget about inviting friends over. Oh, one or two might jump through the hoops once, just to see what it's like inside your big, fancy house—

which they're happy to tell everybody else about—but they won't be back to just hang out, because it's 'too weird.' Turns out other kids don't have gatehouses with guards or need pre-clearance and placement on an admittance list to get in." She ran her fingers through her hair and turned back to him.

"Do you get that your kid can't go for a walk or just ride a bike around the neighborhood? She can't go to the movies or hang out at the mall with other kids. She can't go anywhere by herself because she's always a target. Not just of harassment, but of being kidnapped by some crazy person with a get-rich-quick scheme."

Michael looked stricken. "Myriam was a fluke, Annie, a once-in-a—"

"You can't know that, Michael. You can't ever know and that's the point. Sure, another Russian spy ring might be a long shot—though maybe not, given what you do. But crazies and fortune-hunters? Those are a dime a dozen."

She paused at her front window and watched a mom push a stroller down the bumpy brick sidewalk. Across the street, two little girls drew on their porch steps with chalk. A bicyclist rode past. This was the life she wanted. This was the life she'd fought so hard to have. She turned back to the man who held her heart.

"I can't bring children into that kind of life, Michael. I won't. I won't do it to them, and I won't do it to me."

Her voice was thick with unshed tears, and she had to clear her throat to get out the words that had to be said. "I am finally able to walk down the street without being recognized or hassled. I have friends I can be sure like me for me, and not because they think I can do something for them. I don't have to worry about people sucking up or having hidden agendas. Or keep an investigator on my payroll to make sure anyone who gets even a little close isn't running some kind of scam."

He winced as if she'd slapped him, and her heart broke for the both of them. She crossed to him and placed a hand on his chest, wanting nothing more than to lay her head there and lose herself in his arms. But that's exactly what would happen. She would lose herself all over again.

She looked up at him. "I love you, too, Michael," she said, the painful truth of those words slicing open her heart. She felt his quick intake of breath and her voice hitched. "But I can't do this." Standing on tiptoe, she kissed him gently on the lips. "You are a good man. And you will always be the prince who stole my heart. I'm just not cut out to be royalty. I'm so sorry."

She turned and ran up the stairs before she changed her mind and made a mistake that would surely destroy her.

Chapter Twenty-Eight

Michael sat in his car in a state of shock. He couldn't believe she was walking away from him. Even though she'd forgiven him for the investigation. Even though she loved him. Wasn't love supposed to conquer all? For God's sakes, every other woman he'd dated had considered his money a draw, not a drawback.

The thought stumbled over itself and froze. *Every other woman he'd dated had considered his money a draw.* And not one of those relationships had felt real. He'd always wound up feeling like a means to an end, a path to the prize rather than the prize itself. Hell, that's what had drawn him to Annie in the first place. She hadn't known anything about his money—and once she did, she hadn't cared. She'd simply enjoyed him for him.

He started the car and jabbed at the window buttons, hoping that his usual go-tos of speed and fresh air would clear his mind. They didn't. The traffic and landmarks, the old neighborhoods giving way to suburbs—all of it blurred beneath the harsh replay of Annie's final farewell.

When he reached his own drive and sat waiting for the guard to open the gate, her words blasted through his brain. *Other kids don't have guards at gatehouses or need pre-clearance and placement on an admittance list to get in.* He'd never given a thought to what life for kids would be like in this world. His own childhood had been decidedly normal and whenever he thought about someday having kids, that was the childhood he'd imagined for them. But she was right. Their lives would be nothing like his.

He rolled to a stop in front of his house, but just sat in his car. After a moment, he picked up his phone.

****

The drive took about thirty minutes. Streeter may have agreed to come work with him in St. Louis, but the man didn't like people enough to live there. He kept a small apartment in the top floor of his private office building for those nights he worked late or when the weather was tricky, but home was some twenty-five miles south of St. Louis, outside the rural community of High Ridge.

The gravel road dead-ended at a rambling white farmhouse. Streeter's SUV was parked under a massive old maple tree whose branches spanned a good forty feet. Michael parked next to it and climbed out. He couldn't remember the last time he'd been out here. In the early days, the two of them had spent hours here, drinking beer, grilling steaks, swapping stories and making plans. But life got busier, and those visits became fewer and further in-between until they'd pretty much faded away altogether. Maybe Annie was right. Money did turn people into dicks.

He climbed the steps and rang the doorbell. The door swung open almost immediately.

"You look like hell," Streeter said, after a beat.

"Thanks."

"You're welcome. Come on in. Coffee?"

"Sure." Michael really could have used something

357

stronger, despite the early morning hour.

The inside of Streeter's place was surprisingly comfortable for a life-long bachelor used to bunking in the most extreme of settings. Michael sank into the nearest oversized chair and stared out the picture window at the hills stretching to the horizon.

"Here." Streeter thrust a U.S. Navy mug at him. "I added a shot of whiskey. Figured we could both use one after yesterday."

God bless Streeter.

The older man settled into the chair opposite and stretched his legs out. "You get any sleep?" he asked.

"No. How late were you there?"

"Couple of hours after you left. They took your plane, flew it to one of their secure sites. Didn't think you'd be itching to use it anytime soon, so I didn't argue."

Michael suppressed a shudder. "Right call. And the bodies?"

"What bodies?" Streeter lifted an eyebrow.

Michael gave a rueful smile. "Right. So, what happened to Myriam and Peter? Just in case anyone asks why my assistant and PR guy have both disappeared?"

"Myriam is taking a leave of absence for personal reasons. She won't be coming back."

"And Peter?"

"Suicide. Or possibly an accidental overdose. We'll never know for sure. Turns out he was deep into drugs. Who knew?" He stretched his arms overhead, rolling his neck. "There's no family to deal with, which makes things easier. And I'll drop a few hints that the two of them were an item, just in case anyone is inclined to question the timing. Her lover killed himself. Of course she'd need some time off, especially since they shared a workplace."

Michael nodded. He was so damn tired. "Thanks for taking care of all that."

"David's team did all the heavy lifting. I just locked up after they left." He crossed an ankle over one knee. "So, how's Annie?"

Michael stared at the floor. "Done with me," he finally answered, feeling the weight of the statement settle in his chest.

Streeter blew out a breath. "Well, hell. I thought maybe all this"—he made a vague gesture encompassing all of yesterday's debacle—"would make the investigation issue pale in comparison. That she'd get past it."

"That's the ironic thing. It did. She isn't mad about that anymore. Even said she understood why I felt the need to do the investigation, given the circumstances."

"Then, why?"

"Because I'm rich." Michael stood and walked to the window.

"Come again?"

"Because. I'm. Rich." He repeated it one word at a time, trying to make it soak into his own brain as well as Streeter's. "Said she lived that life with her grandmother and can't do it again. Won't do it again. Talked about how fucked up it was growing up in a media spotlight. Said she wouldn't put herself through it again and wouldn't do it to her kids." He turned back from the window. "She wants kids," he added. "The only thing we agree on, as it turns out." He downed the last of his coffee and looked at his empty cup. "You got any more whiskey?"

"With or without coffee?"

"Skip the coffee. I need to get really drunk today. You mind?"

"So long as you leave that rocket of yours parked under my tree, I don't mind at all."

Michael looked at the long leather couch. "Wouldn't be the first time I've passed out on your couch."

"It would not." Streeter eyed him. "You eaten anything today?"

Michael considered. "Guess not."

"Well, I'd just as soon skip the cleaning-up-vomit part of this feature, so how about I fix us both some food first and then you can work your way through my liquor cabinet?"

"Fair plan."

"And I'll just go ahead and take those keys of yours."

****

The rising sun was flirting with the treetops on the eastern horizon when Michael woke. His tongue was stuck to the roof of his mouth and his head felt like a cracked egg about to spill its contents. He moved his hands to hold it together and winced. Everything hurt, including the growing light out that window over there. A window that was not in his bedroom

He heard movement in the adjoining room and the sound of percolating coffee. Where the hell was he? Gingerly, he lifted his head and peered around. He was sprawled on a leather couch, under a brightly colored Mexican blanket. Streeter's. The previous day's events came rushing back, adding to the pain he was already feeling. He groaned and closed his eyes again.

"Mornin', sunshine." The familiar gravelly voice accompanied the sound of footsteps. "Can't say a night's sleep has improved your appearance all that much."

"Fuck you," he muttered. Or would have if his tongue had been working.

The *ch-ch* chink of glassware against the end table at his head reverberated through his skull.

"Juice, water, and coffee at six o'clock. And here's the aspirin."

Something light hit him in the stomach. He made a move to grab it but missed. The bottle rolled onto the floor with a soft *thunk*.

"Pitiful." Streeter shook his head, making no move to retrieve the escapee. "Biscuits are in the oven to help soak up what's still floating in that stomach of yours, so see if you can haul your ass off my couch." His footsteps retreated in the direction of the kitchen.

A few more muttered profanities later, Michael managed to disentangle himself from the blanket and sit up. He retrieved the aspirin, downed the juice and water, and had finished off most of the coffee by the time Streeter poked his head around the door again.

"Chow's up."

With some effort, Michael pushed himself off the couch and made his way into the kitchen. He eyed the man at the stove piling up two plates with biscuits and gravy, eggs and hefty slabs of bacon.

"How come you don't look like shit? You drank all afternoon, too."

"Metabolism," Streeter answered, setting the plates on the table and plucking the empty coffee cup out of his hand. "Some of us have it, some don't."

"Bullshit," Michael said. "I've seen you hung over as hell." He pulled up a chair. "This smells amazing. Thank God for friends who can cook."

Streeter snorted. "Yeah? How many friends"—he emphasized the plural ending—"you got who cook for you these days?"

Michael looked up, surprised. "Uh, just you, I guess."

Streeter refilled both their coffees and sat down. "Exactly. While you were getting shit faced, I did some thinking."

"Ah-ha! I knew it. You stopped drinking, didn't you? Metabolism, my ass."

"Regular Sherlock, you are. Eat. I need that marinated genius brain of yours to catch up with this conversation."

Michael paused, a forkful of eggs halfway to his mouth. He knew that look. Streeter's time-to-hear-some-hard-truths look. He set his fork back down.

"Go on."

Streeter gave him a long look, then said, "I've known you a long time, Mike. I've seen you build this business of yours from a spark of an idea into a billion-dollar conglomerate."

"And?"

"And, somewhere along the way, it changed you. You used to enjoy life, get excited about stuff. Hell, you used to have friends other than just me."

Michael stabbed at his plate with his fork. "Yeah, well, my girlfriend just got kidnapped and almost killed by a Russian spy who was stealing military secrets out of my office. Not to mention, she is now officially *ex-*

girlfriend because she wants nothing more to do with me. So, excuse me if I'm not 'enjoying life' and all 'excited' about stuff at the moment—"

"I'm not talking about this moment, asshole. I'm talking about for years now. When was the last time you got super-stoked about something? The so-into-it-you-lose-track-of-time kind of stoked?"

"Annie," Michael said softly, his heart breaking all over again.

Streeter's lips tightened. "What about apart from Annie? At work?"

Michael sat back in his chair and considered. "The E-7 design."

"Right. Design." Streeter nodded. "How much of that you still get to do?"

Michael sighed. "You know the answer to that." He bitched about not having time to develop his own designs to pretty much anyone who would listen.

"I do. And so do you."

Michael tackled the biscuit swimming in sausage gravy. "It's a big company, Streeter. There's a lot of business to take care of. Goes with the territory."

"And what do you enjoy about that part of it, the business side of things?"

Michael considered. "Well, building something from the ground up, watching it grow. It's a thrill. You know that. You were there."

"I was. But the creation of something is different than the maintenance of it. I'm talking about now. What do you enjoy now?"

Michael sighed. "I don't know. It's just stuff that has to be done. What's your point?"

Streeter pointed a finger at him. "That right there is

my point, my friend. You don't enjoy the vast majority of what you do anymore. If you're going to choose it over building a life with this woman you're stupid in love with, don't you think you ought to at least enjoy it? That's all I'm saying." He picked up his coffee and took a sip, as if he hadn't just dropped a hydrogen bomb in the room.

Michael stared at him. He stuttered, "I-I'm not choosing it over her. It's not a choice. It's who I am, what I do, my life…"

Streeter's gaze cut back to him. "Nobody's got you duct-taped to that CEO chair. You don't like the territory, change it."

Michael shoved his chair back from the table and glared at the man across from him. "You think I can just walk away? Thousands of people depend on me for their livelihoods, literally, thousands. I have hundreds of contracts to fulfill, a board and shareholders to answer to—one of which happens to be you, I might remind you. What we do or don't do affects the stock market, not to mention the Department of Defense who's relying on us to come through with the planes and equipment they need. I'm supposed to just say to hell with it all and jump ship, consequences be damned?"

Streeter held up a hand. "Could you shut up and listen for a half-second? I'm not asking you to commit corporate hari-kari. Mergers are a thing. Corporate buyouts are a thing. And you don't have to be dying to sell a company. If you could walk away from it all, go back to just designing aircraft like you did in the beginning—in some freelance arrangement or start over building some other new thing—would you want to? Or do you like being the big boss and all that goes with that?" He spread his hands. "Not judging either way, man. Just asking you to think about what really matters to you."

Michael took a shaky breath. Grayson Aeronautics was his baby. He'd conceived it, birthed it, raised it. He had never even considered the possibility of not spending the rest of his life guiding it, growing it, grooming it. But Streeter was right. Maintaining a business was an entirely different venture than building one. In the beginning, he'd jumped out of bed every morning, psyched for what the day would bring. Now, it took an alarm and several hits of the doze button to get him out of bed—and he spent most of his days ticking off a to-do list.

Was he really choosing a to-do list over Annie?

Streeter watched him in that assessing way of his, then pushed his chair back. "I think you have some thinking to do, my friend. Feel free to hang as long as you like. Just put your dishes in the dishwasher before you go, assuming you still remember how to do menial labor." He reached in his pocket and tossed Michael's keys to him. "I'm off to work."

"Hold on," Michael said, a thought hitting him. "What about you? If I did decide to sell, I mean?"

"What about me?"

"Well, in case you hadn't noticed, your career is pretty intertwined with Grayson Aeronautics."

Streeter laughed. "My career was intertwined with you, dimwit. And in case you're not aware, I happen to be very well-off, thanks to this cock-eyed optimist who gave me a twenty percent share in his little start-up and a boss who has overpaid me for years." He grew serious. "Do what's right for you, Mike. That's all you're responsible for. Everyone else will adjust just fine, including me."

Chapter Twenty-Nine

An incoming text chimed on Annie's phone. It wasn't a number she recognized, but the preview pop-up read *Hi, this is Michael.* She froze, her peppermint mocha midway to her mouth.

It had been almost a month since they'd spoken—the toughest month of her life. But she was still upright, putting one foot in front of the other. The trauma therapist was helping. The 'trapped-on-a-plane-with-a-killer' nightmares were becoming fewer and further between, though they'd largely been replaced with erotic dreams about a handsome prince with grey eyes and a wicked smile. Not something she'd complain about if they didn't leave her reeling with fresh heartbreak come morning. But she would get over him. Eventually. She'd pulled her life together before and she could do it again. This too shall pass. Everything did. It was a pep talk she gave herself several times a day.

He'd reached out to her only once, about a week after the kidnapping. She'd asked him not to do it again. It was hard enough to maintain her resolve just on her own. Hearing his voice made it exponentially harder. To his credit, he'd respected her wishes. And he'd come through for James. Nicoletti had dropped the charges. In an especially satisfying karmic twist, Little Wayne made a deal to flip on the not-so-Reverend

Adams, who was now cooling his heels in jail, awaiting trial for drug trafficking. So, all had worked out in the end. All but a happily-ever-after for the prince and the peon.

So much for life imitating fairy tales.

She stared out her office window, her mind spiralling into the 'what-if's. It was familiar, if unproductive, terrain. What if she'd listened to her gut and decided to skip the ball altogether? What if she'd gone straight over to talk to Emily and skipped that fateful drink at the bar? Hell, what if she'd just gotten there on time? She would have seen all the presentations, heard him introduced, known who he was. Then she never would have… Well, she just wouldn't have. Ever. And then none of it would have happened.

But she did go to the ball. And she was late. And she did decide to get that drink. And she definitely did…the rest of it. She had the hole in her heart to prove it.

Jonathan slammed open her office door. She jumped, scattering tiny brown cappuccino droplets across the file open on her desk.

"Geezus, Jonathan, what the hell?"

"Sorry," he said, not sounding it. "Have you seen this?" He shoved his phone in front of her face.

She grabbed a tissue and wiped off her file as she squinted at the screen. "What am I looking at?"

"I set up an alert for Grayson when I got put on Joiner. Never cancelled it."

She shoved the phone back toward its owner. "I told you—"

"He's blowing up. I've had like twenty alerts in the

last five minutes."

Her heart dropped into her stomach. "Oh, God. What happened?"

"Short version? He's stepping away from Grayson Aeronautics. Sold the whole company to Pan-Air."

"Wait, what?"

"Says he wants to get back to his roots, focus on design and the engineering stuff that's his real passion. And here's the wildest part. The money from the sale? All going to charity."

She vaguely heard Jonathan say, "See? Thought you'd be interested," as the room tilted and shrunk to a single pinpoint of awareness…Michael's text. She grabbed her phone and thumbed it open.

—*Hi, this is Michael. I have a new number. And something to show you, as well as a few changes to tell you about. Would you consider meeting me? I promise to keep it brief.*—

Unable to breathe, she quickly typed back.

—*Jonathan just told me. You're all over the news. WTH is going on?*—

His response was immediate.

—*I'd rather explain in person. Can you meet me after work? Say around 6:00 pm?*—

She didn't even think to hesitate.

—*Where?*—

—*I'll text you the address. See you soon.*—

****

The address turned out to be in Kirkwood, technically a suburb of St. Louis, but one that itself dated back to the 1850s. Annie had discovered the area not long after moving to St. Louis and fallen in love with it. A one-hundred-year-old train depot—still a working station—sat in the middle of town, next to an old-fashioned ice cream stand and a bustling farmers' market. Just off the business district, tree-lined streets of old Victorian homes gave off a Norman Rockwell vibe.

Her GPS guided her to one of those Victorians—a soft grey one, with creamy white gingerbread trim on the wrap-around porch and matching rows of overlapping scallops accenting the topmost gable. There was a familiar sports car in the driveway and a familiar figure sitting on the front steps. She turned into the drive and rolled to a stop. Heart pounding, she climbed out of the car.

"Hi," she said, her chest tight.

"Hi," he answered, standing.

He wore faded jeans and a leather jacket. She fought the urge to run into his arms.

Weakly, she motioned to the house behind him. "Is this yours?"

"Acquired four days ago." He grinned. There it was, that sexy crooked smile that haunted her dreams. "Do you like her?" he asked.

With an effort, she pulled her gaze from the man to the house behind him. It was two stories tall—possibly three, depending on what was behind those attic dormer windows. The shady yard was big enough for a flag football game, but not for a gala. There was a porch swing. And kids playing catch in the yard across the street.

"It's perfect," she breathed. She looked back at its new owner. "What are you going to do with it?"

"Live in it. Raise kids in it. Be happy in it, I hope." He smiled and tilted his head at her, looking exactly like he did that first night when he was trying to talk her into leaving the ball with him. The tightness in her chest increased.

"Did you really give your company away?"

He stuffed his hands in his pockets and rocked back on his heels. "Well, I didn't exactly give it away. Pan-Air is coughing up a lot of money for charity. And I'm still very comfortable, money-wise. Just no longer on any 'richest people' or 'billionaire' lists." He gave a little shrug. "I mean, I know I'm all over the news right now, but that'll die down. In a few weeks, they'll move on—this time for good."

He gestured toward the front door. "Can I show you the inside? It's still a bit of a mess, but it's getting there."

She made her way up the steps, her legs less than steady beneath her. "You've already moved in?"

"Partially. It's taking a bit to sort through what to bring and what to let go." He gave her a look. "And there are a few things still undecided that might affect some of those decisions, so it's a work in progress."

"I don't—what—how..." Her tongue was as tangled as her thoughts. Finally, the words got free, tumbling out in a torrent of angst. "How could you do this? Give up everything you've worked so hard for? What if you regret it? Resent it? Resent me for it?"

"Whoa." He closed the gap between them and, running his palms down her arms, clasped both her hands in his. "Take a breath."

She did.

"Yes, this is a big shift," he said with a smile, his easy demeanor a marked contrast to her own near hyperventilation. "But nothing's ever felt so right." He tilted his head again and held her eyes. "You once said you loved me. Do you still?"

She blew out a breath. "The last month would have been a hell of a lot easier if I didn't."

His smile broadened. "It's nice to know I wasn't the only one suffering. Because I very much still love you."

Her heart skipped a beat at the words, even though she'd heard them before and knew them to be true, spoken or not. But love didn't conquer all, no matter what the fairy tales said.

"Michael—"

He laid a finger across her lips. "I say this with love—would you just shut up for a minute? You'll get your turn."

She closed her mouth.

"Sit with me," he said, gesturing to the swing.

She took a seat, and he sat beside her. They weren't even touching, but his proximity had her nerve endings high fiving each other. She tried to focus on what he was saying.

"You and Streeter got me thinking about a whole lot of things, things I hadn't even realized I needed to be thinking about."

"Streeter?"

"When I left your place that last time, I drove out to Streeter's, where I got very drunk and passed out on his couch."

She could respect that. She'd gone through two pints of ice cream that afternoon and gone to bed with a bellyache to match her heartache.

"I can always count on Streeter not to pull any punches. He forced me to consider some tough questions. Like was I actually happy running a business that controlled me more than I controlled it? Did I even enjoy the work I was doing anymore?" He glanced over at her with a wry smile. "Turns out the answer was 'not so much.' Go figure." He chuckled lightly and rocked them back and forth with his foot. "He also pointed out that I wasn't exactly 'duct-taped to that CEO chair'—"

She had to laugh at that, sick humor though it was.

He grinned back at her. "And reminded me that corporate sales and mergers were a real thing, and terminal illness was not a prerequisite. For once, I listened. In the end, it was a surprisingly easy decision. Pan-Air snapped up my offer and, while a few odds and ends still have to be finalized, I'm essentially a free man. I've agreed to finish the designs currently in the works and they've contracted with my new company for first dibs on any of my new designs for the next five years."

"Your new company?" Her mind reeled.

"Wright Designs. With a W."

"Your heroes," she said with a smile.

"Exactly." He grinned. "It felt right to get back to basics. I'm the sole employee. For now." He gave a satisfied sigh. "It feels good. Really good."

He shifted on the swing to face her and reached for her hand. "I want a life with you, Annie. I want to raise a family with you. I want us to have our happily-ever-after. If you want to marry me right now, I'm in. If you want to just move into this house with me and see where it goes, I'm in. If you want to stay in your place for a while and take things slow, I'm in."

He squeezed her hand tighter. "But I also need you to understand this. If you decide you don't want any of that with me—if you're out of all of the above—yes, I will be devastated. But I won't regret any of this. I didn't do this for you...or even for us. I did it for me.

"I want to spend my days doing the stuff I get lost in because I love it so much. I want my kids to have the kind of childhood I had, to get to do all the things and make all the mistakes without the world watching and judging and making constant commentary. I am building the life I want, just like you built the life you want. And I happen to think those two lives could mesh very nicely. I'm hoping you do too."

Tears blurred her vision. She squeezed her eyes shut and when she opened them, he was on one knee in front of her.

"Annie O'Toole, will you take this journey with me?" he asked softly, those gorgeous grey eyes of his locked in on her own like one of his heat-seeking missile systems.

Time slowed and stood still, every detail of the moment freezing into a photograph that would be seared into her memory for the rest of her days. There was no hesitation, doubt or delay, no battle between her head and her heart. For once in her life, everything fell into perfect alignment.

"Long live the prince," she said, a smile spreading across her face. "I'm in for all of it with you, Michael. Now and for ever after."

With a laugh of delight, he scooped her up and whirled her in a dizzying circle. She was both laughing and crying as he slowed, letting her toes slide to the ground and kissing her the way a woman ought to be kissed. She revelled in his touch, realizing that she could and would lose herself in this man, to this man—

over and over for as long as they both should live—and never lose herself along the way.

He rested his forehead against hers and murmured, "This is it, you know. No more farewells."

She sniffled. "I warned you I was no good at keeping a one-night-stand just one night.'

"Thank God," he said with feeling. "So wanna see the inside of our house?"

"I do." She wiped away her tears and grinned. "See what I did there? Practicing."

"Look at you. Always a step ahead." His eyes twinkled as he opened their front door. "Well, come on in. We have a whole life to plan so we should probably get started. Good thing I already have the coffee on."

She sighed in appreciation. "It's like you know me."

He snorted. "Pretty sure that's going to be a lifelong endeavor."

She looked up at him. "Think you're up for it?"

He smiled. "Oh, honey. I'm looking forward to it."

Epilogue

"Wow. It looks like Christmas threw up in here," Jonathan said.

"Thanks, asshole," Annie retorted, taking the proffered bottle of wine and closing the front door behind him as Darrow welcomed the new arrival. "Merry Christmas to you, too." She turned to survey the scene from the entryway. So maybe she had overdone the Christmas decorations a bit this year. She was happy. So sue her.

The house smelled of pine, compliments of the eight-foot balsam fir and miles of pine roping she'd strung across...well, everything.

"Hey, Jonathan," Michael said, crossing to the new arrival with outstretched hand. "Glad you could make it."

"I never pass up an offer of free food and top shelf liquor."

"Smart man," Michael laughed. He gestured toward the loaded table in the dining room. "It's 'graze-as-you-please.' Drinks are on the sidebar. I'll take your coat."

Jonathan shrugged out of his coat. Michael took it and disappeared into the study.

"Bet he misses that butler at times like these," Jonathan whispered to Annie.

She rolled her eyes.

A chorus of greetings made its way round the living room as Jonathan entered. Jax waved from her perch on one of the wide windowsills. Streeter lifted his glass in acknowledgement. Carter, ever the gentleman, stood at Jonathan's entry.

"Carter, I didn't know you were coming. You drove all the way down from Chicago?"

"Geez, Jonathan. You make it sound like our first annual Christmas party wasn't worthy of the trip," Annie groused.

The older man grinned. "Hey, I'm retired. Got nothing but time."

"Oh? And what am I?" The silver-haired woman on the couch beside him raised an eyebrow.

"Ooh, you're in trouble," Annie laughed.

She had been delighted to meet Carter's significant other, a lovely woman by the name of Natalie. They'd all met at Annie's and Michael's wedding, a small, private affair the month before. Jonathan had stood up as her attendant. Streeter had done the same for Michael. And Carter had walked her down the aisle, wiping away her tears with his handkerchief just as he'd done so many times when she was a little girl.

Eleanor had died in September. They didn't go to the funeral, but it sounded like every politico and industry mover and shaker had. Chicago's 1,200-seat Holy Name Cathedral was standing room only according to the news reports, a turnout that would have delighted Eleanor.

Annie was not mentioned in the obituary.

The letter from her grandmother's lawyers informed her that Eleanor had left her exactly one dollar—the lawyerly way of ensuring the disinherited can't claim their omission from the will was an unintended oversight. Annie was neither surprised nor disappointed. But she was gratified to learn that, instead of trying to preserve Barlow Industries in perpetuity, her grandmother had left everything to The Eleanor Barlow Charitable Foundation. Its charter included two stipulations: whatever the money was used for must bear her name—the quest for immortality alive and well, even if Eleanor Barlow was not—and none of the gifts could be used for any program supporting either criminal prosecution or defense. Annie laughed out loud when she read that. Jackson might not be getting his capital resource center, but neither was Nicoletti getting his war chest. Her threat had worked.

Michael came up behind her and slipped his arms around her waist. "You don't have a drink in your hand, Mrs. Grayson."

She rolled her eyes. "Name's still O'Toole."

He chuckled. "Yeah, but to me, you'll always be Mrs. Grayson."

"Mrs. Grayson is your mother," she retorted.

"Ew, now you're just making things weird." He dropped a kiss on the top of her head and released her. "Mrs. C, can you find Annie's lost drink? I want to propose a toast."

The older woman stuck her head out of the dining room, a drink in each hand. "Already did."

Annie sighed. "Where was it this time?"

"On the kitchen windowsill."

"Of course, it was." Annie spent a lot of time looking for misplaced coffee cups and wine glasses.

"May I have your attention?" Michael raised his voice.

The chatter fell silent. Michael took Annie's hand.

"Annie and I are glad you could join us for what we hope will become an annual tradition. This has been—" he hesitated— "a challenging year, shall we say?" He gave a rueful laugh, then looked at Annie and squeezed her hand. "And an amazing one." He returned his gaze to the room. "And you have all been an integral part of the journey. So, we just want to say thank you for your support, your wisdom—" he gave Streeter an almost imperceptible nod at that— "and your love. You are our circle." He lifted his glass. "Long may it live."

"I'll drink to that," Annie echoed with a broad smile.

With a few 'hear, hears' and 'backatchas,' glasses clinked all round.

"And now, I have a special gift for my lovely wife." Michael nodded at Jax, who pulled a gift-wrapped box out from behind the tree.

Annie gave him a questioning look. "I thought we were saving gifts for Christmas morning."

"Well, this one is kind of from Streeter and me, too," Jax explained.

"O-kay…" Annie said. "You know it makes me nervous when the three of you are in on secrets together."

Jax laughed. "I think you'll be okay with this one."

Annie set her glass down. After tearing off the gift wrapping, she opened the box—and froze.

"I found this when, um—" Jax started, but hesitated.

"When I had them investigating your connection to Eleanor," Michael finished. He reached in and lifted out the framed photo of a young couple, arm-in-arm, smiling at each other. Gently, he pulled the box from Annie's hands and replaced it with the picture.

"It's your mom and dad. Probably the only picture of the two of them together."

"It was taken at a fundraiser for the Chicago's old Twilight Theater," Jax picked up the story. "There was an article about it in the newspaper and this was one of the photos they published." She smiled shyly. "We suspect it was the night they met."

Tears welled as Annie traced the face of the father she had never seen. He had her freckles. And her eyes. No, she corrected herself. She had his.

Michael pulled her into his arms. "I know they didn't get their happily-ever-after," he murmured. "But I will be forever grateful to them for giving me mine."

A slow clap started in one of the corners of the room—Annie didn't see by whom—and one by one the others joined in.

"Merry Christmas, Annie," Michael whispered in her ear. "The first of a lifetime together." He ran his thumb across her cheek, wiping away the tears.

She looked up at him. "Do you think they're together, watching us?"

He smiled. "I'd like to think so."

"Me, too. It'd be nice if Grandmother is watching too."

"Seriously?" His eyebrows went up.

She sniffed. "Absolutely." She looked down at the photo. "Because she will hate this."

Author's Note

While I am a lawyer and spent a lot of years doing the very work Annie is doing as a public defender, for purposes of the plot, I've played a bit loosely with the law. In real life, Annie would have been taken off this case the moment her one-night-stand with the victim was discovered—but then we'd have had no story! And while a client *can* waive some conflicts of interest, I stretched that way beyond what would be allowed in real life, to give Annie and Michael their chance at adventure. (Hey, that's why it's called fiction!)

The description of Annie's office, however, is a sadly accurate description of the public defender office in which I worked—complete with ongoing roach infestation (sigh). But I am pleased to say that the current St. Louis public defender's office, and the statewide system of which it is a part, now have much better funding, decent offices, and a separate Capital Division already in place. Progress!

St. Louisans might recognize the location of Michael's 'compound' (as Streeter likes to call it) as Bee Tree Park in South St. Louis County, which is in fact still a thriving park and conservation area enjoyed by many. A number of the other St. Louis locations described in the book also exist, but trademark considerations prevent me from identifying them by name. I suspect you locals can figure those out on your own. And, of course, St. Louis is indeed renowned for its toasted ravioli—as David Aylesbury and Streeter pointed out—so if you're ever passing through, make sure you give some a try!

—*Cat Jameson*

A word about the author...

Cat Jameson is a writer of romance novels packed with equal parts suspense, snark, and spice. A criminal defense lawyer for almost three decades, she draws heavily upon those experiences in crafting her stories.

When not writing, playing with grandkids, or at the metaphysical bookstore she opened as her second act, she's probably off on a road trip with her best friend and business partner in a ten-year-old van named Woo —stopping at every bookstore and thrift shop along the way to load up on things she does not need and has no room for. In other words, finding joy in the journey and having the time of her life.

And if you'd like a bit *more* of Michael and Annie, a fun bonus episode is available to Cat's followers through her website, so check it out!

(That's also where you'll find the *Chasing Shadows* Book Club Discussion Guide.) Enjoy!

****
www.catjameson.com
****

If you enjoyed this story, leaving a review at your favorite book retailer or reader website would be much appreciated. Thank you!